An L.A. Love Story

A Love Story Series

CAROLINE CHRISTIANSEN

Paperback ISBN: 979-8-9854815-0-1
eBook ISBN: 979-8-9854815-1-8

An L.A. Love Story

Edited by: Julie Holt
Cover Design: Caroline Taylor
Interior Formatting: Alyssa Garcia

An L.A. Love Story

A Love Story Series

“We need more cupcake moments!”

Julie Holt

Ava

As I plop into my chair at my audition, I release the breath I've been holding and thank God that I wasn't late. Last night went later than expected. Nannying for the Hollywood elite is no joke. I made good money, but getting home at 3AM wasn't exactly ideal the day of an audition. My agent Shanna at least had the decency to help me update my last headshot, so I have that going for me. However, I'm not a blonde like everyone else waiting to audition. I'm the odd woman out. No shock there.

I'm fairly prepared for my audition. Same song and dance as usual. I'm more of a musical theatre actress, but I'm stoked that more musicals are being made into movies. I miss New York, but I'm slowly learning to love L.A. I pick up a magazine and see it's about the "beautiful people" in the world. My eyes immediately connect with the deep blue ones staring back from the page. Clark Grant. Jesus, Mary and Joseph he's gorgeous. He's wearing a white button-down shirt and his body is submerged in a bathtub so you can't really see anything else. My breath catches in my throat. As sexy as he is on the page, something in his eyes speaks to me.

I know that sounds absurd. He's a famous actor. It's probably photoshopped to make every woman have that feeling, but I feel a connection. I shake my head, laughing at myself for being such a dork. I need to get out more. My agent Shanna would agree. I look over to the interview portion next to the photo, and again I get sucked in. The interviewer asked him about being a single father, and I'm stunned that I didn't know that. He's very tightlipped about his daughter and her privacy, but at the end of the day he's a father first, it's the most important role he's ever played. I find myself drawn to the interview, and then I hear someone clear their throat next to me. I look up and the entire room is staring at me. Oh shit!

"Ava JAMES? Last call!" the assistant says, standing at the door with her clipboard. I grimace at causing a scene and stand up, shoving the magazine in my purse. I start toward the door, and as I make my way toward the assistant, I'm almost plowed over by some girl. People hurry to get out of her way. She looks so familiar, but I can't quite place her. I walk into my audition, and I'd like to say they are all smiles. However, it's more or less a gassy look from everyone. WONDERFUL! I try to lift my spirits and be me, but sometimes it's hard when they look like they don't want to be there.

The audition goes about as well as it could go. I nail my songs and they even ask for another. There was some time chatting among themselves and then they thanked me for coming in. So that's somewhat promising, but who can ever tell with these things? I call Shanna and leave a message. She has about six or seven other clients that she works closely with. A few are bigger names, so she does have some pull. Her family is super connected in town, which helps a lot. I've been to a couple of parties at her parents' house and that's how I met Tammy from the nanny agency I contract for. I like kids. I actually feel sorry for a lot of the Hollywood kids that I've nannied for in this town. I know – stupid, right? However, the truth is I do. It's like they have everything, but yet are missing something they really need.

I was raised a long way away from Hollywood. I lost my parents in a tragic car accident when I was 14 and then lost my grandmother when I was 18. No Hollywood ending here. I grew up fast and left North Carolina as soon as I could. New York City was an adjustment, but I loved almost every second

I was there. There's so much to do. Being the book worm I am, I spent most of my evenings reading or learning lines for auditions. I met Shanna through a mutual friend, and she convinced me that I would have a better shot at my dreams out here in L.A. At first I was hesitant, but after a few years in New York I thought, why not?

Before I even make it home, my phone buzzes. Of course it's Shanna.

"Hey friend!" I answer, putting it on Bluetooth.

"Hey doll face. How did it go? Sorry I haven't listened to my messages yet," she replies.

"Hopefully the audition went well and we can move on with our lives. Now, what are your plans tonight? Mom and Dad are having people over, and I think it would do you well to network a little bit. I think a couple of friendly casting directors will be there. I'd love to get you seen. Not necessarily go around shaking hands and signing babies, but what do you say? Pick you up at eight?" she asks.

"Of course. I have to go home, take a shower and do laundry. I'll meet you at your house? My roommates are hazardous and it's out of your way to come to me."

"Sounds good. Come over about seven and we can pregame here and make sure that you're camera ready!"

I head back to the apartment. It's not much. I don't even like calling it mine. I share it with two other people. For the most part they're never there. One is always at her boyfriend's house, and the other one I think is into some weird stuff. She doesn't seem comfortable doing whatever it is while I'm there. Apparently, I'm at the apartment too often because she's always pissed off while I'm there.

I pull the magazine out of my purse from earlier. I honestly didn't mean to take it, but I went on auto pilot when everyone in the room was staring at me. I open back up to the page with Clark Grant on it. Jesus, it's alarming how a photo of someone this gorgeous can take your breath away. I need to get out more! I see that the article is over a year old now. I look back to the interview and continue to read.

> Interviewer: So you've been a single dad for a few years now. How have you balanced making movies and raising a child alone?

It still stuns me that he's a dad for some reason. Something about that information changes how I see him. Not that it matters what I think of him.

> Clark Grant: My daughter's mother passed away when she was two. We were doing our best at co-parenting. We had our ups and downs, but we stayed connected mainly for our daughter's sake. It has been a little tougher without

a partner to balance all of the responsibilities. Honestly, being a father is the best thing I've ever done, and I wouldn't trade it for anything in the world. I'm also not the first single parent with a full-time job. I've got a team behind me, so I have my advantages. It's been a learning experience for sure though, just like any other parent has experienced. I've found that my greatest joy is coming home at the end of the day and seeing her beautiful smile when I walk in."

Interviewer: I imagine she feels like the luckiest girl in the world to have Clark Grant for a dad. Superhero on screen and at home!

CG: I'm just daddy at home!

Interviewer: Mind if I call you daddy?

I roll my eyes on Clark Grant's behalf. People have no shame.

CG: If that's what you want to do.

Interviewer: I'm just kidding!

We all know she's not kidding!

Interviewer: Anyway. Your last movie was incredible, I have to say. I honestly think you're in the best shape of your life. Our readers were dying when you walked into the shower naked. Those buns of steel memes floating around of you are viral on social media right now. Any words of advice to our male readers wanting to replicate your workouts at home?

CG: Consistency is key! Hire a trainer to kick your ass and a chef to keep you on track. It was not fun getting into that kind of shape, but it's part of what I do. It's what I'm paid to look like on screen. Anyone can do it with determination and passion. I love working out. Maybe not getting as big as I was for my last film, but I had a blast doing it, and I wasn't the only superhero on the screen or training with me, so that added to the enjoyment factor. Also, don't forget to be happy with where you are. We are all lucky to be alive. I can say losing someone close to you reminds you of how fragile life is. I feel like using my time here on Earth wisely.

Interviewer: I can only imagine. Especially losing someone in such a tragic way like you and your daughter did, and so publicly as well. Do you think you'll fall in love again?

CG: I don't know. My daughter's mother and I weren't together at the time of

> her passing, but it's still a tragedy. My daughter lost her mother. It's not about me. It's about her and her needs. We take it a day at a time. That's all any of us can really do in life.

I close the magazine and sit back on my bed. My heart hurts for this man and his daughter. I also hate how intrusive and inappropriate people can be. I'm curious as to what happened to his daughter's mom. I grab my laptop and Google Clark Grant. The number of gorgeous photos that pop up is overwhelming. Geez. I knew about him before. I'm not living in total darkness, but I didn't know anything specifically about him, at least not about his personal life. I look up his Wikipedia page and scroll through. He's British, moved to California when he was 19. Landed his first role at 21. He's been in movies I didn't even realize that he was in. I scroll down to his personal life. I almost feel guilty about prying, but then I remember I'll never meet him. He'll never know I Googled him. Sure, we live in the same town, but the odds of us ever meeting are slim to none. I see his daughter's name is Brooklyn. She's almost five now. She lost her mother when she was around two. Losing a parent at that age, especially your mother, had to be so horrific. I'm so sad for his little girl.

Shanna is putting the final touches on her makeup when I knock on her door. She lives in an amazing little house outside of the Hollywood Hills. It has an incredible view and I wonder if maybe I should be looking for a house instead of an apartment. Most people don't realize I have a nice size savings account because I don't like to splurge. Nor do I act like most of the elites here in L.A. My parents weren't lavish at all. We had a modest home in a very middle-class neighborhood. It wasn't until after they passed away that I realized what kind of financial situation we were actually in. Only then did I start talking to my Nana about what to do. She always pushed for me to get out of town. It was one of her last wishes for me.

Shanna's parents have hired a local jazz band to play tonight and I'm in love! I LOVE big band music. I grab a glass of champagne and head to a bistro table with Shanna. She's like a hawk -- already scanning the crowd. Sometimes I can only laugh at her antics. She's good at what she does, and I have no doubt that she will get me where I want to be when the time is right. I'm not in a hurry, which benefits me but ticks her off. I'm not competitive and I don't feel like I have to go after every part and every audition. I can be picky. I don't think anyone here other than those who know me through Shanna would even know my name. I'm also not humping every influential person's leg here either. Trust me, I've seen it done! I'm embarrassed for them every. single. time.

Shanna and I grab another cocktail and head out back. It's a beautiful summer night in LA. There's a slight chill in the air. I love that about California. Summer nights in North Carolina were way different. Hot, humid, and filled with bugs. Being close to the coastline, you have the ocean breeze, but it can still be stifling at times. A bad evening in L.A. is rare. Shanna's giving me the rundown of who's-who at the party when Tammy comes over.

"Hey, Ava. I'm so glad you're here! I have another family I think will be right up your alley," she says. She always has a family. "I'd love to introduce you if you have a moment," she adds.

"They're here?" I ask, looking around like I'd be able to spot them.

"Well, no. A friend of a friend is looking to retire soon and the family she works for will be looking for a new nanny. They don't even have a profile yet. It's pretty hush hush, but they would be a premier account. She asked me if I thought anyone would fit the bill for the position, and you were the first person who came to mind. Plus, you're here."

"Why is she retiring? Crazy family?" I ask, and Shanna snickers behind me.

"She's retiring because her granddaughter is about to have baby. She's ready to retire and be around for her great grandchild," Tammy says, glaring at Shanna. "And what family isn't crazy?"

"Very true. Yes, I'd love to meet her. Wouldn't

she want me to meet the actual parents? I mean, is that a Hollywood thing? To have the old nanny replace and interview the new prospects?" I ask seriously.

"No. It's not, but this is kind of a special situation. Between you and me, opportunities like this don't come along very often. I can't even tell you the client's name at this point."

"Okay, Tammy," Shanna says, rolling her eyes. "You can have her for 20 minutes and then she needs to be back over here with me. She has better opportunities than changing the Hollywood Elite's diapers."

"She can do both. And do both well, Shanna," Tammy says as she grabs my hand and pulls me away. As we approach a group of people, a few couples smile at Tammy. She is well known for finding clients the right nanny for their family. I haven't found that right fit yet, but 'tis life. I have time to figure it all out. We approach an older group of ladies and a woman with white hair, styled like Marilyn Monroe, starts towards us. She looks me up and down and smiles. I'm curious if I'm being checked out for a nannying position or for something else.

"Hey Lydia, this is Ava," Tammy says as I shake this gorgeous woman's hand. She smiles kindly at me, and I like her already. She looks like an old Hollywood movie star. She's beautiful. Not at all like a soon to be great grandmother. Good for her!

"Hi Ava," she says as we move away from her group of friends and toward an empty table. I take a seat facing Lydia. "I've heard wonderful things about you from Tammy. I am so glad to meet you."

"Of course. To be honest Lydia, you have me at a little bit of a disadvantage. I don't know anything about why you wanted to meet me. Other than you're retiring from your nanny position," I add respectfully. Tammy, Lydia and I sit talking for a couple minutes before Tammy stands up to talk with a couple of people a few tables away.

"I know this is a little different, but my boss doesn't have the luxury to interview a bunch of nannies. In his line of work, he needs someone to go ahead of him. Someone who knows his situation and needs. If Tammy put out feelers for my boss, she'd have a line out her door, plus a couple news outlets asking questions and making assumptions. It's been my job the last couple of years to protect their privacy. I'd love to get a head start to find my replacement so they don't have to worry about that. Tammy said you would be the perfect candidate because you don't get rattled easily and you also don't get star struck at these kinds of shindigs. That's really what's important, other than being good with kids. Their team wants someone who isn't going to be asking for autographs, or worse -- to get her in a movie."

“I can see how that would be an issue. And yes, I understand you wanting to respect people’s privacy. They sound lucky to have someone like you in their life. I can really respect what you’re doing. Is there anything specific you want to ask me?” I ask.

“Not particularly. Are you an aspiring actress?” she asks, smiling kindly. “Tammy said you had an audition today.”

“Yes, mainly for movie musical parts. I enjoy it, but I can also pick and choose what I like. I’m learning and enjoying the process,” I add. She is smiling kindly but seems a little disappointed by my answer.

“I don’t mean this to be rude, Ava, but I’d love an honest answer,” she says. “Why are you here tonight?”

“Fair question. Shanna Lytess is my agent and also a friend. We come to her parents’ parties all the time. I love her family. Also, Shanna likes to network with me tagging along. She likes to show me off if she gets an opportunity. She and her family have been very kind to me, and I respect them very much. Honestly, I’m here because Shanna wants me to be here. I’m also so in love with the jazz bands that they book. And the champagne selection. They have amazing taste,” I say, smiling genuinely at Lydia. She smiles back and nods her head.

“I agree. They have great taste, and I also love a good jazz band. There are some pretty big names in the room tonight, and you've been sitting here with me for 30 minutes talking about a nanny position. I've talked to a couple candidates and none of them were honest with me or at least they didn't seem very genuine. They were more interested in trying to find out who I worked for instead of answering my questions," she adds. We sit and talk for another hour, mainly about how I got to LA and my family history. I find Lydia super easy to talk to and I'm not at all feeling like I'm missing out on anything. Shanna finally finds Lydia and I in the corner chatting. She looks at Lydia shocked and then to me.

Lydia stands up and shakes my hand. "Thanks Lydia," I say, and she nods at me, walking off. Shanna stares at her retreating back and I clear my throat. "Shanna?"

"Do you know who that was?" she asks.

"Lydia?"

"Lydia Maxwell. The movie star. She was a Bond girl, Ava. Lydia freakin' Maxwell," she adds like I didn't understand her the first time. "She's retiring? She's the nanny that's retiring?" she asks, shocked.

"Well, I guess. I didn't know she was a Bond girl. We mainly talked about me and then we talked about our love of jazz music. I've never seen you starstruck, so this is new for me."

"I'm not starstruck. I'm in SHOCK! I knew she

came to some of my parents' parties. You'd never believe she was in her 70's though, right? She's timeless. Who's her boss?" she demands.

"Calm down Shanna," I say as we stand up and grab two more champagne flutes from a passing server. "I'm hungry. Let's find some snacks," I add, pulling her away from Lydia and her friends. I see Tammy walking toward us and I want to eat something before I'm questioned again. We find a table of finger foods that's almost completely untouched. Or more likely the wait staff is hiding somewhere making the table look immaculate at all times. I make a small plate and then hurry to a quiet room so I can stuff my face. Tammy comes in the room smiling at me.

"There you are," she says. "I thought I would have to call you tomorrow. How did it go?" she asks as I start eating my grapes. I don't care who you are, don't get between me and food when I'm hungry.

"Great. Lydia is really nice. I really hope she finds the right fit for her boss. I'm not sure it will be me, but I like her a lot," I answer with a mouth full of grapes.

"I think you'd be perfect. Keep your phone on tomorrow. I know you'll be at auditions, but please answer if I call. I promise it will be worth your time. Lydia leaves for the Dakotas next weekend and I'd love to make sure one of my girls gets the position."

"Did she even like me that much?" I ask, and she smiles conspiratorially.

"Of course she loved you. I wouldn't have told her about you if I knew that you'd be a dud. I can send you to any client's house and you'd come out unscathed," she says, grabbing a grape off my plate. "Answer your phone," she barks as she walks away.

I head back into the room where I left Shanna. She's making out with some random dude. I roll my eyes. She can find a lover at any party. I head back out to the party and grab a water. I've had two glasses of champagne, and I imagine I'll end up getting an Uber back to Shanna's so I can get my car soon. I'm not waiting to see where this love affair goes for Shanna. I take my phone out and set up a pick-up time as I stand at the edge of the yard, looking out at the Hollywood Hills. It's so beautiful up here. I can't help but wonder if tonight is the beginning of something new for me.

Clark

We're sitting around my pool when Lydia comes by with more early birthday gifts since she will be gone by the time Brooklyn's 5th birthday comes around. Brooklyn runs over to Lydia, giving her a big hug and kiss. I can already feel myself tearing up. I wasn't prepared for the emotions that I'm feeling in this moment. I knew it would be sad to see Lydia go. But for Brooklyn to lose another female figure in her life like this is crushing. She loves Brooklyn like she is one of her own and that has meant the world to me. Brooklyn opens her presents and Lydia tells me about her plans for the next couple of days. I've already told her that she's off the hook and to just relax. I want her to enjoy the time she has left in

LA without worrying about us. She slaps me hard on the arm and I pretend that it hurt me.

"You cannot actually think that I would leave without at least trying to find a good replacement," she adds as Brooklyn squeals with delight at her new toys.

"There isn't going to be a replacement, Lydia. No one can replace you or what you've done for us these last couple of years," I say, placing my hand on hers. She starts to tear up, but she stays strong. "I appreciate you more than you could ever know. So please don't feel like you need to do anything more than you've already done. I want this to be an exciting time for you. Another generation is being born into the Maxwell family. This is supposed to be an exciting time, not sad and depressing!"

"I'm not sad or depressed, Clark. Not even in the slightest. I'm excited for us both. I have the perfect replacement for the nanny job. She's absolutely fantastic. Met with her last night," she adds. I whip my head around to face her.

"I didn't offer her a job, Clark. I just did the first round of screening and interviews. She comes highly recommended from Tammy's agency. Plus she's new in town. She isn't going to be snooping around in your underwear drawer. She seems to have a pretty good head on her shoulders, which for this town is like finding a needle in a haystack. I would love to have her over to meet you.

If you like her, have her meet Brooklyn? I know you don't really need help until Brooklyn goes to school, but it would be nice for you and Brooklyn to be able to get to know her better before then. She's great, Clark," she assures me, and I nod. I trust Lydia with my life. More like with Brooklyn's life. Which means her opinion is the only one I'll listen to when it comes to a nanny for Brooklyn. She's never steered me wrong.

"Set it up," I answer back, and Lydia grins. I can't help but notice a twinkle in her eye. I'm not in the mood right now to investigate why. Maybe she's just excited about Brooklyn meeting this new prospect.

We watch Brooklyn jump into the pool over and over again until it even has me exhausted. We head into the house, and I see Lydia's already started boxing up a couple of the things from her room. She has the room upstairs next to Brooklyn's bedroom. Brooklyn, however, is enthralled in whatever TV show with puppies Disney has on, so I know I can talk frankly with Lydia.

"Will Brooklyn like her?" I ask as she turns towards me.

"Yes. That's who I was considering the entire time I was talking with her. She has a pretty incredible story, and she seems like an old soul in many ways. I think you both will like her. I think she's trustworthy, has a clean background check with the agency, and the families she has worked for prior have been some big names around town. She didn't name drop once when I was speaking with her. Honestly, I don't think she even knew who I was, which was such a breath of fresh air for me. I'm sure she'll know who you are. You'd have to be living under a rock not to. But I didn't tell her who my boss was," she adds.

"You mean whose boss *you* are?" I interject and we both laugh. "Cause around here you're the boss, Lydia. You know that."

"Well… doesn't really matter now. I've texted Tammy to set up something with her this week. I've checked with Clayton about your schedule to make sure we get the ball rolling. We can at least make sure we have forward motion with this," Lydia explains.

It seems the train has left the station on this, and I'm on board whether I want to be or not.

"She's somewhat in the industry," Lydia continues. "Actively auditioning, but she seemed to be able to keep that separate when I met her. She may not end up being the perfect fit, but I think it can't hurt to interview her. It will be pretty hard to find someone 'unattached' in this town. Most everyone here is trying to do something other than what they're doing right now. But I think she's pretty well versed in life. Sounds like she would make the right decisions for the right reasons."

"I hope so. Is she showing up without knowing who we are?" I ask, sitting down at one of the bar stools in the kitchen.

"No. I told Tammy that she could tell her who the client was when she set up a time to meet with us. I haven't heard back from Tammy. I'm sure it'll be soon," she says, adding a couple boxes of tea into her packing box. It's sad to see Lydia packing up, but part of me is excited about this next season for us, especially for Brooklyn.

Ava

My phone pings and I see it's a text from Tammy asking if I'm free to talk. When I say yes, my phone rings almost immediately. "Hello?" I say, like I don't know who it is.

"Can you meet Lydia and the client this afternoon?" she asks, and I look at the clock. It's 2:30 p.m. already.

"Yeah, but what time?" I ask. "How dressed up do I need to be?"

"Nothing too snazzy, but somewhat put together. No workout clothes. At least not yet. I've seen you in yoga wear. You may want to wait on giving him a heart attack until after he's gotten to see your personality first," she says dryly. "At least until you land the job."

"Thank you?" I reply, uncertain if that was a compliment. She keeps saying 'he.' What about the mom?

"Please, Ava. Spare me the humility. If you don't know how gorgeous you are by now, then you are not only blind, but also delusional. I mean, you had Lydia Maxwell eating out of your hand last night. Also asking more questions about you after you left."

"Umm…. again. What time?" I ask, rolling my eyes. I don't bank anything on looks. Besides, I've seen where looks alone have gotten other women. It's nothing but trouble. I'll stick to what I've been doing. I'm not looking to land this nanny position on my looks. That would be pure stupidity and not the ideal situation, no matter who the client is.

"Can you meet at 4:30? I know that doesn't give you much time, but if you meet any later I'm worried you won't make it on time because of traffic. I know it's going to be quite the haul. It's about 15 minutes from the Lytesses'. I apologize for the long drive, but if it works out then it'll be worth it, I promise!"

"Yeah. That gives me about 45 minutes to get dressed. I'll give myself a little extra time to get there so I don't hit traffic. Send me the address."

"Will do. Oh, before I forget. The client's name is Clark Grant," she says as she hangs up.

Um… what, now? Did she just say Clark

Grant? I must have heard her wrong.

"Hello?" I repeat into the phone and then look up at my ceiling. God has a sense of humor. I laugh to myself. But I also want to throw my phone across the room. What are the damn odds?

I did not see this coming. I'm glad she told me before I got there, it gives me some time to pull myself together. I'm not one to get flustered, but my God that man is beautiful. I feel my phone vibrate in my hand and I jump. Geez! I need to get it together. It's Tammy sending me the address. She's counting on me to handle myself like a pro and that's exactly what I'm going to do. I've nannied for a few big names, and I really could not care less. This should be no different. It's only because I literally was just googling (and drooling over) him yesterday. I'm going to pretend he's like any other guy I've ever come in contact with. Nothing to see here. I'm cool. I can be calm AND collected, I tell myself over and over again. I'm FINE. I feel like Ross Gellar when he was trying to pretend he was fine, but his voice was coming out all high and squeaky.

I pull my phone out and text Shanna. I was a little ticked off last night that she didn't even call to check in on me. I guess she figured I was the adult I always am and arrived home safely. I text her anyway. She's one of my people, so I let it slide.

Second Interview @ 4:30 with Lydia

Go you!!! Did you find out who the interview is with?

I did. Promise to not flip out? I'm trying to stay calm here!

No promises. After Lydia last night though I'm sure you can't shock me more than that.

Clark Grant

Clark Grant? Like THE CLARK GRANT!!!!

The only one I know!!

Holy Shit balls Ava!! I'd say good luck but I think that ship has sailed.

I'm hoping it goes well. Lord JESUS!!
AND I don't embarrass myself.

Well...that can't be helped. You can be hilarious even when you aren't trying to be.

That's what I'm afraid of. So thank you?

Well. Good luck. Call me as soon as you get in the car!! I MEAN IT!!!

YES MOM!!! Love U!

I put my phone down and head to the bathroom to clean up a little. I've picked out a pretty, casual sundress. Nothing fancy. I don't want to wear shorts and it's too hot to wear jeans right now. I put on my dress and fix my hair, add a little makeup and then look down at my phone. I'm good on time.

An hour later I pull up to the large security gates. HERE GOES NOTHING. I tell the security guard my name and who I'm here to see. He doesn't flinch, which tells me all I need to know. There are a lot of celebrities in this neighborhood and this guy is not fazed at all by this. He makes a call, hangs up and gives me some directions. I thank him and he smiles kindly at me. I feel like I'm getting away with being an outsider here. Until I tell him to wish me luck. It's out of my mouth before I know what I've said, and he breaks into a big grin. I cover my face.

"I'm so sorry. That was unprofessional of me. I guess I meant…"

"Not a worry, Miss. Is it an interview?" he asks, and I nod.

"Nanny position," I add.

"Wonderful family. You'll do great," he replies and hands me my ID back.

I pull through the next set of gates in front of the Grant estate and take a deep breath. I drive for almost a minute through a winding driveway. When I actually come up to the house you can't even see the road I came from. I'm blown away. I knew the house would be big. Probably a mansion, but this is beyond what I could have ever imagined. It isn't gaudy. It's just ginormous. That's a word, right? It looks pretty modern on the outside. I love that it's so private. I'm sure that was on purpose. I park in the most inauspicious parking spot I can find. I almost feel bad parking my car in the driveway. My car is nice, but not nice enough to belong here. I walk toward the house and the front door opens. Lydia is standing there. She's dressed in white linen pants and a cute pink top. She looks perfect and her hair is fabulous. I want to tell her that, but I need to wait until we get to know each other a little better. Then I remember I'm interviewing to replace her, which means I won't be getting to know her that well. That pains me a little because she's been so kind. She ushers me into the foyer and asks me if she can take my purse. I nod and she hangs it inside the coat closet near the front door. I walk with her into the house and see the gorgeous panoramic view from the kitchen.

"Pretty remarkable, huh?" Lydia says. "It's okay. It takes some getting used to. Clark's house is beautiful. I imagine you'll get used to it soon enough. God willing," she adds in a whisper, winking at me.

"I can't imagine anyone getting used to a view like this," I say. "Thanks for the second interview. I really do appreciate it. I enjoyed speaking with you last night."

"You are very welcome. I've already told Clark a little about you. He'll be down shortly. He's giving Brooklyn a bath. They played in the pool all afternoon. She might be a little grumpy, but I promise she's a sweet girl," she adds, and I smile. I have seen my share of Hollywood kids so I'm not worried.

"I'm sure it'll be fine. I can get a little grumpy at the end of the day too," I add and we both laugh.

"Same, Ava. Same," she says. We hear someone coming down the stairs. Brooklyn flies by me and straight into Lydia, almost knocking her over.

"Brooklyn! Easy," I hear the most incredibly luscious voice with a strong British accent chastise her from behind me. I'm trying to focus on Brooklyn, who's holding onto Lydia while staring up at me. I know it might be rude to not turn around and give Clark my attention, but I'm here for Brooklyn. If she and I don't have a good connection, then I might as well turn around and head back out of those pearly gates. I bend down and get on Brooklyn's level. Not too close, but in front of Lydia and Brooklyn.

"I love your puppy dog pajamas," I say, and she smiles happily.

"Do you like puppies, too?" she asks.

"Of course!" I answer. "Who doesn't like puppies?"

"Daddy won't let me get a puppy," she says, looking at her dad. He must be behind me. She's giving him sad puppy dog eyes. WELL CRAP, I think to myself. I hear him laugh behind me. Sweet Jesus, I swear I feel his laugh reverberate in my ovaries. Wow. Yeah... that's gonna have to stop. I swallow and smile at her.

"Brooklyn," he says, laughing, "I think you like the idea of having a puppy more than you would actually like having a puppy. Plus, puppies don't stay puppies forever. You're about to be a big girl at school. Who's going to take care of the puppy while you're at school and Daddy's at work?" he asks as I sit back on my heels. I sit there watching the two of them stare each other down. He's leaning against the wall outside of their kitchen and I have to look away. I already knew what he looked like before coming here. I mean he's Clark Grant. In person though, he's even more beautiful than you could ever imagine. His dark brown hair is a little unruly. Long enough to run your fingers through. Not that I plan on doing that. Jesus, I need to get a hold of myself. I feel myself getting flushed and I don't dare look at Lydia. I know she would see right through me. Brooklyn looks at me and smiles. She points at me, looking back at her dad. OH WOW. So it's like that, huh. I guess I'll be taking care of the new puppy. If there's a new puppy to be had.

"Oh really," I ask and she nods. I wink at her.

"You can do it. It's not hard at all. I watch Doc McStuffins, and if she can do it, so can you," she whispers and then winks back at me, which makes all of us laugh. I sit back on my heels and look up at Clark, who's staring adoringly down at his daughter.

"Doc McStuffins takes care of toys, Brooklyn. Not actual animals," Clark adds, then puts his hand out for me. "Here, let me help you up," he says as I give him my hand. We make eye contact as his dark blue eyes look at me with kindness. Our eyes connect and it almost knocks me back down. I know it's cliché, but there were sparks as our hands touched. I'm surprised it didn't knock me through the glass windows behind me. HOLY SHIT. I'm sure it was just me though. I laugh to myself and rub my hand on my thigh. As if that will make the tingling sensation go away. I glance over at Lydia, who's watching Clark. Clark is looking from me to Brooklyn. I don't know what to do, so I look back down at Brooklyn. She leaves Lydia's side and takes my hand.

"You wanna show me some of your toys?" I ask, and she nods. "My name is Ava."

"Hi, Ava. You can call me Brooklyn. My dad calls me Brooklyn, too. Or Brooklyn Harper Grant if I'm in trouble," she whispers.

"Well, let's hope it doesn't come to that," I whisper back as she walks me toward their TV room. There's a basket full of toys on the side of the sofa. She pulls a couple of toys out of the box to show me. Apparently they're early birthday presents from Lydia. Brooklyn tells me she has a birthday coming up. I'm excited for her, but also sad because that means Lydia won't be here for it.

"I'm going to be five," she says. I sit down next to her and turn around to see Lydia and Clark talking.

"Is this okay?" I ask from the other room and Lydia laughs.

"Are you kidding?" she adds and starts to walk over. "This is exactly what we were hoping for. Brooklyn's vote is almost as important as Clark's," she says sarcastically. He rolls his eyes and looks down at me, smiling. I have to look away and back to Brooklyn. I have to get this under control if I'm going to be able to make this work. He's gorgeous and so kind. I need to get over myself. You can't quite understand until his focus is on you. He could burn a hole into my soul when he turns his blue eyes my direction.

"Five years old, that's so big! Are you excited?" I ask Brooklyn.

"Yep. And I'm going to school. With other kids and everything. It's gonna be so fun. Because I'm so smart," she adds. She shows me all of her toys. I'm sure there's a playroom full of more stuff. I don't know if I should ask her to show me all her stuff yet. Clark and Lydia might have other questions. We are laughing at Brooklyn's wild stories and imagination when Clark tells Brooklyn that just the adults are going to chat. I start to push myself up and he holds out a hand again. Lord Almighty. It's like the best type of electric shock. One that takes your breath away but is so invigorating. I was hoping it was just a one-time thing. I stand up and move toward the wrap around sofa. I sit down near, but not too close to Clark. Lydia is on the other side of him. I can feel the heat coming off his body. I'm not even sitting that close to him, but it warms my skin. I'm scared I'm going to start sweating. I take a deep breath and focus on Lydia.

"So. I've told Clark a little of your backstory. I know you obviously know who you'd be working for. Do you mind if we give you the basics of the position?" she asks.

"Yes. Please," I add, wondering if I should be taking notes.

"It's mostly picking up Brooklyn from school and staying with her until Clark gets home from work. If he's out of town, on set, or has an early call then you'd need to stay overnight so you can be there for Brooklyn when she wakes up. Also to get her to school on time. Most days while she's at school you'll have that time to yourself. There will be times when Clark may need you here to meet someone if his assistant isn't available. If Brooklyn is out of school or sick and Clark can't be here, then she'll need to be with you. You aren't locked down here at the house, but Brooklyn hasn't really been out around town. Her protection and privacy is a top priority for us. I checked your Instagram page. I didn't see a Facebook page or websites for you. I see your Instagram page is open to the public so if you do accept the job, please be mindful of what you post and where you say you are with Brooklyn. If Clark is with you guys, the same rules apply. The job is full time. We know that you have auditions, so hopefully Shanna can work around your schedule here. When Clark isn't shooting, it will be very light. Unless he retires in the near future, then all that could change. There also might be some light travel with the family. Other than that, this is it," she says, pointing to our surroundings. I look at Clark and he smiles when I look at him. He leans back against the couch, looking over at me. I remind myself to breathe as he addresses me directly.

"Please know, Ava, that if you land a role you're wanting, we will understand. This is Hollywood. I'm not asking you to choose between us and your dream job. Lydia said you've been trying to find steady work. I know that can be a nightmare here, so please know we will do our best to make it work if it can. We aren't holding you to a contract or anything. There is no non-disclosure agreement. Nothing binding you to us, there won't be anything to hide. I just ask that you keep our family's life private. If this is the right fit for both of us," he says, looking into my eyes and I know I should look away or to Lydia but I can't. It's like he's staring into my soul. "I just ask that you keep Brooklyn safe and cared for. She's my life," he adds, looking away to Brooklyn. I look over at Lydia since Clark has his attention on Brooklyn. She's smiling knowingly at me. I kind of cock my head to the side in question, but then Clark starts to talk again.

"Ava, I'd love to know what you're thinking. Do you have any questions?" he asks so genuinely that I sit back and look down at Brooklyn. As if she senses me looking at her, she turns to look at me. I don't want to ask any personal questions. I feel like that will come with time. This feels right. Brooklyn stands up, knowing she has my attention, and I give her my hand. She takes my hand and I pull her up on the sofa so she is positioned between myself and Clark.

"I do have a question," I answer, and Clark seems to hold his breath. I'm not sure if he thinks I'm going to ask something personal. I wink at Lydia who seems to relax when she realizes I'm not going to pry.

"Brooklyn, would you like for me to come over and hang out with you when you aren't in school?" I ask, and she looks up, grinning ear to ear.

"REALLY?" she squeals. I nod. Her innocent enthusiasm is heart-warming.

"Yes, really. I'd like to know if you would like that?" I ask. She wraps her arms around my neck and starts to cry. I look up at Clark and Lydia worried. They're also staring at Brooklyn. "Hey," I say pushing the hair away from her sweet little face. "What's wrong?" I ask, and I really am concerned for her. I don't look at Clark or Lydia. I have also known loss in my life. I want this sweet girl to know that I'm here for her. "Hey," I whisper as she sits back. "Are those happy tears?"

"Yes," she nods, and I grab her hand.

"Happy tears are okay, sweet girl. Sad tears are okay too. But this should be a happy moment.

Right?" I ask, and she nods.

"I love having new friends," she adds, looking down at her dolls. "You're my new friend, right Ava?"

"I am, sweet girl. I am." I answer, and she smiles over at me and then to Lydia and Clark.

Clark

I was not prepared for this. I'm so happy Brooklyn is happy. Believe me, it's a relief. I have to admit, I'm impressed. Ava handled it like a champ, and I saw Lydia tear up as well. I grab Lydia's hand and she squeezes mine back. I'm not normally an overly emotional guy, but when it comes to my daughter, all bets are off. Also, Lydia could have given me a heads up about how absolutely stunning Ava is. I'm used to being around beautiful women. I mean, this is Hollywood. But seeing someone as naturally gorgeous and down to Earth as Ava caught me by surprise. When I helped her up earlier, I swear I felt sparks. That's never happened to me. When our eyes connected, I felt my heart flutter in my chest. I'm thinking that's not a good thing for the heart. I can't lie and say I didn't like the way it felt when those gorgeous emerald eyes of hers connected with mine. The way she is with Brooklyn is so heartwarming. I'm not saying I'm going to do anything stupid. I'm just stating the obvious. She's a gorgeous girl. Who also happens to be great with my child.

We decide that Ava should come back in a couple days to hang out with Brooklyn on her own to make sure it's a good fit. Brooklyn was in a grumpy mood earlier, but I'm not sure she will want Ava to leave. I should warn Ava that she might get a little emotional as the night progresses. Lydia goes into the kitchen to make some appetizers for all of us and I join Brooklyn and Ava in the den. They are in Brooklyn's pretend kitchen, and I laugh when Ava asks her for chicken and waffles. Brooklyn looks at Ava like she's lost her mind.

"You don't know what Chicken and Waffles are?" Ava asks, and I sit back and watch the two of them interacting.

"Chicken and waffles? At the same time?" Brooklyn asks and Ava giggles.

"It's actually very good. Maybe I can make it for you sometime?" Ava says watching Brooklyn closely. She laughs again, and when Brooklyn shakes her head, I feel her laugh reverberate in my chest. It's a beautiful sound and I move my body trying to rid myself of the feeling. Brooklyn and

Ava both turn to look at me, and I hold my hands up.

"I'm just wanting to place a to go order!" I say, and Ava smiles at me.

"Sure," Brooklyn gets her notepad and pen and walks over to where I'm sitting on the floor. "Do you have a reservation?" I widen my eyes and shake my head. She huffs in frustration, and I have to choke down my laugh. She looks back at Ava and winks at her. "Well, I guess we can make do for now. But you need to be more responsible, Daddy!"

"Apologies, ma'am!" I say, and she nods in appreciation. "I'd just like a coffee to go." Brooklyn heads back over to her kitchen playset and pretends to pour me a coffee. Ava looks over at me and smiles knowingly. It's the first genuine smile I feel like I've received from a woman in a long time, and I realize that that feels really good. I'm used to being around fake people, but I feel like Ava is the real deal. Brooklyn walks back over to me and hands me my to go cup. I thank her, and she holds out her hand.

"That will be 300,000 dollars." Ava bursts out laughing behind her and so do I. Brooklyn whips around and Ava zips her lips up dramatically. "Is there something wrong with your chicken and…." she whispers to Ava. "…what was it called?"

"Waffles," Ava whispers back and Brooklyn

straightens herself.

"Your chicken and waffles?" she asks, now back in character.

"No, ma'am!" Ava says, saluting Brooklyn and she turns back to face me. She holds her hand out and I put pretend money in it. She nods her head and then walks over to her kitchenette. Ava leans over my direction, and I smile at her, pretending to drink my coffee. "She runs a tight ship around here," she whispers, and I chuckle.

"You have no idea!" I whisper back to her as she pretends to be done with her food. When she leaned over, I had to keep myself from leaning in as well. She smells unbelievable. It's insane. Nannies are supposed to smell like nappies or dirt, or something opposite of the way she smells. My God.

Lydia comes over and tells us that the food is almost ready but asks if I want to show Ava around. I laugh and nod my head. I'm an idiot. Lydia looks at me and smiles as I turn back to Ava. "Sorry. How about we show Ava around, Brooklyn?" Brooklyn looks deeply disgruntled.

"Fine," she says as she walks past us and toward the stairs leading up to the second floor. She gives us an expectant look as I pull Ava to her feet. The zap of electricity between us is still there, and I wonder if she feels it like I do. Ava giggles and walks past me, taking Brooklyn's hand. I smile at Lydia, and she's already smiling at me. It takes me by surprise, but she turns back to what she's doing so I don't have time to ask what that look was for. We give her the grand tour, other than my bedroom. We stop outside for Brooklyn to show her around her play area. Brooklyn is swinging and showing off as Ava and I stand silently beside each other. It should feel weird, but it surprisingly isn't. Why should it, though? She's here for Brooklyn. I mean she's just been hired. We'll be spending a lot of time together, so I'm glad it's comfortable silence and I don't feel like I have to make conversation.

Brooklyn shows us how high she can jump off the swing, and Ava placates her with ooh's and ahh's. I can tell this isn't her first rodeo, so I laugh, agreeing with her sentiment.

"Thanks again," Ava says as Brooklyn starts down the slide. "I'm excited to get to know Brooklyn better. If you don't mind me saying, I know it probably hasn't been easy to be a single dad, but she seems like a really sweet girl." I look over at her a little taken aback. I'm not offended at all, just surprised that she's not scared to talk to me like a human.

"It hasn't been easy, but we've been really blessed in our situation. Not many single parents have the team that I have around me. It was mostly hard knowing Brooklyn wouldn't have her mom there to watch her grow up."

"I can understand that," she whispers, and I

look over at her again. She's watching Brooklyn and she has a distant look on her face like she's lost in thought. "I lost both of my parents at 14. I lived with my grandmother until I graduated from high school and then she passed away. So I'm lucky that I had my parents until I was a teenager. I can't imagine losing a parent as a child." My heart breaks in almost a million pieces for Ava as a little girl. She knows loss as well. She turns to face me, and I nod my head in understanding.

"I'm so sorry, Ava. Thank you for sharing that with me. If it's any consolation I think that makes you even more of a perfect fit for Brooklyn. You guys share something that not many others have experienced in life." She looks back over at Brooklyn and gives her a thumbs up as she does the monkey bars. But then she looks back at me and gives me a small smile.

"Thank you, Clark. That was kind of you to say."

"Yeah, of course. Thank you. I'm honestly glad you're here. I think you'll be a great fit. Plus, Brooklyn is a pretty good read. If she's making you chicken and waffles already, then it's safe to say you're gonna be just fine." I add, and she looks over at me smiling. She has a gorgeous smile, but it would be inappropriate at this point to say so. We both look back to Brooklyn, who's on the monkey bars still. I step up to ensure she makes it across.

She swats me away as Ava and I both laugh at her independence.

We head inside, and I hold the door open for the girls as they cross in front of me and into the kitchen. We stand around the kitchen island eating, and I excuse myself when my phone rings. It's Brian. I told him we had a second interview tonight, so I give him the run down. SHIT. We didn't talk salary. I'm sure she knows we would pay her well, although she didn't even ask. I wasn't planning on this going so well. After Lydia, I figured that it would be hard to find the right person. I don't expect her to stay with us forever. I mean she's stunning, has a great personality and is so personable. It will only be a matter of time before some casting director picks her up or she's booked in a huge movie.

I walk out of my study after speaking briefly with Brian. Brooklyn is watching TV. I join them, and Ava looks over at me. God, I almost forgot the energy between us. I need to reel this in. I'm a professional and I've never had an issue with being professional before. I'm sure as hell not going to start now.

"We didn't discuss salary," I add, and Ava looks to Lydia and then back to me. I see something flash across her eyes. Worry, maybe? Maybe talking about finances makes her uncomfortable?

"If you guys want to talk about that after I

leave, I can wait to hear from Tammy about what you decide?" she adds, and I shake my head. Not a chance, I think to myself.

"I will let Tammy know. She'll get her normal rate. I'd like to suggest something a little different than her usual arrangement for your pay," I say, and Ava looks nervous. "Since what we are asking for is so all over the map. Since you'll be full-time, and you'll have to be flexible with us, at least until we figure this out, I want to start your salary at $250,000 a year," I say, and her mouth drops open. I can't help but look at her beautiful mouth. When I smile, she closes her mouth and looks at Lydia.

"That's too much," Ava says, and I shake my head.

"Not for what we're asking you to do," I insist. "And that's just your starting salary. That doesn't include Christmas, birthday, bonuses, vacation, sick time. You'll also have to travel some, and you'll be staying here a lot while I'm away."

"That's just too much. It's very generous Mr. Grant, I—"

"Why is it too much?" I interrupt. "And please call me Clark."

"I don't know. It makes me feel," she pauses, looking around for Brooklyn. "It makes me a little uncomfortable. I'm nannying your child, not running your business," she adds.

"Didn't I tell you she's the most important person in my life? I think what I'm offering is fair," I whisper as I hear someone walk in the front door. Must be Brian. That was fast.

"Already negotiating, I see," Brian says, looking from me to Ava. "Is he low-balling you?" he asks her sarcastically, and I'm actually offended. "You feel like you should have more than $250k?"

"No," she cuts in sternly. I'm a little taken aback by her tone, but also a little turned on. She's all business now. "I think $250,000 as a starting rate for a nanny is a little absurd, and frankly, it makes me a little uncomfortable. I'm not exactly sure what I was expecting but that's a lot of money. I knew you would pay me a fair salary," she says, softening her tone, unintentionally drawing me in. She has my attention as well as everyone else's in the room. "But that's just a lot for me. Okay?" she asks. I want to tell her I'll pay her whatever she wants, but we're going to do this right.

"This isn't about you, Ava," I say, tuning out Brian's glare. "This is about Brooklyn. It's about what she deserves. This can be between us. I have a mind to ask you why you don't think your time and energy is worth $250,000. I would think it would be worth more, but this is a fair salary for being a traveling and live-in nanny for a lot of the year to an actor in Hollywood. You've seen the house. I'm sure you probably can Google and find out what I'm worth. Don't you think the person taking care of my child should be well compensated?" I ask, and now it's a standoff. I see it in her eyes. Money makes her uncomfortable, but why? I'll find out later. She releases the breath she's apparently been holding, and my shoulders relax.

"Yes. That person I would say deserves to be well compensated. She is worth it," she says looking at Brooklyn, who is fading quickly on the sofa watching TV. "But that's a lot of money."

"Ok," I say agreeing with her. "It is a lot of money. But that's our offer." I win this battle. But I know that there will probably be some battles with her in the future I might not win. She seems to be strong-willed, which is not only great for Brooklyn, but for me as well. This town can wreck you. However, if you have a good sense of who you are and what you want, you are one step closer to your dreams. As I walk Ava to her car later in the evening, I'm a little concerned that she has to drive so far, but it's not my place to say anything. She turns around and gives me a small wave, and my breath catches in my throat. I bloody need to get a hold of myself. I close the door and when I turn around Lydia is standing there smiling knowingly at me.

"I'm not sure what that look is for, but it's not necessary."

"That's fine!" Lydia says as she cleans up around the kitchen. I head to put Brooklyn to bed, and she smiles at me the same way Lydia was. I raise my eyebrow at her and she giggles.

"I like Ava, Daddy!" she says as she's crawling into bed. "She's fun and she's really pretty!"

"Yes, she is darling. Are you happy that she will be your new nanny?" I ask, and she nods her head.

"She smells good, too. She smells like a fairy princess! Or maybe a mermaid!" she says, closing her eyes. She's out before I can finish her bedtime story.

I know she's gone, but in my mind I can still smell the faintest hint of coconut and vanilla. I see that Lydia is gone, so I lock up and sit on the wrap around sofa. I plug Ava's information into my phone. It's been about 45 minutes since she left. I love that she actually ate. I can't tell you how disappointing it is to hang out with women who are scared to eat in front of men. I'm not talking about those who watch what they eat for dietary reasons. I'm talking about the women who won't eat in front of men because they're embarrassed. If a man makes you feel less than because you are eating, kick his ass to the curb. If your friends tell you that you can't eat in front of a man because it's unattractive, find new friends!

I pull out my phone and text Ava before I lose the nerve. I'm just checking to see if she made it home okay.

Hey Ava. It's Clark. Make it home

okay?

Yes!! Luckily there was no traffic…I just pulled into the parking garage.

Perfect! Thanks for tonight! We're all excited!

No! Thank you! And thanks for checking to see if I arrived home okay.
That's very kind of you!

Absolutely. Least I can do. We will see you Thursday?

Yes! I I'm looking forward to it!

Awesome. See you Thursday.
Take care.
Let us know if you need anything.
Not going to lie. This might be overstepping but I don't love the idea of you having to drive so far back and forth. Especially so late at night. I know that's me being a caveman and probably over-protective and I just met

you today.
But I thought I'd be honest.

HAHAH!! You aren't a cave man.
I appreciate that. And I was
honest tonight.
You might as well get to be
honest too!
I'm actually thinking about
moving in a couple months so
that might not be an issue.
But thank you Clark!

Perfect.
That will help me sleep better at
night!
Sleep well Ava

You too. Don't worry about me.
I'll let you know if I need
anything!!

Goodnight Ava

Goodnight Clark!

Ava

I wake up the next morning with the biggest smile on my face. Last night I did a really stupid thing before bed. I did more Googling of my new boss. I fell asleep looking at photos of him. Stupid I know, but I couldn't help it. He's perfect. And what's worse -- or better, depending on your perspective -- he's really nice in person. I wasn't prepared to be this excited about a nannying position. Brooklyn was so adorable. I can tell she and I will be fast friends. When she started crying last night, I was sure that my heart might break in two. She really is a special girl. I'm sure the more I get to know her the harder it will be to step away when I do find the perfect role. I called Shanna on my way home, and I swear she's more excited for me than I am. When I told her that I would have to alter some of my available audition times she was not concerned at all. I figured she would blow her top, but she didn't. She said we could use it to our advantage. Especially when people start to see me out with Clark or Brooklyn. I told her I wasn't using them to boost my chances at getting roles. But in true Shanna fashion, she blew me off. She said soon people all around town would be talking about Clark Grant's new nanny. I told her she was a nut. That's the most ridiculous thing I've ever heard. Who in their right mind would care about some movie star's new nanny?

After a long conversation with a thrilled Tammy, I took a shower before heading off to my next audition. The role I'm auditioning for is okay. I love the casting director, but I'll be honest, this movie has no chance of being picked up by major studio. By the time I get home it's late, and I head to the kitchen for something to eat. My roommate, Ansel is in the kitchen and she's super moody. She must have had a rough day because she's drinking straight from a bottle of tequila.

"Tough day?" I ask sarcastically and she yells some expletives my direction. "Awesome. Sorry it wasn't your day," I say as she slams her bedroom door. "Yep, my day was long too. Thanks for asking!" I yell, knowing she can't hear me.

I decide it's time to look for a new place. I

make a sandwich, grab my laptop and start looking for options online. Most apartments are about the same. I would like to get closer to where I'm working and auditioning. I suddenly realize I probably can pay cash for both a car and for a new place with my salary alone. Not to mention my inheritance. I try not to touch that as much. I hear my inbox ping and it's an email with the details of our agreement from Clark's business manager, Brian. It's all pretty much as we talked about. There's also a couple of lines in the contract about a gas allowance, as well as a signing bonus after the first 30 days. Then a bump in salary after every 90 days. I about choke on my sandwich. WHAT? I doubt it's even worth it to try and fight this with Clark. I think it's absurd, but I'm going to be grateful for the opportunity. I take my phone out and text him.

You're a piece of work you know that?! Just got my agreement from Brian...

Hahahahaha! I've heard worse.
But yes I am.
The sooner you realize that probably the better!

I appreciate your generosity, Clark. I really do. But this is a little over the top. Don't you think?

Not at all. And not a chance we will change it!

Fine. I figured it wasn't worth an argument but you can't blame a girl for trying!

Try all you want Ava. I'm a stubborn old man!

I'm just going to roll my eyes at you from here on that last comment. *rolls eyes emoji*

Oh look you actually did it! You did roll your eyes!
Brooklyn calls those moji's. It's the cutest.

Awww that is pretty cute. Is she doing well?

Yes. She's with Lydia tonight. I just finished with a table read and I'm out at a business dinner with a couple friends!

Oh gosh! I'm sorry! Have a great dinner. Enjoy yourself. See you tomorrow!
Just let me know what time. No rush!

No problem at all. It's just some friends. Seriously text me anytime. I'm pretty good at responding unless I'm actually on set. But you can always reach me through Clayton if you need something and I'm out of pocket. I'll send you his contact info.
Save it to your contacts.

I hear a bunch of yelling from the living area of the apartment. Sounds like Ansel and maybe a boy yelling. I would love to leave her be, but I want to make sure she's okay. She's a horrible person but still human. I would hate for her to be getting attacked and I'm just busy in my room texting with my hot boss! I stick my head out, and the bottle of tequila flies past my head and crashes next to my door. Glad she's drunk or that would have knocked me out, or worse. Ansel yells at me to mind my own damn business and I yell back through the door that I was just checking that she was okay. But NEVER MIND! I grab my phone and see that

Clark responded about five minutes ago.

Also, tomorrow let's shoot for 10.
Is that cool? Give you time?

Absolutely! See you then! Sorry
for the delay.
Crazy ass roommate almost
shattered my face with a bottle
of tequila.

My phone immediately starts to ring, and I almost drop it. Clark is calling me. Holy Shit. Don't panic. I answer and try to roll my shoulders back. Lord Jesus. It's Clark Grant on the phone!

"Hello?" I answer, and I hear some ruffling of covers in the background. Geezus is he in bed?

"Hey Ava," he says and the deep timber of his voice along with his British accent have me internally dying. I mean DEAD. "Ava? Are you okay? Can you hear me?" he asks, and I shake myself back to the now. I'm gonna have to answer his questions.

"Yes! Sorry. I'm here and I'm okay, I promise!" I mutter and try to rein in my female organs and act professional.

"Are you sure? Do you need to leave tonight? I can let Lydia know you're coming if you need to get out. I know you said you were thinking about moving, but we can expedite that process if we need to," he says, concerned. Now I feel horrible for even telling him about my roommate situation. I don't want him to worry. He has enough to worry about.

"No, it's fine, really. I'm in my room. I'm actually looking at apartments and other options as we speak. If I need some backup, I'll let you know. But thank you! I'm sorry for worrying you. It's really okay. I promise!" I utter in disbelief at the turn my evening has taken. I also can't believe Clark Grant is talking to me on the phone. It's surreal.

"I'm serious, Ava. There's nothing worse than not having a safe environment to come home to. Don't hesitate to ask if you need something. It's important to me that you are safe!" He says, and I have to bite my lip as I lay back in my bed and cover my face. Like that's going help!

"Thank you, Clark. You're sweet for offering. I'm hoping Shanna can hook me up with a good real estate agent. She's mentioned it before. I'll get on that ASAP. I promise!"

"Okay. Glad to hear it. If Shanna doesn't have a good agent let me know and I can send some recommendations your way. Brian can help as well, he's connected in that area. I'm dead serious. I know it's not my place. Nor do we know each other well enough at this point for me to step in. But I want to help if I can."

"Well…I appreciate that. If Shanna comes back with nothing, you'll be my next call. Deal?" I say, trying not to make my lip bleed. Lord in heaven, this man's voice is like hot silky honey running all over my body. And he's concerned about my well-being. My ovaries and heart are shouting at this point!

"Deal. Now call Shanna or I WILL!" he says sternly, and I giggle out loud.

"Yes. Sir. Captain. Sir!!" I blurt out before I can stop myself. I slap my hand over my mouth, but then I hear his voice lighten in response. He chuckles, and I've never heard a sound so hot in my life.

"So help me, Ava," he answers. I can tell he's trying to not laugh, but he's finding humor in our conversation. "If she had hit you with that Tequila bottle you would be in the hospital or worse right now." He adds as his voice is almost a whisper. "I told you I was stubborn, but I'm feeling like you might give me a run for my money."

"Okay! Okay! I'm calling her right now. See you tomorrow, Clark. I appreciate your concern for me. I really do!!" I say as I remove my hand from my mouth and can't help the big grin that covers my face.

"Goodnight Ava! CALL SHANNA and let me know if you need anything."

"I will. Goodnight, Clark!" I add and then hang up my phone. I cover my face with my pillow and have to laugh at myself. What alternative universe am I living in right now?

I immediately pull up my contacts and tap on Shanna's name. It's a little late, but Shanna will answer because she's a night owl.

She picks up on the first ring. "What is it? What's wrong?" she asks, and I laugh.

"Why would something be wrong?" I snap back and then remember why I'm calling her. "Clark wants me to call you right now and ask you to find me a reputable real estate agent. He wants me out of my apartment."

"Oh really…what else does Clark want you out of?" she purrs. I roll my eyes even though she can't see me. "And what brought all this on? Did he see that disgusting place where you live? If so, did he see your bedroom?" she replies, barely hiding her judgement of my less than glamorous accommodations.

I cut her off. "Are you done? No. Stop putting your fantasies off on me. I was texting him about the agreement and the schedule for tomorrow when Ansel and her boyfriend got into a fight. I was almost hit in the face with a tequila bottle!" I say loudly.

"Are you shitting me? Your roommates are nuts. I'm with Clark – you need your own place. And like yesterday!! Let me make some phone calls. I think we can fix this by the end of the week or next week. Also, do you want to try and get any of your money back? I know you paid everything up front."

"No, I don't want it back. It's not worth it. I'd rather just get out of here. I wasn't in a huge hurry until I mentioned it to Clark. Next time I'll keep those details to myself. He's a little… overprotective!" I say, trying to decide how best to describe this man I've met only once. But then I remember the sound of his voice on the phone.

"But he's still right. I'll make a couple phone calls and get back with you tomorrow or the next day," she says.

"Of course. Thanks Shanna!"

The next morning, I pull on some yoga pants and the matching top and head out the door. I grab a tea from Starbucks and I'm on my way to Clark's neighborhood. As I park in my designated spot, I grab my bag and head for the door, right as Brooklyn comes bounding out of the house. She almost knocks me over, and I drop my bags to give her a hug back. After collecting my new company card and my binder of all the benefits, we head to the garage to run some errands. Lydia smiles at me as she raises the garage door. I'm unsure of what that look is for, but I find out soon enough. Lydia walks me over to the 4th garage door and drops a set of keys with the Mercedes Benz logo into my hands as I look up at her.

"Do you like your new car?" Lydia asks and my mouth drops open. "Better just get used to it. That's who Clark is. He's a generous guy, and the quicker you come to terms with that the better. Just roll with it. It already has a car seat in the back for Brooklyn." I shake my head and laugh to myself. "It's the new G Class," Lydia says as she walks toward the lit-up SUV. As if I would know what a G Class or any other class of luxury vehicle is.

We head to Target to do some shopping for my new room as well as to buy a few things for Brooklyn. After an incredibly tasty lunch and a shopping trip that would normally give me buyer's remorse (although Lydia insists that it's absolutely necessary,) we head home. She told me Clark wanted to go ahead and have me rip the proverbial band-aid off with the credit card so I wouldn't be hesitant to use it. He apparently knows me well already. Lydia leaves after lunch since she got to the house earlier that day. We swim and swim and swim until I think Brooklyn is going to pass out before dinner from exhaustion. She's got a lot of energy, but when she's done, she's done. She gets a little testy a couple of times, but nothing out of the ordinary or that I can't handle. After I make her dinner, she falls asleep on the couch, and I start to clean up the kitchen.

Clark walks in and I smile at him. He's on the phone and rolling his eyes. I almost laugh out loud at his expression. He might be an actor, but I don't have to ask what kind of mood he's in. Whoever he's on the phone with, he's not happy with. This is the first time I've seen him not laid back and chill. He gives me a pleading look and then walks out of the room still on the phone. I cringe for him. Although I could listen to him talk. ALL. DAY. LONG. That British accent is hard to not appreciate. He could read anything and it would make me melt. I start to clean up in the kitchen when Clark walks back in and sits down at one of the barstools at the counter. I know we literally just met, but it's like we've known each other for ages. When we're in the same room, it's just easy. I walk up to the counter and act like I'm a bartender. I wipe down the counter and then drape the dish towel over my shoulder.

"What can I get ya, partner," I ask in my southern drawl. Clark laughs.

"Oh God. Something straight. Bourbon? Whisky? Scotch? A blow torch?" he answers.

"I think I can help you with the first three, the 4th might be a little dangerous with a four-year-old around." He nods. "Plus, I'm new here, and I don't know where they keep the alcohol. So I'm thinking maybe start with an ice water and then move on to the heavier stuff once I find it," I add, looking in a couple cabinets. "Nothing so far, but I'll find something. Don't you fret!" Clark laughs as he walks to the wet bar in the other corner of the room. Of course he has those fancy decanters and all the expensive stuff. "Ah, I wasn't even in the right area." He grabs a bottle of Jack Daniel's single barrel and a glass.

"You want some?" he asks. *Some of you, maybe.*

I shake my head and turn around so I can breathe deeply. Get it together, Ava! He's your boss. Your very generous, kind, and protective boss. Calm your tits! He pours a small amount in the glass and then heads back to the counter, placing the glass on the smooth surface. "Thanks again for today. Lydia said it went great. She sent a couple of pictures of Brooklyn in the pool. I'm surprised she's still up," he says, walking over to the sofa and kissing Brooklyn on the head. She doesn't even flinch away from the TV. "Tough crowd," he adds and walks back over to the counter to take a sip of his drink. I smile and he seems to relax a little.

"Rough day?" I ask, leaning against the counter.

"Bloody long day," he smiles, but I can see the exhaustion behind his eyes. "My early morning workouts started this morning at five. Gotta start preparing for the next movie. I headed out for an early meeting after that, then I was in a couple fittings and more meetings. Then straight to the table read up until 30 minutes ago," he says, looking down at his watch. "I'm not complaining, I'm just tired." I don't know how to respond, so I just go for honest.

"I know that sucks. And it's hard because you do realize how lucky you are, but at the same time you're still human. You have a young daughter at home who you're raising as a solo dad. That's hard and it's a lot of pressure. You're also running this empire and employ a lot of people, myself included. It's no wonder you're tired," I add, looking up at him and he stares at me with almost wonder in his eyes. I look down. "I'm sorry. I should have stopped at that sucks, right?" I ask.

"No. I was just going to say thank you. But I also was caught a little off guard by how spot on you were. If I complain to people in the industry, depending on where they are in their careers, they can sympathize. If not, they write an op-ed or a scathing email to some magazine about poor little rich Brit can't seem to get his life together. Then If I complain to someone not in the industry it normally goes south because they can't even rationalize what I'm talking about. But you seemed to sum everything up pretty nicely without feeling sorry for me or making me feel like shit. So, thank you, Ava!"

"You're welcome, Clark. And thanks for sharing. Can I make something for you to eat?" I ask, and he looks shocked.

"You cook?" he asks.

"Don't look so surprised. Yes, I cook. Well. Even Shanna has been impressed and she's a hard sell. She grew up with a chef. Cooking is one of my *favorite* things to do," I say and turn to see what's in the fridge. "However, we have a small problem. You have no ingredients to cook with. I'll go to the grocery store next time I'm out and get some stuff to make while I'm here. When do you need me to be here again?" I ask. He looks a little out of sorts, tired maybe. "Do you need me to stay tonight? Sorry we didn't talk about what today looks like for you."

"Ummm...," he says rubbing his hands over his face. "I think we're good for tonight. I still have Lydia tomorrow. I should have most weekends off until shooting starts. We start filming in October and I'll be in and out. But I'd say I won't need much overnight help until Brooklyn starts school in September. The rest of this month and next, I'd say just be on call. I will only need daytime help. So let's say eight to six? Is that okay?" he asks.

"Of course. That's fine. And I picked up a couple things to keep over here, so if I need to stay, I can do it without having to run home." I say, hoping he hasn't changed his mind about me shopping on his dime. "I hope that's okay!"

"What? All of it's okay. Lydia said you were very conservative with your spending today. Which I will say I appreciate. So do Brian and my accountant, but at the same time I want you to feel free to buy what you need while you're here. Anything to make what you're doing for us easier."

"Don't you think that I could use the money you've already allotted for my salary to buy those things?" I ask, and he gives me a gruff look.

"Let's not start this again. Sure, you could. But that's not how I roll, Ava. I take care of my people and whether or not you realize it, you are my people. OUR people," Clark says, motioning to Brooklyn who's passed out hard on the sofa. She lets out a long snore, and we both laugh. "I guess you guys aren't doing a movie night like she wanted," he adds.

"Yeah, I figured not," I answer quietly. "Thank you," I add. "Well since I can't cook anything, do you have delivery services out here?"

"Umm…yes, we do. All kinds of fun stuff around these parts. There's a great restaurant close by that delivers. Do you like sushi?"

"Yes. I do like sushi! I got pretty sick from some bad sushi one time, but I'm sure the quality here is a lot better than where I was."

"Well, the west coast has some of the best sushi. And I've been to Japan," he adds, pulling his phone out. "So here's the menu," he hands me his phone as he writes down what he wants on a note pad. When he's done, I write down what I want.

"You want me to call it in?" I ask and he shakes his head.

"Not necessary. I got this," he adds and smirks at me. "Knowing you, you'll walk off and try to pay for it."

"Not wrong," I yell as he places the call and I head to the TV room to clean up Brooklyn's dinner. I pick up a couple of her toys on the floor and when he walks back in, I'm loading the dishwasher.

"I've kept you pretty late. Hopefully food will be here shortly and then you can head back. I won't need you again till Monday, so hopefully you can rest some this weekend. Any auditions coming up that sound promising?" he asks genuinely, and I'm a little taken aback. He actually sounds interested.

"Not really. The last couple auditions went great, but they weren't the best fit for me. It's tricky to find the right part. It's hard to do musicals well on screen. When it's done right, it's inspiring. When it's not, it's so painful to watch, no matter how talented the cast is. It's my passion, but at the same time I won't die if I'm not working on a project." There's a buzz on the kitchen phone. Must be the sushi.

"I feel the exact same way," Clark says as he walks to pick up the phone. "Sushi time," he says rubbing his hands together. I grab us two glasses of water and then hear a ding letting us know someone came through the gate. Clark heads out to grab the food as I grab two plates and napkins. He brings the large paper bag into the kitchen and starts unloading container after container after container.

"How much did you order?!" I ask.

"You ready to see a magic trick? I can make everything here disappear," he says, motioning towards the bags. "I'm so damn hungry when I'm training," he adds, handing me my two small containers.

"If you can eat all of that, I will certainly be impressed. Do I need to get this on video so you can submit it to E! News?" I ask sarcastically.

"Don't be ridiculous! No one cares about me eating sushi. However, I don't have Instagram, so there's nowhere for me to share all this talent."

"Aw. I'm so sad for you. No audience?" I add sarcastically, and he laughs.

"Yes, the poor pitiful Brit. Every PR person and friend of mine has been trying to get me on the IG, but I just don't think it's for me," he says, finishing off a container of sushi, seemingly without breathing.

"WOW!! I actually think you're going to do it." I'm still working on my first roll and I smile at him as he chows down. It's pretty remarkable and not at all unattractive.

"Are you judging me yet?" he asks. "You kind of look like you want to say something."

"Nah. I'm impressed, Grant! You've almost eaten the four trays from the first bag. That's madness! But, hey, what a gift to have," I add, closing my containers and hopping off the stool to throw them out. "Also, kudos for being a recycler. The world thanks you."

"You bet! So, how's the house search going?" he asks casually, as if he isn't concerned about it.

"Nothing yet. Shanna said she thinks we will have some good prospects by the end of next week. I don't doubt her skills. She is the jack of all trades and will probably come back with some fabulous options for me. I've already sent an email to the apartment complex letting them know that I won't be renewing my lease. Hopefully it'll be a pretty painless process, but my roommates are quite the characters. Makes things not as simple as they should be. I don't have much, so I imagine I can be out of there pretty quickly. I sold the majority of my furniture and a lot of my crap before I moved. I didn't want to have a bunch of stuff in storage. I'll be doing some shopping here in a few weeks, which I'm not too excited about. But maybe Brooklyn can help me pick out some new stuff. That girl and Target are fast friends. She wanted to go up and down every single aisle today."

"She can definitely help you with shopping!

So, what do you think?" he says as I notice that he did clear every single sushi container.

"You did it."

"Told ya," he says, smiling proudly as he walks over to Brooklyn. "I'm gonna put her in bed and then I'll come back down." He lifts Brooklyn off the sofa like she weighs nothing. I'm not surprised, but at the same time those arms are impressive. A lot of him is impressive, but I'll keep that to myself. He joins me in the kitchen about 15 minutes later and sits back down on the bar stool.

"So, tell me about yourself, Ava."

"What do you want to know?" I ask, turning my face to him and he turns his head, looking at me and taking a sip of his water.

"How'd you end up in L.A.? How long have you lived here?"

"I've lived here almost three months. I used to fly out for auditions when I was living in New York. Then I met Shanna, and she talked me into moving to the west coast. I've played a couple of fun roles for Disney and a couple more promising roles in musicals, but nothing to take me where I want to be. I've loved Broadway since my grandmother took me to see Cats and The Sound of Music on Broadway when I was a little girl. Those were the two things that we really had in common. Musicals and musicals made into movies. I know. I should still be in New York City if I love those two things. There's something about doing musicals on film that really intrigues me. For movies and auditions it makes sense for me to be here."

"That's amazing. So you've also lived in New York. Where are you from?" he asks, and I place my elbow on the counter and turn my body so I'm facing him.

"Wilmington, North Carolina. I moved to New York after high school. I didn't want to get stuck in North Carolina. I had dreams and my grandmother really pushed me to follow them."

"That's amazing. Good for you. My parents were really supportive of me pursuing a career, so I really jumped at the opportunity to move to L.A." I hesitate to bring up my parents again at this point. I remember that I still have the new car keys in my purse, so I hop up and grab them from my purse. I place the key in front of Clark, and he looks up at me with a question in his eyes.

"Thank you," I say, nodding toward the keys. "That car will be fun to drive when I'm here."

"You sure you don't want to drive it home? It's yours to drive, Ava. Even when you aren't here. The 4th garage door is yours to use."

"No. I don't trust having that car in my neighborhood. Maybe after I move. Do you like your Land Rover?" I ask.

He leans close to me whispering conspiratorially. Like he's telling me he's going to steal the Hope

Diamond. “It’s okay. I might actually steal your car and drive it around. I want to see if it’s as great as everyone says it is.”

“Well. I think you’ll love it. It’s the only luxury vehicle I’ve ever been in, but I can say even from my lack of experience, it’s amazing.” He looks down at my lips and then stands up, placing his hands in his pockets. I clear my throat and continue. “Plus, I don’t think it’s stealing if you bought it,” I add, whispering back.

“Well, if it’s that great. I might sell my Rover and get a matching G Class,” he says. Luckily I now know what a G Class is. “I have plans to buy a Tesla at some point. But I want something sporty.”

“If you collect all 5 spices then you’ll have all the spice girls. How fun,” I joke, and he fakes being offended with his hand over his heart.

“I’m from the UK, Ava. The Spice Girls are national treasures. If you mock them, I might have to tell you we can’t be friends!”

“Oh, I’m so sorry.” I add dramatically. “I loved the Spice Girls growing up. You just said Sporty, and it made me think of the Spice Girls. You strike me as more of a Posh Spice kinda guy!”

“I’ll take it. Victoria is one beautiful and successful woman. But she’s married to another British Royal Treasure, so she’s off limits,” he says. “As much fun as it is to discuss the merits of each Spice Girl, I need to make sure you get home safely. It's getting late."

"Right! Yes, home. Thanks, Clark. I'll see you Monday, and I promise to text you as soon as I'm home. I'll text Lydia, but please pass on my love and safe travels to her as well. I know you guys are losing someone irreplaceable." I say, laying my hand on his arm. I don't even realize it, but we both look down at my hand, and I move it away quickly like I was touching a flame. He laughs for a second, but I can't help but notice he had to clear his throat. He looks up into my eyes and I feel a zap of electricity between us. I take a step back and almost run into the kitchen island.

"Thank you, Ava," he says, and I can't help but laugh. "For today. It was nice getting to know you a little bit. I'm so glad you and Brooklyn are getting along so well."

"It was fun for me too. I know it's still pretty early with you guys, but it didn't really feel like working today. Brooklyn is an amazing little girl," I add, and he nods. I grab my keys off of the counter. "See you Monday," I say as I walk toward the door. I need to go to bed. I really enjoyed today… maybe I enjoyed it a little too much? The situation I'm in is WAY surreal to me. I'm going to enjoy it while I can though. I feel totally blessed to have these new friends in my life. And I'm not going waste it. I know life can be short and I have every intention of living it to the fullest. Maybe not the way most people would want to, but in my own way. Plus, my hand still remembers what it felt like to touch his arm. NO. STOP IT. I can't go down this road. Not with him.

Clark

Ava leaves and I have to shake myself out of my stupor. She is so easy to talk to. I could have talked to her longer, which is bizarre for me. It's not easy in L.A. to find genuine people. But Ava is different. I know I shouldn't be excited for Monday but I am. It's a conflicting feeling. I'm her boss. She's my child's nanny. There's just something about her. I shake it off and head to my study to work a little. I'm glad I have all weekend with Brooklyn. It's been such a long time since I've had an entire weekend with my girl.

Of course I get called into a last minute meeting downtown on Sunday afternoon and Lydia is sick. I text Ava and groan. I wish I didn't have to do this on her weekend, but I can't help it. She's more than kind about being able to come to the house, but I still feel rotten about it.

When she arrives I meet her at the door. She's wearing yoga pants and a tee shirt. I look up to her face and realize she's looking me up and down as well. She looks away and I hold back the chuckle that wants to bubble up. I don't normally dress up for meetings with Brian, but we are meeting with some new producers today. I'm wearing a button-down shirt and some nice dress pants. I just got out of the shower, so my hair is still a little wet and unkempt.

Brooklyn runs past me and slams into Ava. I reach out to steady her and she laughs. I grab hold of her arm and she places hers on top of mine trying to not fall over. I chastise Brooklyn but it doesn't register. She's talking a mile a minute to Ava, and when I know she's not going to fall over I release her. She thanks me and then follows Brooklyn into the house. I shake my head at Brooklyn but then head back to my room to finish getting ready. When I come out of my room, Brooklyn and Ava are coloring. Ava is giggling and making funny faces at Brooklyn. I love their interaction. I realize that I'm just standing in the doorway watching them when Ava looks over at me. She smiles at me and then down at Brooklyn, who runs to give me a hug. Earlier I was stressed that I have to go to this meeting and leave Brooklyn. But then I know Ava is here.

I know she's new, but you'd think that she's been with us forever the way things just fell into place.

When I arrive home around 8:30, I try to quietly tip toe in the house. I figure Brooklyn is probably trying to go to bed right now. I put my keys down on the counter and grab a bottle of water from the fridge. I hear someone singing and I close the fridge door and try to follow the sound. I walk out of the kitchen and into my room as the sound gets louder. I stop in front of Brooklyn's monitor and look down at the screen. Through the night vision screen, I see Brooklyn lying in bed and Ava sitting beside her. The singing is coming from Ava. I'm stunned. It's the most beautiful sound I've ever heard. She's singing and I stand there too stunned to do anything else. I don't even know what to say. I know she's talented. I've seen video of her that Lydia found online from a musical she was in. Her voice is incredible.

I walk into my closet and change into some athletic shorts and a tee shirt. I notice that she's stopped singing as I head out of my room. She and I simultaneously enter the kitchen. She looks at me and I stop, placing my elbows on the kitchen island. She looks at me like she's waiting for me to say something. I open my mouth, but nothing comes out. She leans against the counter, and I clear my throat. I don't want to embarrass her, but she has me speechless. When she leaves I still can't find words. I'm in awe of her and we barely know each other.

Ava

I leave Clark's house and call Shanna back. She's pissed that I had to cancel brunch today. I didn't have much of a choice though. I mean, my boss called. I figured she would still be ticked off, but she answers as if nothing happened.

"What's up Scandy Mc-Scandal-son!" she answers, and I have to pause for a moment.

"What?" I ask and she cackles.

"So…are you calling to tell me you finally slept with your hot boss?" she asks, and I groan.

"Ugh. You are so exhausting. No I didn't sleep with my boss and you know that," I answer. I haven't left his house yet. I'm still sitting in the driveway. I wanted to call her to talk through our encounter before I left. It wasn't awkward per se.

It just was like he wanted to say something, but he physically couldn't.

"It would be a lot cooler if you did! Lord knows I would have already tried!" she mutters, and I have to smile. She's not wrong, but she's not his type. I blink myself back to reality with that thought. Lord knows I'm not his type either. He for sure dates super models and I am definitely not that. "Ava, hello?" Shanna adds, annoyed. "I was kidding. You know I'd never take a man from my BFF!"

"Shut up, Shanna," I groan as I lean my head against my head rest.

"Uh oh. What's up? I was kidding, but I know you didn't just call me to chat so what's up, seriously?" I tell her about mine and Clark's interactions and she is silent after I'm done. "Hello, Shanna?"

"I'm tracking with you. Give me a second. Okay, what were you doing before you realized he was home? Going through his underwear drawer?" She giggles and I ignore her.

"You know I wasn't. I was putting Brooklyn asleep. He came out carrying her baby monitor in his hand and he just looked like he wanted to say something. But it was like he physically couldn't. I didn't know what to do. I just told him goodnight," I groan, and Shanna laughs knowingly.

"Were you singing her to sleep?" she asks, and I answer yes. "That's it. He was in a trance, you naughty girl. He heard you singing to his daughter.

He's so into you and I think you just pushed him over the ledge," she adds, and I scoff.

"You're delusional, Shanna."

"Sure. I'm the delusional one. He couldn't speak because he'd never heard anything so beautiful in his life. Ava, just trust me. I'm rarely wrong, and I can smell the sexual tension through the phone. You like him and he likes you! It's just that simple." I blow out the breath I'm holding, and I can hear her smiling over the line.

"Anyways, I'll call you tomorrow. I need to start heading home. Find me a place to live Shanna." I start the car and pull out of the driveway.

"Got it, boss," she says, and hangs up.

Clark

Sunday evening I wake with a start. I hear Brooklyn screaming over the monitor. I jump up and don't even bother looking at the video monitor. I'm in her room in 30 seconds. Heart racing, blood pulsing through my body, ears ringing in panic. She's sitting up, crying in her bed. Nightmare. Jesus, it's just a bloody nightmare.

"Baby, daddy's here," I say, getting in bed next to her and wrapping her in my arms. She falls back asleep immediately. I'm wide awake and as my heart rate starts to normalize, I just thank God she's okay. I can't lose her. I don't know what I would do if she wasn't okay. I'll wait and see if she remembers her dream tomorrow. For now, I know she is safe here in my arms. The last thing I remember is holding Brooklyn, and the next thing I hear is a small, sweet voice saying my name. I try to chase after the voice, but it keeps getting farther and farther away. I wake with a start and see Ava standing at the door. Where am I? I look around and I'm still in Brooklyn's bed, but Brooklyn isn't here. I sit up and realize I'm only in my boxer briefs. I pull the covers up and look over at Ava, who looks a little embarrassed. She's staring at my chest and then looks away. She's holding the house phone and I realize it's light outside, which means I overslept. I've surely missed my morning workout and probably my meeting with Brian. SHIT. I hold my arm out so Ava can hand me the phone.

"Brian," I say and he's ranting so loud I have to pull the phone away from my ear. He's irate that I stood him up for our breakfast meeting. He thought I was dead. "BRIAN," I yell back, and he immediately quiets. "Brooklyn had a nightmare last night, and I fell asleep in her bed. I didn't have my phone, so just back off," I mutter, and he releases a deep breath.

"DUDE. I thought something happened to you. It's 10:00, man. Don't be pissed off at me. We couldn't find you. This isn't like you," he says. I look back at the door, and Ava is watching me. When our eyes meet, I give her a small nod and she backs out of the door and closes it behind her.

"I understand. But I didn't stand you up on purpose. I never sleep this late," I say, and he continues on and on. I finally interrupt him and ask him I can call him back in 15 minutes. I need to pee and grab some coffee before I reach through the phone and kill him for yelling at me first thing in the morning. I love his concern, but now he won't shut up and I need a second.

I head downstairs. I can see Brooklyn and Ava playing outside in the yard, and it gives me some small relief to see the nightmare is a thing of the past for my sweet girl. God, I hate when she has nightmares. Most of the time she doesn't remember them, but in the rare instance that she does, it breaks my heart more than it already breaks for my sweet girl. Sometimes it's about her mother and sometimes it's about silly things that I can assure her won't happen. I want to protect her, but there are just things I can't control.

I head outside to tell Ava that I'm leaving, then remember I don't really need to tell her where I'm going. I never told Lydia when I was heading out, but for some reason I want to tell Ava. Like she cares. I also feel like I need to address my lack of speech last night.

"Hey, Ava," I say. She is watching Brooklyn play on the swing set. When she turns around, she looks a little embarrassed.

"Clark, about earlier," she starts, and I hold up a hand.

"It's really okay, Ava. Don't think anything of it. I overslept and Brian was freaking out. I hope he didn't worry you or worse, speak to you the way he spoke to me," I say.

"He was freaking out for sure. I'm sorry," she says apologetically.

"Ava," I say, walking closer to her. "I'm sorry. It's really not a big deal. I'm sorry I wasn't more clothed earlier when you had to bring me the phone. I hope I didn't embarrass or offend you," I say, and she smiles. She makes a small snorting noise as she tries to conceal her laugh, and I smile back at her.

"You're kidding, right?" she asks, laughing.

"What?" I ask, smiling as well. I don't know why we are smiling, but here we are. "Why are you smiling?"

"Why are *you* smiling?" she asks. "I wasn't offended, Clark. Plus most of America has seen you half naked. I hate to break it to you, but it's nothing I haven't seen already."

"Very true, guess you can now say that you know I'm not photoshopped. That'll shut up the talking heads on TV."

"I will make some phone calls. That, along with my footage of you taking down dinner the other night. I'm sure it'll be a hit!" she says.

"Well, I'm glad you still have your sense of humor after this morning. I was only coming out to tell you I'm leaving for the day. I'll be back around

7 tonight. We had to reschedule a meeting from this morning to later this afternoon, so I'll be a little later than usual."

"No problem. Just know that I am going to take Brooklyn to run a couple errands with me today. I need to go look at a couple properties with the agent that Shanna recommended. I hope that's okay?" she asks.

"That's no problem at all. As long as Brooklyn is with you, you can take her wherever you need to go. I know we've only known each other a short amount of time, but you need to know that I do trust you. I don't want the two of you be stuck at the house all day long. I actually like Brooklyn getting out with you. Lydia stayed pretty close to the house. I like that you get my baby out and about," I say, and Ava looks at me with gratitude.

"Thank you, Clark. That means a lot," she says.

"Also, sorry about last night. I was at a loss for words, and I hope I didn't make you uncomfortable." I add, and she looks up at me.

"No, not at all. I was just concerned that maybe I did something wrong?" she adds, and I shake my head, smiling to myself.

"No. Nothing like that. I umm… I came in last night and heard singing and I just have to be honest. I was a little stunned by your voice. I wanted to tell you how beautiful your voice was, but I didn't know how to say it without sounding creepy. I appreciate you singing Ava to sleep. No one has ever done that for her," I say, looking down at her and she nods a little shyly.

"Thank you, Clark."

"Alright. Well call or text me if you need anything. And good luck with the house hunting. I hope you find something great." I give Brooklyn a big hug and kiss. I tell her how much I love her. "Bye, ladies."

"Bye, Daddy," Brooklyn yells back, making the stress from this morning lessen.

I come home Wednesday evening a little early. I figure maybe I could surprise the girls and take them to an early dinner. If Ava already has plans, then maybe Brooklyn and I can have a dinner date. I pull into the driveway and park in the garage. When I get out of the car, I hear giggling at the pool. I love hearing Brooklyn's belly laugh. I love when she's wild and free.

I walk out to the pool area and spot Ava. She's in a bikini, and my breath is sucked out of my lungs. I stop dead in my tracks and stare at her. My God, she's absolutely stunning. I take a deep breath and gather my thoughts. I'm just having a normal reaction to seeing a beautiful woman in a bathing suit. That's all this is. I redirect my thoughts and walk out onto the pool deck. Ava is walking out of the water like you'd see in slow motion in a movie.

Brooklyn spots me and yells my name. I whip my head to her and try to change course. I've got to get my mind right. She waves at me, and I wave back. Ava grabs a towel from one of the lounge chairs and wraps it around her. Brooklyn joins her and Ava sits down to start to dry Brooklyn off. She doesn't make eye contact with me, and I smile to myself. I pray I don't make her uncomfortable. I want her to be comfortable wearing a bathing suit at my damn pool. It's my own shit that I need to reel in. Brooklyn breaks away from Ava and runs to the deep end. Ava starts to stand up and I hold my hand out. She takes it and I help her to her feet. I know she doesn't need it, but I want to be a gentleman. Her hand is still wet from being in the pool and my heart rate jumps up when I feel her wet skin, then remember what she looked like coming out of the water…

Brooklyn yells for me to watch, as she cannonballs into the water, creating the smallest ripple across the surface. I chuckle and so does Ava.

"How long have you guys been out here swimming?" I ask, and she looks down at her phone.

"Oh gosh! Almost three hours. Brooklyn helped me shop today. I promised her we'd be able to swim this afternoon. I guess I didn't realize how fast time flies when you're swimming. The pool is amazing by the way."

"It is. It's one of my favorite things about the house. Brooklyn has always loved water. My father calls her his little fish. She's always loved swimming."

"I can tell. I was nervous with how brave she was at first and then realized she can probably swim better than I can. She's a natural in the water."

"That she is. I'm sorry I didn't let you know I was coming home early. Do you guys want to go out and grab dinner?" I ask, and she looks back to me a little surprised.

"Sure! Let me get Brooklyn out and we can get dressed real quick. Maybe beat the dinner crowd?" she adds. We get Brooklyn out of the water only by bribing her with chips and salsa. Brooklyn and Ava head upstairs to change, and I check my email. They're down in 10 minutes. I'm stunned. Brooklyn's hair is in two pigtails and Ava's hair is in a bun on top of her head. She's added a little mascara and is wearing a t-shirt and cut-off jeans. Brooklyn's in a sundress. They both look sun kissed and I have to gather myself as Ava walks by me on our way to the garage. Ava smells like warm vanilla and coconut. It's intoxicating.

We sit down at our favorite Mexican restaurant close to the house. Brooklyn orders cheese dip and guacamole. Ava laughs at her and then helps her figure out what she wants for dinner. We make small talk while Brooklyn colors on her kids' menu. A few people turn to look at us, but Brooklyn is sitting between us. Not that it really matters. It's our business and no one else's. We've never been out together so I'm sure people will speculate. I need to warn her about the paparazzi though. It can be quite alarming if you've never really experienced that kind of invasion of privacy.

"I should probably warn you that there will be some paparazzi by the time we leave," I whisper as I lean closer towards Ava so other tables don't hear. I can already see people taking photos and videos while we are seated. No one's approached the table, but that doesn't mean they won't. Normally when I have Brooklyn with me, they are fairly respectful.

"I figured that would eventually happen but thanks for the heads up. I'm sure that gets old!" she says as Brooklyn attacks the cheese dip. She giggles at Brooklyn and then looks up at me.

"I'm used to it at this point, but I wanted to make sure that you were prepared."

"You're sweet, Clark. I realize it comes with the territory where you are concerned. I'm sure that they will be more concerned with getting a picture of you than of me," she adds, and I nod slowly. I'm not so convinced. Ava is stunning and I don't think she realizes what people will speculate.

"They will make all kinds of speculations. More than likely it won't be a big ordeal. However, I do feel some responsibility to make sure you feel safe. Especially when we are out in public," I add as she looks over at Brooklyn and then back at me. "I'll always do my best to make sure you and Brooklyn are shielded, but there are some things that are out of my control. Especially when it's been a long time since they've seen me out with a beautiful woman." She looks up at me a little surprised, but then smiles shyly over at me.

"Thank you, Clark."

The food was absolutely delicious. By the time we leave the restaurant there are more than a few paparazzi outside waiting for us to leave. I pick up Brooklyn and carry her to the car; Ava walking a few steps behind us carrying Brooklyn's to-go box. By the time we get back to the car and head toward the house, Brooklyn is falling asleep in the backseat of my Land Rover.

"She's just so damn precious," Ava whispers, and I nod.

"I may be a little biased, but I have to agree. How'd you like dinner?" I ask and she groans.

"Oh my gosh. SO good. I have to admit, I love to eat," she says. Her smile is almost blinding. Her hair has mostly dried, and she has a couple of curly pieces around her face.

"I love to eat as well. As you already know! Is your hair naturally curly?" I ask, looking over at her.

"Naturally wavy is what I'd say. It has a mind of its own. I washed it real quick when we went upstairs. I didn't want to keep you waiting," she says.

"That's refreshing!" I answer, and she turns to look at me.

"Really? How so?"

"Well…I guess I assumed it would take at least 30 minutes. I was shocked you both were downstairs so quickly," I say as she stares out the window. The sun is starting to set, and the sky is gorgeous.

"God, I love the sunsets here. I don't know if I'll ever get used to it!" she says to herself more than to me.

"They're stunning for sure!" I say as we pull into the neighborhood. Ava waves at Anthony at the security booth as we pass, and he waves back cheerfully. I've really never met anyone like her.

"If you don't mind me asking… has it been difficult to date? I'm guessing that social media and paparazzi make it pretty hard to have a personal life," she asks. It should feel intrusive but it's not at all. I can't help but appreciate her braveness.

"It can be. I've never introduced a woman to Brooklyn. I certainly haven't brought a woman back to my home. Communication up front has been key to ensuring everyone feels protected and on the same page about what our arrangement is. Most of the women I've dated or been out with were already pretty established on the paparazzi and L.A. scene. Brooklyn's lost enough in her life though. I'd hate to introduce another female relationship into her life only to have her lose that as well."

"That's understandable. I can't imagine trying to figure all that out in the public eye."

"How about you?" I ask, since we're already talking about it. "Have you experienced the L.A. Love scene yet?" She smiles and shakes her head. I catch myself looking at her lips and then quickly turn back to the road. She's distracting. In the best way.

"How's dating been for me?" she says, looking over at me. "Well, it's been pretty boring actually. I've had boyfriends in the past. When I moved to New York the social scene was hopping, but I never really found anyone that I liked enough to get serious. Plus, my day consisted of auditions, working on paying my rent and then more auditioning. I loved that part of my life in New York. But most of my guy friends were gay, so that kinda took care of the dating issue. Since I moved to L.A. I've been out maybe a handful of times. Most of the time with Shanna and she's such a big personality that I could conveniently slip into the background."

"Really?" I say a little surprised. "I'm actually a little surprised by that."

"You shouldn't be. Shanna is a force to be reckoned with and the kind of men she attracts are not my type of guys. I've met some nice guys at events with Shanna, but I haven't been interested in dating any of them," she adds as I turn my attention back to the road. "Also, I've only been here a few months. Shanna keeps me pretty busy with auditions during the day and Tammy had me working evenings for families. The guys I have met LOVE talking about themselves and who they know. It makes it pretty easy to sneak away. In my limited experience, the L.A. social scene has been slim pickin's. Plus, hearing Shanna's dating stories have me running for the hills and locking my door. I don't feel like I'm missing much!" She leans her head against the headrest, and I smile back at her.

"Sounds like we've had somewhat similar experiences."

We pull into the driveway a little past 7:30. We spent a long time at dinner talking and eating a lot of chips and salsa. I apologize for keeping her later than normal and she waves off my apology. I carry Brooklyn inside and Ava follows me. She walks upstairs with me and then heads into her bedroom next to Brooklyn's. I close Brooklyn's door behind me after I get her tucked in. She was out again in no time at all. I walk past Ava's bedroom and pause in the doorway. She and Brooklyn have spent this week decorating her room and I really like it. I tell her as much as she zips up her weekender.

"Thanks!" she answers in appreciation, and I step aside so that she can go first. "Brooklyn and I have really enjoyed decorating together. She's so much fun."

"She is fun. She's also exhausting."

"I get that. She has a lot of energy. Today around 2:00 I thought I was going to have to have some caffeine. But then she let me lounge in the pool while she played mermaids."

"Mermaids, huh?" I ask as we make it down to the kitchen.

"Mermaids is so much fun. Especially for me. I pretend I'm a mermaid sunbathing and lounge while she goes out to look for food and battle the evil sea witch!" Ava laughs, and I have to chuckle at that. "You should join us next time. It's fairly entertaining."

"I'll check my schedule." I joke, and she giggles. I look over at her. She's standing in the kitchen, but the light from the setting sun is shining down on her. She almost looks illuminated. She catches me and I look away. "Thanks for today, Ava."

"Absolutely. I love it. Honestly I do! I feel really blessed to have met you and Brooklyn. I'll see you tomorrow," she adds, and I nod. No need to say anything else. I walk her to the front door and watch as she walks to her car. I sigh as I shut the door. She's just so damn amazing. I can't help but feel that way. I'm trying to fight whatever feeling this is. I've caught her staring at me a few times tonight. I'm not sure if that's because I am who I am or if it's because of me. The real me, the guy behind the scenes. Without the pomp and circumstance. I'm just me and I feel like I can be that guy with her. At least I did this afternoon. I haven't enjoyed myself like I did tonight in way too long. Things are just so easy with her. That's all there is to it.

Friday morning I have a few meetings that are rescheduled for next week. I hope to get some time at home today to catch up on reading some scripts. I come out of my bedroom and see Ava and Brooklyn in the kitchen singing and dancing. Ava's back is to me, so I lean against the door frame of my bedroom and watch them jump around. Brooklyn is having a blast and Ava is…GOD! I don't even know how to describe her. Brooklyn spots me and points to me.

"Come on, Daddy," she squeals, and I shake my head. Ava keeps on dancing and waves me over.

"Yeah, it's a little too early for dancing," I yell over the music. I push myself away from the door frame and head into the kitchen. I open the fridge and grab some fruit, turn the coffee maker on and pull a cup down from the cabinet overhead. I'm in some athletic shorts and I've forgone my t-shirt. The song stops so they take a break. Brooklyn heads back over to the sofa to play and Ava leans back against the kitchen counter, taking a sip of her tea. I look over at her and then lean back against the counter next to her. We're watching Brooklyn play with her dolls. She's so animated. I look down at Ava and she looks up at me. That instant connection between us takes my breath away every time. I turn to look out the window, but I can feel Ava's eyes on me.

"So did you have some cancellations this morning?" she asks, and I finally take my gaze away from the storm clouds outside.

"I did, thank God. I go in around noon. My trainer's wife is having a baby this morning. So no working out for the next week. I'll probably go on a run and work out here a little later. I let myself sleep in this morning."

"You probably needed that. I wish you could spend some time outside or by the pool. Unfortunately, it looks like it's going to be a stormy day," she says. Just then, a huge crack of lighting hits close to the house. It rattles the ground, and she jumps.

"You okay?" I say, resting a hand over her forearm. She sloshed her tea out of its cup when the thunder rattled the house. She places her cup by the sink and grabs a paper towel. I grab one as well as she goes down to the floor to clean up her spill. I go down to my knees and place my hand over hers. I notice her hand is shaking and she laughs quietly.

"Sorry. I have some serious PTSD from growing up on the Carolina coast. Hurricanes and all. I've always loved storms. But then we had a pretty bad hurricane one year that was a really close call for my family. Sometimes when I hear the loud cracks of thunder, my brain immediately takes me back." She sighs dropping the paper towel on the floor. Wringing her hands together. I take both of her hands in mine, and she looks up at me.

"Don't apologize. We all have stuff, Ava. You're safe here. There's no hurricane anywhere near us. Okay?" I whisper, and she nods her head.

"Thanks. I haven't had that happen in a very long time. Sorry about the floor."

"You realize I have a four-year-old, right?" I say, and she laughs. "There's been more than tea spills on my floors. That I can promise you!"

"I can only imagine," she says as she sits back on her heels. I stand up and place my hand out for her to take. She takes my hand and I pull her to standing. I wrap my arms around her and she walks naturally into my arms. "Thank you."

"Of course. You feel better?" I ask as I also now need to take a breath. I wasn't planning on pulling her into my arms, but it just happened.

"Yes. Thank you," she says as we both take a

step back. She looks up at me and I nod at her. She picks up her teacup and walks over to Brooklyn. I need to put some space between us. What happened was so natural. I wonder if she feels the same way.

Ava

I take deep breath and sit with my back against the couch. Shanna was supposed to come by today and swim, but we had to reschedule. I knew it was supposed to storm, but I didn't realize that it was going to be like this. I can barely see out the window. Clark was so kind and caring earlier when I freaked out and spilled my tea on his kitchen floor. That hasn't happened to me in such a long time. While Brooklyn naps, I decide to read downstairs. Clark left a while ago for a meeting and I'm not sure when he'll be back. I've been sitting here reading my book, but I don't think that I've processed anything I've read. I finally put the book down and get up to make another cup of tea. I keep thinking back to this morning. Clark pulling me into his arms and me resting my head against his strong, muscular chest. It was the most natural thing ever. There was nothing weird about it. So why do I feel like I need to apologize again? We've become so close, so fast. I do find myself thinking of him often. Replaying certain moments in my head that I've had with him. Nothing sexual, because nothing like that's happened. More like… moments. I'll catch him watching me and then he'll smile. Or he'll catch me watching him and I'll smile knowingly at him. UGH…it's kind of frustrating. We're friends. He's my boss. This shouldn't be anything I'm consuming myself with.

I fall asleep on the couch. The sounds of the rain against the window lulled me to sleep. When I wake up, Clark is sitting on a chair in the same room as me, reading a script. He's wearing glasses and drinking a glass of water. His hair is wet and he's wearing jeans and a t-shirt, like he's just showered. His feet are bare and he's got one foot propped up on the ottoman in front of him. He looks over at me and I smile. He smiles back, taking his glasses off and placing them on the table beside him.

"I was hoping to not wake you," he whispers, and I shrug my shoulders.

"Wouldn't be a big deal if you did." I look down at my watch and shake my head. "She must have been tired. It's almost 3 p.m. I should go wake her up so she's not up until midnight tonight."

"She'll be fine. If she's not up by 3:30, I'll go get her. How are you feeling?" he asks, and I sigh.

"I'm good. I know I shouldn't apologize for earlier, but I am sorry." I say as he stands up, coming over to the sofa and sitting on the other side. I tuck my feet underneath me, and he places an arm on the back of the sofa.

"You're right. You shouldn't apologize. You have no control over what happened. My grandfather survived World War II. Anytime there were fireworks in the vicinity he'd have to take something. It sent him back to those war times. A lot of people have triggers for different things, Ava. It's nothing to be ashamed of. I'm just glad I now know about it. You're safe here, and you're safe to share that kind of information with me," he adds.

"I've not had it affect me like that in a long time, so it kind of took me by surprise," I answer.

"It happens. I'm sorry you had that trauma. I know you've had a lot of loss in your life, Ava," he adds. "Will you tell me about your parents?"

"They were wonderful. High school sweethearts, so in love. They were on their way home from a date night when their car was hit by a drunk driver. They were killed instantly. At least that's what the coroner's report said. I pray that's true… that one moment they were holding hands and the next moment they were in heaven. At least that's what I'd tell myself growing up. I moved into my grandmother's house after that. Things were so different. I was just getting to know them really. I was in middle school and learning about my parents as humans, you know. Not just Mom and Dad."

"I'm so sorry, Ava. That must have been so hard," Clark says as he turns his body to face me.

"It was. But I know they're in a better place. I got to spend time with my grandmother for four years before she passed away. She was my best friend. We had so much in common with each other. I adored her. The fall before my parents were killed, there was a horrific hurricane. We almost lost the house completely. It's when I started fearing hurricanes and loud crashes of lightning and thunder together. It was crazy. The wind, the rain. There was no separating the thunder and the lightning. I was so scared. We were lucky though. I remember hearing that from my parents and my grandmother a lot after that. My Nana never said that again until before she passed. I don't think she felt lucky after my parents were killed so tragically. The last thing she told me before she passed was that we were lucky to have those four years together. Uninterrupted time. Those were some really tough years. They taught me a lot. I went to therapy for years to process all of it. It was one of the best things I ever did for myself. I learned to take care of myself. Sometimes the past creeps up unexpectedly though. Thank you, Clark, for being there for me. It was very kind of you."

Clark sighs, wiping a hand down his face and looking down. "We're friends, right?" he asks, and I look up at him confused.

"Yeah, we are. I consider you a friend," I say timidly.

"You'd do the same thing for me as I did for you this morning? Comfort me?" he asks, and I nod.

"Of course," I answer. He moves closer to sit in the middle of the sofa.

"Then you don't have to thank me for being a friend to you, Ava. I have a feeling we're going to be getting closer as time goes by. I'm not just your friend because you take care of Brooklyn. I'm your friend because I think you're wonderful. You are kind and caring. Fun and loving. I like being around you. You don't make fun of me, too much, for being able to polish off more food than a normal human being should," he adds, and I giggle. I nod and he leans forward, placing his arms on his knees and looking over at me. "I'm sorry for all you've been through, Ava. I think it's shaped you into the woman you are now. I think we might be the lucky ones. You've joined our crazy ass team and family. I'm not sure if you need to hear all this or not. I don't want to make any assumptions, but I appreciate you more than you can imagine. I didn't think we'd find anyone quite as special as Lydia was. She was with us through some really tough times. Angela and I had a pretty tumultuous relationship. She had some issues that she never dealt with. No matter how much I tried to encourage her to talk to someone she always blew me off. She had pretty bad postpartum depression with Brooklyn. By then it was already over. We weren't living together, and Brooklyn was with me most of the time. Angela didn't handle her body changing as well as she could have.

"After Brooklyn was born, maybe a year later, we started to see less and less of Angela. It didn't bother me because she irritated the hell out of me. We were together maybe three months before she got pregnant. I tried really hard to make it work. It didn't though. We co-parented as best we could, and I'm grateful that Brooklyn was with me most of the time. I think that was for the best. Angela was adamant," he says, looking around to ensure Brooklyn isn't around. "She was adamant that she didn't want to be a mum. She started getting addicted to plastic surgery and having little minor things done. Eventually it ended up taking her life. She wasn't eating, barely sleeping unless she was taking pain pills. It was sad to watch. She stayed out of the public eye as much as she could. I tried so hard to get her to talk to someone. She never would budge, said she had it under control. When Brooklyn was 18 months old, she was with me in London while

I was shooting a film. Clayton told me that Angela had passed away. Honestly, I wasn't surprised. No one that really knew her was. It's so damn sad to me. I think back on all the things I could have done better. Made her check into a clinic or something. Anything. It took me a long time to realize that I couldn't save her, as much as I wanted to. She died during a procedure. I pray that she went to sleep and woke up in heaven. Completely at peace. It haunts me at times."

"I'm sorry, Clark," I whisper, reaching over and grabbing his hand. He squeezes it reassuringly. I sigh and then hear Brooklyn coming down the stairs. She runs into the kitchen, and then, spotting her daddy on the sofa, jumps into his lap. He leans over, kissing her on the top of her head as she snuggles into his chest. I smile at him, and he smiles back. The rest of the day we watch TV and hang out on the sofa, just the three of us. It's actually quite nice. It feels good to be surrounded by good people. Brooklyn is such a wonderful distraction. I adore her and her father. I also feel so much closer to him since our conversation. I'm planning on coming back tomorrow and swimming with Shanna and Brooklyn. Clark has an appointment and said since it's going to be such a gorgeous day we could have a swim party, just the girls.

The next afternoon Clark leaves, and we head out to the pool. Shanna shows up late, of course. She'd say fashionably late, but that's debatable. We sit by the pool watching Brooklyn swim, and when I look up, Clark's walking toward the pool. He's carrying two bags in his hands, and I giggle. There's no telling with him. He opens the gate to the pool deck and heads over our direction. Shanna purrs and I slap her leg. She acts like she wasn't doing anything, but I KNOW she's going to do something saucy. It's her specialty. I laugh at her when Clark walks over and places the bags on the bistro table. He takes his shirt off and I about have a coronary.

GEEZUS!! He's perfect. I look at Shanna and she whimpers. Brooklyn screams as he runs and launches himself into the shallow end, in a cannon ball. I laugh hysterically as he soaks both Shanna and I. Shanna's no longer laughing when he comes up from under the water and throws Brooklyn in the air, catching her and spinning her around. His wet body reminds me of the magazine article I read not too long ago. I have to remember to breathe. He looks over at me, smiling knowingly, and I shake my head. He's gorgeous, but I pull my eyes away and look over to the bags.

"What's in the bags, Grant?" I yell, and he struts out of the pool. His body is unbelievable. He catches my eye and I look away.

"Let me show you," he says, walking over to the table. Shanna makes a snide comment or two and I slap her leg again.

"OW! You're going to bruise me," she says, rubbing her leg. I give her a warning glare.

"M'ladies," he bows and places a bunch of sushi in front of us. We dig in. Brooklyn comes over every few minutes, and I feed her a California roll before she runs back to play in the shallow end. Clark sits next to me on the lounge chair. I scoot over and we eat and talk about our day. He tells us about a fitting he was just in, and Shanna talks about a horrific date she went on last weekend. Shanna tells us she has to go get ready for an industry party tonight. She invites me, but I politely decline. After Shanna leaves and we've finished our sushi, we are cleaning up as it starts to downpour.

We laugh, trying to gather up our bags, towels and Brooklyn. It's raining so hard I can barely see in front of me. We are halfway up the path to the house when I slip with all the towels. Clark tries to reach out with one arm to catch me as he places Brooklyn on the ground. He slips on the rainy, muddy path and knocks us both down. We're both laughing so hard on the ground that it takes me a second to catch my breath. Brooklyn's made it inside and is yelling at us to hurry up. I'm lying flat on my back as Clark sits up, laughing harder than I've ever seen him laugh. He props himself up on his forearm looking over at me, water dripping from his soaking wet hair. The water running off his muscular chest and arms stops me laughing as our eyes meet. His intense blue eyes take me in. He stands up and holds his hand out to me. I take it, and he pulls me to my feet like I weigh nothing. We laugh again as we walk the rest of the way to the back of the house. He grabs some towels from the laundry room and hands me one as he wraps one around his waist. I start to clean up the floor, but then I hear Brooklyn yelling for me to give her a bath so she can watch cartoons.

"I'll clean up this mess," he says, and I nod walking past him. "Hey. You okay? No injuries from that fall?" he laughs and I shake my head.

"No, just muddy and wet," I say, and then close my eyes as I realize how that sounded out loud. He laughs, and I keep walking. "I'm just gonna go upstairs after that last comment." I add as I walk up the stairs. Good lord, Ava. Why don't you just go ahead and tell him how he really makes you feel?

I give Brooklyn a bath and take a shower myself. Brooklyn heads downstairs and I dry my hair. I don't have anywhere to be, but I'd at least like to get my hair dry before I leave. I pull my hair up into a clip and put on my yoga pants and a crop top. Downstairs, Clark and Brooklyn are sitting on the couch watching a movie. I grab my bags and walk over to them. Brooklyn gives me a kiss on the cheek and a hug. She jumps back in Clark's lap, and he makes a loud groaning noise.

"Easy, baby," he says as she giggles.

"Thanks for dinner, Clark. I appreciate it. I'll see you guys next week!" I add, and he nods. He moves Brooklyn over and then stands to walk me to the door.

"I wanted to show you something before you left," he says, and I have to check my thoughts to stay away from the gutter. I follow him to his study, and he walks behind his computer. He motions for me to join him. He's freshly showered, and the scent of his body wash has my insides tingling. I cross my arms over my chest as I see he's pulled up one of the security cameras on his computer. It's a video from the security cameras showing the two of us falling on our asses earlier in the pouring down rain. We both laugh, and then he looks up at me smiling. He has the most beautiful smile. I look down to his lips and then back to his eyes. The temperature in the room just got about 100 degrees hotter. I clear my throat and then nod towards the door.

"Thank you for showing me that." I add as I start around his desk. "I think we could win some money with that video," I joke.

"Pretty hilarious. Have a great rest of the weekend, Ava. Thanks for coming over today so I could take care of that meeting. I appreciate it," he adds as he joins me at the door of his study. "Also, if you're ever here and nervous. You're more than welcome to come in here and look at the security cameras. I have them strategically placed around the property. The password is in your binder, but I'll also send it to you so you can save it on your phone."

"Thank you, Clark."

"See you next week!" he adds. I turn around, and I can feel his eyes burning into my back. I take a deep breath but don't dare turn back around. He follows me to the front door, and I get in my car. When I climb in, I look over to the door. He's still standing there looking at me. I release the breath I've been holding.

The next week goes by so fast. Between Clark's appointments and Brooklyn's pre-screening for Kindergarten, it's a busy week. Clark gets home around 6 or 7 almost every night. I can see the exhaustion radiating off of him every evening. I wish I could help, but I can't. I have dinner ready almost every evening for him in case he hasn't eaten. Brooklyn loves cooking with me. I really enjoy our time in the kitchen together. Clark is always so appreciative. He's just a great guy.

I take a deep breath Friday morning when I leave the house. My roommate Ansel was in rare form when I left. I think she was coming off a bender or something. It's amazing that she's coming in from a night out as I'm leaving for work in the morning. It's a bad situation, but I'm working on it. I'm just happy that I've finally found a new place. It's not ready yet, but I'm getting so close. I think my roommates are pissed about it, but I don't care. I'm just biding my time.

Clark

What a damn week. When I pull into the driveway Friday evening, I throw the car in park and rest my head against the headrest. I love my life, really, but sometimes people just want too much. Earlier when I texted Ava to tell her I was running behind, she said exactly what I thought she would -- everything was fine and to take my time. So I did. My last meeting was a dinner meeting so I'm full, but I stopped and got some Sprinkle's cupcakes. They'll be a welcome treat for Brooklyn tomorrow, as well as Ava, I hope. I walk in the door with my bag and my sweet treats and it's quiet. I know that means Brooklyn is probably already asleep. Ava is sitting on the couch reading, and when she hears me walk into the den, she looks up at me.

"Hey! Good day?" she asks, and I smile.

"Long day, but a good day because I brought home cupcakes," I say, holding up the box.

"Oh fun!! What's the occasion?" she asks, closing her book and coming into the kitchen. She places the book in her bag and then comes over to me as I open the cupcake box. "Wow. I can smell the sugar from here," she adds, laughing. "Also, Brooklyn tried her hardest to stay awake, but she didn't quite make it. I just took her upstairs."

"I figured as much. She's still in that stage where she could probably use a nap during the day, but she fights it so hard. Then if she does take a nap, she's up till 9 or 10." I take out a cupcake and take a bite. "Help yourself," I add, and she looks down at the choices. She grabs a strawberry cupcake with pink icing. How fitting, she and Brooklyn love the same cupcakes. I got a bunch of different flavors, but I figured Ava would love the strawberry for some reason.

"You never said what the occasion was," she asks, placing a hand on my forearm as we both get high from the sugar wafting from the cupcake box. She takes a bite, moaning out loud, and the noise she makes almost makes me drop my cupcake to the floor. I catch it with my other hand and Ava looks up at me strangely. "You alright?"

"Yeah," I add, clearing my throat. "Must be

getting less coordinated in my old age," I say as I turn around and grab a paper towel to wipe the icing off my fingers. I take a deep breath, collect myself, and when I turn around Ava is giving me a strange look. "Don't look at me like that," I say, laughing. "You almost gave me a heart attack," I add, and she gives me a confused laugh.

"What? ME? Why? What did I do?" she asks, completely oblivious to the noises she made. So I pick up my cupcake and take a bite like she did and then make the same exact noise she made. She covers her mouth, almost spitting out her bite of cupcake. She laughs, heading to the sink to grab a paper towel. "Oh my gosh. I'm so sorry," she says, laughing and wiping her mouth. Now we're both cracking up.

"You don't sound very sorry, no more cupcakes for you," I say jokingly, grabbing the box and putting it up on a shelf that she'd need a ladder in order to reach.

"Maybe that's a good idea," she says, throwing her paper towel in the trash. "Well, I guess I've embarrassed myself enough for the day. Probably time to go home so I can gear up for another day of embarrassing myself. No telling what I'll do tomorrow," she says. "Thanks for the cupcake and the laugh, Clark."

"No. Thank you! And the cupcakes were just because," I add. "No special occasion."

"Just 'cause cupcakes. I guess that's a good enough reason? Glad I'm not on a diet," she says, turning to grab her purse.

"How did the apartment hunting go?" I ask. I know she needs to go, yet here I am asking more questions.

"Great. I actually found an amazing townhouse I liked in Toluca Lake. I think it'll end up being perfect for me. It's in a great location and seems really safe. Well, safer than where I am now."

"Really? That's great, Ava. So maybe these were celebration cupcakes, too," I tease.

"Can we just forget about the cupcakes?" she asks, laughing and blushing at the same time. "And thank you. I move in at the end of the month. I only have a few more weeks with my crazy ass roommates and then I'll be free!"

"No, we cannot forget about the cupcakes," I respond. "They're cupcakes, Ava. It's not their fault they are delicious. You want to take one for the road?" I ask jokingly. "Maybe not a good idea. You could cause a wreck."

"Shut up, Clark," she says, swatting me on the arm. The contact to my arm sends tingles down my spine, but I play it off. This isn't the first time my body has had this kind of reaction to her, and I know it won't be the last. It's more delicious than the cupcakes. I realize we've both gotten quiet and stopped laughing.

"So, no cupcake for the road?" I ask sarcastically.

"No. I'll grab another one…later?" she says, quietly looking up at me. The room suddenly feels very warm. We both step back at the same time, and she grabs her bag. "I'll text you when I'm home," she adds as she heads toward the door. I raise my hand as if she can see me waving goodbye. The door closes and I can only yell an expletive at myself. What the hell was that, Clark? These moments with Ava are the most charged I've had in years. In my kitchen over a damn cupcake. Yes, she's more than that, but I'm her boss and this is exactly what I do NOT need to happen. Not for my sake, not for Ava. Especially not for Brooklyn. The last thing she needs is for me get over my head with Ava and then ruin things. SHIT, I think as I lean against the kitchen sink. I grab my phone and send Ava a text.

Drive Safe!

I know she's driving so she won't text back until she's home, but I need to be more professional. She's a beautiful woman, and I need to get my shit together. But Jesus when she made that noise… who knew someone could be so jealous of a cupcake. I need to get out more. I've got a couple more weeks before Brooklyn starts school and then I'll be prepping to travel. I'll be gone for a while, and

I'll be able to get myself in check. Maybe I need to go on a date?

Ava

WHAT THE HELL WAS THAT? I yell at myself as I pull out of Clark's driveway. I have the entire drive home to run the last 20 minutes through my head over and over again. I don't know if I want to laugh, cry, or throw up. My God I should have just…something? What else could I have done to completely humiliate myself? Making sensual noises over a cupcake in front of your hot ass boss is right up there with… I don't know? I can't think of anything more embarrassing at the moment.

As I wave to Anthony in the security booth, my phone buzzes and I see it's from Clark. GREAT! He's probably firing me for being so inappropriate with my cupcake. He's around women all the time that make complete fools of themselves, I'm sure. Now I'm not any better than the lady the other week who literally stopped and humped his leg as he was walking into a restaurant on Sunset. UGH! I have SIRI read my text to me and it just says, "Drive Safe." I decide to wait to respond until I get home. I need to give myself some time to formulate some kind of explanation of why I was a complete ditz tonight. Maybe I can say I had an aneurysm. No, that's horrible. I pull into the parking garage near my apartment and take a deep breath. On a happy note, I won't have to pay to use the parking garage anymore. I have my own parking spot inside the complex at my new place. Actually two, but who's counting. ME, that's who's counting and I'm excited. But I need to reel it in a little bit with boss man or I'll be finding a new job. I pick up my phone to call Shanna and I have a text from her as well.

CALL ME!

When I call, she sounds out of breath when she answers.

"You're gonna love me!" she says, and I giggle. "Ask me why!"

"Why?" I answer and she goes into an elaborate story about who she just talked to at an industry event. Supposedly there's an audition coming up that she thinks is going to be amazing, but it's pretty hush hush. I try to keep up, but my mind is still on the cupcake.

"Earth to Ava!" she yells, and I sigh.

"I'm sorry," I mutter and give her the rundown of my day after she left. She laughs, and that's not what I was expecting. Nothing ever is with her.

"Sorry, I need to light a cigarette after that story. Remind me not to light a match around the two of you!" she says, and I frown. "Don't even say it, Ava. The sexual tension between the two of you is palpable. I mean, I can't blame either of you. The two of you together would be fireworks. But back to the reason I asked you to call. I'm gonna stay in touch with Eric from casting. I really think he has something big in his back pocket from what information he can give me. I'll keep you updated."

I hang up with Shanna and walk into my apartment. It's absolute pandemonium. Ansel and her boyfriend are fighting again. This time I'm not so lucky. I open the door at the same time someone throws a bottle or maybe it was a lamp. It shatters against the kitchen counter as I walk in and glass comes flying at me. I turn my face from the shattering noise and then glass slams against my shoulder and my hand. It stings immediately and I see blood.

I'm not normally someone who gets woozy seeing blood, but I feel like there is more blood than there should be. I have enough forethought to go to the kitchen and grab one of my hand towels from the drawer. The fighting is still going on, so no one notices that I have even been injured. I walk back out the door, but I know I shouldn't drive. I have my hand putting pressure on the wound on my shoulder and the wound on my hand is just dripping so maybe that means the bleeding is slowing down or maybe getting worse. I can't tell. I know I need to get to a hospital though. I'm sure I need stitches and to get the cuts cleaned out. I see a cab sitting at the corner of the street and I start to run towards it. I'm feeling a little faint, but I'm not really sure what else to do. From the smell inside the apartment, I can only imagine no one in there was sober enough to drive me anywhere. I take a deep breath and then lean over to tell the cab driver I need help. He jumps out and helps me into the car.

"Jesus! Have you been shot?" he yells, attracting people walking on the street.

"No. My roommate was fighting with her boyfriend, and I was just an innocent bystander. I think it was a shattered lamp or bottle or both? I didn't see it coming," I say, a little delirious. He mutters some expletives under his breath and then he's rushing us toward the closest hospital. We are at the emergency room in minutes and when I go to stand up out of the car I almost pass out. Blood loss? Shock? Lord knows. The cab driver helps me into the emergency room and then there is a lot of commotion. I notice my normally pristine gray and white towel is now saturated with blood. Like, dripping. That can't be good. I tell the lady helping me into a wheelchair that I need to pay the cab driver. He waves it off and I insist. "Please grab my purse," I yell at the man who is replacing the towel with something cleaner and looking at my injuries as I'm being wheeled away. I think I'm in a wheelchair. I yell at him that I will find out how to pay him, and then I feel lightheaded so I lay my head back.

I wake up and I'm lying in a hospital bed. I'm in a hospital gown and my arm looks stained a weird color in places. My eye is twitching, which is weird. What the hell happened to me? Car accident? I remember giving them my purse and the nurse finding my insurance card and ID. I remember her looking over at me and then my eyes feeling heavy as I try to keep them open. I think it's because it says the insurance provider is under Clark Grant's name. I remember telling them to call Brian, Clark's business manager, and then I don't remember much. A nurse comes in and asks me how I'm feeling.

"I think I'm okay. I didn't know all of this was going to happen," I say, motioning toward my gown and hospital room.

"You had a pretty nasty laceration on your arm. I'm glad you came in when you did. I'll have Dr. Ashburn come in and talk to you about your injuries. We also called your insurance provider as well as Brian in your phone, since you told us to call him. He said he would take care of everything. So just relax," she says, checking my vital signs. I lie back down and rest.

A little while later, the doctor comes in and tells me about everything going on. Apparently, there are some major blood vessels in your arm, and I got pretty close tonight to severing one. There are a couple of layers of sutures in my arm. I can't feel it now, but it sounds like it's gonna hurt. He says I have to stay overnight, just for observation. I had a blood transfusion because I lost a lot of blood. He says it will help with my recovery, which I guess is good. He tells me a bunch of other doctor jargon, but I'm starting to feel a little tired. They had to sedate me because I had to be taken into surgery. I was lucky. But, my God, this isn't what I was planning. As he is telling me about my recovery time and what is going to happen from here, a disheveled Clark comes into my hospital room. He looks calm and collected on the outside, but I can tell from his eyes that he is anything but.

"Clark?" I ask, shocked to see him. He looks over at me stunned, then to the doctor.

"Clark Grant," he says to the doctor and then turns to me, ignoring the doctor completely and sitting next to the bed. He goes to grab my hand, but it's covered in bandages. "Shit," he says looking at my arm and hand. "What the hell happened?" he asks, and I smile. My eye twitches.

"Will the twitching stop?" I ask the doctor.

"Yes. It's very normal. It could be a combination of a lot of things. The sedation, the blood loss, the shock. I would say it will go away as your body starts to heal. But it's definitely something we will keep an eye on. Your body went through a lot of stress tonight. Rest," he says, looking at Clark. "That's probably the most imperative to your recovery time at this point."

"What happened?" Clark asks, looking at me and the doctor. "The only thing they told Brian was that there was an accident at your apartment and that they were taking you into surgery."

"I'll give you a moment," the doctor says, excusing himself. "I'll be back to check on you later. If you need anything, just let the nurses know!" I thank him and then turn back to Clark.

I replay the night for him, starting from me walking in the door to when I woke up from surgery. He looks absolutely panicked, and I place my hand on his.

"Clark, I'm okay," I say. He starts to talk and then sits back in the uncomfortable looking hospital chair.

"I'm sorry it took me so long to get here. Brian called me and I had to wait for Clayton to get to the house. I didn't want to wake up Brooklyn. Maybe I should have though," he adds, and I squeeze his hand.

"No. Brooklyn doesn't need to be in a hospital in the middle of the night. And I'm not sure you do either. You know you probably alerted the paparazzi by being here," I add, and he rolls his eyes.

"You sound like Brian. He offered to come down, but I told him no. You don't know Brian. He's a great guy, but you don't need a stranger in here right now. I know we don't know each other that well, but I you know me better than you know Brian," he says, muttering to himself. "Have you called Shanna?" he asks, and I gasp.

"Shit," I say, looking around for my phone. "Can you grab my phone?" He gets up and goes over to my purse. I shoot off a text to Shanna. Her phone will be on do not disturb since it's past midnight now, so I just give her an abbreviated version of the night and hit send. I start to say I'm sorry, but he cuts me off.

"Don't you dare apologize. You don't have anything to apologize for, Ava. I'm sorry you are sitting in a hospital bed. Brian was worried sick when he got the call. He was shocked that he was your first call. He was honored, but at the same time worried sick. A little payback I guess from him yelling at me this morning," he says looking down at his watch. "Or yesterday," he adds looking up at me smiling. "Are you okay?" he asks, his thumb rubbing over my palm when I turn my hand over.

"I will be," I add quietly, and he just sits in the chair looking at me. "Are *you* okay?" I ask with a smirk.

"I will be," he says, sitting back and releasing my hand. My body immediately misses the contact and I pull my hand up so it's resting on my lap. "I'm better now that I'm here. Clayton hasn't met you, but he's also worried. Mainly because of my reaction. Then I got here, and I couldn't come back because you were in recovery. SHIT, AVA. They said that the lamp or whatever almost hit a major artery. Also, you are not going back to that apartment. EVER," he adds.

"Well…seeing as all my stuff is there, that seems like a pretty unlikely scenario, Clark."

"Clayton will get your stuff. Or hell, I will. I would go right now, but I'd probably be arrested. I don't want you going back into that apartment."

"Clark," I start to say, but he interrupts me.

"Would you take Brooklyn to your apartment?" he asks, and I close my mouth.

"My point exactly. You aren't going back. Don't push me with this, Ava. You could have died," he adds.

"I won't go back. It's not like I want to, I just don't want anyone else to have to either," I add with a grimace.

"We'll take care of it, Ava. We can buy you all new things if we need to. But for now, why don't you get some rest? I'll go see if the nurse can come check on you. Are you hurting?" He asks and I nod in response, laying my head back. My arm is starting to feel sore and stings a little. He leaves the room and comes back with two nurses. I look up and they are both smiling at me. I'm given some pain medication and told that I will probably become very sleepy. I lay my head back as I see the nurses look over at Clark and then at each other heading out the door. I forgot that he is "*The* Clark Grant." Today he was just Clark, Brooklyn's dad.

"You probably should head back to the house," I say, and he huffs as me comically. "What? There's nothing for you to do, Clark. You need to let Clayton go home. Plus, Brooklyn will be confused when she wakes up in the morning and you aren't there."

"She will be fine. She loves Clayton," he adds. "Are you trying to get rid of me?"

"Yes. It's my life's goal," I answer sarcastically with my eyes closed. I hear him laugh, and then I shiver. I feel a warm hand pull my gown back over my shoulder where it must have slipped. I open my eyes and look over at him. He's looking at me like he did with the cupcake fiasco earlier. His warm hand rests on my shoulder for a moment. My eye stops twitching, but I don't look away from Clark. "I'm not trying to get rid of you, Clark. I just don't want you to feel obligated to stay," I say, sounding braver than I actually feel. I would never say that in any other case. It has to be the pain medication.

"I don't feel obligated, Ava. I should have never let you leave earlier tonight to go back to that apartment," he says, regret showing in his eyes.

"This isn't your fault, Clark. I should have moved out a long time ago. This isn't on you," I add, closing my eyes. "You've been nothing but kind to me since I met you," I whisper as I start to drift off. I shiver again. I'm so cold. I feel someone pull the blankets at the foot of the bed over my body and then a small, tender kiss on my forehead. Or maybe I dreamed that part? Finally, warmth comes over my body and I fall into a deep, painless sleep.

Clark

I lean over and kiss Ava's forehead and then sit back down in the chair beside her bed. She was shivering, so I pulled the blankets over her, poor thing. The kiss on the forehead wasn't planned. I'm not sure where that even came from. I don't regret it. I care deeply for Ava. We all do. I keep telling myself that we've only known each other for such a short amount of time but hell, what do I know? The nurses come in a couple of times, and I do some work on my phone. I have cancelled a couple meetings tomorrow. I'm hoping to bring Ava back to the house with me. She can't go back to that apartment. Over my dead body. And she can't move into her new place yet, I think she said at the end of the month. So I don't know what other option she has.

My phone buzzes. It's Brian. He's calling to check on everything. He says the press hasn't been alerted yet about my being here but to expect paparazzi by the morning. It won't take long. Especially since I'm here with a woman. I tell him it'll be fine, and he laughs at me. I don't want this for Ava, but at the same time what am I supposed to do? Leave her here? Have a car pick her up and take her to the house? That's ridiculous. We are human beings. He tells me he has already contacted Erin, who handles my PR team. Always trying to get ahead of everything, it's the Hollywood Way. We hang up and I lean back in my chair. The doctor comes in at about 2 a.m. and wakes me up. He says Ava can more than likely leave when she wakes up in the morning. His shift ends at 8 a.m., so he's hoping to be able to check on Ava again before he leaves. I thank him and then fall back asleep.

When I wake up again Ava is still asleep. The sun is up and I look at my watch. 6:30 a.m. I rub my hands over my face and then head to find some coffee. GOD what a night! As I walk toward the nurses' station to ask where I can get some coffee, I see Brian walking toward me with 3 cups of coffee in a carrier and a small bag, no doubt filled with food.

"What are you doing here?" I ask as he smiles at the nurses. Back in the room with Ava, he hands me a coffee and then motions towards the bag. I pull out a croissant but put it back in the bag. This is the second morning I will miss my work out. Any more carbs and my trainer will have my neck.

"Here's the plan from Erin and I. You're going to leave in the service elevator. My car is there. I will bring Ava home in your car when she is released. You don't need the extra publicity right now and you definitely don't want to do this to Ava. She doesn't want to be the target of the paparazzi's obsession and the public's questions, especially with you about to leave town and her being here with Brooklyn. ALONE." I start to open my mouth and then realize he's right. I take another sip of my coffee then look over at Ava. "If you aren't careful Clark, I swear you are going to fall for her," he says, not looking at me. I nod. He's not wrong. I've never felt this way before. I want to tell him it might be too late for that, but it's a moot point.

"Yeah, don't want that," I mutter nonchalantly. I don't mean it and he knows it. I haven't been in love with anyone in years, not to mention dated anyone seriously. She's taking care of my daughter. I care about both of them, and we all have a job to do. "I'll see you back at the house," I say to no one in particular. I stand up and head to the door before I can talk myself into staying.

"Good boy," he says, moving to where I was just sitting. I turn around and look at Ava. He throws me his keys and looks over at me giving me a resigned sigh. “I’ll take good care of her Clark, I promise. Besides, she did call me not you,” he says with a cocky grin.

Ava

I wake with a start, reorienting myself to the reality that I am in the hospital and Clark Grant was here taking care of me. My arm is so sore. I look over to where Clark was last night, it isn't Clark. Was it a dream? He looks at me, realizing I'm awake and then tells the person on the phone that he will call them back.

"Doughnut?" he asks, holding his half-eaten doughnut out to me. I shake my head. "How are you feeling?"

"Alive," I say groggily, trying to pull the blankets over myself. Bad call.

"Let me tell the nurse you're up," he says. I look around the room and it's just as I remember it from last night. Then again, Clark isn't here. Maybe he ended up leaving in the middle of the night. Smart. It's better that way. Brian comes back with the nurse, and she starts to take my vital signs. Doctor Ashburn comes in and gives me my discharge instructions. Take it easy for a couple days. He's sending me home with a sling to make it easier not to put any extra strain on my shoulder. He asks me if I need a note for work and I look at Brian. He laughs, shaking his head, and I look back at the doctor and tell him no.

I get dressed in some hospital scrubs, since my clothes were covered in blood. Brian takes me to Clark's car. Well, it looks like one of the cars Clark had in his garage. Maybe everyone in the company has the same cars. I don't know. I can't really concentrate. Brian says that he is going to drop me off at Clark's and then he will have someone go by my apartment and pack everything up.

"Wouldn't it make more sense to stop there now?" I ask. "You know, before you drive an hour to Clark's? And then have to come all the way back here?"

"Yes. Yes, it would. But seeing as how Clark doesn't want you going back to your apartment – and I don't blame him -- I think he would kill me if I even left you sitting out in the car while I went into that damned apartment and got your stuff. Plus, I need to go and get Clark's truck," he says, and I realize we are in the racecar-looking Mercedes Benz. I guess he was in a hurry last night.

"So… he was at the hospital last night?" I ask.

"Yes. Do you not remember?" he asks, and I look back out the window before answering.

"Barely. I think? It's all a blur," I say, leaning my head back on the headrest.

"I'm glad you called, Ava. I'm so sorry that you went through all of that. I'm sure that was very traumatic. Between the two of us, I was honored that you called me. If you tell anyone, I will deny it." I look over at him and he smiles kindly.

"I remember Clark saying something about that. I won't tell anyone. You know that," I add and turn back toward the window.

"Also, Clark didn't want to leave. I showed up this morning," he says a little mischievously.

"It's okay. I think that was a smart move."

"I knew I liked you. You're smart, Ava. Got a good head on your shoulders."

"Thank you, Brian," I say, laughing. He's not wrong. Sometimes I'm too smart for my own good. Last night is a little blurry, but some things aren't. I'm okay with that. For now, they can stay that way. "Would it be better for me to stay with my friend Shanna?"

"Don't be ridiculous. Clark will insist you be at the house. We will do everything we can to help you recover, Ava. I know it may be a little difficult for you to be as mobile as you were before your injury. If we need to get a temp while you recover, we will. Whatever we need to do to make sure you and Brooklyn feel comfortable."

"Now who's being ridiculous, Brian? I watch Brooklyn, I'm not training for the Olympics. I'll be fine. I might be a little slow, but she's not so little that I need to be carrying her all the time. Dr. Ashburn said I would be back to normal in about 10-14 days. Then Brooklyn will be heading to school. I'll get my sutures out and life will be great. Clark will be heading off to Vancouver to shoot the movie and Brooklyn and I will be fine. Everything is going to be great. I'm going to be okay."

"Thatta girl," Brian says, and I smile. "You're such a trooper. Never would have thought you almost died last night."

"I didn't almost die. Geez, you Hollywood folks are dramatic. I could have died if I went to my bedroom and fell asleep maybe? But I didn't almost die. I just lost a lot of blood."

"Whatever you say, Ava," Brian says as we hit the freeway. I'm hummed to sleep by the sound of the car's engine and conversations from last night come back to me dreamlike. I wake up alone. I'm in a parking lot. I'm in Clark's car, but Brian isn't here. I look around and see I still have my purse and my phone. Where is Brian? Finally I see him come out of a store with a big paper bag. He opens the door and smiles at me.

"I thought you had left me here," I say, and he shrugs his shoulders.

"I think you and I both know that would never happen. But I figured we could go ahead and pick up your prescriptions and some food that will be easier to digest. Sometimes you can get really nauseated after being sedated. So I picked up a couple things to make you some soup. Or… well, Clark said you cook, so you can make you some soup."

"You don't cook?" I ask, laughing.

"No. I don't cook. I have business lunches and dinner meetings. Grab coffee in the morning and doughnuts when I'm feeling saucy. That's about as close as I come to cooking," he says, and I smile.

"Wow. That's really….special."

"You're special," he says sarcastically back to me. I like Brian. I'm glad he has a sense of humor.

"I know, right?" I say as we pull up to the security gate. I know this isn't home, but I feel a sense of relief knowing I'm here.

"You okay?" Brian asks.

I nod. What could possibly be wrong?

We pull into the driveway and I recognize Shanna's car out front. GREAT. What is she doing here? I get out of the car with a little help from Brian, and Shanna comes out the front door looking pissed.

"What the hell, Ava!"

"Calm down, Shanna. I'm fine," I say as Brian

and I walk towards the door. Clark and Brooklyn follow her out. I feel a little overwhelmed with all this welcome. I take a deep breath. I don't know why this makes me feel a little emotional. The pain medicine?

"You're right you look fine," she says sarcastically, pulling me into a hug. I yelp, and she lets go. "Sorry."

Brooklyn scrambles down to give me a hug. Clark tells her to be easy and she is. He looks at Shanna, and she has the nerve to look a little sheepish. "Do I need to tell you to be easy as well?" he asks, and she blushes. She looks at me and I laugh. "How are you feeling this morning?" Clark asks me as Shanna moves so that Brian can walk into the house. I shrug and he puts his hand on the small of my back, ushering me into the house. Inside the house there are flowers everywhere.

"What is this?" I ask. Clark tells me that word got out and people are sending flowers after hearing about an accident with Clark's nanny.

"These are from Shanna," he says motioning to a small bouquet of roses. "These are from Shanna's parents," he says showing me a box of flowers that cover a small section of the kitchen counter. "These are from Tammy, those are from Brian and these," he says motioning to a large bouquet of lilies, peonies and roses, "are from Brooklyn." Brooklyn beams at me, and I lean down and give her a kiss on the head.

"Thank you, sweet girl," I say, and she gets all excited. "They are beautiful."

"Daddy let me pick out the colors," she says, touching one of the flowers and I wink at her. Clark comes around and sits on a stool, pulling me so I can sit on the chair next to him.

"What do you need?" he asks. I shake my head. I feel myself getting emotional, and I will not break down in tears. I WILL NOT BREAK DOWN. He nods, realizing from my watery eyes that I need a minute. He leans over and kisses me on the head. "Let's make Ava some soup," he says to Brooklyn as they walk into the kitchen, leaving me sitting on the barstool and Shanna eyeing me suspiciously.

"You want to go upstairs and lay down?" she asks, placing her hand over my bandaged one. I know you've had a rough night, Ava. It's okay to be a little overwhelmed." I nod my head and I show her the way upstairs. I tell her about last night and then she tells me how Clark contacted her parents and they got in touch with her this morning. She was worried sick. Like everyone else, she has insisted on going to get my stuff today. "You actually look good in scrubs," she says, and we both laugh. I feel like at some point I will break down and have a good cry, but not yet. Not with everyone around. I pull myself together and about that time I hear a knock at the door. Brooklyn and Clark are standing in the door carrying a tray with some soup, crackers, and a ginger ale next to a cup of ice. I give them a small smile. Gosh I haven't been taken care of like this since I was a young girl. It makes me tear up, but I pull it together. I thank Brooklyn and she crawls up on the bed with me. Clark excuses himself and tells me to call him or text if I need anything. I eat a bite of the soup and it's good. Really good.

"Did your daddy make this?" I ask Brooklyn and she nods.

"He makes this for me when I'm sick." I look up at Shanna and she is watching us.

"Can we watch Mickey Mouse while you eat?" Brooklyn asks, grabbing the remote and turning the TV on.

"Of course," I say.

Shanna sits down on the bed. "So are we gonna talk about what's actually going on here?" Shanna whispers, and I look at her like she's nuts. "Oh, don't look at me like that. The sexual tension between the two of you is palpable, Ava. You could cut it with a knife. AND," she whisper screams at me, "he kissed you on the head."

"He was just being caring, Shanna. Don't get ahead of yourself. He was really worried about me."

"Don't preach to me about worry. He called my parents, Ava. Clark Grant called MY PARENTS at seven this morning trying to find me. That's not normal," she says, smiling at Brooklyn when she turns around and looks at her. Brooklyn gives her a nasty look and then looks at me and smiles. When Brooklyn turns back to Mickey Mouse, Shanna looks at me and grabs a cracker. She takes a bite and then leans back.

"Don't start, Shanna. I'm Brooklyn's nanny. Clark leaves in a month for a long shoot in Vancouver. He cares about me, sure. I would be concerned for him too if he was in the hospital. So would you," I say patting her hand.

"Semantics. But no… I'm onto you Ava," she says, looking down at her watch. "I have to make a phone call and then I'll be back. Then I will help you shower and change into some new clothes. Smart to have clothes here. Stay overnight often?" She asks with a smirk on her face. Ugh, this woman.

"No. Not yet," I say and she bats her eye lashes at me. I stick my tongue out at her at the same time that she sticks her tongue out at me. I do love her, although she's a pain in my butt.

After I finish my lunch, Brooklyn and I are sitting in my bed watching Mickey Mouse when Clark comes in. He knocks on the door frame.

"You don't have to knock," I say, smiling at him as he walks in.

"Shanna said you needed my help," he asks,

and I give him a confused look. “No?” He says at my confused expression.

“I don’t think so,” I say, and he leans against the dresser in my room looking over at Brooklyn.

“Is she bugging you?” he whispers, and I shake my head.

”Never!”

“I wonder why she said you needed me to help you?” Clark asks, crossing his arms over his chest.

“Where is she?” I ask, and he tells me she left. “What?” I ask and he nods.

“Why? What did you need? I can do it, Ava. All you have to do is ask,” he says puffing his chest out theatrically.

“No, I’m fine,” I say a little put off, although I smile at his theatrics.

“Ava, don’t be ridiculous. What do you need? I promise you I can take care of it. Just ask,” he says, and I smile at him.

“She was going to help me shower,” I say, and he pauses, staring at me for a moment. Then he clears his throat looks down at me in my scrubs and then back up at my face and smiles.

“Okay… well…” he says, trying to figure out his next move.

“Like I said,” I laugh, “I’m fine. I’ll figure something out.”

“No. No, No,” he says, trailing off. He holds a finger up as he thinks. “We can figure this out. I’m sure we can do this. You probably want to shower. And I'm here to help," he says working out in his head as he is saying it out loud. I just laugh at his slow panic.

"Clark," I say, placing my hand on his. "I think you need to relax. You're stressing me out!"

"Clayton!" He exclaims loudly and grabs his phone out of his back pocket. He starts to make a phone call, and I look at him like he's lost his mind. Clayton, what? "Hey Man. What are you doing right now?" he asks. Clayton must have put him on hold. "He's on the other line," he whispers to me.

"Clark. Are you asking your assistant to come over and help your nanny, who he's never met, to shower?" I ask incredulously. He can't be serious.

"No. I mean, yes. But his boyfriend won't mind," he says.

"Clark, that's crazy. Hang up the phone," I say, and he shakes his head.

"He wants to meet you anyway. Two birds, one stone," he says laughing.

"I swear, Clark. Hang up the phone." I get out of bed and try to grab the phone.

"NO," he says sternly. "Get back in bed. Ava, what are you doing?" he says as I stand up and almost fall over. He wraps an arm around my waist and pulls me up so my forehead rests on his chest. I'm so dizzy, I think as I put my good hand over my face. The blood must be rushing to my head because I have a hard time catching my breath. Clark puts the phone down and picks me up, placing me back in the bed. He sits me down gently on the edge of the bed, and lifts my chin so I'm looking at him. It takes me a minute to really focus my eyes on him and he looks so worried. "There she is," he says. "SHIT, AVA! You scared me to death." We are interrupted by Brooklyn. Clark drops his hand from under my chin.

"Are you okay, Ava?" Brooklyn says, coming to sit on her daddy's lap on the edge of the bed. "Daddy was holding you like he holds me."

"Yes, sweetheart I'm fine," I say, moving a piece of hair that fell in her face and putting it behind her ear. She moves off her daddy's lap and goes back to the end of the bed to watch Mickey. We hear someone yelling Clark's name, and we both look over at Clark's phone on my dresser. Oh yeah, Clayton. "Clark," I say, and he stands up. "Clark," I urge again and he grabs the phone.

"Clayton," he says, and I sit up. "Can I call you back?" After all that. "You what?" he asks Clayton on the phone and then goes to my window. "Ah, yes. See you in a few minutes."

"I guess he's here?" I ask with a lack of humor, and he nods. "Well I guess that takes care of that issue."

"I guess so," Clark says, clearing his throat. "Ava, please don't get up and especially that quickly again. I'm sorry if I worried you with calling Clayton, but I was just trying to help. I promise," he says reassuringly.

"I know you were trying to help. I'm not offended, I just think that maybe helping me shower is not the way he wants to meet me the first time."

"Apparently you haven't met Clayton. He loves a good problem," he says as I hear someone bounding up the steps. "Here he comes," he whispers with a smirk. He's looking at me with a twinkle in his eyes and I just lean back huffing. "I hope you're ready!"

Clark

Clayton is one of my favorite people in the world, so I'm curious to see what Ava thinks of one of my closest and dearest friends, and of course what Clayton thinks as well. Clayton started working for me before I became "who I am" to the world. He believed in me when a lot of people didn't, and to me that means more than anything. He's been a devoted and loyal friend from the beginning and I'm eternally grateful to him. Clayton comes bounding into the house, and I can already feel his energy. Ava gives me an uncertain look.

"Clark. I will figure out my shower situation," she whispers at me, and I laugh. "Clark," she whisper-yells in a warning tone.

"I'm not going to make a stranger bathe you,

Ava," I say, because I wouldn't do that to her. I know I panicked earlier and it's not like Clayton wouldn't offer to do it anyway. He's Mother Teresa in a man's body! I hear him bounding up the stairs calling for us and I smile. "In here Clayton!"

"Where's my favorite Baby Brookie?" he yells, and Brooklyn jumps off the bed and runs into the hall to greet Clayton. She and Clayton LOVE each other. They are two peas in a pod. Clayton could sit and watch hours and hours of Mickey Mouse with Brooklyn, and I love him for it. He's a Disney fanatic, probably because he himself is a magical person. He comes in the room holding Brooklyn's hand and smiles at me and then Ava. "Oh wow," he says looking at Ava and then to me. Ava may have had a pretty rough and traumatic night, but she's still effortlessly beautiful. "Shut the front door, you GUYS!!"

"Clayton, meet Ava. Ava, meet Clayton," I say, and Ava sits up a little and swings her legs over. "Ava," I warn, and she gives me a shush look.

"Hi Clayton. It's so nice to meet you. I've heard wonderful things about you. From both Clark and Brooklyn," she says and Clayton motions for her to stay seated. He sits next to her and pulls her into a soft hug.

"Ava. It is so nice to meet you. I have heard about you as well. But apparently someone left some things out. Like how gorgeous you are. I mean you're so cute I could put you in my pocket and carry you around," Clayton says looking up at me. "Clark. You rascal. What were you thinking leaving out so much detail?" he says, and I give him a confused look.

"What?" I give him a warning look.

"Ohh. I'm making daddy mad," he says conspiratorially. I resign myself to my fate. With Clayton it's easier that way. "Listen honey, we are going to let you rest. I brought stuff over to cook tonight. Brooklyn is also going to let you rest," he says over his shoulder to Brooklyn. "Right, Boo?" Brooklyn gives her sweetest smile and an enthusiastic nod.

"Thank you," Ava says to Clayton and then he shoos me out of the room.

"We will be downstairs if you need anything," I say, and Clayton tells me NO.

"You will be going to your table read, and I rescheduled your workout to this afternoon. Brooklyn and I will keep Ava company. We will get her cleaned up, and then Marco will be over later this afternoon to help me cook a magical meal for us. I can't wait for you to meet Marco. He's my little cupcake," he says dreamily and I laugh as I grab Brooklyn's hand to take her downstairs. Apparently I'm working today. Damn, I love this guy. He's taken care of me for years, and I wish everyone had a Clayton in their life.

"She LOVES cupcakes," I say winking at Ava

as she gives me a warning look. Brooklyn says she wants a cupcake, so we head downstairs to get one. Maybe I'll make a special delivery and bring another one up to Ava before I leave. A guy can dream.

"I sense a story," Clayton says to Ava in a sing song voice. Ava groans and I hear her fall back into her fluffy pillows. Brooklyn and I head downstairs, and I grab her a cupcake as I head to my bedroom to pack up my stuff.

Clayton

I adore her! I adore her! I adore her!! I knew immediately when I walked in and she was smiling at me that I liked her. The poor dear had a rough night and I intend to make her feel safe and loved today while I'm here. Although I'm sensing there's a lot of love already being felt in this house between her and our favorite leading man! The way he looked at her… he isn't fooling anyone. I feel like he should have told me by now how absolutely stunning his new "nanny" is. I leave her to rest and go downstairs to find Brooklyn, but I run into Clark in the kitchen with his bags.

"Oh no you don't," I say as he acts like he is about to leave. "You have an hour before your table read starts. They know you had a close friend in the hospital last night, so they'll forgive you if you are running a little late. Which you won't be because you have plenty of time. I want to know why you've been keeping this light of your life away from me," I ask, and he rolls his eyes.

"I haven't been keeping her from you, Clayton. She's been working for me for like a month. And she isn't the light of my life. That's Brooklyn. Calm down."

"Lies," I say and lean against the kitchen counter. "You have feelings for her. I can tell. I can see it in those beautiful ocean blue eyes of yours." He tries to deny it, and I just snap at him to stop. "Don't waste your breath, Clark. I have feelings for her, and I just met her. She's a breath of fresh air. A real woman. Not one of the Hollywood tycoon hunters you're used to. Lydia isn't an idiot. She's not going to hire a grandma to replace her. She's going to make sure you have someone fitting in your life. It's time, Clark. Whether you want to admit it or not. I'm not saying rush into anything. Don't look at me like that, Clark Grant. I will slap that look off your face," I say as he tries to get testy with me. "All I'm saying is don't second guess yourself. Just enjoy yourself. You deserve happiness and you've beat the hell out of yourself for long enough. Upstairs you looked happy, and you were laughing. You winked at her for heaven's sake. It's the most adorable thing I've seen from you since Brooklyn.

So do me a favor. Shut up. I don't need a response from you. Go to work, come home to Momma, and just feel it out," I say with my arms outstretched. He walks into my hug, and I pat him on the back. "There there, be a good boy! Listen to Momma. Dinner will be ready at seven."

"Thank you, Clayton," he says begrudgingly. I know inside he's smiling. He's such a good boy and this Momma is so proud of him. "Take good care of our girls," he adds as I grab his keys and hand them to him.

"Always. And just in case you were wondering, those emerald green eyes look at you the same way that you look at her." He turns around, and I put a finger up to my lips and shush him. He huffs and jerks the door to the garage open. I just smile to myself and then when I know he's out of the driveway I grab myself a cupcake and go to sit with Brooklyn. "Oh, I love this one," I whisper to Brooklyn as we sit and watch Mickey Mouse. We say CHEERS as we toast our two cupcakes, like you would a celebratory drink. I love my baby Brooklyn.

After about two hours I head upstairs to check on Ava. I gave her my cell phone number, but she said Clark already sent it to her. I told her to utilize it any time she has a need. Brooklyn was having another snack while watching a movie, so I felt like it was a good time to head upstairs. I see Ava trying to sit up and I "tsk tsk" at her.

"I'm not just here to look pretty, Ava Baby," I say, rushing into the room. She sits up and I push her hair behind her ears. "There we go. Much better. Do you want to try and take a shower?" I ask, and she laughs. I stop there and know there's another story, and I'm sensing it has to do with our Prince Charming. "Okay. After we get you this nice, well-deserved shower and out of these scrubs, I need to know everything that's happened thus far in your life. I need all the details. All leading up the moment I walked into this room. We need to catch up. You're going first and then I will follow suit. It only makes complete sense if we are going to be spending a lot of time together. But first…" I stand up and hold my hands out, waiting for Ava to agree. It's time to get this sweet girl a shower. She has dried blood on her neck and in spots around her wrist.

After a quick shower, I help her get some fresh pajamas on and then grab a chair to dry her hair. She has the most beautiful dark brown hair and I tell her so. We sit on the bed, Brooklyn included, as she tells me her life story. From her upbringing in North Carolina, to her short stint in New York, to moving to LA a couple months ago. We touch on all the details of Clark, and she tells me she's just grateful for the opportunity and how incredible her experience has been thus far. I hear the cupcake story as well, and now I'm really excited to see how all of this plays out. She would like to pretend that she and Clark are just friendly, nothing more, but I can sense more on the horizon. They can play it this way if they like, but Momma knows best!

Ava

I LOVE CLAYTON. I need a tee shirt with that on it! He's just the best. He's been downstairs for the past hour working on dinner. Brooklyn fell asleep on my bed for about an hour while Clayton and I were talking. I got to hear all about him and he's just wonderful. When I was telling him my life story so far, he was so attentive and I think he was actually really surprised with parts of my story. But I've persevered and I'm here to tell it. I've never really opened up like that to many people. I gave Lydia an abridged version and Shanna knows a lot, but that's about it. But Clayton. He knows everything now! And I'm okay with that. I feel like I know him pretty well, too. I put down the book I've been reading because I'm scared I'll fall asleep and miss dinner. After Clayton has been working on it all afternoon, I'm not going to do that to my new friend. I start to sit up and hear someone clear their throat.

"How are you feeling?" Clark says from the doorway. I look up, startled. God he looks delicious. He must have just finished working out. He's in a fitted sleeveless shirt and some athletic shorts. He's so muscular and defined. He's tall and sexy. I hear him clear his throat again and my eyes snap up to meet his.

"Want to share something with the class?" he asks with a smile on his face. He walks into the room and I start to sit up. "No ma'am," he warns as he comes over to the bed and helps me sit up. He's very close and I can feel the warmth of his body and smell his still-damp skin. It's a very overwhelming scent, but I can't help but take a deep breath. He sits back on the bed and looks down at me with a grin. "Did you just smell me?" he asks. Not at all upset, more amused.

"No," I say, laughing it off. "Although you could use a shower," I add, but I want to tell him not to. I think he smells amazing and manly. It's comforting, safe.

"I can see you had a shower," he says, smiling down at me. "Clayton is finished with dinner and Marco is here. You ready for more company?" he asks. He gives me his hand to help me out of the bed. I give him my hand so he can pull me up. He places his hands on my waist to steady me since my shoulder is still bandaged up. I put my sling on and he helps me make sure it's secure.

We head downstairs and I meet Marco. He's so beautiful, I can see why Clayton is so in love with him. He's very Italian and very attractive. All dark hair and dark eyes. I find out he's a stylist and I love him. This might come in handy one day for me. I need all the help I can get in that department. I mean of course I can dress myself. When I'm not injured. I just don't have that touch with fashion like I can tell Marco does. He's dressed casually but pristine. You can tell he could make anyone fabulous!

Dinner is incredible. Marco and Clayton cooking in the kitchen is a wonder. I LOVE cooking as well, but this is authentic Italian cuisine. They spared no expense, even down to the fancy wine which I can't partake in because of the pain medication, but everything is amazing. I'm so full that I'm glad I'm wearing pajamas. We sit around talking while Clark takes Brooklyn up to bed. Marco and I get to know each other a little better as Clayton starts clearing the plates away. After a while Clark comes back down and joins Clayton in the kitchen, helping him clean up. I can't help but watch how his body moves. I turn my attention back to Marco and he's smiling at me.

"They're pretty amazing, aren't they," he says, leaning close to me, knocking gently into my good shoulder.

"Yeah," I say with a small smile. He asks me if I'm ready to head back upstairs and I nod. "That's probably a good idea. It's a little after 8 and I need to take another pain pill. My shoulder is getting sore again." We start up the stairs giggling about nothing really when I hear Clayton tell us to wait up. He joins us on the stairs and the three of us head into my room as I get in the bed. I'm on my normal side and Clayton and Marco crawl in beside me cuddled up. We turn on a movie and I take one of my pain pills. We are about 15 minutes into the movie when Clayton brings his phone out.

"It's time for a Grant Productions team photo op. For Instagram of course," he adds as we huddle close together. I give them my IG handle and they both add me immediately and vice versa. He posts the photo and then we go back to watching the movie.

The next thing I know it's dark in my room and I'm alone. I look at my phone and see it's way past midnight. My shoulder is hurting, and I need some more water to take another pill. I could take my glass into the bathroom, but I would rather have some orange juice or something. I head downstairs and realize this is my first night in Clark's house. It's a little surreal, but then again this entire month has been surreal. I turn on the kitchen lights under the cabinets so as not to make it too bright. I open the fridge and grab the orange juice. I close the door to the fridge and see a small light from the master bedroom area light up. His door was open. CRAP.

"Sorry," I whisper loudly when I see him appear in the doorway. "I was trying to be quiet. I didn't realize your door was open."

"I left it open for a reason," he says. "In case you needed something. I normally sleep with my door open. In case Brooklyn needs me or has a nightmare." He comes into the kitchen, and he isn't wearing a shirt, so of course I notice his strong, tanned, muscular chest. I turn back to my orange juice and take a sip, swallowing down my pill. "Are you feeling okay?" he asks. Damn. I should have just filled my glass up upstairs. He's really sexy.

"Yeah," I say, a little groggily. "When did Clayton and Marco leave?"

"About 10. Clayton fell asleep, so Marco had to drag him out of here. I think he wanted to stay," he says smiling "I think he's pretty taken with you."

"I adore him," I say looking up over at Clark and into his eyes. I'm talking about Clayton, but part of me feels like I'm referring to Clark. He's looking at me seriously and then after a long moment blinks and smiles.

"Sorry. I'm glad. Do you need anything else?" he asks, and I feel like we aren't talking about my shoulder, but I shake my head. The tension in the air palpable.

"Did I wake you?" I ask as I pick up my glass of orange juice.

"No. I was reading some scripts that Brian sent over earlier. I got pulled into one in particular and got carried away. I know I need to go to bed. 5AM will come early tomorrow." He says looking at the clock in the kitchen. "Clayton plans to come back, so I hope you're ready for that," he smiles.

"Of course. I'll be good, Clark. Thank you for everything," I turn to walk away and Clark moves forward a few steps and grabs my uninjured hand pulling me into his arms. It's not sexual. It's more comforting than anything. His bare chest beneath my cheek is so warm and safe. I wrap my uninjured arm around him and lean into him. We stay there for a minute. He leans down and kisses the top of my head. Again, it's not sexual at all. He mostly just seems relieved I'm okay.

"I know that you've had a crazy 24 hours. I'm here if you need to process anything, Ava. Don't feel obligated, but I want you to know I'm here. I know it's a weird situation because I'm technically your boss, but please know that you can come to me if you need anything. Seriously. I could sense you started to get upset when you got home earlier.

I'm sure it was overwhelming," he adds, and I nod.

"Yeah. So many different emotions. I'm grateful to be okay. I'm also grateful to be somewhere I feel safe. All the flowers, lunch being made for me. It's just a lot. Not bad a lot, just a lot of love here," I pause and take a deep breath. "Last night was scary. I wanted to pretend to have it under control, but I guess I didn't realize how out of control everything actually was," I say, looking up at him. He releases me so he can look at me. We stand there, looking at each under for what feels like a few minutes but I'm sure was only seconds. "If I didn't have you and your team there to help me, to be there for me… I don't know what I would've done. I count myself lucky to have you – all of you -- in my life, Clark. I've spent a lot of my life taking care of myself, but I finally feel like someone else cares for me," I add. He smiles genuinely down at me. Leaning his back against the kitchen counter and crossing his arms in front of his chest.

"I'm glad you feel cared for, Ava. I'm sorry you've had to endure a lot of life feeling alone. I know I'm-- our team is lucky to have you. If I'm being honest…" he says, "I know we are still getting to know each other, but I'm grateful for your trust and giving us a chance to get to know you and vice versa. We do care about you and want you to feel safe here. Please know we will do whatever it takes to keep you and Brooklyn safe," he says seriously, and I smile up him. I walk back into his arms, and he wraps them securely around me. I stay there for a couple seconds and then start to feel sleepy.

"I just took a pain pill. I should probably head back upstairs while I can," I whisper with a smile on my face. Lord knows I'd love to just stay here with my head on his chest. But I need to be smart about this. There isn't anything sexual about what just took place, but if I stay here long enough, I may not make the best choices. He releases me and I step back. "Thank you, Clark," I say as I turn to go upstairs, not bothering to turn the light off. I need to be upstairs, like NOW! I crawl into bed and take a deep cleansing breath. I'm going to need to keep my distance and be more careful for a couple more weeks. Then Clark will be traveling, and this won't be an issue. Right?

Clark

DAMMIT! I'm falling hard for her. It's too early to feel this way, right? It's been almost two months since she started working for us? It's been two weeks since our midnight kitchen encounter after her injury. I can honestly say I don't think I've cared about another human being, other than Brooklyn, the way that I feel and care for Ava. She and I stay up after Brooklyn goes to bed, talking and sharing stories about our day. It's nice. Not necessarily romantic, more like two friends hanging out. I look forward each evening that I don't have an event or dinner so we can spend that time together. I've learned so much about her. We've fallen into a rhythm with her living upstairs. It's never been weird or awkward. Our encounters are always very friendly and filled with humor.

Clayton has been at the house a lot more. He brings his laptop over and works from the house so he can hang out with Ava. The two of them have become inseparable. Ava's friend and agent has also started to come over to the house to spend time with her. I love it. My house has never felt so full.

Brooklyn starts school next Monday and although I'm excited for her, I'm also a little sad that Ava won't be at the house as much. I like knowing she's here, that she's safe. Ava gets her sutures out on Monday while Brooklyn is at school, and then she'll be moving into her new townhome. I know I should be excited for her, which I am. I love the idea of Ava having her own place. That's important. But…I also feel a little lost about it. Clayton can tell I'm a little off because every time he mentions using the truck to get Ava's stuff to her new place I get a little moody. I tell him to shove it, and he tells me to play nice with the other kids. He's right though. I need to relax and let it go.

I'm heading back to the house from my fitting at the studio when my phone rings. It's Clayton.

"Hey man," I say over Bluetooth in my car.

"Hey. Everything is squared away. Three weeks and you leave for Vancouver. You shoot from the end of September now till the beginning of November. Then there will be a small break for the holidays with some reshoots on location that you'll need to fly back and forth for, but nothing too strenuous. Then we'll be back for Christmas in L.A. and shooting will be done. You excited? Last movie to fulfill your contract on this franchise. There will be a LOT of PR and interviews after shooting is done, so be prepared for that. This will be a long season of publicity before the movie comes out, but that'll be at least another year from now. But I think it'll be totally worth it," he says, and I smile.

"Thanks, man. I appreciate you arranging all of that," I say, and then we hang up. I'm stoked to get this last movie rolling. It's bittersweet. It's been a long road and it's changed my life for the better but I'm also ready to move forward. I want to look at other options for myself. Maybe take a year off? I don't know. What's nice is I don't have to make a decision right now. I can even take on some smaller roles and get my feet wet in some other areas of acting. Who knows? The freedom to figure out my next move will be nice.

I pull into the driveway and see everyone is at the house. All of my people are here, and it's nice to have this while I can. Clayton of course will be with me in Vancouver for the most part. He will come back and forth, and I'll obviously be able to as well, just not as often. Ava and Brooklyn will come and visit, or more accurately, Ava will bring Brooklyn.

When I get into the house it's all laughter and

talking. You'd think a party was going on but it's only, Ava, Clayton, Marco and Shanna. They are sitting around in the den drinking wine. I walk in and yell, "Honey, I'm home!"

I hear Clayton laugh, and he yells back. "How was your day, sweetie?" I come into the den and sit between him and Ava. Marco asks if I want wine and I shake my head. Shanna continues on about her last blind date and it has us all rolling. She is quite descriptive. It's hilarious and also horrifying at the same time.

"You know, Ava. Benji has a really cute friend. He was actually wanting us to double with you," she says, and it gets quiet. I feel like I should encourage her, but I also don't want to. It's not any of my business. She's an adult. I look down at her and she is staring daggers at Shanna. I chuckle, if you can call it that. I was trying to hold in my laugh at Ava's reaction, but I couldn't. She's pretty damn cute when she's mad, especially if you point it out to her. Clayton excuses himself to take the empty bottles into the kitchen. Marco joins him and Shanna just looks expectantly between Ava and I. I'm not sure what she is expecting, but I just smile back at her. She's not going to get a reaction out of me over something like this. I expected this to happen eventually with her. She's always trying to push, but apparently she doesn't know it takes a lot for me to break.

"Anyway," Marco yells from the other room. He and Clayton are getting ready to head out. Ava stands up and walks into the kitchen, and when I begin to stand up Shanna stops me. She has quite the nerve. Maybe it's the wine? I might be calling her another cab home tonight. This isn't the first time, and I'm sure it won't be the last.

"Easy," I say looking into the kitchen and watching Marco, Clayton and Ava saying their goodbyes. Shanna lets go of my arm, apparently remembering herself.

"That doesn't make you mad," she says, looking up at me, "what I said about Ava dating?"

"Is that your goal?" I ask, and she looks confused. "Apparently you don't know me very well. It takes a lot for me to get mad. Ava doing what she wants with her life would make me happy, not mad. Just like Clayton and Marco doing what they want with their lives makes me happy."

"Okay," she utters sarcastically, and I keep walking into the kitchen. I grab a water from the fridge and say goodbye to Clayton and Marco. The next couple of weeks are going to fly by and even though I'm going to be out of town for a while, knowing I have these wonderful people in my life makes everything worthwhile. Shanna gets on my nerves, but only because I think she's trying to get under my skin. Ava and Shanna settle back in the den, and I head to my bedroom. I'm going to shower and get ready for bed. I'm glad I have the rest of the weekend before Brooklyn goes to school. I know Ava has everything ready for Brooklyn, so I don't have to worry about anything. She even took Brooklyn by the school today to remind her of where she will be going next week.

I'm getting out of the shower when I hear a knock on the door. I'm wearing a towel around my waist when I open my door. Ava is standing there. She looks down at my towel and then up at me. I grin and she rolls her eyes.

"Yes Clark, you're hot," she mutters, and I laugh.

"Wow. That was quite forward, Ava. Anything else you want to share with the class?" I ask, leaning against the door frame. She gives me a sarcastic smile and pushes my shoulder playfully.

"No. I just wanted to apologize for Shanna. When she drinks, she gets pretty mouthy," Ava says, and I shrug my shoulders.

"I'm not at all offended by Shanna. She has her opinions and I have mine. She can say whatever she would like. No harm, no foul," I add, and Ava looks up at me. She looks like she's got more to say, but so do I. "Ava, I do care about you, as does everyone who was in the house tonight. Shanna included. If she wants to set you up on a date or wants to try to get under my skin, then she's welcome to do those things. It's up to you if you want to go on a date. It's up to me on whether or not I take the bait Shanna throws out there. I really adore you, Ava. I'm not going to pretend I don't. If you want to go on a date, I would hope Shanna would set you up with someone great. Not a blind date. She doesn't even know the guy she was trying to set you up with. She was just trying to ruffle some feathers. You're an incredible woman, Ava. 95% of the men in this town are scum. I'd hate it. Partly because I'm a guy and I know how most guys think, especially in Hollywood. Also because I have my own selfish reasons, but that's my problem. I'm too old to play games and I'm not going to be ruffled or offended by something someone who doesn't know me says. Do you even want to go on that date?" I ask, reaching over to tuck a loose strand of hair behind her ear.

The contact with her skin is like an electric current touching my skin. I cross my arms across my chest and remember I'm still in a towel. "Hold on. Give me a second," I say, leaving Ava standing in my doorway. I know she can see me, but I don't care. I drop my towel with my back to her and then pull on a pair of athletic shorts. I turn around and she's shaking her head smiling at me. "Too much?" I ask as I join her back at the door. I walk past her into the kitchen and sit at the bar, turning to face her. She sits on the bar stool next to me and then swivels her chair to face me. "Now where were we?" I ask, and she smiles. "Ah. Does Ava actually want to date?"

"I don't want to go on that blind date," she says, smiling at me. "If I wanted to, I would. But I don't, especially after the horror story Shanna just told us. That doesn't sound like anything but a waste of my time."

"Okay. Anything else you want to talk about?" I ask, and she laughs.

"No. I think I'm good. I just felt bad because I don't want things to be weird between us," she says, looking me in the eyes. I just need to rip the band aid off. "I care about you a lot as well. I think you know that!"

"Ava. Everything between us is fine. Shanna was obnoxious, but your reaction to her was pretty entertaining. If you aren't wanting to date, then no one should be putting pressure on you to do so. Not Shanna, not Clayton or Marco, especially not me. When you're ready to date, you'll let people know." I say, and she smiles.

"I didn't say I'm not ready to date. I said I didn't want to go on a blind date with that dude," she adds, a bit more bravely than I think she was prepared for. Huh, is that so?

"Ok. So you do want to date?" I ask, trying not to smile. "Anyone in particular you'd want to date?" I ask, trying not to smile.

"Maybe?" she says, turning to face forward. I

turn her bar stool so she has to face me.

"Maybe?" I ask.

She shrugs her shoulder. "I'm not in a hurry to date, but I'm not avoiding dating. It's a weird situation. I don't know."

"You don't know, or you aren't ready to talk about it?" I ask, and she just stares at me. "Can I be honest?" I ask, and she nods.

"Look, the last couple of years I haven't been ready to date. Not after my situation with Brooklyn's mom. That was pretty scarring to me. She's not here to defend herself or to give her side of the story, but it was rough. I did love her, but we didn't like each other most of the time and it didn't end well. Up until I met you and started to get to know you, I haven't wanted to date anyone. Like at all. I wasn't interested, and I didn't feel like I was missing out on anything. Until you," I say, making sure she hears me.

"I would love to take YOU on a date. I've thought about it a lot. However, there are a couple of things that are keeping me from jumping in headfirst. One, I'm about to leave for months. It would be unfair for me to do that to anyone. Especially someone I already know and care about. Like 'Hey let's go on a date. Oh, you had a good time? Great! Me too. Now we can't see each other consistently for the next couple of months. Two. You work for me, or you're technically employed by my company, but same thing. As professional as I wanted to keep things between us, it's been very friendly between us since the beginning. You and I just clicked right away. We have from the first evening I met you. At least that's how it was for me. I'm not trying to speak for you and your experience." I pause to see if she's already put off by my forwardness, but she seems to be waiting for me to continue.

"Third, Brooklyn. She has a lot more to lose if this were to not work out the way we would hope it would. Brooklyn adores you. She would be devastated if you left, especially if it was because of me. Not saying I expect it wouldn't work out, but the odds are stacked against us. And lastly, you! I adore you, Ava. I think the world of you. But I didn't know if you were ready to date. I feel like we're already pretty close and getting closer by the day. I love being around you and I think you're one of the most breathtaking women I've ever been around. I'm not sure you understand how absolutely incredible you are. I'm in awe of you. But I didn't know where you were with all of this. I figured you realized you and I had other… not necessarily obstacles, but things and people to consider. I would be honored to take you out, Ava. I could give a shit what other people think. Honestly, dating you, regardless if you are my nanny, doesn't matter to me. I respect you. What you do for Brooklyn and I is something I will always appreciate. You mean the world to us, Ava. If we did date and it didn't work out and you didn't want to continue working with us, I would make sure that you were set up well. I would make sure you weren't left jobless. I'm not going to fire you because things between us didn't work out. It's just not as easy as it apparently seems to someone like… let's say Shanna. Her flippant remarks and opinions are unnecessary," I add and stare back at Ava. "Did any of that make sense?"

"Yes. It makes a lot of sense," she says, releasing the breath she was holding. She's close enough that I feel her warm breath on my skin, making chills appear across my chest. "I mean, of course I'm attracted to you. What woman, or man for that matter, wouldn't be? Of course, in a perfect world I would love to go on a date with you. You and Brooklyn mean the world to me. Which is exactly why I wanted to make sure we were okay. I haven't said anything to anyone about dating. I know people aren't stupid. There is something more between us. I would have a lot to lose if this didn't work out between us. And you ARE about to leave," she adds, and I pull her bar stool closer to mine so that her legs are in between mine. "You're one of the most incredible men I've ever met, Clark. Kind, caring, gorgeous. And everything you just said is, wow. I don't really have more words other than that right now. I'm grateful that you also understand what's at stake here. I just didn't want you to think I'm not interested. Because I do want to date. You."

"It would also be pretty damn selfish of me to assume that you would want to wait months for me to come back. I'm game to take this as slow as you want to take it. I'm taking my cues from you, Ava," I say, putting my hands on top of hers. "We don't have to explain anything to anyone. I'm fine to just keep going down the road we're already on. Or we can pull off on the side of the road and check the map if we need to park it for a bit," I say, laughing. That kind of made sense.

"That's an interesting analogy, but I think I understand," she says, laughing with me.

"What do you want to do, Ava? I'm not going to be dating anyone else, but it would be pretty selfish of me to ask the same of you. You should go out on some dates. Have that hellish Hollywood experience. I'm not saying it'll work out in my favor. I might have to get pretty drunk knowing that you're out with the assholes from around here. I can't stress that enough. Men in this town suck. However, if you just want to see where things go between us, we can keep moving forward. Slowly and at our own pace. I want to do what you want to do, Ava. I know what I want, but I also know what we're up against."

"It's enough to know that you care for me like

you do, Clark. I'm not going anywhere," she whispers, and I lean forward, kissing her on the top of the forehead. "I can see myself falling hard for you, Clark. I don't want to get hurt, but I would like to see where this goes. We don't have to do anything so drastic. I just want to be here with you. Especially while you're here. Like this," she whispers, and I pull her into my lap. I wrap my arms around her and she snuggles into my arms. We fit together perfectly. Of course we do. I love having her in my arms and I miss her when she's not there.

"Ava," I say gently after a couple minutes. She looks up at me and I smile down at her. "I've already started falling for you. And I don't want you getting hurt. I know how that feels and the thought of anyone, especially me, hurting you is painful." I lean down, kiss her on the forehead and then pick her up. "What do you want to do now, Ava?" I ask, standing in the kitchen with her in my arms. She looks at me as I pull her closer so we're almost nose to nose.

"Watch a movie?" she suggests, smiling. "Seems pretty safe?"

"God, I hope so," I agree, and carry her into the den. I place her on the couch and then sit down, pulling her feet into my lap. I let her find something on TV and after ten minutes of searching, she throws the remote at me. "What? Nothing good?" I ask as she laughs.

"You'd think with all the damn channels you have that I wouldn't have any issue finding something. But here we are," she says sarcastically. I scroll through the movie channels and she tells me to stop.

"Absolutely not," I say laughing at her. "We aren't watching any movies with me in it."

"The hell we aren't," she says, crawling up and grabbing the remote from me. I grab her uninjured hand and pull her so she's laying beside me on the couch. I wrap my arms around her and she lays her head on my chest. I resign myself to fate and we watch my first attempt at becoming a superhero. I'm not sure when we fall asleep, but I wake up to find Clayton staring down at us. I don't have my phone or my watch but the clock on the TV says 6:50.

I put my finger against my lips and then scoot out from behind Ava, but she wakes up. She sits up quickly and then looks at the time. She grabs the blanket and covers herself back up but not before she says hi to Clayton.

"Why are you here?" I say as kindly as possible as I head into the kitchen to make coffee.

"Nice to see you too," he says gruffly, but I don't respond. I don't need to. Not with his sass and definitely not his running commentary. "Your second suit fitting is this morning! We're supposed to be at Tom Ford at eight. You didn't answer my email last night when it was rescheduled, and you didn't answer your phone last night or this morning. So I thought I would come over and make sure that not only were you okay, but that you were ready for our appointment. Marco is meeting us there."

"Okay. Well I didn't get your email and my phone is in my bedroom. And as you can see," I say, motioning to the sofa. "I was not in my room last night. We fell asleep on the couch watching a movie." I turn to make my coffee and once I have it ready and in hand, I turn back to Clayton. "Also, I'm more than okay," I smile, and so does he.

"I can see that, and I can't wait to hear about this. But you need to shower and we need to leave in fifteen. So drink quickly. You can fill me in in the car."

"Fine," I add begrudgingly, but I don't go to my room, instead I head back over to the sofa and kiss Ava on the head. She turns over, not opening her eyes. I move the hair out of her face, and she smiles. "Have a good day, Ava. Apparently, I have stuff to take care of."

"Don't worry about us," she says, rolling over and getting comfortable again. "We will be fine. Brooklyn should be up pretty soon, and we are going swimming," she says, smiling sweetly.

"You in a bathing suit. I'll be sad to miss that," I add. I lift her hand and kiss the palm, then tuck her arm back under the covers. I head to my room, but not before I take a sip of my coffee and look over at Clayton who's staring at me, mouth agape. "Ten minutes, Clayton. Give me ten damn minutes."

Ava

The last couple of weeks have been amazing. Brooklyn started school and she is so proud of herself. She's doing amazing and I know I've only known her a couple months, but I'm completely stoked for her. Clark and I are still much the same. Toying on the edge of wherever this is going to go. We're not publicly dating -- we watch movies or sit up late at night after Brooklyn goes to bed. I've moved into my townhome thanks to Clark and the guys. I stay there half the time and the other half I fall asleep on the sofa or in my room here at Clark's. If it's too late, Clark doesn't like me to leave, and I get it. I love how much he cares about me. I know he's falling for me and I've fallen hard for him. But. I have to remember realistically where we are. He leaves tomorrow for Vancouver, and I'm glad in a sense that we played it safe. Clayton has been fussing over us like a mother hen. He hates leaving all of us as well, but Marco said he would come and check in on us. It's all been pretty magical so far. Brooklyn is sad that her daddy is leaving tomorrow, so I've set them up on a little daddy-daughter date this afternoon. Clayton is here packing Clark's bags with Marco. There are a couple of events that Clark has to attend while he's in Vancouver, so it's all suits and fancy stuff. The thought of Clark in those clothes makes me a little flustered so I go and do laundry.

It's about 8 p.m. when Clark comes in carrying Brooklyn. She's out cold. Clayton and Marco left about an hour ago to grab dinner. Clark has to be at the airport at five in the morning for their flight, so it's going be an early wake up call for him. Clark heads upstairs with Brooklyn and I smile at him, continuing to read on the couch. When he comes back downstairs, he seems a little teary. He sits next to me, and I place my hand on his cheek. He leans into me, placing his hand over mine and closes his eyes.

"What's wrong?" I say, and he lifts his gaze to me. Unshed tears pool in his eyes.

"I was trying really hard to be strong, but Brooklyn broke down crying in the car and I had to pull over. She was crying and I was crying. God, it was a disaster of a drive home. I just never want to leave her. You would think it would get easier, but as she becomes more and more aware it just gets harder. I don't want to leave her."

"I know. I'm so sorry. But we will come visit you as soon as we can. Her fall break, a couple weekends here and there. It'll be November before you know it. We will FaceTime you as much as your schedule will allow us. Don't worry about her, Clark. I know that's easy for me to say, but I will protect her with my life," I add as I feel myself getting teary as well. I've never seen Clark this emotional and my heart breaks for him and his sweet daddy heart. "You are a wonderful father, Clark. She knows that. The time will go by so fast, and she will be so busy with being a big girl and school. I'll keep her busy, I promise." He pulls me into his lap, and I wrap my arms around his shoulders.

"God, Ava," he says, pressing his nose into my hair. "I don't want to leave you either."

"I know. I don't want you to leave, but it's all going to be fine. I love how much you love us," I whisper. He lifts his head, holding my face in both his hands.

"I should have done this a while ago," he says as he gently presses his lips against mine. At first the kiss is gentle, and then we just sink into it. A mixture of neediness and sadness. "Forgive me," he says against my lips when we pull apart.

"Forgive you for what?" I ask. That was quite the first kiss.

"For not kissing you sooner. For leaving. For not telling you that I love you," he adds with a sad smile.

"There's nothing to forgive, Clark. This is our life right now. I'm not worried about it. Yes, I want you to stay. Yes, I'm excited for the next time I'll get to see you. For when I can be with you, and you can really be with me. But I don't feel robbed of anything, Clark. People travel for work all the time. I love you," I say, and he kisses me hard. My back hits the cushions on the back of the sofa and then I feel Clark tenderly kiss my forehead, my cheeks and my lips.

"I love you too, baby. You mean the world to me, Ava."

"I should have said it sooner," I say as he pulls me back in his lap.

"God, we're a mess," he says. "Sleep with me tonight," he whispers in my ear and I pull back, surprised. He laughs. "I mean sleep *in my bed* with me tonight. I don't mean have sex with me, Ava. I just want to be with you tonight. We can watch a movie, or we can just stare at each other for all I care. I just want to sleep in my own bed tonight. It's my last night in my bed for a while, and I want you with me." He leans over and kisses me again chastely.

"Okay," I answer, and he pulls me up, carrying me into his room. I haven't really ever been in his room. Not because it's "not allowed," but because I haven't really ever needed to. He pulls some clothes out of his drawers and heads into the bathroom. I don't know what side of the bed he sleeps on, but I can see he has a couple books and scripts on one side of the bed and the other side is pretty empty. I choose the side with nothing on the bedside table. He opens the door at about that same moment and he's wearing some sleep pants and no shirt. I smile at him and groan.

"Really, Clark?" I ask, laughing a little.

"You need me to wear a sweatshirt and a chastity belt?" he asks as he crawls under the covers.

"I don't think a sweatshirt would really make a difference when it comes to you. Also, a chastity belt? What are you, from the 17th century?" I ask, and he laughs.

"I could be. Maybe I'm a vampire." We both laugh and he rolls over to face me. "I just want to hold you, Ava," he says, pulling me under the covers. "What do you want to watch?"

"I don't care," I say, placing my hand on his face. He has about a day's worth of growth on his face, and I love the way it feels against my hand. "You are so beautiful, Clark."

"So are you, Ava. God, so are you," he says pulling me into his side. "Are you tired?"

"Yes and no," I answer, and I feel his chest vibrate beneath me.

"Explain that for me," he says, turning me to face him.

"Yes. I'm tired, but I also can stay up and watch a movie. Or just talk. What do you want, Clark?" I ask and I'm a little afraid of the answer. Not because I'm scared of him or what he wants, but because I'm scared we want the same things. And I'm not sure I'm ready for those things yet.

"You look nervous, Ava. What I want, I have. You, in my bed, with me. Where I know you're safe. Where I can hold you and reach out and touch you if I want to. Where you can roll over and be close to me if you get scared in the middle of the night. Where we can be together. That's what I want. Anything else is a bonus for me, and to be honest I'm not sure you're ready for the other things I want," he says smiling shyly at me. "And I'm not so sure I'm ready for that either."

"How can you read me so well?" I ask, placing my hand over his heart.

"Because I can. You can read me just as well, Ava. What do you want?"

"Kiss me, Clark," I whisper, and he pulls me so that I'm flush against him. I lose track of all time and space. "Clark," I whisper against his lips. "I need to tell you something."

"What is it?" he says, looking at me kindly.

"You can tell me anything Ava, surely you know that by now," he adds.

"It's nothing serious. I just feel like I need to tell you that I'm a virgin," I say, and somehow I know he will handle it like he handles everything -- with gentlemanly grace.

"Thank you for telling me," he says, leaning over and kissing my nose. "I certainly don't think differently of you because of that. If you weren't a virgin I would still respect you, but I will sure as hell respect the fact that you're a virgin. We absolutely aren't ready to go down that road. I'd at least talk to you about anything beforehand." He props himself up on his pillow and looks deep into my eyes. "Ava, even if you were ready tonight, I wouldn't let it go there. It would be really disrespectful of me to have sex with you and then leave for months. I have no intention of causing more hurt than the next couple of months are already going to be for us. You are so important to me, and we will never do anything sexually until I know you are not only ready but that we are on the same page about it. I can't afford to screw this up with you, Ava. I am going to do everything in my power to ensure that we take this slow. I want us taking our time and at our own pace, specifically in the physical department. We have all the time in the world, Ava."

"I know," I reply. "I don't share that with many

people. It just doesn't really come up in conversation. It's just that, I have never really met anyone that I wanted to be intimate with, until you. I've had boyfriends. I always knew that I wasn't going to be sticking around North Carolina or New York for that matter, and I didn't want to get stuck in a relationship with someone that would make it harder for me to leave. Plus, the guys weren't that great and the ones that were were gay," I say, and we both laugh. "All that to say, I do want all of those things with you," I add as he leans over and kisses me gently on the lips.

"I'm not in a hurry, but I'm also not a virgin. As you can tell by Brooklyn," he says against my lips, and I smile.

"I figured as much," I say, and he smiles. "Plus, I've seen your love scenes in a couple movies. I know you're not actually having sex with those women, but it's hard to imagine that you don't know what you're doing," I add, and he laughs.

"I'm experienced, Ava, but I'm also not a man whore like most men around this town. I've been intimate with 5 or 6 women since I've lived in L.A. I came to L.A. pretty young. I lost my virginity in what you would call my high school years. Nothing memorable. I've had some great relationships, and I've had some toxic ones. But I can honestly say I've never felt the way I feel about you with anyone else, which makes it easier to wait. I know what we have here is special, and what you have to offer is special. You being a virgin just makes it that much more so. If this is something you eventually want to share with me then I'll be honored. But we have time Ava to make those decisions. Later."

"Thank you, Clark! I love you," I whisper, and his face brightens into a huge grin.

"I love you too, Ava. And I'm gonna miss you so much!" he adds as he leans over and kisses me deeply.

When I wake up it's light outside and Clark is gone. I know he had an early morning, so I'm sure he didn't want to wake me. I press my fingers against my lips and think back on all the kisses from last night. I love kissing him and we did a lot of that last night. I could kiss him forever and I know that one day soon I will get to kiss him again. God, he's incredible. I'm the luckiest girl in the world.

I hear Brooklyn over the monitor and know she's either starting to wake up or playing in her room. I sit up and realize that I'm in Clark's bed. I don't really want to have that conversation with Brooklyn yet, so I get up to head into the kitchen to make some tea. When I stand up, I notice a note sitting on the bedside table. It has my name in Clark's handwriting, so I take it into the kitchen with me.

My Darling Ava,
You were resting so peaceful-

ly, I didn't want to wake you. Thank you for sharing what you did with me last night. And thank you for letting me hold you through the night. It meant the world to have you in my arms. I fall more and more in love with you every day, and I count it an honor to have your heart and for you to have mine it's yours, Ava. If any part of me has ever belonged to another person it would be my heart, to you. I pray that this time apart is short, and as you said last night, that it goes by quickly. I look forward to seeing and speaking with you soon. I'm looking forward to the next time I'm able to hold you in my arms and kiss you. You are exquisite, Ava. If you get lonely, crawl in my bed and have a cupcake. And please take a picture and send it to me! Give my love to Brooklyn. Remind her how much her daddy loves her and that I will be back soon. I'm looking forward to when you guys come to visit.

I love you!
Clark

P.S. I have ordered a surprise for you! It will be here in Vancouver when you arrive. I'm so very excited my green-eyed goddess!! And yes, I will spoil you as long as you let me be yours! And maybe beyond that. It brings me such joy to think of a future with you!

I about fall into the floor reading the note. Of course it sounds sexier as I imagine hearing him saying these things in his British accent. I will keep this forever. I know how lucky I am. I take a picture and send it to Clayton and Marco in a group text. I know Clayton is currently with Clark, but I don't care. It's given me such life. At the moment, I feel like could do anything in the world. Brooklyn comes downstairs as I am putting the note in my purse.

"Good morning, angel," I say, and she smiles.

"You're here!" she says, surprised.

"Where else would I be?" I ask, putting some honey in my tea.

"I thought you would go with Daddy?" she adds, and I shake my head.

"Nope. You're stuck with me sweet cheeks," I say as she climbs on the sofa, grabbing the remote. I help her find Mickey Mouse and then go make some breakfast for her. I'm not sure what I expected the weekend to look like. I know the high from my time with Clark and his love note will soon dwindle. Of course I'll be sad about his absence, but I also know that I need to keep Brooklyn busy. Our first day without Clark is upon us. I can either look at it like that or this is just one more day closer to being back in his arms. My phone starts to vibrate. It's a text message from Clayton.

Ummm... are you kidding me right now!!
I'm dying of romance and unshed tears

My God my heart about burst reading it.

He loves you so much and I'm so glad I get to hang around the two of you while you guys figure all this out. There are going to be some really heartbroken men and women in this world.

I can only imagine. Hopefully we can keep it hush- hush for a while. I'm also not too worried about it because I love him so much. I didn't know I could love someone this much. Plus he kissed me for the first time last night.

Honestly I'm shocked the two of you went as long as you did. But how romantic. He's been floating on cloud 9 all day and now I know why!! Haha!! You should frame that letter, Ava. If you don't, I will. I'll even have it put on a t shirt if you'd like?

Not necessary. But I'll be

keeping this letter forever.

Well..let me know if you change your mind.

How was the flight?

Great. Pretty uneventful. We just got to set.

Awesome. Well, I'm going to text him since I know you guys have landed. But I wanted to share the note with you!

Ok! We love you!!

Brooklyn and I love you too!!!

I put Brooklyn's breakfast on a tray and let her sit at the sofa to eat. Then I head back to the kitchen and sit down to text Clark.

Are you trying to kill me, Clark Grant? That was the most romantic note I've ever read. I'm literally speechless. You are the most amazing man ever! Also, Brooklyn is doing well. She's eating breakfast and watching Mickey Mouse. Clayton said you guys are on set. Please don't feel obligated to text back when you are super busy. We understand. And we love you!

We go about our day playing outside and in the pool. Later we head inside in the late afternoon and take showers. I went to the grocery store while Clark and Brooklyn were on their daddy/daughter date, so I have meals planned for us for the week, but I do want to get Brooklyn out of the house. I tell her we are going to go somewhere special and she's excited. I look down at my phone and am a little disappointed that I haven't heard from Clark today, but I know that shooting sometimes can go 12-17 hours a day. I haven't heard from Clayton either so I'm sure everything is fine. I'm new to this so I just need to figure out what "normal" is and then go from there.

Brooklyn and I head to a Mexican restaurant and eat an early dinner before the weekend crowd sets in. On the way back to the house we stop by Target and get Brooklyn and I some activities to do for the weekend. I know I could get everything off Amazon, but we are out so it won't hurt since Brooklyn loves to shop. We spend an hour or two in Target and then head back to the house. We arrive at home, and it's a little nerve wracking being here in this big house all by myself with Brooklyn, but I tell myself to be brave. I start to get a little nervous, so I call Clayton for support. I know he will laugh, but I call him anyway.

"Hello, my favorite angel," he says, and I laugh. "You doing okay?"

"Oh, yeah. We are good, I just have a question," and he laughs. "Is it normal to be so nervous the first night in this big house all by myself with Brooklyn?"

"Oh, sweet baby Jesus, yes. But you are so capable, and you could not be safer in Clark's house. I know it can be a little much the first couple of nights. Set the alarm. The house will tell you if a door is unlocked or if a gate is opened. Plus, there are two security guys that circle the neighborhood all night and even during the day. Nighttime can be a little scary, but you are safe baby girl. I promise," he says, and I take a deep, calming breath. We are in the garage. So I know he's right. I could not be safer. I know what it's like to be on my own. It's not that. It's just that I haven't been here alone yet.

"Thanks, Clayton. How is it going?" I ask, biting my lip. I hope he doesn't hear the other questions in my voice.

"It's good, baby girl. The first couple weeks are crazy. I spent half the day getting us set up in the hotel suite. It's gorgeous. Can't wait for you to see it. Also, Clark hasn't stopped today. Like literally

I've seen him maybe 20 minutes while he ate dinner. Then he went right back to set. He's got a late work out tonight and then he will get about 5 -6 hours of sleep tonight before his 5 a.m. call time. Then it's rinse and repeat like this for the first 4-6 weeks. He will have a small reprieve during a few weekends more than likely, but other than that it's gonna be hardcore, honey."

"Yikes! That sounds aggressive!" I say, and feel a small amount of relief. He's really busy. "Well, take care, Clayton. We love you," I say as I grab our Target bags and head for the door to the house. We get inside and I smile, closing the door and locking it behind me. I know I'm safe here.

"You too, baby girl! And just know, Clark is very rarely with his phone. Just know that's normal. He loves you. We had a great talk earlier and I'm so tickled about all of this. Don't ever doubt how much he loves you, Ava. I know he looked at his phone earlier, but I haven't seen him on his phone at all today. He will ALWAYS text you back. Just might take him a while to get to it. He's laser focused while on set."

"Thanks, Clayton. I'm glad he has the distraction."

"Night night, baby girl," he adds.

Brooklyn and I stay up for a couple more hours playing with a puzzle and watching TV, then I put her down for the night. I'm sad she didn't get to talk to Clark, but I also get that this is how life is in this business. I'm glad I'm able to be here with her. I pour a glass of wine to settle my nerves and then take her monitor from Clark's room and go sit on the back deck. I'm about to take a sip and enjoy my evening when my phone rings. It's a FaceTime from CLARK!

Clark

"Hey, Ava!" I say as the picture comes into focus. "Can you hear and see me okay?"

"I can," she says as she props the phone up so she can see me handsfree. God, she's just stunning. Even over FaceTime. "How was your day?"

"My day was long but amazing. Tell me how you and Brooklyn are first? You look beautiful by the way. I probably should start with that." She smiles shyly at me and then sits back.

"Our day was wonderful, and we are good. Brooklyn is asleep. I'm sorry yours was so long. How is everything going in Vancouver so far?" she asks and takes a sip from her wine glass.

"Great. I'm still getting settled and into a

rhythm, but in a week or two I'll be cruising. Just takes a little while for me to get comfy in my surroundings. The older I get, the harder it becomes. What wine did you choose? How is your shoulder and hand doing?"

"So many questions," she laughs. "Just fine. I barely notice my shoulder. I have a pretty crazy scar on my shoulder but nothing that really bothers me. I'm sure it'll fade with time. I picked up this wine at the store the other day when I was out. It's okay, probably won't choose this one again. I can say this though, the bottle was really cute. The wine however, not so great. I opened it, so I might as well try and finish it," she says, laughing. I adore her.

"Ava, I have an entire wine cellar in the basement. You know this," I add, giving her my best stern face even though she knows I'm not at all stern. "Next time just go down there and pick out a bottle. If you don't know what to choose, text me or Clayton, or Marco. They're also pretty knowledgeable. You don't even need to let me know. Clayton restocks every month."

"Clark," she says giving me a blank stare. "I'm not drinking one of your hundred-dollars-a-bottle wines. Clayton said you have bottles worth like a thousand dollars down there. I'd be scared I'd accidentally choose one of those. I feel safer in my price range," she adds, and I laugh.

"Who cares, Ava. You deserve to drink great wine. You are there by yourself with Brooklyn. Next time you want a nice red with dinner or if you have Shanna over, grab a bottle of Stag's Leap or Silver Oak. If you want a great white, go to the wine fridge and grab a bottle of Cakebread. Those are all great wines and are pretty middle of the road. If you forget, call me," I say. Then I realize she's laughing at me. "What? I want you to drink great wine, Ava. You are too beautiful to have a cheap wine headache. It'll be worth it, I promise."

"Ok. I'll keep you updated on where I land on the wine issue. Brooklyn had a wonderful day, by the way. Of course she misses you, and not to make you jealous, but she's enjoying our girl time," she adds, and my heart could beat out of my chest.

"I'm so happy, Ava. I love that the two of you are getting so close and that she's able to enjoy herself with you while I'm away. Makes being away easier to bear," I add.

"Thank you for my note this morning, Clark," she throws in. I prop my chin on my hand, watching her. "I will probably frame this and put it beside my bed and read it every morning and every night when I feel lonely."

"Are you lonely, Ava?" I ask, my voice lowering to almost a whisper.

"Sometimes. Just like everyone else. But I don't feel lonely when I'm here. I feel safe. I'm a little nervous about my first night here by myself with Brooklyn, but I think by the end of the week I'll be laughing at myself for ever being nervous in this safe house. With your state-of-the-art in-home security system and security personnel driving through the neighborhood at all times."

"You are always safe at the house, Ava. You and Brooklyn both are safe. The house will let you know if a window or door is open or unlocked. The house will also do scans throughout the night. If you need anything in the middle of the night or during the day, please call me. I don't want you to be scared."

"I know. I'm used to living on my own. I probably shouldn't have said anything. I don't want you to worry. I just, I don't know. I'm a little uneasy. Maybe because it's still all so new," she adds.

"I wish I was there to keep you and Brooklyn safe. Believe me. I wish I was there," I add, my voice trailing off as I think of being there with my girls. I clear my voice and take a sip of my water. "I'm sorry I wasn't able to text you back earlier. I was in the zone here. It won't always be like that. These first couple of weeks are always a little more on the crazy side and then things seem to lighten up in the middle of shooting. Then, toward the end, if we are on schedule with any reshoots needed, we end up just hanging out. The way things are looking right now we might be working straight through every weekend, but I'll keep you updated. Definitely want you guys to come up for Brooklyn's fall break though," I add, and she nods.

She gets up and grabs her wine glass, telling me to hold on a second. She comes back, grabs the phone and walks upstairs. I see her turn on the hallway light and I think she's next to hers and Brooklyn's bedrooms from what I can see. She looks at the phone and holds up a finger next to her lips, silently shushing me. She walks next to Brooklyn's bed and shows me my sweet girl sleeping in her bed. God, she's such an angel. I stare at her for a minute just taking in how absolutely angelic she is when she's asleep. When she's awake she's a force to be reckoned with, but while she sleeps, I'm always taken back to when she was a baby. So little. When she was a toddler, I was so scared she would get hurt or fall down. Then she lost her mum. After that it was just the two of us, but now it's the three of us. Ava backs out of her room and heads back downstairs. She's sitting at the kitchen counter, and I thank her for letting me see Brooklyn.

"Aren't you exhausted?" she asks in a whisper, and I can only laugh.

"Trying to get rid of me already?" I answer back sarcastically, and she rolls her eyes.

"I'm not the one who was up at four this morning. Now it's after 10:00 at night and you have to get up in a couple hours to work out before heading to set," she says sternly, and I see someone has been in touch with Clayton. I'm glad she knows my schedule. I want her to know where I am and what I'm doing. I don't want her to worry, and I want her to know if I'm unavailable it's for a good reason. "I'm not worried, Clark. I love you," she says, and I feel my face light up with pure joy.

"God baby," I say rubbing my hands in front of my face. "I love you, too. You have no idea. I'm sorry I didn't say it more before because now I won't be able to tell you or Brooklyn in person how much I love and adore the two of you until I see you again. That could be a month away," I add, and she smiles sadly. "Well, you are welcome for the note. It's all I had the energy to do this morning, I was so tired. If I could have written you a book I would have, but I ran out of time. Are you at the house all day tomorrow?" I ask and she nods.

"I'll be here after I drop off Brooklyn at school. I'm going to be doing that sweet girl's laundry tomorrow and then catching up on some reading. Very busy day," she says sarcastically.

"Glad to hear it. Well, keep me updated and get some sleep. I pray it's restful, I know you are a little apprehensive being there by yourself tonight. Call me if you get scared."

"I will," she says, kissing her fingers and pressing them to the phone. I do the same and then tell her goodnight. We hang up and I lay down on my bed wishing I was back home but grateful for the opportunity to finish out the franchise. I love the cast and crew. Most of them are more like family so we have a blast, but it's still work. I close my eyes and I'm out.

A couple weeks into shooting everyone is in a rhythm. We are on schedule, which is great, but we have a way to go. It's an absolute blast, but I miss my girls and tell almost everyone. No one but Clayton and Marco have met Ava, other than my team, so I'm left to give them all the details on how amazing she is. I tell Clayton that I want him to go ahead and book the flights for Brooklyn and Ava since her fall break is coming up in October. I HAVE to see them. Brooklyn is wearing me out about when she will get to see Daddy in person. I can't hold her off much longer. It's not that I don't want to see her, it's the complete opposite actually. I just feel like the week of fall break will be better for me because that week is already pretty light on the shooting schedule. I will also be able to spend the time I want with my girls. MY GIRLS. I keep saying that over and over in my head and I've started to say it out loud as well. Everyone wants to meet her. I'm sure some are curious, but more or less everyone is just happy for me. They've known me pre- and post-Angela, and I'm grateful to have the support of my friends.

One evening after a light day on set, I head out to dinner with a couple of my friends and crew from set. After a couple rounds of drinks and appetizers we sit around catching up. One of my least favorite people on this movie is a guy named Kyle. He is trouble with a capital T. He can't seem to keep it together, and as the franchise has progressed, he's gotten worse. He asks how things are going in the lady department and I just laugh.

"The lady department? That's not a very great transition into this conversation, Kyle. Might want to work on that," I add as the waiter comes back to the table to ask if we want more drinks. I don't trust this guy at all. He would run to any tabloid source in order to get his name out there. I tap out and a couple others close out their tabs as well. Kyle orders another drink, and we all smile knowingly at each other. We know full well where this will lead. This isn't the first time he's ended up drinking too much or mixing alcohol with whatever he's doing on the side, making an ass of himself or us.

"Oh, come on," Kyle says, a sly smile on his face. "You smile like a little bitch every time you look at that picture on your phone. You used to have more game than that, Clark. I'm a little disappointed that you'd give all that up because some lil' Twinkie showed you a little attention," he says, goading me, but I just sit back waiting for the show to play out.

"I did have more game in my 20's and early 30's. I'm a dad, Kyle. I don't have time for games, nor do I want to play them."

"Yeah, let it go, Kyle. He's happy, dude. Just be happy for him," Vivienne says from across the table. She's a really cool chick, and I'm glad she decided to come out with us tonight. She's been one of my costars and a great friend since the beginning of the franchise.

"I'm happy for him, Viv. Let me just make my point," Kyle says, slurring his words. "Everyone is curious about this chick. She's a normal civilian. I just don't want you to settle," he adds, and although I understand he's loaded, most people have more tact.

"I'm not settling in the least, Kyle. You don't have to worry about me. I promise you I'll get by," I say a little sarcastically. I motion for the waiter to bring his check and he nods. There are some paparazzi outside already, and the last thing Kyle needs is more negative press. He's been in and out of trouble this year and he needs to get a handle on things. This was supposed to be low key dinner and drinks with friends, not an all-night bender.

"I'm not ready to leave yet, Clark. Why are you being such a bitch? I can close out my own damn tab. Just because I asked about your new fling doesn't mean that we have to call it a night," he adds, and I ignore him. Viv nods at me that I did the right thing, and I look down at my phone, pretending to be doing anything other than going further down this rabbit hole with him. "Come on guys," he says sitting up and looking at all of us. "I didn't mean to put a damper on the evening. Don't be mad at me. I love you guys," he says, slurring his words again and I wince. Tomorrow morning is going to be rough for him. It amazes me that some actors that haven't made a name for themselves are more douchebags than A-list actors. At least that's true on this film. Every single headliner on this film is a class act. Kyle, with his supporting role is an asshole. Not only to fellow actors, but also to crew and staff. I'd love to say that people who act like that eventually get their own, but that's not always the case. Not in Hollywood at least.

"You're being an ass, Kyle," Jay says as he signs for his tab. Kyle won't be coming back out with us again. This was a mistake. This was supposed to be a laid-back evening. We are also still working and representing our movie. Some people can't handle their liquor and should probably focus more on their work. Case in point with Kyle.

"Shut up, Jay. I'm always an asshole. I'm just

asking pointed questions, and if Clark isn't comfortable talking about his young, hot nanny then he can tell me to shove it." I laugh at him, and Kyle laughs as well, thinking I'm agreeing with him. He stands up a little shaky and says he's heading to the bathroom before we leave. No doubt to throw up if I'm reading him correctly. When he leaves the table, Viv leans over and tells me I handled him like a pro.

"I'm not worried about him or what his opinion of me and my choices are. However, I will make a stink if he delays production because he can't get his sloppy ass out of bed tomorrow. My girls are coming in town next week, and I'll be damned if they have to reschedule because he's once again acting unprofessional," I add as Jay nods.

"Agreed," Jay answers as everyone at the table stands up and heads toward the front of the restaurant. I'm not even a little bit buzzed, but after Kyle's BS tonight it makes me want a glass of something stronger. He's hell bent on starting some shit so he can have some kind of press coverage for starting crap on set. Up until the last movie we did, we had no one in the cast that was drama. Then Kyle joined and it's been a shitshow where he's concerned. However, it's the last movie and most everyone out in the real world watching these films are fooled by his shenanigans.

Behind the scenes is a different story, people

are not fooled in the slightest. He's a dick and exactly the kind of guy I was telling Ava she'd run into if she dated in LA. He's that good-looking, landed great roles, heartthrob that has women fooled into thinking he's the parts he plays. The dude is an asshole who'll bed almost anyone, and it sucks to have to babysit him on a day-to day-basis. Even his team has a hard time controlling him. If we had left him behind, there would have been hell to pay, and I'll be damned if he drags my name or my people through the mud with him. Dude's got some major insecurity issues. I don't blame him for his issues. Everyone has their own issues. But he feels the need to blame every person in the world for his problems instead of dealing with his shit and taking ownership when he messes up.

We head back after Kyle finally makes it into the car. There's no doubt that the paparazzi got some pretty unflattering shots of him getting in the car. He had two women all over him and of course he brought them along. Where the hell he found them on the way to and from the bathroom is beyond me. Now I've got one of his hangers-on trying to drape herself on me. I give Viv a pleading look and she tries to stifle a laugh. We're getting out of the car at the hotel and hanger-on #2 tries to grab my hand. I shake it off but keep my head down as to not create any fuss. I'm not at all in the mood for this. I pull my arm out of her reach and Viv comes in between her and I to shield me from her pulling me to her. God, Kyle is an idiot. Knowing him he probably paid this woman to do that. When we get inside, I walk straight to the elevator. It's after 11. The hotel won't allow paparazzi to infiltrate their lobby, but that doesn't mean that some fan can't get a photo, and then it'll be all over social media.

The next morning during a break on set, Clayton comes over to me and shows me his phone. It's a picture from last night. Kyle with the two women all over him climbing in the car last night. Hanger-on #2 trying to grab me and then Viv wrapping her arm around me as we walk into the hotel. Nothing too damaging. The photos of Kyle stumbling into the lobby aren't great. Clayton mainly shows me the photos that I'm in.

"What an idiot," I say as I'm sitting in my trailer. "He was an absolute nightmare last night," I add and Clayton laughs.

"Why anyone is surprised is beyond me. That's why I didn't want to go. You got lucky that Viv is such an angel. If not, it would be you and the girl with her boobs falling out of her dress, which is actually not a dress but a shirt, walking into the lobby. That would be bad news for a lot of reasons."

"No doubt about that," I add, and I grab my

phone to thank Viv. She tells me she's always there to help and I smile. It's nice to have good friends.

"I just don't want Ava to get hurt because you were placating Kyle. He's nothing but trouble," Clayton says, and I nod.

"Yeah. I want to avoid that as well. We literally went to dinner and drinks. We had to close out his tab and then when we were waiting on him for at least 30 minutes, out front he shows up out of nowhere with these two chicks, one who was pulling at me."

"I'm not surprised about that. I mean women pull at you all the time. Wouldn't be surprised if Kyle told them to do that. I'm just saying, the women getting out of the car with you guys. It looks like you were with them is what concerns me. Ava doesn't need to see that. I've already warned her about how the pap's will try and get a photo like that even if there's nothing to really see. However, you also gotta help me out here. Make sure that there aren't women like that in your party. I don't care if you have to tell Kyle where to stick it. You need to be careful, Clark," he adds, and I whip around and give him a rundown of Kyle last night. Every little snide comment and the shit storm he could create if I started something with him.

"I don't mean to put that on you, Clayton. I can't stay locked in my hotel room, but I also want to make sure Ava is protected. Kyle knows she's my nanny. I honestly could give two shits less what he thinks, but I will be damned if he tries anything with Ava and her privacy. That's already at risk. It's only a matter of time before I get pulled under because Kyle wants more publicity."

"We will protect you and Ava the best we can. I can tell from the photo that you are trying to shake the woman off. Everyone knows you and Viv are just friends. You guys have been in this franchise together since the beginning. She's in a serious relationship and no one is going to say otherwise. But I'm just a little nervous, Clark. I don't like Kyle at all. I think it's gonna end up blowing up, and at Ava's expense."

"I'll move heaven and Earth to protect her, Clayton. You know that! I love her. I could see myself spending the rest of my life with her. I'm not going to screw it up if I can help it," I add, and I feel my blood pressure boiling.

"I know you will do anything to protect her, Clark. Shit, I know that," he says as he tries to rein me back in. "All I'm saying is that I'm worried that someone, not you, is going to use your private life and turn it into a side show for their benefit. Kyle's rising star is starting to fade. Enough people know he's a risk to cast on any big production and he's getting pressure from all angles. He's a wanna-be Clark Grant and we all need to be careful. Especially with Ava and Brooklyn coming up soon.

God, I hope that goes well," he says, sitting down and scrolling through the photos from last night. "If not, you might have to get ahead of the story if he tries to go to the press with details of you and Ava.

"If it comes to that I would do it in a heartbeat. I just need to make sure we protect my girls, Clayton. You have permission to do whatever it takes," I add, and he nods. I know he will.

Ava

Brooklyn and I are on a private jet. I repeat a private jet. Just the two of us. This is crazy. I'm trying not freak out, but this is crazy. I usually love October. The weather starts to cool down and it's such a fun time to be out and about. The fall candles, the leaves start to turn and football season is in full swing by then. This is my first fall in California. The weather in California seems to always be great, but now I'm heading to Vancouver, and I'm told to bring my heavy jacket. Who knew! Apparently, we are skipping fall and going straight to winter? When we land a few hours later I can tell it's cold and rainy from the view outside my window. Brooklyn is so excited to see her daddy that she hasn't even noticed the change in weather. As we deplane, I see Clark and Clayton get out of their rented Escalade, and Brooklyn runs to her daddy. I smile seeing the two of them embrace. I know this has felt like a lifetime for Clark. I'm glad we were able to bring Brooklyn to see him. Clayton gives me a big hug and a kiss on the cheek. I've missed my guys so much. As I'm pulling away from Clayton, Clark grabs my hand and pulls me into his arms. His warm, strong and safe arms. I melt into him as his scent overwhelms me. Clean, warm and a hint of expensive cologne. I find myself tearing up. I was not prepared for this kind of emotion seeing him again. I knew I was excited to see him. My god how I've missed him, but this is new. He lifts my chin to look at him and I blink away tears. He kisses me gently on the lips and I do not miss the unshed tears in his own eyes. I give him a small smile, and he wipes away the tears from my face. He missed us as well.

As we head toward the hotel, Clayton tells me we are going out to dinner after we unpack. Clark is on a call and doesn't seem too pleased with whoever is on the receiving end of that call. I look at Clayton and he just shakes his head. I'm sure I'll hear all about it soon enough. Clayton sits in the front with the driver, and Brooklyn and I are in the back with Clark. As we pull up to the hotel, I notice a couple of photographers. I didn't realize that there would be photographers waiting outside the hotel. I guess I should never be surprised, but they seem to recognize the SUV as we approach. Clayton gets out first and then Clark gets Brooklyn out of her seat and carries her in his arms. Why they would want to photograph a child is beyond me. I wait a little behind Clark and Brooklyn and grab Clayton's hand as we get out of the car. I don't look at anyone but Clayton, and he gives me a big HERE WE GO smile which makes me laugh. God, I've missed him.

We get up to the room and after a quick tour by Clayton, we stop in front of the floor to ceiling windows, and I take it all in. The suite has three bedrooms with a large living space and kitchen in the center. The panoramic views of downtown Vancouver and the waterfront are stunning even on a foggy and rainy day. I bet when it's not raining it's breathtaking. It's not that I don't love rain. It just makes it seem so much colder. I head into the third bedroom since Clayton is set up in the second. Clark is obviously in the master bedroom. I need to unpack Brooklyn and my things, so Clayton comes in and chats while I get us settled.

"I noticed you hung back a bit when Clark and Brooklyn got out of the car," he says, leaning against the wall beside the chest of drawers. I look up and he's smiling, but he's got a question lingering in his eyes.

"I mean… I'm not trying to start anything with

the press. Not because I'm not ready for that, but because well…Clark and I haven't really talked about it. I know that would change a lot more for him than it would for me. I don't know, I don't have to be glued to him every time we are out and about. Honestly, I just kind of decided to hang back on a whim when I saw them rush the car."

"I thought it was pretty smart. I know Clark is in love with you. I'm a little peeved at him for not giving you more of a heads up about it though. You guys probably should have talked about it before you got here," Clayton says, closing the drawer after I place Brooklyn's jeans in it. "I know he's used to it. But you aren't."

"I'm not worried about it. They don't know about Clark and I. I know how I feel, and I know how Clark feels. We're taking it slow," I add as I walk to the door and close it so Clayton and I can talk. Brooklyn and Clark are catching up in the other room and I don't want to disturb them. "I'm not offended, and I'm not necessarily worried about them getting a photo of us together either. Eventually they'll put two and two together. Heck they do that with people who aren't even together. We aren't trying to hide anything. You know that. It's just that…we haven't really talked about paparazzi. I guess I just don't have an opinion on it."

"Well, you should. I know the two of you love each other, but you need to be on the same page.

Clark hasn't been very hush-hush on how he feels about you while he's been here. He hasn't sent out a press release or anything, but he's definitely not hiding anything. I love that about him. But unless you are ready for the kit and caboodle that comes with his life, then the two of you need to be pretty careful while you're here. I get that he's shooting a movie and that's a hard time to try out a relationship, but this could affect your future too, Ava," Clayton adds as I turn to face him after I hang up my clothes. "Auditions, the roles you receive, how people perceive you. Clark's already established in the business and he's made a name for himself. You haven't, doll. You need decide if that's something you're truly ready for. I'm not saying it'll ruin your career. I just want someone to be thinking about you, Ava. You have a choice in this," he says as I come to sit on the bed. "Please hear me say Clark is actively thinking about you. It's not that," he starts, and I place a hand over his.

"I love him so much. I'm not going to NOT be with him because I might miss out on a few opportunities. I mean, before I met Clark, I was having a hard time finding great roles anyway. It would be a little silly of me to miss out on both. I feel like the right opportunity will come along when it's right. I'm not saying I would give up everything to be with Clark. I know that's ridiculous. Especially this early in our relationship. There will be certain compromises that I will have to navigate as we figure it out. But I CAN say this. I appreciate you Clayton for thinking of me. It means the world to me." He sits next to me and wraps his arms around my shoulders, squeezing me tight.

"It's hard because I love and adore the both of you. Clark doesn't want you to have to compromise anything to be with him, but that's not very realistic. I think he's trying too hard to protect you when what he really needs to do is just find out where you are with all of this. I think it's hard when your relationship is new and the last couple of weeks it's been virtual."

"Yeah. We've touched a little bit on his life and the other things that come along with it. But I guess we just need to feel it out before we make a call on anything. If I had my vote, I would just be with Clark. I love him. But I know it's not that simple of a decision."

I change out of my yoga pants and sweatshirt and into some black jeans. I pull an off-the-shoulder sweater and some booties on as well. After I put on a little bit of makeup and run a brush through my hair, I feel like I'm ready to go. Clayton is on cloud nine because Marco is coming tomorrow. He had a meeting with a client that he couldn't move so he didn't fly up with us, but I'm so excited for all of us to be together. I help Brooklyn get changed into a cute sweatshirt dress and some warm leggings as Clark comes in and smiles at us. He's dressed in blue jeans and a long sleeve henley that's fitted to his incredibly muscular frame. He's wearing boots, and I realize that I've never seen him wearing boots. It's actually making him a little taller. He's statuesque and my God, he's so beautiful. From head to toe he's perfection. I catch a whiff of his cologne and it's such a sexy scent. He clears his throat, and I look up to see him trying not to laugh at me.

"Ava, if you continue to look at me like that, we are going to be late for dinner," he says with a sexy grin on his face.

"Sorry. But have you *seen* you?" I ask as Brooklyn runs out of the room when she hears the theme song to Mickey Mouse come on the TV in the living room.

"I have. Have YOU looked in the mirror, Angel?" I turn around and he's looking me up and down. "God Ava, you are so stunning," he says as I laugh. You'd think it had been a year since we'd seen each other. He pulls me into his arms and kisses me on the forehead. "You smell amazing baby. You ready to grab some dinner?" I nod my head, not wanting to move from his arms. "I would love to stay like this forever with you Ava, but I need to make sure my girls eat a good dinner." He lifts my chin giving me a sweet kiss on the lips and I feel my body warm all over. "We also need to talk while you are here about the press and photographers outside. We should have talked about this before you got here, but I didn't even think about it. Please forgive me. They are more than likely going to get photos of us if they haven't already. I know you know that comes with the territory, we've talked about that. But I want to make sure I'm able to protect you the best I can," he adds, and I lift up on my toes. I grab his face, bringing it closer to mine. I kiss him hard, and he wraps his arms around my waist tighter. His hand goes under my sweater and presses warmly against my back. It feels like lighter fluid to my senses. I breathe him in, pulling his hair and he groans. "Ava," he moans against my lips, pulling back. "We have to stop. Brooklyn and Clayton are in the other room and I'm trying to take this slow."

"I know. I'm sorry," I say as I take a step back from him, but he pulls me back into his arms.

"Don't apologize for passion, Ava. One thing we won't have to worry about is the chemistry between us. But we will have to worry about getting too carried away. I need to know how you feel about the paparazzi. We are about to head into the lion's den, and I need you to be as prepared as possible. You have a choice here, Ava."

"I don't really think we have a choice with the paparazzi, Clark. If you're asking me if I'm ready to be with you publicly, I am. Why don't we talk more about this after we get back from dinner, when Brooklyn is asleep. You know I love you. I know I want to be with you. But I also know we need to take this slow, and it will be hard to control the narrative once the press gets a hold of that," I say, and he nods. "I don't care if they photograph us together. I love you."

"I love you too, Ava. Let's talk later tonight. I want you to know I want you however I can have you. If that means not touching in public, but then getting to hold you in private, I'm okay with that. I'm not worried about how this will affect me. It'll affect you more. I want you to know what you're getting yourself into. Love won't be our issue. It's going to be people outside our circle, the media, paparazzi, that will be the issue. People with too much damn time on their hands. Before I was in the entertainment business, I never would have thought someone would try and destroy another human just to sell magazines or for views on social media. Unfortunately, there are people out there whose entire life mission is just that. If I can protect you from that, I will. But I can't protect you from every negative of being with me," he says a little sadly, and it breaks my heart. I reach up, touching his cheek and he turns his head, placing a simple kiss to the palm of my hand. I pull him to sit on the edge of the bed with me.

"Clark. You are worth all of that. We will figure

it out together. I know you can't protect me from everything. I know you want to, but you can't. Aren't I worth it to you?" I ask, knowing what his response will be, but I'm trying to prove a point here. He looks taken aback and he becomes even more serious.

"Of course you are. I would move heaven and Earth for you."

"Then you should know that I feel the exact same way. We don't have to make any drastic decisions right now. We have the luxury of taking this at our own pace. Let's just go eat and let whatever happens happen. I love you," I say leaning into him and kissing him chastely on the lips before grabbing his hand and pulling him to his feet. "Now let's eat."

We head to a very luxurious steakhouse and it's delectable. We didn't encounter any paparazzi on the way into the restaurant, but Clayton told me we won't be so lucky on the way out. We are sitting at a large table toward the back, near the kitchen, so we aren't situated in front of a window. They had a private dining room, but Clark told them that wasn't necessary. Clayton and I are sitting on one side and Clark and Brooklyn are on the other side. Brooklyn is watching a movie on her iPad and the three of us are enjoying a bottle of red wine. I've missed this so much. I love and adore both Clayton and Clark. We sit and talk for an hour over appetizers. I haven't laughed this hard in a long time. Clark gets a steak bigger than my head, and Clayton and I both get the Salmon. It's cooked to perfection. We all take a bite of Clark's steak, and it melts in my mouth. I moan and Clark and Clayton have a hell of a time making fun of the noises I make over food. It's another CUPCAKE fiasco, but I laugh along with them this time. We've been at dinner for around three hours, just sitting and talking over dark chocolate and raspberry cheesecake when Clark's phone rings. It's Brian. Clark tells us he will be right back and steps away to take the call. Clayton and I are still laughing when his phone buzzes as well. He looks down at his phone and then up at me.

"Looks like the time has come little lady," he says as he opens his Instagram and we see someone has tagged him in a photo. The picture has also hit a couple of news sites. Someone in the restaurant has taken a picture of us tonight at our table. He tells me not to look around, but the photo already has 200,000 likes. Not to mention someone has tagged me in the photo. After Clayton copied both Marco and I in a photo of the three of us in bed a month or two ago, I had a huge jump in followers. So far everyone has been super kind. Mainly because at the time they saw me as a non-threat. I haven't posted any photos of Clark because that's not my M.O. I also don't post photos on my account of

Brooklyn. I have posted pictures of Shanna and I, Clayton and I, as well as a glass of wine with the view from Clark's backyard. But most people don't catch where the photo was taken. Once a picture of Clark and I gets out, if it gets out, then I'm sure the mood surrounding me will change. The picture of Clayton, Marco and I had the most likes on my account. I already have over 100,000 followers alone because of Clayton and Marco. Before that photo I had maybe 300 followers. The photo is a picture of Clayton and I laughing, and you can see the back of Brooklyn's head and Clark is grabbing my arm laughing. I mean, from the vantage point of the photo it just looks like three friends who work together having a good time and laughing. Most of the photos are of Clayton and I. Anyone who follows Clayton on IG knows that he's gay. He's not hiding anything. Why should he! The next photo is the same photo, but it's zeroed in on Clark's hand on my arm. It's already been picked up by at least four entertainment sites. We've only been in the restaurant for a couple hours talking and drinking, so it's unbelievable to me that news travels that fast. But there's no news. I'm not even sitting next to him. I'm sitting next to Clayton. And it's not like his touch was even in the least bit sexual. It was more like him reaching out because he's laughing so hard. Clark comes back and looks pissed.

"I'm sorry. Brian called to tell me about the

photo. I can see you've already seen it. Well, we knew this would happen. How are you feeling about all of this?" Clark asks me and Clayton turns to look at me.

"Honestly, I'm fine. They didn't get a picture of the two of us, Clark. If anything, it's speculation at this point. Even if they did…I don't care!"

"Okay!" Clark says, placing a hand over mine. "Good," he says, releasing the breath he was holding, and I start laughing. He looks over at me curious, and I look over at Brooklyn who's starting to nod off. "Why are you laughing?"

"Because of your brooding on the way back to the table. What if I had said I wasn't okay with it?"

"I guess I expected you would be okay with it. But Brian was freaking out!" Clark starts to say, and I grab his hand squeezing it gently.

"Let's not worry about what anyone else thinks and feels but us," I add, and he smiles over at me. He lifts my hand up and kisses it gently. The restaurant has cleared out considerably since we first arrived.

"Deal. Thank you, baby," he whispers, and I wink at him.

"Why don't you take Brooklyn back to the hotel. It's way past her bedtime," Clayton says, smiling at Clark. "Ava and I will finish our drinks and pay for the check. We will see you back at the hotel? It's supposed to be a nice day tomorrow so we can all venture out and do some fun things. Until then, we love you. Go put your princess to sleep," he says to Clark. He agrees and picks up a half-asleep Brooklyn. Clayton and I can either walk back since it's not too far or we can get a cab. Clark leans over and gives me a kiss on the lips showing he's clearly over the people who can't seem to give him the privacy he deserves, and then he puts a hand on Clayton's shoulder, giving him a thank you without having to say it.

About 30 minutes later, Clayton and I finish our wine and pay the bill. As we are leaving there are still some paparazzi, so we decide to grab a cab. I try to act like I don't see them as we wait, but they literally try and get in your face. The doorman from the restaurant comes out and tells them to back up if they are going to be invading our privacy, which helps. The cab comes and I hop in first. Clayton closes the door and gives the driver the address to the hotel. As we pull away from the curb, Clayton looks at me laughing.

"As always, this is going to be a fun adventure, Ava," he says, grabbing my hand. "Are you okay?"

"I'm fine. I just have to get used to it. It doesn't bother me and I'm not going to fight it. If this was about them respecting Brooklyn's privacy, I could understand that, truly I could. But Clark and I are two consenting adults. I don't have anything to hide," I add as we pull up to the hotel and see more paparazzi. "As long as our safety isn't at stake, who cares?" Clayton opens the door and grabs my hand. We head into the lobby with flashes of cameras popping around us. A couple people in the lobby turn to see who we are and then, not recognizing us, go back to their business. The doorman stands in front of a couple of paparazzis trying to get a shot inside and I can tell some expletives are exchanged between them.

When we get back in the suite, Clark is sitting on the sofa in the den reading a book. Brooklyn must already be asleep. Clayton says he's turning in for the night, and I walk over to Clark who pulls me into his lap on the sofa.

"Baby, I'm sorry I got irritated over the photos taken tonight. It isn't that I don't want to be photographed with you. I just thought we would have more time. I know this doesn't really change a whole lot for us right now, but they are going to be on our case from now on. I know you love me, Ava. I do. And you know that I love you. But are you truly ready for all this?" he asks as I turn in his lap so I can look into his face.

"Clark. I knew what I was getting myself into the moment I started working for you. I didn't go into this blind. I'm a smart woman and I can handle myself. If you're worried about me, then it's wasted energy because I'm ready for whatever happens. We can't control everything, despite what

Brian and your team think. You have more experience than I do with the press. But I don't care. I don't have to answer to anyone. I don't have to answer questions. I agree we should take this slow. I don't plan on changing anything because of press. I understand if you have to change your plans. But you need to understand that life is too damn short for me to get worked up because people realize I may not end up being a background character in this whole shebang. I'm going to be myself and love who I want. I'll be more careful and aware, but me."

Clark pulls me closer, rubbing his hand up and down my thigh. "Ava. Please hear me say this very clearly. I am ready for this, but I've seen how ugly the press can be. While people say they don't believe everything they hear in the press. Sometimes they do. I don't think anyone can be fully prepared for this kind of attention and press, but I'm ready. They make up things you didn't say or twist your words. They go after people who know you and quote people who don't know you. It's quite a production. I don't want you to have to trade your dreams for mine. I don't want you to have to trade the roles you could end up getting to be with me. I know that's your decision, but I don't want that for you. I'm not saying that's going to happen, but it could. I love you too much to stand in the way of your dreams. That doesn't mean I don't want us to be together. It's just hard, because I want both," he says, leaning over and kissing my bare shoulder. "I don't want to lose you. I want to see where this goes. But I also want to be smart about this. I will walk beside you, Ava, and my team will be your team. Regardless of what happens. But you need to know that we are right on the edge of this launching into the world." He leans over me and he kisses down my collarbone. It takes my breath away, so I lift his face so we are looking into each other's eyes.

"I can't concentrate when you do that Clark," I say, and he smiles back.

"How do you think I feel with you in my lap and your arms wrapped around me? I'm partial to wanting to keep you safe in my arms and the other half of me wants to ravish you. Such is life."

"Sorry," I say sarcastically as I try to move off his lap. "You kinda did that to yourself though. You're the one who pulled me into your lap." He gently pulls me back.

"Well. That's it then," he says as he wraps his arms around me. The rain has stopped, and the moon is now more visible through the clouds. "I love you, Ava. Please always remember that."

"I love you too, Clark," He kisses me behind the ear and I realize we've been sitting here for a while in the quiet. "You ready for bed?" I ask and he nods.

"Are you coming with me? Or do you want to sleep in the room with Brooklyn? As you know there are two beds in Brooklyn's room, so I won't be offended if you want to stay in there. I have an early phone call in the morning, but I promise not to wake you if you stay with me tonight," he adds, pressing his warm lips to my shoulder. "I also promise to be on my best behavior," he says laughing. I know he will, but when his lips are on me it's hard to concentrate.

"I would love that, but what if Brooklyn comes in in the morning? What do you want to do?"

"Well. I guess we can tell her that you're my girlfriend and that sometimes when people are in love they sleep in the same bed. Is that okay with you?" I turn and smile at him. I can't help it.

"Yes," I say, my lips against his. "That's okay with me." He lifts me up and carries me into his room. I realize my pajamas are in Brooklyn's room. He pulls out one of his t shirts and hands it to me. I head to the bathroom and change into it. I need to wash my face, so I use some of the hotel's supplies. They are all luxury and expensive brands so I'm sure they're fine. I see some of Clark's face lotion and use a little of it. I brush my teeth with the extra toothbrush and then walk out of the bathroom. Clark is sitting on the edge of the bed in his pajama bottoms with no shirt. I lean against the door frame, taking him in. He looks like he should be in a magazine. His hair is a little messy and his body seems to shimmer in the soft light. I love wearing Clark's shirt. It makes me feel sexy, and I love that it smells like him. He holds out a hand, and I walk to stand in front of him.

"You are so beautiful, Ava. Even in zero make up and wearing nothing but a tee shirt. You were exquisite tonight at dinner, and you are just as beautiful now. How did I get so lucky?" he looks me up and down. I'm not wearing anything under his shirt, and I know I should be more nervous but I'm not. He stands up with me and I wrap my legs around him. He stops and looks at me with a twinkle in his eyes. "Jesus. Ava, are you not wearing any underwear?" I smile, shrugging my shoulders. He looks up at the ceiling as if he's trying to muster some inner strength. He holds me with one arm and pulls the covers back, crawling into bed with me. I unwrap my legs from him so we can lay face to face, but I place one leg over his hip so we can still be close. He rubs his hand up and down my leg, stopping at my hip. "Not going to lie. This is going to be harder than I imagined," he says smiling, and I press into him.

"I can feel that," I say, smiling at him. He rests his forehead against mine, laughing.

"Ava," he growls against my lips. "You know what I mean."

"I know. And I don't intend to make this more

difficult for either of us, but I also know that we are only human. My God Clark, you are the most beautiful man in the entire world. Your body is like it's been chiseled out of marble. I can't help but want to touch you. I love that this is mine to touch," I say running my hands over his chest. "I promise to be careful, I know you're only a man, Clark, and your strength has its limits, but I do want to touch you. And I want you to touch me. I'm yours, Clark," I say looking from his chest into his eyes.

"I'm yours too, Ava. I have been since the moment you walked into my house. I fought my feelings as best I could. Then I decided it wasn't worth it to waste my time fighting something as strong as what we have. Once I touch you and we cross certain lines it will be more difficult for us to want to stop. I will do my best, but I'm only human. And you smell divine," he says as he leans down to kiss me. He pulls me into his side so that I'm lying with my back to him. My shirt has risen up a little so it's around my waist and not covering my butt anymore. "God, AVA," he says as he moves his hand from around my waist over my bare hip. "God help me," he says, his lips against the back of my head. He pulls his arm from under the covers to pull me closer to him, as if that was even possible. His hand is on the outside of the comforter and I agree that it's probably safer there. I'm just relishing being back in his arms. I smile to myself as Clark turns the bedside light out. His scent is intoxicating. I love the feeling of being safe in his arms. I honestly don't care anything about the paparazzi because I have this with Clark, and no one can take this feeling away from me.

Clark

The next morning I slip out of bed while it's still dark. I have a phone interview with a magazine out of New York, so with the time difference I have to be up early. They offered to come out to the set, but I told them I was taking a long weekend to be with my daughter so I wouldn't be on set as much. Plus I didn't want them in the hotel with Brooklyn and Ava here. The interview takes about an hour, and I answer all the pertinent questions. Clayton and I feel like it went really well. I really do enjoy doing interviews and TV show appearances. It's only when things start to get a little too personal that I become a little uneasy. I'm able to play it off, but sometimes I'm shocked with what people are comfortable asking. We are getting ready to wrap and I'm ready for the normal "Are you dating anyone/are you single" question. I get that all the time, even when Clayton or my PR team says I won't be answering any questions about my personal life. So when the interviewer asks me if I'm single because it's "what their readers really want to know," sometimes I wonder why they don't lead with that question. I laugh and say that I'm not single, but that's all I will comment on that subject at this time. He thanks me for my time, and I get off the phone. I get up to get some coffee and Clayton follows me.

"Wow. I mean, I was expecting you to say no comment." He hands me the creamer and I pour some into my mug.

"No need to lie. It would be disrespectful to Ava to say I'm single. I'm not single. But that doesn't mean I have to go into details."

"Very true. I hope you're ready, Clark. Also, since it's supposed to be somewhat nice today I have a driver on standby. I know you'll do some walking, but I'm not sure if we will be able to fully avoid all paparazzi. Marco will be here in an hour and then we can leave. I know it's still a little early, but I thought we could show Brooklyn and Ava the waterfront areas and do some shopping. Maybe a little lunch out and then you could take them to the set for a while, let them see where you've been the last month or so. Thoughts?" Clayton asks and I nod.

"Sounds good."

I stop to look out the window as the sun is starting to rise over the water. It's beautiful and part of me wants to go get back in bed with Ava. So I do. I tell Clayton I'm going back to bed and he smiles, looking back down at his phone. I walk back into the bedroom and because the bedroom is still dark, I don't turn the lights on. I just crawl back in bed and it's so warm. I could probably go back to sleep, but I won't. I just want to lie here with Ava. She rolls over and faces me. Her eyes are still closed, and I move the hair from her face and lean down to kiss her lightly as to not wake her. God, I want this forever. I do. I could wake up every morning to her and fall asleep with her in my arms every night. It's too soon to ask her to spend the rest of her life with me, but I do have a surprise for her. It's been sitting in my suitcase since last night. I pulled it out of the room safe yesterday before they arrived, but I want to wait to give it to her when the moment feels right. It's nothing huge, at least not for me. I hope she likes it. I saw them while I was at my jewelers to get Brooklyn a gift and thought about how beautiful they would look on her. When Ava and I started to become a little more serious I went ahead and bought them. I couldn't imagine them being on anyone else. She doesn't really wear earrings so I'm hoping the diamond studs surrounded by tiny diamonds are something she might want to wear. She starts to stir and then blinks up at me. I realize I was just lying here watching her sleep. She smiles and I lean down to kiss her nose.

"Hi," she says sleepily, and I lean down to kiss her cheek. I love kissing her.

"Good morning beautiful," I say, smiling down at her. "I have something for you," she widens her eyes and we both laugh. "Obviously not what I meant." I get out of bed and grab the box out of my suitcase. She sits up, and I sit in front of her as I hand her the box. "I didn't know if you remembered I had a surprise for you when you got here. Didn't think about it last night." I whisper, and she leans over and kisses me on the lips. She opens the box and gasps. "Do you like them?"

"Are you kidding? They're beautiful," she says, running a finger over the diamond earrings. "I've never had anything so beautiful," she adds, and I smile down at her.

"Neither have I," I lean over and kiss her under her ear. "They aren't as beautiful as you are, Ava. When I saw them I thought of you. I hope that you like them. Please don't feel obligated to wear them, but I would be honored if you would accept them."

"Clark, I love them. I hope you don't judge me for putting them on right now," she says, a little embarrassed.

"Not at all, baby. Go put them on!" She hops

off the bed and stands in front of the dresser mirror to put the earrings in. Once she has them in, her eyes fill with tears and I feel a little overcome as well. They are stunning on her, bringing out her emerald eyes. She looks at me in the mirror and a tear falls down her cheek. I come to stand behind her and wrap my arms around her. I know she isn't sad. She's the most appreciative person I've ever met and it's heartwarming. I want to spoil her. I want to take care of her.

"They're beautiful on you, Ava."

"Thank you, Clark," she says, turning around and kissing me. She heads to the bathroom and I sit on the bed thinking. God I'm ready to sign my life over to her already. She comes out of the bathroom and comes to sit next to me. "Sorry I needed to brush my teeth. Thank you, Clark. They are perfect," she says as I look down at her.

"They are only a small token of my affection for you, Ava. They really are beautiful on you. They are only the beginning so please be prepared. Every time I see something and think of you, chances are I will buy it," I add, and she laughs.

"Okay," she says, kissing me on the cheek. "I need to get dressed," she adds.

"You get dressed. I'm going to shower. I'll be out soon, angel."

Clayton

Ava comes out of Clark's bedroom wearing nothing but a tee shirt and then I see the diamonds in her ears. Of course I squeal. Is there any other reaction to your sweet girl sporting new diamonds? The answer is no!

"Oh my god, darling," I say, getting up from my laptop and walking over to her. "So much to cover, but let's start with the earrings. They are stunning on you, Ava. My god they're perfect. Not to mention you in nothing but his tee shirt. Do I even need to ask?" I say, kidding around. Ava and I have talked about where she is with all of that and her inexperience. I know Clark is a gentleman. It's one of the endearing things about working with him. I don't have to worry about him being an asshole or blow back from him sleeping with a bunch of floozies. He's a good guy and there aren't many left in this industry. I know he respects Ava.

"They're beautiful, aren't they," she says smiling at me. She really is stunning. She can pull off the no makeup look better than most. "I didn't want to go wake up Brooklyn by getting my pj's. Plus I enjoyed sleeping in Clark's shirt. I could smell him all night."

"Someone's got it bad," I add. Brooklyn comes out and runs to get on the sofa. We turn the TV on, and I love that she didn't even notice Ava is only in a tee shirt. She's normally very observant, but I think she's used to Clark and Ava being touchy and feely together. It's not like they hide it. She probably just assumes it's normal. I don't think she would be upset about it. There's a knock on the door, and I know that has to be Marco. I open the door and Marco is standing there with a big smile on his face. I couldn't be happier to see my sweetheart. I give him a big kiss and hug as he comes into the suite. We waste absolutely no time. We grab more coffee, and he tells me about how yesterday went with the new client he just landed and I'm ecstatic for him. He deserves all the amazing things life brings him. He's so talented. We are catching up when Clark walks out of his bedroom and there seems to be a very different air to him than there was last night. I know that is all due to

Ava. Him falling in love with her is the best thing that's ever happened to him, aside from Brooklyn. He smiles at me and then gives Marco's shoulder a squeeze. I love my guys! He walks over to Brooklyn and turns the TV off and I am shocked. You do NOT turn off Brooklyn's cartoons. He kneels down in front of her, and I wonder what is about to happen. Marco and I sit there staring.

"Brooklyn, I need to talk to you about something, okay?" he says to her, and she stands in front of her daddy, nodding. "How would you feel if Ava was daddy's girlfriend?" he asks and I gasp. It's the sweetest thing him talking to Brooklyn about all this.

"Does that mean Ava won't be with me anymore if she's your girlfriend?" Brooklyn asks sadly, and I feel a little weepy at the conversation. Clark smiles and shakes his head.

"No, baby. Ava will still be with you, but she will be with daddy too."

"Then she can be your girlfriend," Brooklyn smiles and Clark nods, relieved.

"Good. Because I am in love with Ava," he adds, and she gives him a big hug.

"I love Ava too!" Brooklyn says and I lean my head on Marco's shoulder. He pulls me in for a hug and I realize I'm crying. This sweet little family has been through so much and I love that Ava is now a part of their redemption story.

"Ava loves you too, baby."

"Does Ava love you?" she asks, and I see Ava has come out of her room.

"She does," Clark says as Brooklyn hugs her daddy's neck. Clark is looking at Ava with a smile on his face. Ava smiles sweetly at Clark and heads to the kitchen to make her morning tea. Once Brooklyn's cartoons are back on, she sits down to watch. Clark comes into the kitchen smiling at me as he walks behind Ava, turning her around, dipping her and kissing her hard. It's the most dramatic scene I've seen from him, which makes me laugh. These two are the best.

"Well, that was the most adorable interaction I think I've ever seen," Marco adds as he places his coffee cup in the sink. He rolls his suitcase into our bedroom, and I follow him so we can have some time alone before we head out for the day.

Ava

Today has been magical. Being with everyone is like being with the family I never thought I would have again. The earrings from Clark are gorgeous. I love them so much and wearing them makes me feel so special. I can't believe he purchased those for me. Clark is holding Brooklyn's hand as we walk around Vancouver checking out the sights. We stopped to watch the boats at the park and then went a toy store to buy a couple things for Brooklyn. It's a pretty gorgeous day. It's still chilly but the sun is shining so it's been really nice. We haven't encountered any paparazzi today, but I know that will be short lived as people are starting to notice Clark. Most are pretty respectful, but one or two ask for a photo or an autograph. It's a little past lunch time, and we finally decide on a restaurant. It feels good to sit down. Brooklyn is sitting between Clark and I, with Marco and Clayton sitting in front of us. We eat some of the best Thai food I've ever had. I mean, so delicious that I have to force myself stop eating. We have more walking to do, and I don't want to make myself sick. As we head out of the restaurant a couple of people stop Clark, but I take Brooklyn's hand and we keep on walking. Clayton has called the driver to pick us up, and honestly, I'm a little relieved. Not because I don't enjoy walking, but because they are taking us to set.

When we arrive on set, we first go to Clark's trailer. It's so luxurious that you almost forget you are in a glorified RV. Then we spend the rest of the afternoon walking around set. It's so cool to see the different sets and behind the scenes. I always find this so interesting. They are still shooting today, but Clark isn't on the schedule. I meet a couple of his co-stars and they are all so sweet. One person I love is Vivienne. She's so incredibly down to earth. I know she and Clark have been in many movies together, and they've been close for a long time. She seemed genuinely excited to meet me. She told me that if I am ever in Santa Monica, I should call her up. I tell her I will, and then we continue walking around where we can. We've been on set for about an hour or so when I notice someone who looks familiar walking toward us. I immediately feel Clark tense beside me.

"He's an asshole, Ava," Clayton whispers in my ear and I nod in acknowledgement. "He's the only ass on set. Be prepared. He's the one I warned you about, okay?" he adds. Kyle Wright. It's amazing how he has the public so fooled. Women want to tame him, and he really knows how to play that card well. He bends down to say hello to Brooklyn first, then looks up at me and then to Clark. The look he gives me sends shivers down my spine, and not in a good way. He stands and talks to Clark and Brooklyn for a minute, but he keeps looking over at me. I turn around and speak to Marco, who is giving Kyle a nasty look. Marco faces me and smiles kindly.

"Where do we want to eat for dinner?" I ask Marco as Clayton turns to look at me.

"Good idea. Let's decide if we want to eat out or get takeout. I'm fine with both. But I'm also game to put on my pj's and get some great wine and food from downstairs in the restaurant. Marco, you've been traveling today. What are you feeling?" Clayton asks and Marco is about to respond when I see a couple other actors come over and start talking. Enough to distract Clark, and Kyle takes advantage of the opportunity to come stand next to me. He puts an arm around my waist, pulling me to his side and says hello. If he wasn't such a creep, I'd be flattered, but I've been warned.

"It's so nice to finally meet you." He drops his arm so that it brushes against my ass. I look up at Clayton, who saw him do it, and he grits his teeth. Clayton is about to say something, but I move a little closer to Marco and turn to face Kyle.

"I'm Ava," I say taking a step back and Clayton gives Kyle a warning stare.

"I've been wondering if and when I'd get to meet you," he says. He seems like he's on something. His eyes seem like they're having trouble focusing. He's putting the charm on, and I'm sure that works on his unsuspecting prey, but it won't work on me. I'm unaffected by him and his greasy character. He's absolutely nothing compared to Clark. It's actually comical that anyone would even entertain that notion. He's been talking about himself for about five minutes when he realizes that I'm not really listening. "Sorry," he says sarcastically. "I forget that you probably already know all of this. You look like a magazine reader." A couple people who walked up with Kyle laugh, but I turn back to Marco who nods toward Clark.

"I think we should probably head out," Marco says and reaches for my hand.

"Uh-huh," I add, forcing a smile. "That's nice, Kyle. Hope everything goes well for you."

I turn around and hear him say loudly to the guy standing next to him. "I didn't realize she would look as good leaving as she would coming. If you catch my meaning," he says laughing. I want to turn around, but I look up at Clark, who's talking to another actor. Luckily he missed that last comment. I reach out, taking Clark's hand and he looks down at me. I wink at Clark, and he pulls me into his side, wrapping an arm around me and leaning down. I think he's going to kiss my head, but he whispers in my ear.

"I'm about five seconds from murdering him. What a disrespectful little shit. I'm sorry about him. Are you okay?" he asks, and I nod. Apparently he didn't miss everything.

"Don't make a scene, Clark. That's what he wants. But if he brushes up against my ass again, I think that I might punch him in the face myself," I say as Clark looks down at me with a 'you can't be serious' look.

"Are you kidding me?" he says, swearing under his breath. I look down at Brooklyn, and Clark follows my line of sight. He nods. Now is not the time nor the place. "Let's get out of here baby," he adds as he picks up Brooklyn. He doesn't let go of my hand. I turn to Clayton and Marco, who looks like he's about to spit nails. Kyle is smiling at me, but I don't smile back.

"Hey, we have to go or we're going to be late," I say to Clayton and he nods. He and Marco say goodbye to a couple other people and then head our direction. I hear Clayton yell, “WHAT A DICK!”

“I’m so sorry,” Clark says turning to me. “That will not happen again. The next time I’m on set Brooklyn will not be there so it will not be as nice of an interaction between he and I. I’m just sorry you had to interact with him like that. I’ll handle this on Monday when I’m back on set. I’d like to do it now, but I’ll be making a formal complaint on Monday.” Clark stops looking down at Brooklyn, then to me and shakes his head. “Actually, give me a second. Marco, take the girls back to the trailer. Clayton, come with me,” he adds, and Marco and I stop and take Brooklyn’s hand. We head to the trailer, and Clark and Clayton head back toward the group.

Back at the trailer, I look over at Marco a little apprehensively. He smiles encouragingly at me, and I release the breath I’ve been holding. This isn’t how I wanted this visit to go. I didn’t want it to cause a stir, so this is a little depressing to me. Yes, Kyle was out of line and yes, he did mean to brush his hand against my ass. It was inappropriate and out of line, but I don’t want to be the actor’s girlfriend that causes a stink. I have conflicting feelings. If it happened to someone else, I would absolutely feel that Clark is in the right to go back and have words. However, I’m feeling like I caused this. Even though I know it’s not really even about me. Marco and I sit with Brooklyn and she plays a game on my phone. Marco takes my hand and I look up at him appreciatively.

"Don't do that to yourself. You look worried and you shouldn't. You didn't do this. Kyle did this to himself, and Clark absolutely has every right to defend you honor. He touched you inappropriately and you shouldn't have to say anything. We witnessed it and Clark will handle it. If Clark had seen it, he would have made a scene. Clark is a gentleman, and he'll make a point. No one will be surprised, and no one will be thinking anything but how unfortunate it is that Kyle had to ruin your time visiting your boyfriend on set. It's Kyle, not you. So don't look like you did anything wrong. You and I both know he was out of line. He always is. I'm sorry that he did that, I really am."

"Thanks, Marco. I'm sorry it happened as well. I wish it didn't. I didn't want to cause a scene."

"Too late for that. They shouldn't have hired Kyle Wright if they wanted to protect their film and the integrity of everyone on crew. I'm so sorry, angel."

Clark and Clayton walk back in at that moment and they are both laughing about something. Clark closes the door behind him and comes over to me, lifting me up and placing me on his lap.

"I'm so sorry about all of this, Ava. He was out of line and he deserved to be called out. I didn't want to do it in front of you and Brooklyn, but I hope you understand why I did," he says and I nod.

"I've been around assholes before. I appreciate you doing that. I'm just sorry that it caused a scene."

"I'm sure you have been around assholes, but he has no right to touch you without your consent, Ava. That's not okay. That kind of behavior on set and off set is unacceptable. There wasn't a scene. He heard me out, and it will not happen again. I also did it in front of the people who needed to hear it. They will handle it from here. It's not just you, Ava. I'm sorry, baby," he says, brushing my hair behind my ear.

"I appreciate it, Clark. But you aren't the one who needs to be apologizing."

We arrive back at the hotel and Clark grabs my hand and I nod at him. I'm ready for this. Clayton and Marco exit first and then Clark, Brooklyn and I. I try to pretend the photographers aren't there. Clark holds tight to my hand and I just focus on the steps ahead of me. We get into the lobby and Clark pulls me into his arms, kissing me gently on the lips.

"You okay?" he asks, and I nod, smiling up at him.

"Absolutely!"

We head upstairs and make a bunch of popcorn. We order appetizers and drinks from room service and then cuddle up on the sofa. We turn on a family friendly movie, and about 15 minutes into the movie Brooklyn falls asleep so we try to find something else to watch. We are having a hard time finding anything, so Clayton turns it off so we can sit around talking. About an hour goes by and Brooklyn wakes up, so we turn her movie back on and head into the kitchen to sit around the dining table. Marco and Clayton want to stay in, so we plan on taking Brooklyn somewhere fun.

We are getting her ready when Clayton comes in and turns the TV on to an entertainment channel. There's a still on the screen of Clark and I heading into the lobby holding hands, and I just laugh. Geez, that was fast. It literally only took a couple of hours for the photo to go live once it was taken. We just look at each other and Clark shrugs his shoulders.

"I'm happy if you're happy baby," he says to me, and I wink at him. Clayton turns the TV off and then leaves the room. I'm not gonna worry about it because I have Clark. Brooklyn, Clark and I are all changed and heading out the door when Clark holds up his phone. It's Brian. He smiles and answers it.

"This better be good if you're calling me while you are supposed to be on vacation, Brian," Clark says, smiling down at me. It is what it is. Brian must be sensing that Clark is in a good place, so the call is short. I hear Clark mention my name and that we were aware and not worried about it. I fuss with Brooklyn, who wants me to hold her. I pick her up and she smiles at me. She kisses me on my nose and I kiss her on the nose as the elevator doors open. I think the most important factor here is Brooklyn and how she is doing with all of this. She seems happy as a lark as we start to head out the door. I see Clark's driver hop out and stand in front of our car to help us get into the car. I put Brooklyn in first and then climb in after her. Clark closes the door and goes to sit in the front. I see flashes of light everywhere as people take Clark's picture. He waves at a couple of people, then we pull away from the curb and into traffic.

It takes about 15 minutes to get to dinner and it's a Hibachi restaurant. Clark helps us out of the car and into the restaurant, but not without him leaning over and kissing me first, as he opens the door. I love this. I feel like we are dating, but as a family. I would LOVE to eventually go out just the two of us, but I'm also perfectly content with spending time with Brooklyn as well. She's just as much a part of us as Clark and I are. And if it wasn't for her, I would never have had the opportunity to meet Clark, let alone be dating him. Gosh that's crazy, I think as I run that statement over in my head. I'm dating Clark Grant. Like officially dating him. I've never been in a serious relationship like this. Nor have I ever felt about anyone the way I feel about him. Watching him and Brooklyn together is so good for my soul, and it makes my heart swoon. I haven't thought about having kids. It's just not something I ever really thought about. I've nannied throughout my life, babysat, but it wasn't something I seriously considered as an option for myself. The thought of Clark fathering a child of mine is outrageous. I love and adore Brooklyn. I've only known her a few months, but the thought of loving a child more than I love Brooklyn is crazy to me. I'm not sure where these thoughts are coming from. I guess just seeing Clark and Brooklyn like this together and dating him at the same time just warms my insides. After dinner of course there are paparazzi outside. We just walk straight through to the car and hop in. Clark heads back to sit in the front while Brooklyn and I sit in the back. I notice the paparazzi are still more interested in getting a photo of Clark, so I kind of appreciate him heading to the front.

Once we are back in the suite the rest of the night is uneventful. We sit up talking and watching TV and then head to bed. This time I grab pajamas before Brooklyn goes to bed. It was a fairly long day, but Clark and I still cuddle for a while in bed before we fall asleep. There's a strong possibility that my body is starting to crave Clark's touch. When he kisses me, I want more and when he touches me gently I want him to touch me more passionately. I know that's completely normal. I don't want to push him. I know he's being respectful of me and wants us to take it slow. I get that. It's such a relief to be with someone who isn't just trying to screw around with you, but at the same time, I need him. My body needs him.

I head to the bathroom the next morning and I've started my period. I guess that solves the issue of seeing where things go while I'm in Vancouver. I laugh to myself thinking that this is just typical. I'm starting to come to terms with the fact that maybe my body knows better. We are pretty lazy today. Everyone is tired and Brooklyn is so cranky. I start to pack our things since we are leaving tomorrow morning. Clark comes in and starts to help me pack. We continue to pack in comfortable silence when Clark comes up behind me. He kisses a trail up the side of my neck to behind my ear and whispers, "It goes without saying I don't want you guys to leave. You know that, right?"

"We don't want to leave you either, but Brooklyn has school and you need to get back to work," I say, turning in his arms. "Plus, the quicker you are done with the movie, the quicker you'll be home."

"That's true. But I still don't want you to leave. I loved having you here with me, Ava. I'm going to miss having you in my bed at night and next to me during the day."

"I'm gonna miss you too," I reply. "I might

have to sleep in your bed when I get back to LA. Just to feel close to you," I say as I kiss him back.

"God, yes. Please do. And send pictures. I want you in my bed. Regardless if I'm there or not. But if I'm not there, then yes, please sleep in my bed and sleep on my side," he says, smiling against my neck, then kissing down my throat.

"Calm down, Casanova. You aren't going to be there, remember?" I add, laughing as he pulls back.

"Six more weeks until my next break, and then I'll be coming home to visit for a long weekend. God, I can't wait."

The rest of the afternoon we spend lounging around the suite. It's pretty cold out today so we aren't too keen on going out and walking. Clark asks if I'd like to go out just the two of us and I smile. *Of course I would!* He tells me to get ready. I put on a sweater dress, my booties and minimal make up. Clark wears some slacks and a button down and he looks incredibly handsome. Clayton tells us to take our time, that they will be fine tonight. Marco is staying another week, so they have plenty of time to do couple stuff once Brooklyn and I leave. Clark will be on set, so I'm excited for Marco and Clayton. They are the most precious couple ever. Clark helps me into the car and this time sits in the back with me. The photographers are going crazy, and I'm honestly a little nervous about it. I know it's just part of it, so I'm hoping to eventually get used to it. Clark laughs with me when we get in the car and then he looks me up and down. I know it's just the thrill of it being just the two of us, but I really want to tear his clothes off when he looks at me like that. I look away and he grabs my hand.

"It's our first date," he says smiling at me, and I look back and grin. "And if you keep looking at me like you want to rip my clothes off it's going to be really difficult for me to keep the promises I've made to myself…" I squeeze his hand back and he laughs, "…and to you!"

"It doesn't really feel like we are on our first date. We know each other better than most on a first date. But I'm excited," I say as I lean my head on his shoulder.

We arrive at our destination in minutes. It's a beautiful French restaurant. We sit at a table near a window overlooking the water. The restaurant smells divine and the view from the window is stunning. Clark speaks fluent French, so I let him order for me. It's incredibly attractive to be with someone so worldly. My grandmother would be so proud that I'm not stuck in North Carolina, but rather out in the world with someone who's actually seen the world. I would love to travel. I'm not sure when or how, but it's on my list.

"Where all have you traveled, Clark?" I ask him as the waiter brings some bread and wine (probably expensive) to the table.

"I grew up outside of London, so I was able to travel a lot. My parents were really into traveling. We traveled a lot by train. It was cheaper to get from one place to another. I've spent a lot of time in France and Spain. Some time in Germany. After I moved to the US, I would vacation in Mexico and the Caribbean. For work I've been to almost every country because of press tours. I mean I think the only place I haven't been is North Korea," he says laughing. "And I'm not upset about that at all. I love to travel," he says smiling at me. "How about you?" he asks, and I laugh.

"This will be easy," I say, smiling at the waiter as he brings our appetizers. "I've only been out of the country a handful of times, this time included. I've been to Canada twice, Mexico once, the Bahamas and that's about it. When I was a kid we would go visit theme parks, but I haven't really spent much time out of the state I've lived in. North Carolina and New York for a short season. Now I'm in LA, and that's about it."

"Do you want to travel more?" he asks, and I nod.

"Yeah, hearing you speak French to the waiter made me realize I'm a little out of my depth here." He reaches across the table, taking my hand. He runs his thumb across my palm as I talk. It's so comforting and also very sensual. "I was just thinking about how much I'd love to travel."

"Well, you have vacation time, Ava. Why don't you travel? Or maybe when I'm done with the movie we can go on a trip together," he suggests, and I blush. "Would you like that?" he asks.

"I'd love that. Thank you."

We eat the first course of our meal and talk about how the movie is going for him. Apparently Kyle is more of a problem than I realized. He tells me he is sorry again for how Kyle behaved. I believe him, but I've never had anyone stick up for me like this. I change the subject so that we are moving in a different direction. He tells me that the press tour for this movie is going to be crazy. Since it's the last movie, they are pulling out all the stops. I tell him how excited I am for him.

"Really? Are you seriously excited for me?" he asks, laughing as our plates are taken away.

"I am. I mean, of course we will miss you. But I'm excited for you to promote your movie. I'm excited for you to be able to put a big red bow on the franchise you've been a part of for years. I'm also selfishly excited for you to wrap all of it up so you can be home with us for more than a month or two," I say, reaching across the table. "And I'm excited for what the future holds for you." He leans over, pulling my hand to his lips so he can kiss my palm.

"Thank you, Ava. That means a lot to me. You

know, I've never really been with anyone who's been a fan of what I do. The benefits, yes, but what I actually love to do," he says, looking at me and smiling. "You're the first."

"I'm sorry for that, Clark. You need someone who is for you. I hope I can be that support for you. I know you support what I do now," I say, mock fluffing my hair and he laughs. "But I can imagine you'd be a great partner where my dreams and passions come into play."

"Of course I would. Ava, if at any time you decide that you want to find something else to do, I'll be your biggest cheerleader. Would Brooklyn miss having you as a caregiver? Absolutely. But I think you being around in general is more important to her. She's a big fan of you and so am I. Your happiness means the world to me, Ava. I love you," he says, and I want to crawl over the table and kiss him, but we are in a nice restaurant. I'm not wanting to draw more attention to us than is being drawn already. I've seen a couple of women eye our table, and I just smile to myself. He's MY boyfriend. I know how lucky I am.

"You know, if for some reason we don't work out," I say with a smile on my face so that Clark knows this isn't me leading us into a downer conversation. "You will have ruined me for every other man. I've never been with someone who thinks about others as much as you do."

"I'm okay with that," he laughs. The waiter brings dessert, a chocolate soufflé and a trio of sorbets. The raspberry sorbet is my favorite. I'm about as stuffed as stuffed can be, so I have a couple bites of each and then tap out. Clark finishes them off like a hummingbird and I laugh at him. It really is incredible what all this guy can put away. Clark pays the bill and we head to the door. The maître d' tells Clark that there are a lot of photographers outside, and that we are welcome to exit out the back. Clark looks at me and I shrug my shoulders. He thanks him, grabbing my hand, and we head out front to the car. The driver is already waiting for us with his hand on the door handle so we can hop in quickly. I'm glad he did because there had to be at least 15 photographers out there. We speed back to the hotel, and I thank Clark for an incredible night. When we get back Brooklyn is already asleep, but Marco and Clayton are sitting in the den enjoying a bottle of wine. I change into my pajamas and join them. Clark comes back out about the same time in a pair of designer pajama pants, and I snuggle up to him on the sofa. This is my last night with Clark for a while, so I want to cherish every second. An hour later Marco and Clayton head to bed, so Clark and I sit on the sofa and continue to talk about life. I swear we could sit and talk for hours and it's so incredible to have someone I can connect with on an intellectual level. Not just an attraction. Clark literally carries me to bed about 15 minutes later, after we clean up in the living area. We both lay there staring at each other and then I start to tear up. I'm not sure what pushed me over the edge. Clark pulls me into his arms and just gives me the time I need to cry.

"What is it, baby?" he asks gently in my ear. "You can tell me."

"I don't know. I guess I'm just emotional with everything this weekend. Mostly I feel like I'm gonna miss you. Miss this," I say, and he wipes away the tear falling down my cheek. "Maybe I'm just extra emotional because I started my period but…ugh. I just feel a little overwhelmed," I add as I sit up so I can get my shit together.

"I don't envy you at all, Ava. I can't imagine having to endure everything women have to, but that doesn't mean that I can't be empathetic. Is there anything I can get you?" he asks, sitting up as well. "I don't look forward to the day I have to explain periods to Brooklyn. I just know she isn't going to be thrilled at being inconvenienced every month." This makes me laugh because it's so true. It's what I need to get it together. I smile at him and he looks deep in my eyes and kisses me. "Your eyes are so beautiful after you've been crying. I'm going to miss you. The first six weeks went by pretty quickly so I imagine the next six weeks will go by just as quick." We have a pretty heavy make out session, and then fall asleep in each other's arms. I wake up to Clark telling me it's time to get up. It's about 7:45, and we have to leave for the airport in less than an hour. Ugh, I was having an incredible dream. I'm not sure what it was, but now that I'm looking at a half-naked Clark I'm not sure my dream could beat this.

By the time we arrive back in LA, it's early afternoon and Brooklyn is done. She's done with every single aspect of travel and wants to park herself in front of the TV. I change her into her pj's and let her do just that. I unpack everything and start a load of laundry. Tomorrow is a school day for her, so I need to make sure we are ready for tomorrow morning. I have a missed call from Clark and a text message. He said he got a notification that we were supposed to get some bad storms tonight.

We aren't planning on going anywhere so we are good. Thanks for letting me know. I haven't even looked at my phone, sorry. I'm finishing up laundry and Brooklyn is watching cartoons so don't worry about us. We will be safe.

Thank goodness. I miss the two of you already.
Glad you are home safe baby. I'll call you tomorrow
Love you, Ava!

Love you too, Clark! Sweet dreams!

You too. Dream about me!

Always! :)

Clark

The next couple of weeks fly by. Part of me is a little sad the last movie of this franchise is more than halfway done. The other half of me is so damn excited I can't stand it. Like I said in a couple of interviews this week, it's bittersweet. I'm asked more and more often about Ava in interviews, and I can only smile and tell them that I'm no longer single and I'm very happy about that. It's sometimes a little weird to talk about Ava when she is unaware that I'm talking about her. But like she and I have talked about in the last couple of weeks, it's all part of the job and I'm happy to tell the entire world how incredible she is.

The week before I'm supposed to fly home, I have a sit down interview with a major magazine I'm doing the cover for. Clayton and Marco are here with me in a different suite of the hotel to do the shoot part. It's a reputable magazine, so I'm happy to do it. After a light lunch I head down a floor for the interview. It's going really well until the last couple of questions.

"So our readers of course are going to want to know about your relationship status. Can you tell us if you are on the market, Clark? We've been hearing buzz of a new lady in your life." she asks, and I laugh.

"Off the market sounds so medieval. Like I'm a steak you can pick up at the store. I'm not single. I haven't been single for a while. And yes, I'm very happy. Ava is the most incredible woman I've ever met."

"I feel like what we just heard here, friends, is the sound of a million hearts breaking around the world," she says, and I don't respond. "How does your daughter feel about you dating the nanny?" she adds, and I feel like walking out and ending the interview. My daughter is always off limits. She's watching me, and I want to say 'no comment,' but I also know if I don't answer that, people will assume that the interviewer hit on a sore subject. Which she did. This is completely unprofessional.

"I don't really like to discuss my daughter in interviews, but my daughter and Ava are very close," I say, a little more short than I would like.

The interviewer has the audacity to act like she's sorry, but I know she's not.

"Oh I'm sorry we can strike that question from the interview if you'd like," she says, recrossing her legs and smiling at me with a sly twitch of her lips.

"You know what's on the list of things I'm not willing to talk about, and my daughter is one of those. Her private life is not a cover story. You will not use my daughter to sell magazines. If you want to ask questions about my dating life, that's fine. But you will always leave my daughter out of it."

"That's true. That's not something we want. Again, I apologize," she adds, looking over my shoulder to her producer. She nods and we call the interview done. We shake hands and then I head back upstairs and into the suite. Clayton growls and I just laugh. People will push and push until they get what they want. I'm not sure what Brooklyn's opinion about me dating Ava has to do with franchise movies. I call Ava and she answers on the second ring. I lay back on the bed and release the breath I've apparently been holding.

"Hey, baby! I was just thinking about you! How did the interview go?" she asks, and I smile. I love that she remembers my schedule.

"Great day, horrible interview and interviewer," I say, recounting this afternoon and she listens to me ramble on for probably too long. She's quiet and I wonder if I lost her. "Ava?" I ask, looking down at my phone.

"Clark, I'm so sorry. I love you, baby," she whispers, and my heart almost bursts from my chest. God, she loves me.

"Baby, you have no idea how much I love you. How was your day?" I ask, and I hear some clanking of pots and pans.

"Well… let's see. Drop off and pick up with Brooklyn was uneventful, but I feel like I'm being followed. Paparazzi maybe? There's always this black Acura that follows me to and from the neighborhood. They don't ever come in the neighborhood, but either I'm being followed by this same car or there are a lot of black Acuras everywhere I go," she says, and I'm at full alert.

"I'm not liking this," I say. "Ava, did you let security know?"

"I let security in the neighborhood know, and I let Brian know earlier today. He said he would check on it. I know if there is anything to figure out, he will figure out what's going on."

"I'm glad you told Brian." I say, and I'm a little peeved that he didn't immediately call me.

"I mean, they aren't doing anything other than following me around. I'm assuming it's paparazzi, but they aren't taking my photo. Or at least I don't think they are, unless they are taking pictures of me driving. I don't feel comfortable enough to stop and see what they're doing or to leave my car. I've literally been going to Brooklyn's school and back. I'm not taking a chance where Brooklyn's safety is concerned. I just think it's weird. Why would they want to get a picture of me out driving?"

"Who knows. Baby, you did the right thing. I'm glad Brian is taking care of it. You can trust him to handle it. I know when we were in Vancouver, he told me he wanted us to have more security especially when you and I were out together. Mostly because people are interested, and if people are interested, then that means paparazzi see dollar signs in getting the photos people want to see. I'm not having you out there unprotected. Clayton hasn't seen any photos of you or any stories, and I have my PR people checking up on all of that. I'm sorry, Ava. I know that can be scary," I say, and I hear her laughing. "I cannot wait to kiss you, baby. And hold you in my arms. To touch you," I add, and she stops laughing.

"I want you to touch me, Clark," she whispers and I sit up.

"You do?" I ask, clearing my throat. God, this woman drives me the right kind of crazy.

"Of course I do. Why wouldn't I want you to touch me? I was wanting you to touch me in Vancouver, but I started my period, so the timing didn't really work out. Are you excited about Thanksgiving?" she asks, and I shake my head trying to clear my head.

"Whoa Whoa Whoa. Let's go back," I say, trying to steer the conversation back and she laughs.

"To Thanksgiving?" Damn this woman! She's detouring the conversation on purpose.

"Yeah. I'm real excited to talk about the turkey. No, AVA, to you wanting me to touch you in Vancouver. Did I know this?" I ask, not remembering her telling me any of this in Vancouver.

"No, I don't think we talked about it. At least I don't think we did. Of course I wanted to, and I did want to bring it up. Then the next morning I started my period, so I didn't feel like it was necessary to tease you," she adds, and I groan.

"God, baby. I want to touch you so bad. Where do you want me to touch you?" I ask, rolling over onto my back.

"Everywhere," she says quietly, and I groan again.

"God, Ava. This is going to be long damn week," I add, and she laughs.

"Clark. I don't know why you seem so surprised. You know I want you to touch me. Or at least I would think that you would already know this. I want you to touch me and I want to touch you." I place my hand over my face. We are too far away from each other to have this conversation.

"I'm going to need to go and take a cold shower after this conversation is over," I growl into the phone. She's laughing at me, and I have to smile. She's beyond adorable.

"You do that, buddy," she adds. "I'm not sure why you'd be shocked that I want you to touch me. But I feel like we are going around in circles here. I need to get little lady into the bath and then get her ready for bed. So…how about we pick up this conversation when we are in a 100-mile radius of each other!"

"Probably a good idea," I say.

"Goodnight, Clark!" We tell each other how much we love each other again and I feel like a teenager. I need to take care of a few things. Starting with a cold ass shower. I know I will sleep like a baby tonight. After my cold shower I fall fast asleep. I don't remember all of my dream, but I can imagine it won't be half as incredible as actually touching Ava for the first time in real life. My dream was incredibly sensual, but what I do remember is the ring Ava was wearing in it. It made me wake up with a smile on my face. Not to mention touching Ava in my dream, that I won't forget for a while. I don't have sexual dreams often, but God, I miss her. I've never felt this way about anyone. Ever. I need Clayton to help me out with a couple things. I have an idea of the pieces I want to try and find for Ava. I think it'll be perfect. She will think it's too much, but no one else will. Clayton is going to love it too. This kind of thing is right up his alley. In my dream she was my wife. The thought of spending the rest of my life with Ava would literally be a dream come true. I know we don't have to rush, but I know this the direction I want to take this.

Clayton

"Are you serious?" I ask Clark during a break we have in the trailer the next morning. Clark is doing a huge fight scene this morning and his energy is getting on my damn nerves. I swear Ava is the best thing that's ever happened to him.

"Dead serious," he says, drinking some water. "Contact the jeweler, I think his name is Silas. Same guy we got the earrings from. I want a couple pieces put together for Ava. I want a matching necklace to the earrings he sold me. I want a ring. Same design. Around three carats in the center diamond. Tell him not to worry about sizing it yet. If you can try and pull a ring sizing for Ava in the next couple weeks, that would be perfect. We have time to get the sizing right. Nothing is happening with the ring yet, but I do want to have it. I know it'll take him some time to get the design right. Also, I want to find an emerald and diamond jewelry set for Ava. Oh, and since we have a couple parties coming up, I want Marco to go ahead and start thinking of gowns for Ava. I want at least three dresses for her to choose from. You and Marco can decide fabrics, but I think Ava would be absolutely stunning in emerald green." He's talking and I'm keeping up, but where the hell did this come from?

"Ok. I'm thinking let's do the three dresses in satin. An Emerald one for sure. Marco can make those, easy. And with Ava's body, they will absolutely stun. Maybe a velvet long sleeved emerald dress as well. A black satin dress too. Good call, Clark," I say as I'm typing a note to myself. "But can I ask where all this is coming from?"

"I had a dream last night. Maybe more of a vision. Ava, in an emerald green dress with matching diamonds and emerald jewelry. And then on her left hand she was wearing a diamond ring with smaller diamonds surrounding it. God, she was incredible," he says, and my God, he's serious. "Did you write all that down?"

"Yeah, I got it, boss. But I feel some prying questions coming, and I don't know if your break is long enough for you to answer all of them."

"Probably not. I'm going to spend the rest of

my life with Ava, Clayton."

"You got that from a dream? You guys haven't even slept together yet, Clark. You haven't even been living with each other long enough to make this kind of decision."

"I'm not asking her to marry me over Thanksgiving, Clayton. I'm just getting prepared. I want to spend the rest of my life with her. And no, I didn't get that from a dream. But seeing us together in my dream made me realize it. I want to feel that way with her the rest of my life. I don't need to spend six years with her to figure that out. I can figure that out from here, now. She's the best thing that's ever happened to me. I will be asking her to marry me eventually. Just not yet. I want to make sure she's ready for all this!" he says, motioning around the trailer and him in his costume. "I just know, I know she's the woman I want to spend the rest of my life with. And no I don't need to sleep with her to figure that out either. I want everything with her. The good, the bad, the in between. I want her, forever."

"Well. Shit," I say as I wipe away a tear from my eye. "I might just start getting a little emotional, Clark. When do you want the ring ready?" I ask, and he stops to think.

"Christmas?" he asks, and I look up at him.

"WHAT? That's next month Clark." I say, clearing my voice. I hope Silas can get his ass in gear because Clark doesn't mess around.

"I'm aware, Clayton. You think I'm moving too fast?" he asks, not really caring about my answer, and I shake my head.

"Actually, no. I think this is exactly the right move and she's exactly the right woman for you. I want this for you as much as you do. I just… I don't know, I'm a little shocked. I figured I'd have to slap some sense into you in order to get here. And here I am being slapped," I add, and he nods at me, not really listening. When Clark makes his mind up to do something, he goes for it full speed ahead. I sit down at my laptop and set up a time to chat with Silas, as well as make preparations with Marco for some fittings next week with Ava. All of this new information is making me so damn excited, but I need to keep my head on straight. We've got a lot of moving pieces right now. But I can NOT wait to call Marco and tell him all of this.

Ava

I'm standing in front of a mirror with Marco and Clayton looking at the reflection of someone who is not me. I mean it's me. It's just a very upgraded version. The woman in this dress looks confident and untouchable. Marco finishes pinning the dress so he can make the necessary alterations. A couple days ago he came by the house and took my measurements and then told me he'd be back in a couple days with some things to try on. I smile at Clayton who was working on his computer on the bed, but is now looking up at me in awe.

Clark and Clayton came home yesterday, praise Jesus. Clark went straight into a couple of meetings first thing this morning as well as into town to do some interviews. His mom and dad are supposed to be coming in town this week for Thanksgiving and I'm really excited to meet them. I've talked to his mom a couple times. Mainly for Brooklyn's sake, but I'm excited to meet her face to face. Clark wants me to attend some award shows and parties coming up for work, so I'm excited to see how these dresses turn out. Marco brought a couple of different designer dresses for me to try on as well, and it's surreal to be wearing them. The ones that worked, we kept, but some of them didn't work because I'm just not as tall as the majority of Hollywood. Marco brought a satin dress today for me to try and as soon as I put it on it took my breath away. It's a satin, emerald green dress, low cut in the back, thicker straps on my shoulder to support me since I can't wear a bra with it. Clayton stands up smiling and walks over.

"Clark was right. Emerald green is the perfect color on you. Look at your eyes," he says as we stare at my reflection in the full-length mirror.

"Clark picked this out?" I ask, and Marco laughs, shaking his head.

"No, Honey. This is a Marco Laurentes original. He told Clayton what he thought would look amazing on you and I created this little masterpiece. I don't often get to create anything from scratch, but Clark is allowing me to use my gifting on you," he says with a wink.

"You made this?" I ask, and he nods, looking

back down at some of the stitching. Clayton stands back with him and they talk behind me about the bottom.

"It's going to be perfect, Marco," Clayton says through a huge grin. "I think you need to replicate this one with more colors. This style really flatters our girl."

"I agree, it's great. I'd love to try a couple other things, but this will be *perfezione*," Marco says, his Italian really coming in strong when he's in the zone.

Once I'm back in my yoga pants and a long sleeve tee shirt I head downstairs. Marco leaves with his goodies to finish up and is floating with excitement. Clayton brings his laptop downstairs and works next to me as I read a book. Brooklyn plays with her toys and the silence is so nice. This morning Brooklyn was in a rare mood, so I'm glad she was able to get it together. I think she was just hungry, which I completely understand. I get a little moody when I'm hungry as well. Clayton has been booking hotel rooms, flights and meetings since he got here.

"You've been a little quiet, powder puff. Something bothering you?" he asks, and I realize I'm not even looking at my book. I'm staring off into space.

"Hmm?" I say looking over at him. He's got his laptop closed and is looking at me with a concerned grin.

"You've been staring off for the last 10 minutes into outer space. Something's off," he adds, sitting up and crossing his legs on the sofa. "Talk to me, baby girl."

"Sorry. Lost in thought. I haven't told Clark yet," I add, turning to Clayton. "I've got a big audition coming up for a part I would kill for. I'm a little nervous, but I'm also kinda excited. I've auditioned with their team before, but for a different film. This would be for a supporting role. It's a Frank Sinatra biopic. I'd be playing Ava Gardner if I got the role. It's pretty exciting to think about. I'd actually get to sing, even though Gardner wasn't known for her vocal performances, but there would be a song, two actually."

"Ava, that's amazing! Ava playing Ava," he says with wonder in his voice, and I smile.

"I know. It's not lost on me. But if I get it, it shoots in New York. Well, for half the time, and then in LA the other half," I add.

"Don't freak out yet, babe. First get the role. You know Clark would do anything to support you," he adds, a little confused. "Why do you seem so…apprehensive?"

"I don't know. It's just that…"

"What? He's head over heels in love with you. You have to know that!"

"I know, and I'm head over heels for him too.

And Brooklyn. That's the problem."

"How in a world full of problems is that a problem, angel?" he asks, moving the laptop and standing up to look at a storm rolling in in the distance.

"Because I wouldn't be able to nanny at the same time," I add as Clayton turns around laughing.

"Ava, darling. Nannying isn't your dream, and it isn't what Clark truly wants from you either. Don't ever be scared to tell Clark anything. Especially when it comes to your dreams," he adds. "He is your biggest champion. You are safe here, Ava. Regardless if you nanny for him or not."

"There's a love scene, Clayton. And I'm reading with the lead actor tomorrow."

"So what? Clark's done love scenes before. It's not as sexy as you think it is. Is the lead actor Kyle Wright?" he asks, laughing. I roll my eyes. "That would be the only issue."

"Gross, no," I add. "It's with Dalton Calhoun." Clayton stops laughing and whips around.

"Wait, what?" he says, coming over and sitting on the ottoman in front of me. "Dalton Calhoun is playing Sinatra?"

"That's what Shanna told me. They want me to come in from the other auditions I've had with them. I don't want this to create any weirdness, and I sure as hell don't want Clark to feel like he needs to put in a good word for me. I want to get the role on my own. When I looked up Dalton, there were all these pictures of him and Clark. I didn't even realize they were that close," I say, and Clayton smiles.

"He's one of the most musically talented men you'll ever meet, Ava. If he's playing Sinatra, this production will be legit. You realize that, right?"

"I know that. That's why I'm nervous. I sure as hell don't want people to think I got an audition or the role, if I'm lucky enough to get the role, because of Clark's relationship with Dalton." I look at Clayton and he stands up. I ask him what he's doing and he's pacing. He motions to me to give him a minute, so I lay back on the sofa and just wait for him to stop pacing.

"Okay. Here's what we're gonna do. The audition is tomorrow, correct?" I nod and he continues with his plan. "You're going to tell Clark only about the non-specifics. If he asks you to tell him more, tell him Clayton said no. Tonight we are going to film you and I rehearsing your lines and your song. Then we will edit it and post bits of it tomorrow after the audition or on your way. We can decide as we go. I will mention in the video somehow that Clark doesn't know. That way when we tell people he didn't know, you have proof he didn't actually know. It'll be on social media for all to see. Plus, once people see how talented you are it won't matter because they will see you got the role for your talent, not your taste in successful men. He's not going to love the idea of you doing a love scene with one of his oldest and best friends. However, Clark is a professional. He will want this for you, no matter what. We just need to raise up the Ava Army so when the haters start squawking it'll shut them up. Okay?" he says with a gleam in his eyes.

"I'm willing to try it your way," I say, laughing as he hugs me.

"Dalton Calhoun, huh?" he adds, walking over to the kitchen to pour himself another cup of coffee. "I'm not gonna lie, I kinda want to see this movie already. I know you aren't in the entire movie. But my god, this will be fabulous."

After Clayton leaves later that evening, I've got everything I need to ensure this plan goes off without a hitch. Clark comes in from a long day and he looks exhausted. He's hanging up his keys in the kitchen when Brooklyn runs over to him and jumps in his arms. I stand up and walk over, wrapping my arms around the two of them and he leans down to kiss me.

"Good day?" I ask, and he sighs against my lips.

"Better now," he replies as Brooklyn jumps down and runs back to play. "How about you, baby?"

"I have a couple things to talk to you about, but after Brooklyn goes to bed. She's only got another half hour of energy left in her," I say, and he eyes me warily. I turn back around to grab my book from the table and slip it in my bag. Clark picks up his parents from the airport tomorrow morning, so I have the day off. He's said numerous times that I can stay at the house, but I told him I'll come visit. Of course I want to be here, but I also want to give them some space.

"Please stay tonight," he asks, pulling me back into his arms. "I want you here with me. I know you want to give my parents some uninterrupted time with me and Brooklyn, but I desperately need you here with me. My parents know we're dating, Ava. They want to meet you," he adds, and I smile up at him.

"And they will meet me. I can't stay tonight. I have an audition in the morning and when Brooklyn goes to sleep, I will tell you more about it. I know I'll end up staying over while your parents are visiting. I just can't tonight."

"Okay. I'm curious about this audition. You've had auditions before, but this feels different. Why does it feel different?"

"It is. But I can only tell you so much tonight. Clayton told me to tell you no. So don't try anything. But I will tomorrow after my audition is over. Just promise not to ask too many questions," I add, and he smiles.

"No promises, baby. Not where you're concerned. I'm excited if you are," he says, eyeing me. He kisses me again and wraps his arms around me. "Did you eat?" he asks, and I nod.

"We had pasta. There's some leftovers in the fridge if you want me to heat some up for you."

"No, I have something I need to talk to you about as well." Great. Now I'm a little nervous. I smile at him, and he winks at me. God, he's hot. He's wearing jeans that hug his godlike physique and those boots from Vancouver. It's definitely chilly here in LA. Not as cool as it was in Vancouver by far, but in the 50's. He's wearing a cream henley and a watch that looks like it cost more than my car. His hair is a little longer than usual, like you could run your hands through it and grab a handful. He is watching me watch him, smiling knowingly at me. He sits on the arm of the couch and places his hands on his thighs. He sighs looking at me and I can only stare.

"Baby, you gotta know when you look at me like that it makes me feel like I'm on top of the world. You get that right? You make me feel like the luckiest man in the world while at the same time like you want to rip my clothes off."

"Both are true," I say, smiling at him. He groans and then holds his hand out. I take it and he pulls me in his arms. He smells delicious and I tell him so.

"So do you, angel. He runs his hands from my

waist to lightly graze over my butt and I smile at him. "And this," he says as he moves me closer to him. We are pressed firmly together, but I lean back a little to kiss him. "You in yoga pants, baby, is hot as hell. This ass is out of this world!" I laugh and he brings his arms around my waist, lifting me as he stands up. We kiss gently for a couple moments and then he puts me back down. "I'm going to change, baby. I'll be back shortly."

After Clark puts Brooklyn to bed, he comes back downstairs and pulls me into his lap. I cuddle up, just enjoying the feel of his arms around me. I feel safe and loved. I have never felt anything other than those things with Clark. It's kind of his specialty. I realize how lucky I am and I'm scared to lose this. But I know if I do lose him then he was never mine in the first place. I feel better after talking with Clayton earlier. But this is Clark. He'd be a lot to lose.

"Talk to me, baby," he whispers in my ear as he turns me so we are sitting next to each other.

"My audition is a pretty big one tomorrow. It's for a major movie. I can't tell you the specifics, I just need you to trust me. I even have a video to put on my Instagram tomorrow. Mainly so that people will know that you didn't know about it. I just need you to trust me. I'm really excited about it. But you need to know if I do get the role, that… well….some things will be different," I add, looking into his eyes.

"Okay," he says, unaffected. "I trust you, Ava. I also realize that nannying isn't your only gift. I knew that before you even interviewed with us. Lydia found some YouTube videos of you singing. I knew that you were amazing before I even met you, Ava. Just like I know how amazing you are now. I don't want to lose you, Ava. If we are talking about things being different because you won't have time to Nanny, so what? All I want is you. All Brooklyn wants is you. We will take what we can get. I want you to follow your dreams and live those dreams out. I've said it before, Ava. I'm not going to be the reason you don't do all of the things you want to do. I will only be the man beside you cheering you on and supporting you. I believe in you. Can you tell me anything else about tomorrow?" he asks and I shake my head.

"No, but I can tell you that I'm excited, but also a little nervous. They've specifically asked for me to audition for this role. I've auditioned with them before but on other productions, but this is big. A new role. A role that will take me away from LA for a while," I say looking down. He pulls my chin up, smiling at me, and kisses me lightly on the nose.

"Don't look down. You have nothing to look down about, Ava. Where would the movie be shooting?" He asks. "Can you at least tell me that?"

"New York, LA and possibly London," I say as

I cuddle deeper into his arms. "I don't want to lose this Clark," I add. "I don't even have the role yet and I'm already scared to lose you. To lose Brooklyn. I love being her nanny. I love being your girlfriend."

"And we love you, baby. If you get this role you will not lose us, I promise you that. Here's a little tidbit of information you may not know. I have a place in New York, and I have a place in London. I will be there, if and when you want me to be there. This isn't an issue for us, Ava. Not to me at least." I turn around and kiss him hard. He pulls back after a few moments and looks at me with love and adoration in his eyes. "Baby. I love you. I'm not going to let something like you traveling for work bring us down. Please know I will fight for you, Ava. This isn't something I would fight though, I want this for you. Now, if you have anything else to add, about the audition please let me know, but I've been dying to talk to you about something since you left Vancouver," he says, and I sit up facing him. "I want you to move in with me, with us, Brooklyn and I. She and I both agree. It makes sense for you to be here with us. We both love you. I want you here with me, in my bed, every night I can have you there. You know how I feel about you, Ava. I'm serious about us. You don't have to make a decision now. Think about it, please." I can only stare at him. I'm not shocked. Or maybe I am?

But then I shake off my stupor and my excitement bubbles up.

"I want to move in with you, Clark. Nothing would make me happier than to live with you," I say happily. "And Brooklyn." He pulls me firmly to him, kissing the top of my head as I snuggle into his arms. We stay wrapped up in each other's arms for what feels like forever and then he kisses my head again.

"I'm glad we're doing this, Ava. I also know tomorrow is a big day for you. I will not push you for more information, but you better call me after your audition. I'm excited for you, baby. My parents fly in around 10 a.m., but if you want to come over afterward, I'd love to finally introduce you. Also, the specifics of when you are ready to move in with us are up to you. I'm ready anytime."

"How about after Thanksgiving?" I ask, and he squeezes me gently. "Yes?"

"God, yes. Get a good night sleep angel. I'll be praying tomorrow goes well for you. I'll miss you tonight, but I'll get to have you here soon. I can't wait," he adds, and I smile.

After a long, heated kiss goodbye and one short walk to my car, I get in and head toward my townhome. Funnily enough, since moving in I haven't been able to stay there much, but I'm excited to get some alone time so I can prepare for tomorrow. I pray the audition goes well, but as with anything else in the entertainment industry, I know I can only do my best. There's so much that's out of my hands. As I'm crawling into bed, I sit down and take a few deep breaths and thank God for this opportunity. I also thank God for Clark and Brooklyn, for the friends that I do have in my life right now. I've been so busy the last couple of months I haven't really had the time to go to church. I wonder what Clark would think about me taking Brooklyn to church while he's out of town. Maybe this weekend? It's always very centering for me to go to church, to be able to worship with other believers. I could use a good worship service right now. I find one of the pastor's podcasts that I love on my phone and then sit back in bed and listen. It always puts life in perspective for me. Afterwards I fall asleep, my nerves gone and my heart centered.

The next morning, I post my clip to Instagram like Clayton and I talked about and then head out for my audition. I text Shanna while I'm waiting and then look over my scene. As I'm sitting there, I get a text from Clark.

Knock em dead baby. Clayton just got me signed up for Instagram. I'm new to this so be

patient with me. I watched your video, angel. I'm so freaking excited for you. Call me when you're ready. And know I'm with you on this and so proud.

You've got this! I love you!

I don't text back. But I smile knowing I have the support of the man I love. I'm ready for this next chapter, whatever that means. I stand up when they call my name. I smile at the casting director and then over to the piano player. I've auditioned many times in this same room. The piano player's name is Mark. He has played for a couple of my auditions, so he winks at me. I hand him my sheet music and give him an excited smile. I love this song and can already see performing it in my mind. I start to sing and let the song take over. I feel like it takes me to a different place entirely. No casting directors or crew watching and judging me. Just me. The song, the vision I feel so deeply for the music. It all comes together so seamlessly. I'm asked to sing something else a cappella and I do. I always have a couple of songs ready just in case. Apparently, I chose wisely and sung something a little jazzy, since this movie will be about the old Hollywood days. After I'm done, they sit talking for a minute, so I grab my music from the piano player. I put my music in my bag, and as I turn back around with the scene in my hand they smile at me. I notice Dalton Calhoun is also sitting at one of the tables, but I try not to look at him. He clears his throat and addresses me.

"You've got a spectacular voice, Ava. Let's do this scene and see how it feels," he says, and I nod at him.

We read through it a couple times and then we stand up and act out the scene. I follow his lead and have to say our chemistry is great. Nothing like the chemistry Clark and I have. I'm not sure you can recreate that on film, but I try to use what I know about Ava and Frank's tempestuous relationship. I know from what I've researched that she was known to be a firecracker, so I try to emulate that. We try the scene a couple different ways at the direction of the casting director, and each time they turn and talk about the scene. In between the readings Dalton and I make small talk. It's hard to pretend he isn't Dalton Calhoun, but I do my best. I try to remember he's just another human being and if anything, being with Clark has prepared me a little for this moment. The casting director stands up with another page and hands it to me. Oh dear.

"Now. You're aware that Frank and Ava had a pretty steamy, but also tumultuous relationship. Fire and Ice. They were the love of each other's lives. I want you to read through this scene with Dalton a couple times and then let's see what happens. I know you just received it. But I'd like to take the fire and ice and see what we can really do with it." He leans up against the table and then watches as Dalton and I look it over and read through it a couple times. I realize I'm going to really need to be on, so I move around a little bit trying to shake off any nervousness or tenseness I have for this scene. This is my moment. I look at Dalton and he nods to me. I feel like he wants me to do a good job. Better yet, it feels like we both want that for each other without even saying it. This scene is fire and ice, just like the scene calls for, so we jump right in.

After a couple of read throughs, I look up and half the table is smiling and the other half are just watching blankly. It's hard to read, but I look to the casting director in case he has more direction. He's just looking at me. I start to feel like someone should say something, but no one does. I look at Dalton and he smiles at me. He nods and then walks back over to the table. I felt like we knocked it out of the park, but I could be wrong. I've never had such incredible material. Dalton was amazing. I can tell that he will be the perfect Sinatra. This is supposed to be an all-star cast. They could have their pick of actresses for the role of Ava Gardner. I just hope that I get the opportunity to see where this goes. The casting director turns to the assistant behind him and writes a couple things down as he speaks. I turn around and put my paper back in my bag. I just have to do something with myself. I'm glad it's not silent, but at least put me out of my misery here.

"Congratulations, Ava," I hear Dalton say and I turn around, looking at him shocked. "You ARE our Ava Gardner." I immediately sit down next to my bag and gasp, tears coming to my eyes. I did it. Dalton walks over to me and gives me a hug. Then I sit around talking with some of the producers. Mark comes over and gives me a hug and I thank him. I think I cry at one point just from exhaustion and relief more than anything else. I'm so excited. I look up at the ceiling, thanking God, and I can't wait to call Clark when I get in the car. The assistant tells me they'll be in touch with Shanna, but Dalton is super stoked. They want me to come in again soon and meet with the director and a few more producers, and I just keep nodding and smiling. After years of crazy auditions and not getting the right parts I finally feel like I've landed the role of a lifetime! I know they have other actors coming in to read for other parts, so we all say our goodbyes, but Dalton pulls me aside on my way out the door.

"You gonna call Clark?" he asks, and I laugh looking up at him. "You didn't think I knew?"

"I didn't know. I told him I couldn't give him any specifics about the audition because I wanted to make sure I did this the right way," I add, and he smiles. We stop outside of the door and I see Kya Strong sitting in a chair outside the door. At first she stares daggers at me, but then she sees Dalton and her eyes widen in disbelief. She catches herself and pastes a big smile on her face, but he doesn't say anything. I'm not sure if he caught it or not but I give him my attention, ignoring her.

"We saw the video you posted," he says, nodding toward the other people in the room. "Smart PR. Get ahead of it. You were incredible, Ava. This is going to be a lot of fun. I told them I wanted someone new, someone just like you. And here you are," he says, holding his arms out. "Congratulations, Ava. I can't wait to work with you. Tell Clark I said hello," he adds as we hug. After the scenes we just shot, a hug seems comfortable with him. We definitely have a connection. Not necessarily romantic or sexual, just great chemistry. As I walk away, I turn around and Kya is watching me. She remembers herself and stares back at the door as her name is called. I turn back around and smile to myself. I get in the car and the first person I call is Shanna. I know she's waiting to hear back and when she answers the phone she's already squealing.

"I knew it would go amazing. My god you were in there for almost 2 hours," she says as we squeal back and forth. "Crap. That's my other line. Look, I'll call you here in a bit with some more details but way to go, Ava. I knew you were destined for the spotlight!"

We hang up and I drive over to Clark's. On the way there I call Clayton and he's super pumped. I tell him I'm on my way over to Clark's. I send Clark a text to ask if they're home. I wanted to call him, but I figure I might as well tell him in person.

We're home, angel. Come on!
Did you eat lunch?
Are you coming straight from the audition?

I am! Was going to stop and grab something.

No need. Come home, baby. I'll have something for you here.
We love you! Can't wait to hear!

When I pull into the driveway, it does feel like home. Last night in my townhouse it just felt off. I guess because I haven't spent a whole lot of time there. It feels right being at Clark's. My heart is here, so of course it feels like home. I start to walk up to the door and Brooklyn runs out and jumps on me.

"Ava! Kiki and Sonny are here," she exclaims when she's in my arms and I smile down at her.

"I bet they are so excited to see you. Did you pick them up from the airport?" I ask.

"Yes, and we took them to lunch. I'm so happy everyone is here!" she adds, jumping down and taking my hand. "They can't wait to meet you." Clark appears in the door. I smile at him and he smiles back.

"Well?" He asks with his arms open. "I'm dying to hear how it went."

"I got it!" I yell as he pulls me in his arms, spinning me around and kissing me.

"I knew it! Baby I'm so proud of you. So damn exciting. I can't wait to hear more about it, but first, some very important people want to meet you," he adds as he closes the door behind us. Brooklyn runs into the den leaving Clark and I in the foyer. Clark wraps me up in his arms. "Let's meet my parents and then you and I are getting out of the house for a bit. I want to hear about everything. Don't leave anything out!"

I meet his parents over sushi. Clark ordered, so there's plenty and we have a blast getting to know each other. Lloyd and Chelsea Grant! They are absolutely perfect. I can see why Clark turned out to be such a stellar human being. I'm not saying he's perfect, but he's damn near close, and he's perfect for me. I get to hear how they got their grandparent names and it's the cutest. They adore Brooklyn as any grandparent should. I hear they'll be visiting for about two weeks, depending on Lloyd's health. I knew from Clark that his dad had been sick for a while. This will unfortunately be his last trip out west. He's been battling lung cancer for years and it's getting harder and harder for him to travel. All things considered though, he seems to be in good spirits. We sit around and talk for a while and then Lloyd goes to lay down. Brooklyn and her Kiki head outside to play. It's a really nice day, so Clark asks me to go on a walk. We drive to a nearby hiking spot and get out of the car.

Clark

As Ava and I head up to the top of the trail we are in comfortable silence. There are a few other people on the trail, but for the most part it's just me and my girl. On the ride there, Ava recounts her audition, and I could not be more proud of her. As we start up the trail, I grab her hand and she looks over, smiling at me.

"Baby, I'm so excited for you." We keep walking and she's beaming. I know that feeling well. I remember the feeling I had after I landed my first major movie role. Life feels surreal. It's a new beginning and you have this feeling like everything is about to change. As we walk, we talk about what the next couple of weeks look like. They don't start shooting from what she knows for another six months. So late spring, early summer, is what she's being told. I keep looking at her, and I think her smile could light up the entire west coast. I will do anything in the world to keep that smile on her face. When we get to the top of the trail to the overlook, I take my phone out and take a picture with Ava. "I need to post my first photo."

"Well, I'm happy to help." She helps me post the photo and then I put my phone away. We stand there for a bit, in awe of our surroundings. I walk behind her and take a photo of her looking out over the canyon. The wind is blowing through her hair, and she looks so content. It's a great look for her. Happy. Proud. Expectant. She turns to look at me and I send her the photo. She looks down at her phone and then smiles back up at me.

"You should post that picture with a caption about the future Ava. Your world is about to change. You should try and capture these moments and share them. People need that kind of hope." I come up behind her and wrap my arms around her. She posts the picture with the caption *Taken by the love of my life. At one of the most exciting times of my life. Excited for the future, my friends. Life is about to change. Love, Ava* <3

She wraps her arms around my neck, pulling me into a deep and heated kiss. I could die happy here. A few moments pass by and then I pull back.

"Easy, baby. I don't want a passerby to get the

wrong idea and post a picture of me completely aroused by you," I say, pulling her close so she understands my meaning. She laughs against my lips staring up at me. "Thank you for sharing your moment with me, angel. I'm honored. I can't wait to watch this new journey unfold for you."

We head back down the trail back to the car. I let Ava in and then get in, looking down at my phone. HOLY SHIT. One million likes and I have a missed text from Clayton.

Congrats Boss. You're breaking the internet

Not really. But thanks. I think it was all Ava

Sure blame it on her. You still got it, Boss!

How proud of our girl are you?

Ecstatic! So deserving. Just stoked to work for the both of you. But I feel like we need to prepare her for what's to come.

We will. I want her to enjoy this moment. I'm gonna take

her out to celebrate. After Thanksgiving. I'm gonna have an official celebratory dinner party. I want her to really enjoy this. And I want us to be nothing but supportive. This is going to be fun.

You're the best kind of human Clark.

See you Thursday! Happy almost Turkey Day

Ava and I head back to the house after a small celebratory dinner at one of my favorite restaurants. It's a hidden gem. I did notice a couple people pull out their phones when we arrived. Ava handles it like a champ. I'm glad she understands this life. This business tears more people apart than it brings together, at least where relationships are concerned. It's hard, but Ava seems to handle it with grace. Ava got her movie, I'm wrapping up mine. She's moving in with me at the end of the week! I haven't told her that I'm going to be taking some time off after the movie wraps. Tonight isn't the time and I don't want her to think it's because she landed this role. I wanted this before I even met Ava. Brooklyn needs some more time with me before I dive into a new role. I can't stop smiling though. The direction

Ava and I are heading is so exciting. This is what I want. She's what I want. I've never wanted anything more for myself or for Brooklyn. I'm also so excited that she's going to be in a Dalton Calhoun Production. Such a small world.

Ava leaves a little after seven to head back to her place. Mum comes into the kitchen as I'm sitting there checking my phone. 2.5 million likes on Instagram. The photo of me and Ava is everywhere. I'm smiling down at the photo when my mum sits down next to me.

"I'm happy for you son," she says, and I turn to face her.

"Thanks, Mum. I'm happy for me, too. And for Brooklyn."

"I really like her, and I love how happy she makes the two of you. She seems like an amazing woman. She really does love you both. I know that's not tough to do, but I do know good relationships in your line of work are hard to find. I have to say as your mum I worry about you in this industry. However, I can see that you've found yourself a rare gem." I take her hand and squeeze it lightly in appreciation.

"I didn't think I could have both. I thought I'd traded love for success. I had Brooklyn and I was grateful for that. Most don't even get that. I had Brooklyn, I had my career, and I was starting to believe romance was only in the movies. But I found it. Better yet, we found each other. Thanks to Lydia."

"You know. After Lydia left one evening, she called to tell me that something amazing was on the horizon for you and Brooklyn. I didn't understand what she meant but now I do. She wanted you to have everything. And she believed you could. You just didn't believe it yourself. Now that I've met Ava, I understand. She loves you just as much as you love her. So she moves in Friday, huh?" My mum says smiling knowingly at me.

"She does. She also just landed a role in a movie. I'm really excited for her, and she did it without my help."

"I'm happy for the both of you, Clark. Look, it's getting late and I'm still on London time. Thanks for flying your dad and I out. He's not doing well. I know you know that. His doctor thinks he's got about 6 more months left. I know this trip meant the world to him. To get to see you and Brooklyn again. He's made his peace son and I hope you know how proud he is of you," she adds, a tear falling down her cheek.

"It's ok, mum," I say, wiping the tear away. "You loved him well. And he you," I add as she nods. "I was so blessed to have the both of you as parents. Most don't get that lucky. We will be here for whatever you guys need. I hope you know that. I hope you know how much he loves you. He still looks at you like you are the most precious woman on Earth. You guys loved each other really well."

"We did. He's the greatest man I've ever known. He's not gone yet," she says, smiling as I hand her a tissue. "We still have some time. But I want you to know that we love you and that your father is so proud of you, not just of your career, but of the man you've become. The father you are to Brooklyn. I know us being so far away has been hard. We always knew you were going to do something amazing with your life. And you have," she says, smiling as Brooklyn comes and climbs up in her lap. She kisses Brooklyn and Brooklyn asks her to tuck her into bed.

The next morning, we hang out all day with my parents. Dad takes breaks when he needs to, but mostly we sit around playing games and eating great food. Mum asks me if we will need any help with food for tomorrow. I shake my head. Marco, Clayton and I will be working on the turkey from early morning till our late lunch is ready. Marco is making a couple sides and Ava said she would make some sides as well. It just warms my heart that tomorrow I will be eating Thanksgiving with my best friends and family. Then Ava will be moving in with us. The sun has set, and my mum comes back down after snuggling with Brooklyn and shares a glass of her favorite wine with me. I sit back and thank God for my life and the lives of those around me. I'm incredibly blessed. Ava asked if I would be okay with us finding a church for the three of us to attend and I'm completely on board. I haven't been to church in a while. It's not the easiest for me to find a place where I can attend and not feel like people are watching. Ava has some ideas and I'm game to figure it out. I have so much to be thankful for and I'd love to get back to church.

Thanksgiving Day is a blast. Ava comes over first thing in the morning to watch the parade on TV with us. Marco and Clayton arrive a little later to help prep the turkey. While Clayton is getting the turkey into the oven and the other sides prepared, Marco pulls me aside. We walk back into my office, and I think it's to give me the bill for Ava's dresses. He pulls out a small box. We both look down at it and then I look up at him laughing.

"Look, Marco. I love you, but I'm more in love with Ava," I say, joking. He slaps me on the chest. I open the box and see it's a wedding band with small diamonds around the center. It's gorgeous. "When?" I ask and he smiles up at me.

"I was hoping you could help me out," he adds,

and I nod. "I'd love to propose to Clayton today. Maybe while we are going around saying what we are all thankful for? Then I will get down on one knee and ask the love of my life to marry me. My hope is for us to have a small service here overlooking the Hollywood Hills. It's where we first fell in love. I don't know when Clayton will want to marry, but I want to do it soon. In the next couple of months. Clayton told me you plan on eventually proposing to Ava. Maybe around Christmas? We don't want to overstep things for you and Ava, but I want this to be very special for Clayton. He deserves that," Marco says, getting a little teary.

"Of course. After you and Clayton decide when you want to have the wedding, Ava and I will make sure it's perfect. Whenever you want. We will make it work," I say, giving him a big hug. "As far as me proposing to Ava, the ring will be ready in a couple of weeks. I heard back from Silas yesterday, actually. I want to propose on Christmas Eve. I'm not sure about Ava, but she starts shooting in late April or May. I don't know if she will want to get married before shooting starts or after, but I'm guessing they'll need her for a couple months. I just don't know. It's up to her on what she wants to do. I'd go to the courthouse tonight, but this isn't about me," I add, laughing.

"Thank you, Clark. You've been so supportive of us. Also, I cannot wait for you to see Ava in her

Emerald green dress. Of all the dresses I've fitted her for, that one is special," he says, kissing the tips of his fingers like he just made his mum's spaghetti.

We are putting the finishing touches on our Thanksgiving fixings, and I know everyone is hungry. Ava made a couple casseroles, picked up a cake and the ham this morning. Marco looks nervous, so I come behind him and put my hands on his shoulders, squeezing reassuringly. He seems to relax a bit and I smile. He knows that Clayton will say yes. It's more or less the nerves of such a big moment. They've been together for years, they already live together --they are practically already married. This is just to make it "official." We place everything on the table as everyone gets situated with their drinks. I raise my glass and thank everyone for coming.

"Before we dig in, I'd like to tell everyone thank you for being the most incredible family. Mum and Dad for coming in town to be with us. Clayton and Marco, for being with me almost every single day. Clayton, you put up with more than any normal human should, and I love you dearly for it. Brooklyn, my darling, you are everything a father could ever want in a princess. I'm so thankful for you." She smiles sweetly at me, and I blow her a kiss. "Lastly my sweet Ava, I love you with all of my heart. I'm so glad you came into our lives." I lean over and give her a kiss and then look beside me to Clayton. He says what he's thankful for and then turns to Marco. I take a deep breath. Suddenly I'm nervous for him. He stands up, grabbing his glass, which starts to shake, and then thinks better of it and puts the glass down. Ava looks at me warily and I wink at her.

"I'm also so thankful for all the love at this table. You all are truly family. Being Italian, that's a big thing for me. I could not be more blessed. I love you all. Clayton," he says, turning to his love, who's smiling at him. Poor guy has no clue. "You are the love of my life. I cannot imagine a world where you are not the sun in my sky and the stars in my night. I have loved you from the moment we first saw each other over the sales rack at Barney's all those years ago. The first time we kissed, time stood still and life has never been the same since. I know how we feel about each other. I want to make it official so that the whole world knows you're mine and I'm yours," he says, getting down on one knee and pulling the box out of his back pocket. "Clayton, make me the happiest man in the world and marry me." Clayton gasps and so does Ava. I look over and she's smiling with tears in her eyes. I grab her hand and she squeezes mine back. Clayton grabs Marco's face, giving him a big kiss as we all cheer.

"Yes!" Clayton exclaims. Marco opens the box

as Clayton and Ava both gasp. "And yes again," he says looking down at the ring. Ava comes around to give them both a hug. Everyone is so excited. I love how much they love each other. It's been inspirational for me and in my life. We finally sit down to eat once everyone has hugged and admired Clayton's band. I give him a big hug and tell him how happy I am for him. He winks and I smile. He knows my time is coming up soon as well. I hope Ava can feel that too. I feel it deep in my bones and I know Ava does too. When we look over at each other, I can feel that she's just as ready as I am.

Ava

Today was amazing. I think I've said it a million times to Clark, who smiles and laughs every time. It was amazing to have Thanksgiving with friends who feel like family. This time last year, I was eating a Hot Pocket in bed, watching Netflix. Not that that wasn't great. It was lazy and relaxing, but this year I'm surrounded by the most incredible people in the universe. I can honestly call them my people. We didn't really make it all the way around the table, so when Clark and I climb into bed that evening, I tell him it's my turn.

"I didn't get to say what I'm thankful for," I say as he sits down on his side of the bed. He's only in his sleep pants, so I'm a little distracted.

"What are you thankful for, angel?" he says,

smiling over at me. "And why are you so far away?" he reaches, over grabbing my hand and pulling me closer.

"Cause you're distracting, Clark," I say. "You and all your sexiness are distracting."

"Tell me more," he says, pulling me closer. I giggle, trying to wiggle out of his arms. After kissing me, he rolls us back over so I'm lying next to him.

"Calm down, Casanova. I'm thankful that this year I wasn't alone on Thanksgiving," I whisper, and his smile fades. "I don't mean that to make you sad. I enjoyed my time alone. Probably more than most should. But I didn't know what I was missing. Until you," I say, and he pushes my hair behind my ears, leaning closer to kiss me lightly on the lips. "I'm thankful for you, Clark. For introducing me to your people and letting me into your world. I've never really had friends like this until you. I love you and your family more than I could ever imagine I could love another family. It's so nice to be part of that with you. Clayton, Marco, and Brooklyn. But mostly I feel part of something special, something bigger than myself. When I'm with you, I know I can do anything in the world. Mostly because I have your love and support," I say with tears in my eyes. Clark kisses me hard and I whisper as a tear falls from my eye. "So thank you. Thank you for everything." He sits up and pulls me into his lap.

"I love you more than anything, Ava. You are my family. We all love and adore you so much. Never stop telling me how you feel, Ava. It makes my world go round to hear you say how you feel and how much you love me. You don't realize what a starving man I was before I met you. I didn't realize what I didn't have until you came in with your bright light and beautiful smile. You are perfect, Ava. Perfect for me, perfect for Brooklyn, and my family. And one day soon, don't get nervous, baby," he says with a playful warning, but he still looks serious. "One day, Ava. I will get down on one knee and ask you to spend the rest of your life with me. I want that. I want you forever, Ava," he adds, and I feel my heart start beating hard in my chest. It's what I want too. To hear him say it out loud makes my head spin, in a good way. "One day, Ava. I will stand at the end of an aisle and watch you walk down it to me. You'll make me the happiest, luckiest, most blessed man in the world. Until then, I want you to make sure you are ready. I know you have a lot already going on, but I love you, baby. I want you more than I've ever wanted anything in the world. Can you do that for me? Can you make sure this is what you want?"

"I can. And I will," I say, smiling and kissing him back. We have a very hot and heavy make out session and then Clark rolls us over so we are laying side by side again. I'm catching my breath and coming back to Earth as he pulls my chin gently so I'm focusing on him.

"I want us to wait to have sex until we're married," Clark says, a little out of the blue. He knows where I am on all of this. I want the same thing. I know marriage isn't far off for us, so it's not like he's telling me we will have to wait forever. It actually makes me relax a bit. I didn't know I would have that reaction, but it's how I feel too. Deep down I know that's the right decision for us.

"Okay," I say a little breathlessly. "I'm good with that, Clark. Thank you."

"You are beyond sexy and it takes every bit of restraint I have to wait, but God, Ava. I want this to be special for you. I feel like if we take it slow it will be better. Are you okay waiting? I feel like you relaxed a little when I said that." I sit up, trying to clear my head a little.

"Yes, I can wait. Maybe not a very long time. I know what I want and it's you. I want to make sure you want that too, and you're not just saying what you think I want to hear because you think I'm not ready. I'm ready, Clark. I want you so bad, but I also think I can wait if it's what we both want."

"Then let's wait. We don't have to rush anything. If something happens, amazing. If it doesn't, then great. I would love nothing more than for your first time to be with me, as your husband. I also know that's pretty old fashioned, but I'm kinda an old fashioned guy. No surprise there. Are you okay with that?"

"Yes. I want my first time to be with you, as my husband," I add as he beams back at me. "Just do me a favor." He leans over and turns the light off and we crawl towards the middle of the bed towards each other.

"What's that?" he whispers into the dark.

"Don't wait too long!" I say, and I feel him pull me closer to him. I can tell he wants me now but is restraining himself. He laughs quietly and so do I.

"I won't, baby." He kisses me on the forehead and then turns me so we are cuddling. I fall fast asleep thinking about how lucky I am.

The following weekend Clayton and I go to lunch while Clark packs his bag for his last month on set. I'm excited that he will at least be coming home for Christmas. I know this round on set is only a couple of weeks, but I'm already sad about him leaving. Clayton and I are on our first round of margaritas when he asks me if I'll be his maid of honor. I place my margarita down and grab both of his hands.

"I would be honored, Clayton. You're like the sibling I never had and always wished for," I whisper, and he laughs. "You're like having a brother and a sister!"

"Oh, I'm both for sure," he says and we clink our margaritas. "I gotta say, I'm so excited, Ava. Did Clark tell you we want to get married in your backyard overlooking the Hollywood Hills?" he says dramatically, and I shake my head.

"No, he didn't, but I want to hear about all of your plans." I want to know every single detail. We talk for an hour straight about his hopes and dreams for the wedding and ceremony. I can only swoon. It's perfect. Perfectly him and Marco. They plan to wed on New Year's Eve and make it one big party. Clark told him to spare no expense and that doesn't shock me at all. Clayton is honestly the sibling Clark never had and always wanted as well. Clark is Clayton and Marco's best man and Brooklyn is the flower girl. This is going to be so much fun!

"Word on the street," Clayton whispers as he starts on his second margarita, "is our little Brooklyn might be a flower girl twice in the same year." He sits back up and I laugh.

"I think you might be right," I whisper back conspiratorially. "I will ask her if she wants to be. She might just want to stand next to her daddy. Gosh, I haven't thought that far ahead. The last Clark and I spoke he told me to be thinking about us getting married. About the real possibility that he is going to ask soon. To be honest, there's not a lot to think about. I'm ready, Clayton. I've never been more ready for anything in my life," I add. "It's really hard to believe that Clark and I have only known each other since July, but it's true. It's almost been six months. I think we just want to experience all the rest of what life has to offer for us, together. I'm almost 30 and Clark is in his late 30's. No better time than now!"

"That's really the best way to do it. I mean, who knows how long you have in this life. Why wait for it to make sense to other people? You have to do what feels right for you and Clark. Also, did you send the contracts over to Brian and the team to look over for you?" He asks, changing the subject.

"Yes. Brian said everything looked great and we should be good to move forward any day now. I'm so excited, Clayton."

"Hell, I'm excited for you. That also gives you to the first week in May to get your ass in gear for the film. I know they said not to change a thing and I LOVE that. Women back in the old Hollywood days were so glamourous. I can't wait to see what they do with you. You are going to be an absolute bombshell. I hope you are ready! You're in a Dalton Calhoun Production. Can you believe it?" he asks, and I squeal a little bit.

"It still seems like a dream come true. My part only shoots for six weeks in New York. Can you believe that? I spend six weeks in New York, come back here and then shoot for two weeks here. Then two weeks in London on a sound stage. I'm such a lucky broad," I say with an old Hollywood flair.

"Yeah, you are! Also, how amazing is this guacamole?" he adds and I nod. Mexican cuisine is the best.

"It's amazing. We need this at your reception!" He looks up, gasping in acknowledgement and nods his head. We have the best ideas!

I head back to Clark's and plan to spend the entire night kissing him. I'm going to miss him. I walk in and he's sitting on the sofa with his glasses on reading a script. I stand there looking at him, taking him in. He's so damn sexy, especially with those glasses on. He doesn't look up, but smiles.

"Are you going to just stand there, angel, or are you going to come over here and kiss me?" he asks, not taking his eyes off his script.

"I might," I answer as he takes his glasses off and puts his script down on the table beside him.

"Well, I hope you come in for the real thing," he says as he leans back, putting an arm on the back of the sofa. I put my stuff down and walk toward him.

"I'm gonna miss you."

"Come here, baby," he says, pulling me into his lap. I lean back, relishing how our bodies feel together. Like we were meant to be together. "I'm going to miss you, too. I'll be back in three weeks. Then it'll be Christmas, then it'll be New Year's Eve and then we will ring in the New Year together.

It'll be a blast and I'm going to get to kick off the New Year with you. I'm so glad you're here."

"Me, too. I hope next year is as great as this year has been," I say.

"Oh, it will be. I can promise you that." Turning to him, I grab his face and kiss him, holding nothing back. I straddle his lap and wrap my arms around him. He pulls me so our bodies are flush together. I grind against him, and he groans against my lips. I do it again and he flips us over so he's laying on top of me. He slows our heated make out session into sweet kisses. Lightly kissing my cheek, my nose and my forehead.

"If we are going to make it to our wedding night, Ava, you are going to have to understand that grinding against me like that is going to literally make this the hardest time of my life," he says, laughing against my cheek.

"Oh, I'm sorry. I thought you might like it," I say sarcastically as he laughs.

"You're kidding, right?" he says, laughing and pulling me up. "I love having you anywhere close to me. You know that. Especially when you rub against me like that. Let's go to bed, baby."

"I just can't help it with you," I say as he sweeps me up in his arms and carries me into the bedroom. He throws me on the bed, and I land in a big fluff of pillows and comforter. I smile as he pulls his shirt off and jumps into the bed as well. He folds me into him and then leans down kissing down my neck to my chest and back up again. I gasp as he gets back up to my neck and then he holds my face, staring down sweetly at me.

"Let's get our pajamas on," he says, pulling me up. I head into the master closet with him. It amazes me that I walk into this closet and my stuff is here. Like everything is here! These are all of my things. In Clark Grant's closet. In my closet. I need to work on that. I pull my shirt off and head to my chest of drawers to pull out a tee shirt. Clark wraps an arm around me from behind and pulls me to him. "Let me," he says. He unfastens my bra and then lowers both straps until they fall off my shoulders. He leans over, kissing both of my shoulders where my straps were. Then he's gone and I can hear him open a drawer behind me. He slips one of his soft tee shirts over my head and I put my arms through. He kneels down in front of me and smiles up at me. He takes both of my shoes off and then sits staring up at me. "May I," he says with his hand on the button of my jeans. I nod bravely.

"I need you to say yes or no, Ava," he whispers, and I clear my throat.

"Yes," I answer down to him. He unbuttons the button of my jeans and then unzips them. He places my hands on his shoulders and then pulls my jeans slowly down my legs. I hold onto his shoulders as I step out, leaving me in only his t shirt. Everything is covered, but this is the most sensual experience of my life. Looking at Clark down on his knees smiling up at me with his sexy grin. I could melt right here. He starts to stand up, and I press my hands down on his shoulders. He lifts an eyebrow up at me in surprise and I laugh. "You forgot my underwear," I whisper. He looks down to the ground, groaning, and then smiles up at me.

He runs both hands from the outside of my ankles to my calves. Then up to my thighs where they lightly brush against my ass. I bite my lip to keep myself from moaning. If this is any indication of what kind of lover Clark will be, you can go ahead and sweep me into a pile in the corner somewhere until I come to. I look down at him and he grins. His touch means everything. "I was wondering when you were going to look back at me. Keep your eyes open, Ava," he says as he hooks his fingers in the sides of my underwear and slowly pulls them down my legs. I step out of them, and Clark throws them into the hamper on my side of the closet. I'm watching him closely as he leans forward, not taking his eyes off of me and kisses me right on my pubic bone over his t-shirt. He turns his head and pulls me so that I'm flush to him, breathing me in. He wraps his arms around my body, and I place my hands on his head then run my hands through his hair. We hold each other and I feel like it takes me about a minute or two to breathe again.

He stands up, smiling a wicked smile down at me and I release a long breath. SHIT!

"Geez, Clark," I whisper as he pulls my face to his. He kisses me and I put my hand on the button of his jeans. He pulls back looking down at me with a question in his eyes. "Only fair," I say, a little more brave than I actually feel. I want to undress him. He untangles himself from me and holds his muscular arms out.

"I'm all yours, Ava," he laughs. I reach down and unbutton his jeans and then I slowly unzip them. He doesn't take his eyes off mine. I start to move to my knees, and he puts his hands under my arms, pulling me back up gently. I give him a pouty face and he shakes his head. "I don't want you on your knees in front of me, Ava." I place my hands on his jeans and pull them down until they are to his thighs. Then he wraps one arm around me and pulls his jeans down with the other. I look up into his eyes and he walks us backwards so that we are standing next to his chest of drawers in the closet. He pulls out a pair of sleep pants and then lets go of me. He pulls his boxer briefs off so he's standing in front of me in all his masculine glory. My heart about leaps out of my chest. He's perfect. He doesn't look away, just pulls his sleep pants on. So I walk forward and place a kiss right over his heart. He picks me up and I wrap my arms around his neck, kissing him sweetly on the lips.

We walk back into the bedroom as he turns off the closet light. He lays me on the bed and crawls on top of me. "I meant it when I said I'm all yours, Ava. That was one of the sexiest experiences of my life. I know you aren't going to believe me. I cannot tell you how badly I want you. But not tonight. Your hands on my body is the sexiest and sweetest feeling in the world," he adds as he holds my face so he can kiss me. I kiss him back passionately until we are both groaning. God, I want this moment to last forever. "I pray it will be everything you dream it will be, Ava. I can tell you this. I can feel it in my bones. We will be great together. Have you ever talked to anyone about their first-time experience?" he asks, and I roll over so we are facing each other.

"Yes. I know it will hurt the first time and there will probably be blood. I've heard over time the pain goes away and then that's when the real passion begins," I add, and he clears his voice.

"That is all very likely, but I will make sure you are ready so that it will be as painless as possible. I don't want to hurt you. But I promise you I will do everything I can to make sure that our first time together is as painless as possible. We will take it slow," he says, moving a hair that fell over my face behind my ear. "The thought of hurting you is repulsive to me. I'm going to need you to trust me. I've never taken anyone's virginity, Ava. You can be damn sure I'm clean. I haven't been with anyone in well over a year. Before that I was with Angela. I'll say this though. I've never had as much passion and intimacy with anyone as I've had with you!"

"Thank you, Clark. I know you will," I say as he leans to turn the lights off.

Clark

I've died and gone to heaven. That's all there is to it. I've fallen for an angel and she's transported me to heaven. That's all I can think as she falls asleep in my arms tonight. I didn't know I could feel like this. I also didn't know I could be this aroused by undressing a woman. When she went down to her knees, I couldn't handle it. It's not that I don't think she will ever be on her knees. That would be stupid of me to think. But I'm not ready to see her like that. For some reason it didn't feel right. I want to protect her. I know that she doesn't necessarily need my protection, but my god I want that woman. I'm so damn in love with her. I feel so undeserving of her love and what she has to offer. I guess that's why I feel so protective of her innocence. I have a hard time falling asleep as I think about the next few weeks coming up. I'll be busy but then hopefully I'll be home and back to my girls before I know it. These are going to be the longest three weeks of my life.

With one more week left in Vancouver I'm getting so close to heading home to my girls. Luckily Kyle finished shooting his scenes with me a week ago, so I haven't had to see the dumbass much around set. He apologized. I forgave him but told him to stay out of my way. I have patience, but it only goes so far with assholes like him. He's telling people he's heading to rehab after he finishes here, but I feel like he's only trying to get back into everyone's good graces. Last I heard he was in LA racking up thousands of dollars at bars and even tried to charge it to the studio. What an idiot. He's really a lost soul, but I'm not the guy to save him. I catch him watching me all the time and it puts me off a little. I've been around guys who have been attracted to me, but this feels different. Darker. More sinister.

I head back to my trailer after a long day of shooting and Clayton is giggling like a school girl. He pulls out his mobile and it's a picture of Ava's engagement ring. God, it's stunning and it's even better than I imagined. I smile at him and feel my emotions are all over the place. I imagine getting down on one knee and giving this to her. It's going to be the highlight of my year.

"So boss, what's the plan? We can pick it up on the way home from the airport if you'd like," he says, knowing I'll have a hard time waiting to give it to Ava.

"I want to propose on Christmas Eve," I tell him, and he sits back, holding his mobile to his chest.

"Yes!!! It's so perfect. Then a week later, I'll be getting married. Then after my honeymoon we will plan yours and Ava's wedding. Oh my gosh! What a way to kick off the New Year. It's perfect," he says, standing up and pulling me into a hug. He shows me the other pieces I asked Silas to make and they are all incredible. The emerald and diamond jewelry set will be perfect on Ava. I also can't wait to give her the matching necklace that looks like the earrings I've already given her. I didn't want the diamond as big as the engagement ring diamond. Clayton said it would look gaudy and he's right. "FYI Boss, the ring ended up being 3.5 carats. Plus all the diamonds surrounding it. Silas thought that any bigger and her arm might break. Plus, she's going to have a diamond wedding band. You want her to be able to wear it. Not for it to wear her." He laughs and I smile over at him.

"That's perfect. God, he did an amazing job," I add and pull him into another hug. "And you. You did a great job relaying what I wanted. Let's pick it up on the way home if we can. I'll put it in the safe in the office when we get back home.

That's a wrap! The following week flies by and our shooting schedule is a breeze. Everyone is so excited, but also a little sad. It's the end of an era for those of us who started filming the first movie of the franchise almost 10 years ago. It feels good to be wrapping the movie with everyone on set. It's an incredible day. We sit around talking, signing parts of the set and taking all kinds of pictures. After a couple hours of celebrating on set with the crew, we head to our respective trailers. I shower off the day and then change into my jeans and hoodie as Clayton finishes packing up our stuff. We have our driver picking us up in 15 minutes, so I help him pack up. There's a knock on the trailer door, so Clayton opens it and Kyle is standing there asking to speak with me. I walk behind Clayton and put my hand on his shoulder so he moves. I sit down on the step and wait to hear what he has to say. I'm not inviting him in. He can say what he needs to say right here. There are people still walking around finishing up around their trailers. This probably isn't the privacy I'm sure he was hoping for, but this is as good as it's going to get for him.

"I just wanted to say thank you. You could've had me fired off the movie or killed my career in your interview a while back. I've made some pretty big mistakes the last couple of months, specifically on set. I know I've been careless with my words and my behavior. I just want you to know I AM aware, and I am going to try and get help. I'm sure like everyone else, you don't believe me, but I am going to try."

"I appreciate the apology. I'm not the person you should be apologizing to. However, you need to understand that you've been out of line and I'm not okay with it. Not just the way you treated Ava, but how you treat people in general. Take care of yourself, Kyle. You only get one shot at this life. Don't waste it being a jackass. Get the help you need." I turn around and close the door. I look over at Clayton and he has his phone out recording what just went down.

"Can't be too careful with that one. I want this on film in case something else backfires. That was big of you, Clark. You don't owe him anything. You could have slammed the door in his face. I'm glad you didn't. I have a feeling there aren't many people in his life that hold him accountable. But you also can't be his savior. He has to do the work," he adds.

We grab our bags and head to the car waiting outside. It's time to head back to the hotel and pack up. The weather in Vancouver has taken a turn for the worse and it's snowing heavily. If we are going to make it home tonight, we are going to have to pray that there's a break in the weather. I know a couple other people are flying out as well.

The wrap party has been moved back to LA due to the weather. We decided to fly out tonight. I'll be in bed with my baby by midnight. I'm so excited. I'm going to be home with her soon. I might have a couple of overdubs or possible reshoots but as far as the big picture is concerned, we are done. Later next year we will film the bonus features like interviews and extras, but I couldn't be happier with how everything turned out. The press tour won't happen for at least another year or so once the movie is closer to being released, but we are officially in post-production. After leaving the hotel Clayton and I head to the airport. It looks like we are still cleared for takeoff, so I climb up in the plane with Clayton and we take our seats. Clayton is just as excited as I am. I wanted to surprise Ava, but I also don't want to scare her when someone enters the house late tonight. I know she's probably already put Brooklyn down for the night since it's a little past eight. She may already be asleep herself. I know Brooklyn had a big day with it being her class Christmas party. Next week is Christmas

Eve and my god I could not be more stoked. We were going to grab Ava's jewelry on the way in, but Clayton talked to Silas and he said we could pick it up tomorrow since we are coming in so late tonight. I can't wait to see Ava. I grab my phone and see that it's on its last bar. I text Ava quickly before we take off and then put my phone beside me and fall asleep.

Coming home early baby.
We will be home a little after midnight!
Can't wait to see you! I Love you!!

Marco

I wake up to incessant ringing from my cell phone. It's around 9 p.m. when I look over at my phone. I had fallen asleep on the sofa after I heard from Clayton that they would be heading back tonight. I pick up my phone and see that I have 10 missed calls and numerous texts. What in the world? One of the texts is from my new assistant, Mary Beth. She's asking me if Clayton and Clark are okay and tells me to turn on the news. I'm so confused. I turn on the local news and check a couple sources online. They are reporting a crash during take-off at Vancouver International Airport. I turn the volume up and hear the reporter talking. *It appears to have happened during take-off. The private plane slipped off the runway and caught fire. No more in-*

formation at this time. We will report back once we have more information. No word about casualties or survivors at this time. I look back at my phone to see what time Clayton said their plane was due to take off. No specific time. SHIT. I immediately feel sick to my stomach. I text Mary Beth back and tell her I don't know. I haven't heard from him. I dial Clayton's phone and it goes straight to voicemail. I place my head in my hands and start to cry. What am I going to do? My poor sweetheart. I pray it isn't their plane, but there's no way for me to rule it out either. I pick my phone up and call Ava.

Ava

I hear my phone buzzing again beside me and I roll over and grab it. Seeing it's Marco calling, I sit up and try to orient myself. I miss the call but see I have six missed calls. Two from Shanna, four from Marco, and a text from Clark.

Coming home early baby.
We will be home a little after midnight!
Can't wait to see you! I Love you!!

I smile down at the text and get all kinds of excited to see him. I wasn't expecting him until tomorrow night, but I'm so glad he's coming home early. Brooklyn will be thrilled to see him in the morning. I'm excited to see him tonight. My phone rings again and it's Marco. I answer it, a little dazed from falling asleep and then almost immediately being woken up by my phone. I look at the clock. It's a little after nine.

"Hey, Marco," I say, my voice groggy.

"Hey, Ava. Are you watching the news?" he asks, and I can tell he's been crying. My stomach drops immediately. NO.

"I'm not. What's wrong, Marco," I ask, my body is starting to feel tingly. It's like when you almost get in a car accident or when you see a car crash happen near you.

"There's been an accident in Vancouver. They're now reporting that an actor's private plane crashed during take-off. I don't know any more than that. Crews on the ground are now reporting no survivors, but I haven't heard anything official yet. I've tried to call Clayton and Clark, but no answer. Brian is calling authorities in Vancouver, but he hasn't reached anyone who can give him more information. I'm so sorry, Ava. I don't know if it's them. It's hard to tell at this point," his voice breaks. He sounds so far away and my head feels heavy. I feel my stomach lurch and I run to the bathroom. I barely make it to the toilet before throwing up everything in my stomach. I still have my phone in my hand, so I drop it like it's scalded me. I continue retching until my stomach is completely empty. I sink down on the floor and crawl into a small ball, my body shaking and my heart shattered. I cry harder than I've ever cried in my entire life. NO. Not Clark. Not Clayton. Not Brooklyn's only surviving parent. Not the love of my life. DAMN everyone for leaving me. DAMN everyone who I've ever loved dying on me.

What feels like an eternity, but is actually only minutes later, my phone vibrates against the cold bathroom tile. A text from Marco.

> **I'm coming over. Disarm the doors, Ava.**
> **We will get through this together. I love you!**

I open the security app on my phone. Disarming the alarm, I lay my head back down on the cool tile floor. I call Clark, but it goes straight to voicemail. I don't even have the energy to hang up, I just cry and cry until my eyes feel like they will be swollen shut forever. I leave my phone on the bathroom floor. I don't need it anymore. I have no energy to do a damn thing but walk to the mirror. The woman staring back at me isn't me. She's a shell of the woman I was becoming since knowing Clark. There's a small part of me that believes the reports could be wrong. But I'm a coward, I can't turn the TV on. I don't want to hear his name over the TV, confirming that my dreams and hopes for us have been crushed. I can't move. I'm paralyzed with fear. I can't imagine how scared and terrified they must have been in those final moments. IF this is true, Brooklyn will need me to be strong. I wash my face and brush my teeth, pretending I'm stronger than I actually feel. I have to take the next step. I have to be strong for Brooklyn, for Marco, for myself. I clean myself up and then walk into our closet, heading straight to his sweatshirts. I pull on one that smells like him and tears spring back into my eyes. I walk into the den and turn the TV on. It's just as Marco said, but nothing new to report. I mute the TV because I can't listen right now. I head to the coffee maker and turn it on. I'm sure someone will want coffee at some point. I don't have my phone, but I'm not sure who I'm expecting to call.

The snow is coming down in Vancouver and they're calling for a whiteout. Marco walks in the door and immediately we are in tears holding each other. 'This isn't happening,' I tell myself. I'm sick to my stomach and I'm not in the mood to talk. I can only stare at the muted screen. Marco and I walk over to the sectional and sit down. He asks me questions and I can only nod or shake my head. His phone rings and it's just another curious person. I'm starting to get angry and I'm glad that I don't have my phone. I just want Brian to get the information and get back to us. I know I should text Shanna back, but what am I supposed to say? I know nothing more than the people watching it unfold as I am. Why haven't we heard anything? I don't even know what time it is or how much time has passed.

I get up and go into Clark's bathroom, getting sick again and again and again. I brush my teeth again, grab a washcloth and turn the cold water on. I wring out the washcloth after I've submerged it in cold water and press it against my flushed face. It only makes me feel a little better, but it's temporary. I'm no longer throwing up anything of substance. It's just air and emotions at this point. I look down at my phone and see I have 15 missed calls and 10 text messages. None of them are from Brian. I take my phone back into the den with me and sit next to Marco. He gets up and makes himself a cup of coffee. I can't stomach anything, so I just lay down, staring at the TV. I put the washcloth on the back of my neck and try to breathe.

"Why is there no new information?" Marco whispers with tears running down his face. "Why can't they give us more information? This is ridiculous," he says as he looks down at his phone. "Brian was supposed to call me right back." That can't be a good thing, I think to myself.

"He's probably on the phone with authorities," I mutter, feeling defeated. I have never felt like this before. I have had many family members die in my life. In accidents, due to old age, but this cuts so deep that I'm not really quite sure I'll recover. He was my future. He's the only man I've ever loved. Closing my eyes, I feel a fresh wave of tears start to flow. The next thing I know, Marco is kneeling in front of the sofa his arms wrapped around me. We are both holding on by a thread. My head is killing me, and I am drained. Marco's phone rings and he almost drops it trying to answer it.

"Is it Brian?" I yell, sitting up quickly and regretting it. My head swims and I feel like I'm going to pass out. It's been almost two hours of us sitting around with no new information. How is there no new information?

"It wasn't them," he says, falling to his knees. I join him there. A fresh wave of tears envelops us both. We hug and cry and hug some more. It wasn't Clark and Clayton's plane. It was a plane of actors, but their plane took off right after Clark and Clayton's. Clark and Clayton took off at 8:05 and this plane took off at 8:25. Same airport, different private plane, different actors. It took Brian a while to get through to the right people. Marco hangs up the phone after repeating everything Brian says to me. I just lay all the way on the floor. I'm devastated for the families and friends of whoever was on that plane, but I can't help rejoicing that it wasn't Clark and Clayton's plane. My mind is mush.

After a long while Marco and I make our way over to the sofa. We are sitting watching the news still when the confirmation comes across the screen. It wasn't Clark and Clayton's plane. They are now confirming the plane to be that of Kyle Wright, his pilots, his assistant and two other guests. I gasp and so does Marco. That's terrible. He was so young. It's hard to celebrate that it wasn't Clark, Clayton and their crew when others really did lose their lives. But honestly, I'm relieved. I'm relieved that Clark and I have more time. That it wasn't Brooklyn's dad. It wasn't our sweet Clayton and that I will get to see Clark tonight. I don't think I'll be able to sleep tonight. I just don't think that's going to be possible. I sit back on the sofa, and we turn the TV off. We both lay there for about ten minutes. Marco grabs his phone and starts replying to messages. I'm sure I should too, but I can't. I have zero energy. He puts his phone down and chuckles.

"Phone's now dead, but I don't care." We sit there for a few minutes and Marco goes to grab my phone. I'm letting my body catch up to what my brain now knows as I feel my phone vibrate. I look down and it's Clayton's name. I immediately start crying. I just can't help it. Clark and Clayton are okay. I answer and he's hysterical.

"Oh my god, Ava. Marco's phone goes straight to voicemail. We just heard about Kyle. I'm sorry. Just got off the phone with Brian. He told us for the last couple hours they were speculating that it was our plane," he says, and I can't say anything, I'm just sobbing. I hand the phone to Marco. He's crying, I'm crying. I start to feel sick again. I run to the bathroom, but nothing is coming up. My body and nerves are shot. About five minutes later Marco comes in into the bathroom.

"They are on their way. They called us as soon as they landed. Clark's phone has been dead since they took off in Vancouver, and Clayton's phone didn't have any service on the plane. Clark wanted to talk to you babe, but I told him you've been getting sick all night. He's coming home darling," Marco says as I lay on the bathroom floor shivering. "He's alive, Ava. They're on their way here," he says, grabbing a wet rag and dabbing my face. "It's going to be okay."

I know it's shock. I sit up as Marco sits down next to me, our backs against the bathroom sink. Who knows how long we sit there. I brush my teeth again for like the fifth time tonight, then we go back into the den. We are sitting, holding each other when I hear the door open. I look up to see Clark and Clayton in the doorway. The four of us crumble. Clark kneels down in front of me, tears in his eyes, looking me over like he's in shock at the state of my distress. He pulls me in his lap, rocking me back and forth as I cry and then he cries.

"Baby. It's okay. I'm here," he whispers to

me. I feel him pick me up as I whisper to him how much I love him. He carries me into the bedroom and puts me in bed. He's still fully dressed, but I hear him kick his shoes off, then he crawls into bed next to me as he covers us up. I've stopped crying, and thank God, I've finally stopped getting sick. I inhale his masculine scent and the softness of his hoodie. I finally fall asleep or pass out, one of the two, and have zero dreams.

I wake up a couple hours later. It's still dark and I'm in bed alone. For a moment I think that maybe it was a dream all along, but I see Clark's suitcase next to the bathroom door. I think back on the night's events and I'm happy that it doesn't immediately make me sick. Maybe my stomach is turning around. I climb out of bed and walk into the kitchen. The light is off, but I know exactly where he will be. Upstairs with his sweet princess. I quietly climb the stairs and peek around Brooklyn's room. He's sleeping next to her in her bed. He's such an amazing daddy. God, to think what Brooklyn could have lost last night. I crawl on the other side of Brooklyn so that she's in between Clark and I, and fall asleep.

When I wake up, Clark and Brooklyn are still asleep. It's a little past eight, which is pretty normal for Brooklyn on weekends. Yesterday was a big day for her. She was so tired when she got home from her class parties. I climb out of bed and head downstairs. I'm making my tea when Marco and Clayton come out of the guest room. They are holding hands and look like they didn't sleep at all either. They see me, and Clayton comes over to give me a long hug. We start to cry again, and I feel like I may not ever stop. I feel swollen and depleted. Marco looks about the same. I pour my tea, adding some honey, and join the two of them with their coffee on the back porch. It's cold this morning, but it feels good. I sit back and place my tea beside me to cool a little. Clayton tells us when they were in the air they had someone notify the pilot of a crash in Vancouver, and only as they were about to land they heard it was Kyle's plane.

"We had no idea that the entire time we were in the air, people thought it could possibly be our plane. Clark panicked, his phone was dead. I called Marco as soon I could, it went straight to voicemail. Luckily Brian was able to relay to you guys what he learned from authorities in Vancouver. We called Brian as well. He was able to put a statement together. Ava, I called you as soon as we got off the phone with Brian. I heard you crying and then Marco lost it, said you had been getting sick since nine when he called to tell you about the crash. Clark was a mess. Hell, we all were a mess. We could not get here fast enough. Then to see the two of you like that when we got here," Clayton says, wiping his tears away. I start to tear up as well thinking about last night. God, what a night. He tells us about Clark and Kyle's last conversation yesterday. About Clark telling him to take care of himself.

"Where's Clark?" Marco asks, and I tell him upstairs in Brooklyn's bed.

We sit there quietly. No one talking, just cold, exhausted and drinking our hot beverages. I don't want to move. I don't want to talk. I don't want to do anything but sit here. After I finish my tea, I tell them I'm going to head back to bed. My stomach still feels weak. The thought of eating anything makes me feel nauseated. We all are just dazed, that's the only way to describe it. Emotionally hungover. I barely remember seeing Clark last night. I remember feeling him -- holding me, crying with me. I remember feeling his lips on my head as I fell asleep. I sit on the edge of the bed and feel his presence. I look up and he's standing in the doorway to the bedroom.

"I'm so sorry, baby," he says to me gently as he walks to sit beside me. "I can only imagine what last night must have been like. I love you, Ava. I'm so sorry," he whispers in my ear.

"It's not your fault," I say, my throat sore from getting sick so many times last night. "I love you, Clark. I thought we had lost you forever," I say, tearing up again. "I was so mad. I'm so damn tired of losing the people I love. You guys are the only family I have left," I say as he pulls me toward him so he can hold me. He's here. Everyone's safe. Everyone's here. I can rest now. I feel so fragile, but I know with every inch of my being that I would rather be fragile here than strong anywhere else in the world.

"You are my family," I hear Clark say, and I open my eyes. He places a hand on my head, leaning over and kissing me gently. "I know that I can't promise you that you won't lose me. I know that's not realistic. But I can say this, Ava. I'm here with you now, and you are here with me. I hope that you don't have to cry like that ever again, Ava. It was devastating to see, to hear you were so sick. I've known grief myself, baby. I've known loss, but the thought of losing you, losing Brooklyn… What you must have been feeling last night. If it was me in your shoes last night, I would've reacted the same way at the thought of losing you so tragically. Not when I was hoping we had our entire lives to spend together. I pray the next time you are that upset is when you lose me 60 years from now. After a lifetime of loving each other. Why don't you get some rest, angel? I think you'll feel better," he says as I pull my body against his, but I'm still so cold. "Wait right here, baby," he says as he walks into the bathroom.

I hear him start the bath and I smile to myself. He comes out and walks over to me, pulling me up to stand. He pulls my sweatshirt and tee shirt off over my head, his eyes never leaving mine. He pulls my sleep shorts off and I'm standing in front of him naked. He grabs my hand and pulls me into the bathroom. The temperature difference between the bedroom and the bathroom is about 10 degrees and the bath is steaming. He helps me into the bath and then walks over to my sink, grabbing a pony-tail holder. He pulls my hair up and then kisses my shoulder. I lean back once I'm almost completely submerged. I feel the warmth in my hands and body start to come back. Clark kneels beside the bathtub and rubs my cheek with his thumb. "I need to run out for a minute. Will you be okay until I get back?" he asks and I nod.

"I'll be fine," I say as he smiles sadly. He leans over, kissing me gently on the lips and I'm so grateful he's okay. The bath was the right idea. I needed the extra help to get my body warm again.

"Brooklyn is still eating breakfast and watching cartoons with Clayton and Marco. They're going to stay until I get back, and before you say they don't have to stay, they don't want to leave yet. Marco is exhausted as well. I have a feeling we will all be napping today. Brooklyn seems tired too and I've heard all about her party from yesterday. I'll be back soon, baby," he whispers. I stay in there for about 30 minutes before I get out, dry off and put on one of Clark's tee shirts. I crawl in bed and fall asleep quickly.

Clark

I don't want to leave her, but I need to. I need to pick up my packages from Silas before he gets too busy with the Christmas rush. I can't believe Christmas is already next week. It's one of my favorite holidays. Ava, Brooklyn and I put the tree up after Thanksgiving since we knew I'd be leaving so soon afterwards. I can't wait to be able to just sit and look at the Christmas lights on the tree. It's so relaxing to me and there's this wonderful nostalgic feeling. With mum and dad not coming for Christmas this year, it'll just be the three of us. Marco and Clayton are going to visit Marco's family in New York, so they won't be back until a couple days before their wedding. I was hoping Clayton and Marco would be here when I proposed to Ava, but I'm also excited to have this moment with Ava and Brooklyn. I pull up to the jewelers and park out front. I head inside and there are a couple other customers inside. I wait until Silas notices me and then he waves me back. He takes me back to his office and I smile as he shows me the jewelry, piece by piece. The emerald set is incredible. So is the necklace that matches the earrings I bought Ava a couple months ago. Ava hasn't taken them off and I'm so honored that she loves them so much. When he pulls out the diamond engagement ring, I look up at him in awe.

"It's perfect, Silas," I say and he nods. The center diamond is perfect. Yes, it's a large round cut diamond, but it's not too much. At least I don't feel that way. The smaller diamonds circling the center diamond were the right call. It makes the ring really stand out and look one of a kind. I love it and tell him so.

"It is. She must be perfect as well," he says kindly.

"She is that. I'm going to ask her to marry me Christmas Eve. Wish me luck."

"Can't think of a better Christmas present to receive than that ring right there," he says tapping on the now closed ring box and I smile.

"She's my present this year," I say. "That will be the best Christmas present!"

Clayton

I'm alive. I'm alive when that could have easily been our plane. Why wasn't it our plane? Marco and I stayed up all morning talking about it. I can't seem to move past it. Kyle was a pretty big asshole, but he didn't deserve to die. Why? I'm glad he got to speak with Clark yesterday. I didn't really take him seriously, but I'm still devastated for him. Today is a bust. Marco went back to bed, and Brooklyn and I have been sitting in the den watching cartoons. Well, she's watching TV and I'm staring off into space. The thought of losing Marco is almost too much to bear. I can't imagine what he and Ava went through last night.

I went in and checked on Ava a little while ago and she was still fast asleep. Praise the Lord. Marco and I are getting married in two weeks. I would go to the courthouse right now, but it's Saturday and we want a big celebration. We leave Monday for a week in New York with his family, and then we'll be back in LA for the week of the wedding. Clark is sending us to Tahiti for two weeks for our honeymoon. I'm so excited. If there was ever a doubt in my mind of how much Marco loved me, last night solidified that. He was devastated and so was I. Clark comes home and he's smiling from ear to ear. It's contagious. This is a good distraction from the night before.

"I'm going to have hard time waiting a week to ask her," he says, looking around to make sure she isn't in the room.

"I bet. Is it just as beautiful in person?" I ask, standing up and walking into the kitchen. We head into his study where he keeps one of his safes. He closes the door behind us and opens everything up so I can see them. I'm stunned. No words. Which is saying a lot for me. The engagement ring is beautiful, flawless. It will be beautiful on her. As he pulls out the other pieces, I look at each one, imagining her wearing them. I think my favorite is the emerald set. He places everything in the safe and then locks it.

"Thank you for everything," he says as we walk back into the kitchen. "I couldn't have done this without you, Clayton."

"Of course. And thank you, Clark. We are excited to be marrying here. We appreciate you letting us do that," I say as we head into the kitchen to make lunch.

"We are more than happy to do it. I'm sad you won't be here on Christmas Day. But you'll be back soon enough." We start to make a big salad and some soup. Marco comes out of his room and into the den, where he just plops back down again. I laugh and Clark smiles over at me. "I'm glad you guys are here," he says, and I place my hand on his shoulder.

"We're glad to be here, Clark. Sad to be missing Christmas Eve," I add with a wink, "but I know it will be super special. Try and get that on film if you can."

Ava

I wake up to someone moving the hair out of my face. I sit up feeling like a different human. Clark asks me how I'm feeling, and I smile a little weakly. My first real genuine smile since early last night.

"I feel so much better and cozy," I say, looking up at him. "Thank you for taking care of me," I add as he smiles down at me.

"I love taking care of you. I wish it was under different circumstances, but I do love it. Let's get you dressed. I've made lunch. Marco and Clayton are still here, and Brooklyn just went down for a nap. She was a mess for some reason."

"I can only imagine. She was exhausted last night. I saw that you went and slept in her room.

I think you're the best daddy in the world. I know you were worried about me, but how are you feeling?" I ask as he pulls me up and we head into the closet. I find some sweatpants and pull them on as he stands in the doorway watching me. I turn and smile at him as he takes off his shoes. He's wearing a pullover and some black jogger pants. He looks absolutely delicious. I walk over to his side of the closet and grab one of his zip up jackets and pull it on.

"I like wearing your stuff." I walk over to him and wrap my arms around him. "They smell like you."

"I love seeing you in them. Makes me happy, baby," he adds as he leans down, picking me up. I wrap my legs around him as he places his hands on my butt. "I also LOVE this," he says, squeezing gently while kissing up my neck. "I love all of you!"

"Glad to hear it," I answer against his lips. "But let's eat and don't be offended if I don't eat a lot. My stomach is still a little weak from last night."

"Don't push yourself. Have a little soup," he says as he lets me go and we walk hand in hand to the kitchen. I sit up at the counter and he grabs me a bowl of soup. It's delicious. Just like him. Warm, safe and comfortable. Tastes like home.

"It's yummy," I exclaim, and he winks back at me. Clayton and Marco are eating a salad. I watch

Clark make a bowl of salad and a bowl of soup. He sits down next to me, and I smile up at him. He's just perfect. I love how much he can eat. I also love him. So damn much.

Christmas Eve arrives quickly after the trauma of last week. We have a very lazy week leading up to Christmas. It's a lot of lounging in pajamas and eating in front of the tree. Also reminding Brooklyn that she can't open any presents yet. I can't wait for Clark to see what I got him. I may have gone a little crazy for both he and Brooklyn, but I love it. I'm a sucker for Christmas time. It really is the most wonderful time of the year. Obviously we are in LA, so it's not snowing, but at least it is chilly outside. Cool enough to wear a sweater and jeans in the evenings. Not that I've put on real clothes all week. The three of us have literally changed from lounge wear to pajamas and back again. Clark has had a lot of phone calls and well-wishers this week since the mix up with the devastating plane crash. He's grateful that people are relieved that it wasn't him, but it's almost like the Greek tragedy of losing Clark Grant in a plane crash was a letdown to people since it ended up "just being Kyle Wright." The media really hasn't been kind. Clark has mixed emotions about it. I think he's trying to figure out how to navigate his feelings.

Clark, Brooklyn and I pre-made our Christmas Day sides. We decided to grill steaks tomorrow instead of a big Christmas Day dinner. It's only the three of us, and Brooklyn wanted chicken nuggets and macaroni and cheese. Clark and I decided to make a big mac and cheese casserole and some other sides to go with our steaks. Brooklyn has been on Clark all day about when she can open a present, and I giggle every time. She's relentless! She's wearing him down, so I pull him aside and tell him that every year when I was growing up, we were allowed to open one present on Christmas Eve. I told him I got her some fun Christmas pajamas and that we could let her open that so she can wear them tonight. He agreed, so we are making some hot chocolate and setting everything up for Santa to come tonight. Brooklyn is so excited about the reindeer coming. Clark rolls his eyes. He didn't grow up with such an emphasis on Santa Claus, so he's not a huge fan. I chuckle and tell him it's just for fun. He's scared she will resent him when she finds out Santa isn't real.

"She won't grow up being mad at you once she hears Santa isn't real. It's really just Christmas magic while they're little." He leans over and kisses me as we head into the den with our hot chocolate. We sit down by the Christmas tree. It's all lit up and I love it. Watching Brooklyn playing around the Christmas tree while Clark and I cuddle, I couldn't ask for more. I hand Brooklyn her box and she jumps up and down excitedly. She tears it open and even though it's just Christmas pajamas, she's still so excited.

"They've already been washed Brooklyn. You can put them on now," I tell her as she runs upstairs to put them on. I stand up to go grab another present for her under the tree. It's something small for her. She's back down in no time at all and I hand her the other box. She rips it open and it's a framed picture of her and her daddy in a princess frame. I knew she would love it because it's covered with glitter and sparkly gems. She squeals and heads back upstairs to put it in her room. Her Christmas Eve energy is inspiring. She's back downstairs wanting another present and we tell her only one more. She opens up the box and it's one of the Disney princess baby dolls she's been wanting. She's ecstatic and Clark opens the box for her. Once Brooklyn and her baby doll are settled and playing, I stand up and grab a box for Clark. It's a large box and he smiles at me.

"It's nothing big," I say, and he laughs looking at the box.

"It looks big," he replies as I hand him the box.

"I meant it's not a huge present. It's just something I'd love for you to open tonight," I add as he puts his cup of cocoa down and opens the box. He pulls the canvas print out of the box and looks at the collage of photos of the three of us. It's a pretty large canvas of black and white photos of him and Brooklyn, Brooklyn and I, and then the three of us together. He's in genuine awe looking at it.

"Ava. I love it."

"I thought you could maybe put it in your office since it's black and white. Ya know, so you don't get lonely in there while you're working," I add, and he stands up to give me a hug.

"It's very thoughtful, Ava. I love it so much. We don't have nearly enough photos of the three of us together. This is only the beginning of these canvas collages." He stands up, kissing me on the head and I kiss him back tenderly. "I'm going to put this in my office, baby. I'll be right back." He turns and walks toward his office, and I smile at his retreating back. I sit on the sofa with my hot chocolate watching Brooklyn play. She is so in love with her baby doll and I'm so happy she loves it. Clark comes back in the room and smiles at me. I turn back to Brooklyn who's now introducing her baby doll to her other dolls. I'm laughing at something she's singing when I notice Clark fiddling with something in the kitchen. He has his back turned so I figure he's having trouble with something.

"You alright in there?" I ask, laughing.

"Never better," he adds as I turn back to Brooklyn, who's sitting with a big smile on her face, talking to her dolls. Clark comes into the den and says, "Alright, your turn. You haven't opened a Christmas Eve present."

"Oh, that's not really necessary." He rolls his eyes at me playfully.

"Nice try, Ava. Brooklyn you ready?" he asks, and I fully expect them to break out in some kind of choreographed song and dance.

"This one is from me," Brooklyn says, and I see Clark smiling down at the two of us. I open the box and it's a drawing Brooklyn did. It's the three of us holding hands and on my left hand is a giant gem with what looks like sparkles and fireworks coming out of it. I giggle and look up at Brooklyn, but she's smiling knowingly at her dad.

I'm smiling, unsure of what's going on when Clark gets down on one knee in front of me. My body goes cold, hot and then shocked. My hands immediately cover my mouth and I have to remind myself to breathe. I take a deep breath, smiling at Clark. I cannot believe this is happening.

"Ava. My beautiful Angel. You are our family. You are the best thing, other than Brooklyn, to ever happen to me. I love you more than I thought I could ever love another human. I didn't think I could have love like the love we have together. I want to spend the rest of my life loving you and making you as happy as you make me. You're one of the most selfless, caring, compassionate, warm, loving and beautiful women I've ever had the honor of knowing. I would be honored. We would be honored," he says, looking over at Brooklyn, who's smiling at me. "If you would officially join our family. Marry me, Ava. Make me the luckiest, happiest, most blessed man in the world by being my wife." I'm still in shock. He reaches into his pocket for a box, but I nod wrapping my arms around him before he can pull the box out.

"YES!" I say, and he laughs. He holds me hard to him, kissing me and smiling at me.

"Baby, you haven't let me open the box yet," he says, laughing again. I'm still in his arms as he pulls the box out and opens it. My mouth drops open and I'm pretty sure I say something inappropriate. It's beautiful. It's HUGE. And so, so sparkly.

"Oh my god, Clark. Oh my god," I say, looking up at him. "It's beautiful." He slides the ring on my finger, and I collapse into him, knocking him over so we are lying in each other's arms on the floor.

"I can't wait for you to be my wife," he says against my lips as we kiss. "Come here Brooklyn," he says, pulling me up and onto the couch. She jumps up and hugs the two of us. The three of us sit there under the tree wrapped in each other's arms. I hear voices, but I know that it's only the three of us here, so I'm confused. I look over at the kitchen and Clark laughs. He pulls me up and we walk into the kitchen where I see his phone propped up but hidden. Clayton and Marco are on FaceTime. Clayton is crying and Marco is jumping up and down. I squeal and so do they. Clark walks over to where he's got a separate camera set up and turns it off.

"That was the hardest five minutes of my life being quiet for that long!" I hear Marco say.

"Perfect ring for the perfect girl," Clayton exclaims. After we talk for a couple minutes, they head to a Christmas Eve church service with Marco's family. We tell them Merry Christmas and then go back into the den. Brooklyn continues to play as I lay with my back against Clark's chest. I keep looking from my ring to him and then back again. It's surreal.

"It really is the perfect ring for you, Ava," he says as he lifts my hand to his lips and kisses it gently. "I had it designed specifically for you. I knew the earrings were beautiful on you, so I thought that the ring would be perfect too. I can't wait to spoil you the rest of my life."

"Six decades of spoiling, huh?" I ask and he laughs.

"You remembered that. Yes, at least 60 years," he says, pulling me into his arms. "I'm so happy, Ava. I knew the moment you moaned eating your cupcake that I would one day ask you to spend the rest of your life with me," he says, laughing. I lean up, slapping his chest playfully as he pulls me back to his side. "When the accident happened with your old roommate, I knew then I couldn't lose you. Things became quite clear for me then. Faster than I imagined they would, but I think I always knew."

"I knew as well when you stayed that night in the hospital with me. I thought there's no way that I could know something like that that quick. But I did. I remember you kissing my forehead when you pulled the blankets up. Since then, I've been falling more and more in love with you everyday. I've never been more sure of anything in my life."

"Listen Ava, this is the only wedding I ever want to have. I want you to have anything and everything you want. We can have a big wedding, small wedding, medium wedding. Anything you want. Whenever you want. Wherever you want," he says, smiling at me. I turn around so we're facing each other.

"Clark, I honestly didn't think this was something I'd ever have for myself. I didn't think I would want to have anything like this. Not when I lost my parents at such a young age. When my grandmother passed away, I was terrified of losing anyone and anything else. I think I wanted to avoid that kind of hurt ever again. If you don't fall in love, then you can't have your heart broken. But all of this happened so, naturally. This is your wedding too, Clark. And Brooklyn's," I say, giggling. "What do you want?" I ask Clark.

"I want you. I want you to be happy. If I could have any wish at all. I would love to not wait too long. Please don't make me wait years," he says. I shake my head.

"Is April too much of a wait?" I ask, and his smile is almost blinding. He's beaming.

"April is perfect. Is that enough time to plan what you want?" he asks and I shake my head.

"I don't have many people to invite. I say we do a small ceremony somewhere and then take a honeymoon before I leave in May for New York," I suggest.

"I think that's perfect," he says, leaning over and kissing me tenderly. "Also, I haven't told you this yet, but I've decided to take the next year off. At least not signing onto any new projects to film next year. I just want to be with you and Brooklyn right now. I wanted to take a break anyways, but after the last couple of months, I think this is the right move for me. I'll still have some contractual things to take care of with this film, but nothing that will pull me away for long stretches of time. When you go to New York, I want us to go with you. Since you're shooting in the summer it won't be a lot for us to come with you. Would you mind?"

"Are you kidding? This is the best news ever. I love that. I can't wait to see your place in New York," I add as he smiles knowingly in my direction.

"You mean our place?" he says. He's right, this will be my place too.

"I'm going to have to get used to that. But yes, on one condition," I add.

"Anything, Ava," he adds, and I smile back knowingly at him. He looks at me warily and I giggle.

"You can no longer pay me to be here," I say as he frowns.

"What do you mean?" he asks, and I smile sarcastically at him.

"My salary. All of that money. I can't accept money from you, Clark. Have Brian stop the deposits. It's a little weird to pay your fiancé to watch your child."

"Okay. You do know that we will be sharing a bank account when we get married though, correct?" he asks, smiling slyly at me. "So while you won't be getting a salary, you'll have access to more money. Because it will be OUR MONEY," he leans in and whispers conspiratorially against my lips. "But yes. I will have Brian cancel all of that. But it's semantics, Ava, because while you think you are one-upping me, you actually have access to everything. What's mine is yours, and I plan to put your name on everything. The houses, the cars, the accounts. Everything," he says, and I sit up ready to give him hell. "And before you get all defensive. I know you don't care about those things. I know you care about me. I'd sign everything over to you tonight, regardless if we were married or not. I'm glad we are having this conversation now though. You need to prepare yourself for it. Be prepared to be spoiled. I've said it numerous times in hopes that you'll get used to it, but I'll say it again, Ava. Everything that is mine is yours."

"Fine," I say reluctantly. "April?" I ask.

"April, baby," he says, kissing me so passionately that it knocks me on my back. He pulls away after a few long seconds and stares down in awe at me. "What do you want to do with your townhouse? Obviously you can keep it. Don't sell it on my account. I think it's a great place," he adds, and I shake my head.

"Doesn't feel like home. I'll sell it. As well as my old car. I'm assuming you are allowing me to keep my 'nanny-mobile?'" I ask, and he laughs.

"Hell yes, you are keeping it. If you want to trade it in for something else, do it. I think you look sexy as hell in that car, though. In fact, I test drove the black one in that class and loved it. We could be twins! I might still want a Tesla though," he says, thinking out loud and then remembers himself. "I'm not sure. Haven't gotten that far. But yes, please sell your old car. Or donate it to the church, whatever you want. The credit card I gave you is more for business purchases not personal purchases, so I'm going to have the bank add you to my personal accounts. I'd love for anything you want or need to come out of our account. You are welcome to open your own account if you'd like with your earnings and income from projects. I know you also have a trust fund from your grandmother's estate. Whatever you want to do that is fine with me."

"What's mine is yours, Clark," I say, and he rolls his eyes.

"Good grief, woman," he says, kissing me. "Fine. No separate accounts. Touché."

"Great," I say, feeling like I won the argument, but at the same time I know he's right. I went from a six-digit yearly salary, to millions of dollars or more, bank account. I don't even know how much money he has.

"What is it?" he asks with a wary smile on his face.

"I don't even know how much money you have," I ask, and he laughs. "Sorry. That came out wrong. It's not anything I ever really cared to know. It feels weird to even talk about, but I know you have a lot of money. It would be absurd to think you weren't well off. I just don't know."

"You don't have to worry about money. OR real estate investments. Or anything else," he says, looking over at me. "If you want me to have our investments guy pull up a round number for you on where we are financially, I can have them do that," he says, grinning at me. He's kidding, but I still slap his chest. "We can sit down in the New Year and go over that. I'll say this… the next couple generations of Grants won't have to worry about their finances."

"Don't be ridiculous. I don't even really need to know right now," I say, and he laughs. "I merely asked because there are things I still don't know about you. I know we will learn more about each other as we go. I know how generous you are. You give a lot of money to different charities and organizations, but I don't know everything yet. I'm not worried about it. I just want to know you. I want to know all the things."

"We will. We have time. While I do give a lot of money away, it's because I feel like I have a responsibility to give back. To whom much is given, much is expected," he says and I smile proudly at him. He's not just putting up a front. He's serious, and I love him for it. He's the best kind of human. "Do you want to know anything else?" he asks.

"Actually, yes," I say as I grab the remote. "What Christmas movie are we watching tonight?" He calls Brooklyn up to the sofa and she climbs in between us, smiling as we turn on ELF. Something light-hearted and funny. Perfect. We all snuggle into the couch, and I look down at my hand smiling. If this was a movie or a TV show it would pan out right here and then fade to the credits with Happily Ever After written across the screen. I squeeze Brooklyn a little and she giggles, leaning back into me. Clark looks over at the two of us smiling and I smile back.

"Are you guys going to have a baby now?" Brooklyn asks loudly. Clark and I both look at her simultaneously and then up at each other holding in a laugh. "Do I get to choose if I want a brother or a sister? How does that work?" I cover my mouth, about to laugh and he glares at me.

Clark

This is exactly the kind of moment when Brooklyn would show up in all her glory! I give Ava a warning look to not laugh, but then find myself laughing as well. Here's the thing. I don't know if Ava wants to have a baby or not. I don't really have an opinion on it. If she didn't, that would be fine with me. If she did, we'd need to figure out what she wanted to do. I'd love to have a baby with Ava, but she did just sign on to do a movie. I'm not young per se, but I'm also not that old. Brooklyn looks up at me expectantly and I smile.

"I think Ava and I need to talk about that first, Brookie," I answer, and she shrugs her shoulders nonchalantly.

"Okay," she says, unaffected by my answer,

and goes back to watching the movie. We settle back down to watch, but I can't concentrate on the movie now. I shouldn't be so side-tracked by this, but I keep wondering how I didn't ask this before. I guess Ava is right, there are a lot of things we haven't discussed. This is one of those things you probably should discuss though. I would be happy either way. It's not necessarily a discussion about finances or space. The thought of Ava and I creating something together would be a beautiful thing. But we also have each other and Brooklyn. We are already a family. We both have careers. Ava just booked her first major motion picture. They haven't started shooting yet, but I don't know. I guess I could take this topic in a lot of different directions.

The next thing I know, Ava is pausing the movie and I turn to look her. Brooklyn is asleep so I pick her up and we both take her upstairs. We tuck her in, and Ava leans over, kissing her forehead.

"Merry Christmas, Angel," Ava whispers. She tucks Brooklyn in, and I fall even more in love with her, if that's even possible. This is why I fell for her in the first place. The way she loves so deeply and so effortlessly is such a gift to us. I lean over and kiss Brooklyn as well. I turn off the lights as we head downstairs. I grab Ava's hand, pull her into me and kiss her hard.

"Merry Christmas, my beautiful fiancée'," I

whisper and she beams.

"Merry Christmas, my beautiful fiancé," she says back to me. She lifts up on the tips of her toes and wraps her arms around my neck, kissing me deeply, then reaching under my shirt. Her hands are so cold that it makes me gasp. She tries to pull her hands away, but I press her hands against my chest, warming them against me.

"Don't stop touching me," I say, pulling her towards me. I back us up so we land on the sofa. Then grab her legs so she's straddling me.

"I want to sleep naked with you tonight," she says against my lips, and I groan.

"I want that too," I whisper as we pull apart. "But no funny business," I add sarcastically, making her giggle.

"I promise to be on my best behavior," she says, smiling up at me as I pull her to my side.

"It's not you I worry about, Ava, it's me. I want to make sure we're ready. We only have four months until we get married. If we start sleeping naked together, and you touch me like you do, I'm gonna have a hard time controlling myself. I'm not saying I can't. I'm just saying it will be a testament of will." I kiss her gently. "I love that you trust me. I don't want to give you a reason not to."

"I trust you, Clark, and if something happened it wouldn't be on you. You're my fiancé now. Yes, I do want to wait to have sex until we get married, but I also want to touch all of you. We can make it another couple months. I just want a little more of you," she says.

"I want more of you too, Angel," I say as I pick up our cups and take them to the kitchen. We head into the bedroom, and I smile over at her as she stands by the bed. "What do you want, Ava?" I ask as I pull my shirt off, tossing it on the chair in the corner of the room.

"I wanted to do that. Like another Christmas present for me to unwrap." We both laugh as she fake pouts. Then she smiles at me as I walk over and wrap my arms around her.

"Then you may open one more present tonight," I say against her lips. "You get this forever, baby," I add. "There's no rush!"

"I know, but I still want to see all of you," she says. "And I want you to see all of me."

"Damn, Ava," I whisper as she reaches for me and I take a step back. "Ava, do you trust me?" I ask as I grab her hand. "I mean really trust me?" She stops in front of me, sitting on the bed.

"With my life. I wouldn't be marrying you in a couple of months if I didn't," she whispers, looking into my eyes. I kneel in front of her, smiling. "On your knees again?" she asks. I untie her sleep pants and then pull her so she's standing directly in front of me. I pull her pants down slowly, not taking my eyes off hers. I stand up and pull her shirt off gently. I pull the straps of her sleep bra off her shoulders and kiss the marks they left. I gently peel the bra over her head and now she's standing in front of me completely naked. She looks a little nervous. She starts to look down, but I pull her to me. I lift her chin, smiling down at her as I kiss her lips tenderly.

"You are so beautiful. Please don't be nervous. You have an incredible body, Ava. I wanted to see all of you as well," I whisper as I run my hands up the side of her body until I reach her face. I gently crawl on the bed with her and then lay her down beside me. "Are you okay?" I ask, my breathing becoming a little shallow. She nods. I kiss her gently on the lips and make sure that she's still with me. "Do you want me to touch you?" I ask, and she breathes out a *YES*. I swallow hard and smile down at her. Turning on my side so I'm lying next to her, I lightly run my hand against her cheek, and then let my hand gently slide down to caress her elegant neck and over her collarbone. I'm holding all of my weight on one elbow so I can watch her, all of her. She's watching me as I touch her, and I can tell that she's just as affected as I am. I continue my path down her body and as my hand lightly runs between her breasts. I can feel her heart beating beneath my fingers. I lean down and place a gentle kiss between her breasts. Leaning back up, I kiss her lips softly as my hand runs over the swell of her breast. I let my hand completely cover her breast and then move to the other breast as she starts to move a little under my touch. She moans into my mouth, and I let my hand gently stroke one breast and then move to the other.

"Yes, Clark. Please don't stop," she whimpers as my hand moves down to her stomach. Slowly my hand moves lower, running smoothly over her pubic bone and then between her legs to her sex. She whimpers as I move, gently stroking my hand between her legs. Her back bows off of the bed and I can tell it won't be long before my beautiful Ava finds her climax. I lean over, continuing to gently caress her so I can watch her. Her eyes are blazing when they meet mine. The pull between us is so strong. She closes her eyes and I kiss below her ear, down her neck, and over her collar bone. She's whimpering louder as I move to kiss gently between her breasts, my finger slipping gently inside her sex. She's so incredibly tight, so I start with only one finger, then gradually move to two. I pull one nipple into my mouth and then the other as she cries out, finding her finish. She lies weightless and panting, trying to control her breathing. I continue to kiss down her body, stopping at her pubic bone and then back up. I kiss her tenderly on her soft lips and then both of her closed eye lids.

"Open your eyes, beautiful," I whisper against her lips. She opens her eyes, and my sweet girl looks completely sated. "How was that?" I ask and she smiles, giggling a little self-consciously. She rolls toward me, trying to hide her face and I laugh. "Oh no, you don't," I say, moving her so I can see her face.

"That was amazing," she says, beaming at me. I kiss her gently and pull her next to me. "I'm going to run to the bathroom real quick and then I want to touch you," she says, and I shake my head.

"Baby, I'm fine. That was a treat for me too, you know," I add as she climbs off the bed. I notice she doesn't cover herself, which makes me proud that she's comfortable with me seeing her body. She closes the door and I roll over to my back, releasing the breath I was holding. That was amazing. God, I love my life. She opens the door again and walks back over to me, smiling.

"I want to touch you, Clark," she says a little shyly. I grab her hand and pull her onto the bed.

"Okay. But first you need to know this isn't a tit for tat kind of situation with us, Ava. That's not how I operate. I don't want you to ever do something because you think it's 'my turn,' or you think I want something from you. I'm not that kind of guy, and we aren't going to have that kind of relationship. We are getting to know each other. Just like we are getting to know each other's bodies better. I enjoyed the hell out of that, Ava. Watching you fall apart under my touch. My god, I can't tell you how absolutely stunning that was. I could do that all day, Ava," I say as she blushes. "That was one of the sexiest moments of my entire life. I've never had a more intimate moment with someone." She looks down and I lift her chin so she's looking at me. "I'm serious. There's a difference in having a one-night stand with someone and when your main goal is to watch the woman you love come alive under your touch because it's what you both want. When it isn't about you and it's about the other person's pleasure. I've never been more turned on in my entire life, Ava. We have the rest of our lives to explore each other's bodies and we will. You can be damn sure about that. It's going to be very hard to not touch you after this, Ava. When I close my eyes, I can still see you coming apart. The sounds you make, the way your body feels, the taste of your skin on my lips." She rolls into me, still naked and wraps her leg around mine, kissing me hard. I groan, kissing her back with everything I have to give. I roll on top of her and slowly grind my hips onto her and hear her gasp. I lean up on my elbows smiling down at her. "We have forever, Ava," I add, kissing her and rolling over onto my side of the bed with her still in my arms. I turn the lights off and she giggles.

She moves her hand lower so that it's under the band of my pants and resting on my ass. What was funny before is no longer funny. "Looking for something?" I ask as I slowly roll on top of her and kiss her gently on the lips.

"No. Nothing specifically. Just wanting to touch you," she says, and I smile against her lips as her other hand slowly runs down my back joining her other hand on my other ass cheek. "Let me touch you. Please."

"I love your hands on me, Ava," I whisper as I roll onto my back so she's straddling me. "Touch me, baby."

Ava

"Touch me, baby," he says as I place both hands on his chest after he rolls over. I lean down, kissing him and he places both of his hands on my legs, gently rubbing circles on the inside of my thighs with his thumbs. I kiss his neck, down his chest and over his heart, feeling it beat fast under my lips. I place both hands on the side of his hips, moving down the bed to have better access to his body. "AVA," he warns, and I smile, continuing to kiss my way down his stomach, across one hip and then to the other. His stomach is hard as a rock under my lips, and I wonder how hard all of his body will be. I mean I can see he's hard everywhere, and I do mean EVERYWHERE, and a lot larger than I anticipated.

I kiss every muscle of his stomach, down the delicious V of his hips and then look up at him. He's smiling, shaking his head. "Don't do it," he adds, laughing at me, and I smile. I lean down, placing a gentle kiss over his sweatpants, feeling the hardness that is straining against his clothes. He groans and I start to kiss up his body as I feel him start to relax. He wants us to take our time, but I have to touch all of him. As I reach his lips, I kiss him hard like he did to me and then reach under the waistband of his pants to grab HIM lightly, but confidently. He groans again against my lips as I gently run my hand up and down him. He places a hand over mine, steadying me. I continue my assault on his mouth as he rolls us over, my hands naturally falling off of his body. He grabs my hands, pulling them over my head as he kisses up and down my neck to my breasts and then back up again. As he is loving my body, I wriggle beneath him as he holds both of my wrist in one of his hands and runs the other hand in between us, touching all of me. I whimper, not able to think straight and then he covers my mouth with kisses again.

"It's hard to think when you touch me, Ava," he says panting against my lips. "How about you?" he asks as I groan.

"What?" I ask, and he laughs.

"Exactly. Okay baby, you got to touch me," he says, rolling over onto his side and propping his arm under his head.

"I wanted to touch you for longer." Rolling onto my side as well, I look deep into his deep, dark, blue eyes. "Why didn't you let me," I ask, and he leans over, kissing me on the nose.

"Baby, I wanted you to continue touching me. It's really hard for me to control myself when you are touching me like that, though. When you're kissing me like that, when you're making the sounds you were making," he says with a groan. "I love you, Ava. It'd be so easy to take this across the finish line with you, but I want to savor every moment. I want to make sure you are ready. I want your body to be ready for me, sure, but I want your mind and your soul to be ready too. I want to possess all of you. Not because you're mine to possess, but because it will be so much better that way," he adds, running a thumb over my lips. "Please trust me. Merry Christmas, angel," he whispers, smiling at me. I smile back, knowing he's right. Knowing we want all the same things and we DO have time. It will be much more enjoyable for the two of us if we take our time and he's not having to question whether or not I'm ready for that next step.

"I love you," I say as he rolls us over so we are cuddling front to back.

"I love you too, angel."

The next morning I wake up to an empty bed. I look down at my hand and see my gorgeous engagement ring. I smile thinking about everything that's transpired in the last 24 hours. I'm the luckiest freaking woman in the world. Clark Grant is my fiancé and he loved on me so well last night. God, what a night. I sit up, putting on my pajamas and heading to brush my teeth. Thinking back on last night, even though I was naked, Clark was a gentleman while we slept. He gently rubbed his hand up and down my hip and kept me close to him all night. At one point I woke up and his hand was gently wrapped around my waist, his thumb caressing over my ribs. Clark is an easy guy to cuddle with. Not only is his body pure perfection, but the man beneath the body is perfect too. I head to the kitchen and see Clark and Brooklyn sitting on the couch. I'm a little disappointed he didn't wake me when he got up, but Brooklyn is still waking up and playing with her baby from last night.

"Merry Christmas everyone," I say groggily as I walk into the den.

"YAY! Can we do presents now?" Brooklyn asks now that I'm awake. "Daddy wouldn't let me check my stocking or see what Santa brought until you were up," she adds, disappointed, and I laugh.

"Mean ole daddy," I say, leaning down and kissing Clark. He rolls his eyes at my comment. He pulls me into his lap as we watch Brooklyn open her presents from Santa and her stocking. He kisses the side of my neck and I look at him with a warning glare. "Easy Casanova," I say against his lips as I get up to make a cup of tea. Brooklyn is showing Clark all of the toys from Santa, and he does a great job of acting surprised. I giggle to myself as I turn around and see Clark watching me. I lean against the kitchen counter, smiling back at him. He looks so happy. I'm happy too. He's empowering me to be the woman I always wanted to be. I mean I have him, I have a career doing what I love, I have Brooklyn. Through him I have a family now. Clayton, Marco and Brooklyn. I'm safe here. He turns back to Brooklyn, who needs him to open something. So he just tears the box open. I laugh that he didn't get up and open the box with a knife. What an animal. He's just perfect. He stands up, coming into the kitchen, placing a hand on either side of the counter, boxing me in. He leans down to kiss me.

"Good morning, fiancée. Did you sleep well?" he asks, and I smile up at him. "I did, in case you are wondering, baby."

"I did too. I'm a little overwhelmed by all these feelings, if I'm being honest."

"I know how you feel. I thought a lot about it

yesterday, last night specifically. Touching you was the highlight of my year, Ava. I'm not even kidding. The highlight of my life is that you're still wearing my ring this morning," he says, pulling my hand up to his lips and kissing it.

"This ole thing?" I joke, smiling up at him as he kisses my ring and then places my hand against his heart.

"You still love it?" He asks as he presses his hand over my hand that's resting on his heart. I can feel his heart beating under my hand and I feel emotions bubbling up. I roll my eyes at him though.

"My god, Clark what isn't there to love? It's flawless. It looks like it should be in a museum. I'm going to have to be careful whirling this thing around. I could do some serious damage with this rock on my hand."

"You ready to open your other presents?" he asks, and I look down at the front of his pants as I take a sip of my tea. He laughs, shaking his head at me, then kisses me on the forehead. We walk hand in hand into the den and I sit on the couch as he grabs the presents. He starts distributing them, and I think he's a little shocked that he has a good number of presents as well. I'm sure he's not used to that, but things will be different now. He's so used to taking care of everyone else, but I want to be there to take care of him too. Clark starts to open his presents and smiles at the ones from Brooklyn.

She picked them out and I can tell he cherishes every one of them. I open my presents from Brooklyn first since she's so excited about them. One that makes me tear up is a set of matching outfits that she and I can wear together, specifically some matching pajamas. I tear up, giving her a hug, and she jumps up and down. I adore this sweet girl. I can't wait to spend the rest of my life helping take care of her and raising her alongside Clark.

Clark places a large box next to me and I smile at him. It's so heavy. I put the box on the ottoman. "I swear, Clark, if this is jewelry I am going to spank you!" I say under my breath so only he can hear me. He spits out a little of his coffee, laughing, and then sits back watching me with a huge grin on his face. I rip the wrapping paper off and see that it's a large white wooden jewelry box. It's beautiful. I mean stunning. Clark helps me pull it out of the box and I have no words. I don't think I'll ever have enough jewelry in my lifetime to fill it, but I know Clark will do his best. I walk over, kissing him and thanking him.

"I thought you might need that," he says. I give him a sarcastic glare that says 'I'm sure.' "You've got more," he says, motioning to my pile of presents and I shake my head.

"Your turn. You haven't opened those three from me," I say as he grabs the first box. It's light and I smile.

"Guess it's not diamonds," he says laughing. He opens the box and it's a piece of paper. It's a confirmation page and itinerary for a flight in 3 weeks to go visit his parents outside of London. He looks over at me with tears in his eyes. He stands up, smiling at me, and picks me up, squeezing me hard. "Baby, that's so thoughtful. Thank you," he whispers in my ear.

"You're welcome. Your mom and I talked while she was in town. I know your dad isn't doing well. So I wanted you to be able to go spend time with him while you can. Brooklyn and I can go or you can go on your own. Depending on how your dad is feeling. It's up to you," I say and he nods, wiping a tear away. It's not that Clark couldn't book that on his own. He certainly can. It's that I cleared his schedule for him with Brian and Clayton so he can go and spend time with his family. He grabs another present and takes a deep breath. The next box is a new designer trench coat for winter that Clayton and Marco said hasn't even hit stores yet. He's impressed. "I imagine visiting London in January that'll come in handy," he says, nodding towards the trench coat. "Thank you, Ava," he says, smiling again and picking up the last box. He opens the small ring box and looks up at me in shock. It's a gold signet ring with his family crest on it. He leans back against the chair he's in and looks at me, stunned.

"Ava," he whispers, and I stand up, walking over to him. I take the ring out of the box and slip it on the pinky of his left hand. I lift his hand up and kiss it gently. He pulls me in his lap, wrapping me in his arms. "God, Ava. I don't think we'll ever top this Christmas," he says, whispering down into my hair as his lips press kisses against the side of my head. I roll over so I can wrap my arms around his neck.

"Next Christmas I'll be your wife," I whisper, and he beams down at me.

"Good point, angel!" We just sit for a moment looking into each other's eyes. "I imagine every single day going forward will be the most magical time on Earth."

He stands up with me in his lap and grabs the remaining boxes that were next to me on the sofa, putting them next to him. He hands me a small box, about the same size of the box my engagement ring was in, and I turn around as he laughs. "Just open the damn box, Ava." I tear the paper off to the sounds of him laughing behind me and see it's from the same jeweler. I open it and it's a necklace. The same design as my engagement ring and my earrings. Except that the gems are the same size as my earrings. It's honestly perfect. The diamond in the center with small diamonds around it is so classy. I lean back, pulling his head to mine so I can kiss him.

"Thank you," I say as I take the necklace out of the box and have him clasp the back. It hangs just below my throat and it's gorgeous. He then hands me another box. This one is the size of an iPad and I smile. I bet he bought me an iPad. I smile at him, and he beams back conspiratorially. "iPad?" I ask confidently and he shakes his head. I stop smiling. I rip the paper off and it's a large box with the same jeweler's name on the front. I open it, gasp and then close it. "This better be costume jewelry, Grant!" I say turning to him. He sits back, smiling knowingly at me. I open it again, seeing the diamond necklace with an emerald hanging tear drop style in the center with matching emerald and diamond earrings. I touch the gems and feel like I'm going to pass out. This is insane. "You are nuts, Clark," I say, turning in his lap to face him. "My nut!" I laugh.

"Relax baby, they are insured, and they will go beautifully with the gowns Marco designed. Also, they match your beautiful eyes," he says, kissing me chastely before leaning back in his chair.

"Clark, they're too much. But you already knew that I'd react this way," I add, smiling. I release the breath I'm holding and look at him. "Thank you. They are crazy, but also so beautiful," I say, closing the box. "These should be in a safe somewhere, and not in a jewelry box," I say, and he nods.

"They can go in the safe in the closet. I promise you, Ava, I plan to buy you enough fun stuff for your jewelry box too. This will go in the safe as well," he says, handing me another small box. I drop my head against his chest and he laughs. This is becoming a thing with him. I think he likes my reaction more than anything else. I open the box and it's a matching emerald and diamond ring. The emerald shining back at me is stunning. The lights from the Christmas tree reflect off of it like a mirror. "It's a set, Ava," he says as he wraps him arms around me. "They go with the other emerald and diamond jewelry pieces."

"Thank you, Clark," I say, sitting up a little warily. Most women would kill for these kinds of gifts. I'm just not used to it. I've never received jewelry in my life. Nor have I been the recipient of anything so grand in my entire life. This kind of treatment will take some getting used to. "I love you. Now, let's lock up these gems and find a fun movie to watch."

Brooklyn FaceTimes with her grandparents as Clark and I clean up around the den. The evening comes and goes, and our steaks were amazing. Clark can really grill a steak well. We are sitting on the edge of the bed getting ready for bed, talking, when my phone rings. It's Shanna. I sent her a photo of me wearing my engagement ring Christmas Eve, but I haven't talked to her today.

"Merry Christmas," I say as she jumps right

into giving me the business about letting Clark post the photo on his IG before I did. I laugh at her, but she's serious. Last night Clark and I took a romantic photo of us with my engagement ring in the photo, and it was quite a popular post. He's getting better at the whole Instagram thing. "Who cares, Shanna. I will post something soon. I'm not worried about it."

"Yeah. But you need to be capitalizing on this. This is monumental, Ava. The movie announcement will go out in a couple weeks, and we need material to keep your followers entertained. I'm already working alongside the studio for some publicity photos and some magazine articles. It's gonna be a great year, but you need stay on top of all this. I'll be in touch after the first of the year, but I wanted to tell you that Mom, Dad and I are super excited for you. Our company is so proud to represent you," she says, and I look at Clark, who's watching me, smiling warily. He gives me a thumbs up, asking me if everything is okay and I nod.

"Thanks, Shanna. Have a wonderful Christmas and New Year's. I'll see you next year," I say and she laughs.

"We will be seeing a lot of each other, girl. You're gonna be a STAR!" she says with an old Hollywood flare as she hangs up. I laugh, replaying the conversation with Shanna to Clark. He sits on the edge of the bed and takes my hand.

"You're already a star, Ava. Don't let the industry make you think they made you one. They are just appreciating what we already know. If you let them believe they made you a star, then that means they can take that away from you. And they can't."

"Thank you, baby," I whisper as he lifts me up, placing me in bed. "I'm so stuffed from dinner. You're a great griller, Grant" I say as I curl up under the covers next to Clark. His warm chest feels so strong under me and I'm grateful.

"Ava. I forgot to ask you about this last night. With all the touching and kissing. I got a little distracted. But I do want to know something," he asks, and I roll over to face him. I place my chin on his chest and he rubs a hand down my hair and then back up. "Do you want to have kids?"

Clark

She sits up next to me and I take her hand. She looks down at her hands and I place one of mine over hers. I turn her hand over, running my finger over her palm. She looks up at me and I smile. "Whatever you want, Ava, I'm fine with. I have you and I have Brooklyn. IF you don't want kids, I don't feel like we need anything more. I'll be content with it just being the three of us. IF you do want kids, I'll be thrilled as well. I'm in a place in my life where we can go either way. It's really up to you, angel."

"I don't know. I mean, I didn't really give it much thought to be honest. I didn't think I would find anyone that would make me feel the way you make me feel, so I didn't think I would ever get married. And kids? My gosh, that wasn't ever something I thought was in the cards for me."

"We don't have to decide right now. I just want you to know that either way, I'm here with you," I say, lifting her chin up. "I love you. You and Brooklyn are enough. I don't want anything more from you unless it's something you want, too. So please hear me when I say -- if you don't know, that's okay too. We can cross that bridge when we get there. Hell, we aren't even having sex yet," I say with a small chuckle. "However, I want to be there to support you. I want to be there if you want to process it. You aren't alone in this decision. This year will be busy enough for you with your movie, a wedding, and any other roles you want to pursue. So it's not like I feel like you need more on your plate. But please hear me say, you will not be alone in this decision, either way."

"I don't want to be on birth control. I'll say that," she adds and I nod. Interesting.

"There are other ways of being careful," I say, smiling and she blushes. "You and I will need to be on the same page though. I'm sure you already know your body pretty well, but we can track it together if you want," I say, not wanting to push. "You know, when you're ovulating and on your periods."

"I agree. I'm pretty in tune with my body. I know friends in the past have had an app to keep up with their periods and ovulation. I'm pretty regular. So," she says trailing off and I smile at her.

"You're sweet as hell, Ava. It's amazing that someone so sweet can also be as sexy as you are. It's your body, Ava, but I want you to know you aren't alone here. Ever!"

"Thank you," she says, cuddling up to me. "When I know, you'll know. Until then let's just go with maybe? I know I'm not opposed to having kids. I think I just need to figure out how soon. I know you're never fully prepared to be a parent, but it is nice to know I have a partner in this. Someone to help me as we figure these things out."

"I am always here, Ava," I say, turning off the light and kissing her forehead.

It's Clayton and Marco's Big Day. I'm completely stoked for the two of them and their journey here. I smile as Clayton and Marco say, *I DO!* Looking over at Ava, I wink and she blushes. She looks beautiful in her red chiffon dress with a faux fur stole over her shoulders. Marco's doing, of course. My darlings will never be out of style as long as Marco and Clayton are around. It is sunset and the sky is a perfect pink, purple and orange for their "Kiss the groom" moment. We all cheer and then the two of them walk hand in hand up the aisle toward the back of the yard. The reception is both inside and down in the yard under heaters for those that want the full reception experience. The large tent we have set up is big enough for tables, chairs and a dance floor. Clayton and Marco invited around 100 people, so it's a pretty great evening. I pull Ava to my side as we head to the dance floor after Marco and Clayton's first dance.

"You look beautiful, Ava," I whisper as I pull her close and she leans her head on my chest. "In a couple months we will be having our first dance as husband and wife." She looks up at me beaming, and I'm in awe of how breathtakingly beautiful my sweet angel is. "It's all I could think about during the ceremony. You're all I can think about."

"Same. I can't wait, Clark. I know it's only four months away and it'll fly by, but I'm so excited." I lean down as she lifts up on her toes and kisses me gently. The song ends before we know it and Clayton pulls her away from me so they can dance together. I laugh at the two of them dancing as the DJ starts to play some 90's pop songs. I stand back and watch them as people come and congratulate me on the engagement.

We put Brooklyn down a little before midnight. Ava and I hang close to the house so we can keep an eye on her since we have people inside the house. People normally won't venture upstairs, but we don't take any chances. I have Brooklyn's monitor in my pocket as we socialize with those inside the house. People crowd around the TV inside as we prepare to watch the ball drop. I turn to watch Ava and thank God for her. I wave her over to me and pull her to my side when she approaches. I lean down, kissing her before the count down even begins. We are still kissing after the ball has dropped. It isn't until a buddy of mine yells for us to get a room that I flick him off and continue to kiss my gorgeous fiancée.

"Happy New Year, Ava," I say against her lips as she smiles up at me, contentedly. I feel the same way after kissing her.

"Happy New Year, Clark. I can't wait for what this year brings."

Ava goes to bed a little after 1:00. There are still about fifteen people in the tent dancing and carrying on. I know I don't have to stay up, but when you have people at your house it feels strange to go to bed when they're still milling around. I head down to the tent and see that Clayton and Marco are still dancing in each other's arms. They're smiling and staring deep into each other's eyes. I stop, smiling at them. I'm so damn happy for them. They are my people. The catering crew and most of the guest are now leaving. I smile as a couple passes me, thanking me for a great New Year's Party. It's almost 2 a.m. now and I sit down to get off my feet for a minute. The song ends as Clayton and Marco walk towards me. I give them a hug and they head out to their waiting Town Car. They didn't want a big exit, which was not expected. They wanted a laid-back reception and that's exactly what they got. The DJ packs up and then it's just me picking up some cups and dropping them in the garbage. I have a crew coming tomorrow afternoon to clean everything up, but it's still my house. I turn around and Ava is standing there watching me, wrapped up in a blanket. I smile at her she walks towards me. I grab my phone, turning on some Etta James and then I reach for her hand.

"Dance with me," I say as she puts Brooklyn's monitor on one of the tables. I hold her in my arms and she lifts up to kiss me. I pick her up and she wraps her arms, legs and blanket around me. I hold her and the blanket around us as I kiss her with the passion of a starving man. She pulls my hair and I groan into her mouth. I'm not sure how long the song has been over, but she pulls back catching her breath. I smile at her as she tears up. "What's wrong, angel?"

"I'm just so damn happy," she whispers, and I nod in agreement, kissing her gently.

"Me too, baby. Me too," I add as I carry her up the path to the house. "Let's go to bed."

Ava

Clark left early this morning to do some re-shoots and interviews in Vancouver. He's only supposed to be gone three days. Then he'll be back to drop Clayton off in LA and pick up Brooklyn and I to head to London to visit with his family. He got an update from his mum that his dad wasn't doing well. He was originally going to leave at the end of January, but now there's a change of plans. His team was happy to work around. We are only two weeks into January and Brooklyn's first full week back to school. She's so happy to be back. I think she was bored with Clark and I at the house. I went to a Pilates class and lunch with Shanna to discuss the next couple months. I've missed my Pilates classes. When I was in New York I was taking a mat class twice a week. Now I'm lucky if I get one in. Everything seems to be falling into place, which I'm completely stoked about. As we were leaving, I did notice a couple of photographers take a photo, mainly aimed at my left hand. Shanna is unaffected by the attention, welcomes it almost. However, it does put me a little on edge. We never figured out what the deal was with the guys following me months back, but they stopped a little before Christmas. It's no longer a concern of ours.

When I pick up Brooklyn from school, her teacher tells me she's been acting a little more tired than normal today. I put her in the car and she immediately falls asleep. By the time I pull into the garage, she's starting to feel a little warm. I take her temp and it's already at 102. I change her out of her school clothes, running her a lukewarm bath and then change her into her favorite pajamas. Before putting her to bed, I head downstairs and grab a cup of juice and put it by her bed while calling her pediatrician. We make an appointment for the next morning. I pray that all she needs is some rest and it's only a 24 hour virus. I text Clark that Brooklyn isn't feeling well and I'll keep him posted. I go downstairs to make some of Clark's Chicken Soup and clean up her bag from school. By supper time Brooklyn still isn't up so I go in her room and she's burning up. I take her temperature again and it's 103. I call the pediatrician and they ask me to go ahead and bring her in. I wake her up and strap her into her car seat before heading to the doctor.

THE FLU! Poor baby girl. She's complaining that her body hurts so bad and since we caught it early, they were able to get her the medication she needs to hopefully shorten her time sick. I pick up her prescription and then head back to the house. I sit her on the couch and feed her some soup. After she has something in her stomach, I give her the first dose of medicine. She's a little dehydrated, but I think she's hanging in there. I have no symptoms so far but I'm not sure how long that will last.

By day three she's doing a lot better but is not completely well. She still has a cough, but her body aches and fever are gone. Clark is worried but I tell him not to come home. He doesn't need to get this, especially if he wants to go visit his dad. This isn't a trip with his parents that he can just reschedule. Time with his dad is running out, and fast. Clayton flies home and Clark heads to London to visit with his dad. I promised him I would let him know if anything changed. Brooklyn talked to her dad every day and seeing his concern for her is the most heart-wrenching experience to watch. I know he wants to be here with us, but he really needs to be with his dad.

By the next week Clark's father has passed on. Clark said he passed away in his sleep and while he's devastated that his father is gone, he's so glad he's no longer suffering and in pain. His dad didn't want a memorial service or funeral, just to go without a fuss and people knowing he lived a good life. After a few days with his mom, Clark comes back to LA. We pick him up from the airport and head to the house. He's in good spirits but I'm sure he's putting on a brave face for Brooklyn.

When we get home, we head to grab some dinner at a nearby restaurant. On our way out, people stop Clark to let him know how sorry they are for his loss. By the time we get home he's a little distraught. I go get Brooklyn ready for bed. She's a little cranky, but I think she's had a rough week as well. Recovering from the flu can be tough on anyone. After she's down I head into the bedroom and see Clark putting his clothes away. I come over and we silently put his clean clothes away and put his dirty clothes in the hamper. I take his hand afterwards and kiss his palm gently. He looks exhausted and I want to give him space but let him know I'm here. He leans over, kissing me on the head and then walks out of the closet. I release the breath I'm holding and turn off the closet light. When I step into our bedroom he's sitting on the edge of the bed. I walk in front of him, and he wraps his arms around my waist. I press his head gently against my stomach. He starts to cry, and I whisper that it's okay. After a few minutes he sits back and looks up at me. The look in his eyes breaks my heart.

"Baby. I'm so sorry!" I whisper and he nods.

"Me too. I'm so glad he's not suffering anymore, but I miss him like hell! He was an amazing man!" he whispers back and I pull him against me again.

"I know. I'm so sorry!" I add and we stay there for a few minutes. We eventually crawl into bed. Clark holds me close to him. I'm glad I can give him this. There's not a whole lot I can do or say to make this better. But I can do this!

I wake up and Clark isn't in bed. I look over at the clock. It is after 1:00 a.m. I head into the kitchen where Clark is on a Zoom call. He looks over at me smiling and then wraps up his conversation. "Sounds good, Brian. Keep me updated on that. I agree that would be the opportunity of a lifetime." He hangs up, smiling at me and gets up to pull me in front of him. I don't know what I'm looking at, but then I see the name on the script.

"BOND?" I ask and he laughs.

"Yes, Bond. They want me to come in and read for it. It doesn't shoot for another 18 months, so I can still take this year off. I told Brian I would be interested in looking into it for sure. I wanted to run it by you and see what your thoughts were," he adds, and I roll my eyes.

"Please tell me you're kidding," I say, and he shakes his head. "Of course you can do whatever project you want. You don't need my permission. Also, why have this conversation so early?"

"Brian. He's a night owl. I told him I was good to catch up now. He's been at an event." Clark answers and I shake my head. "Also, I'm not asking your permission, per se, Ava. I'm wanting to start a conversation with you about something that could possibly happen. Would you talk to me about a project you were going to audition for?" he asks.

"Well, I didn't give you the specifics of the last one, but I did talk to you about it."

A few weeks later we are heading to a gala that was supposed to be around Christmas, but with the death of Kyle Wright they pushed it back. My hair is in loose waves around my shoulders and I'm wearing my emerald satin dress and my matching emerald and diamond set. To say I'm decked out in all my diamonds is an understatement.

"You're dripping in diamonds, darling!" Clayton says as he zips up the back of my dress.

Clark walks into the bedroom and stops dead in his tracks, looking me up and down. The way he's looking at me you'd think the paint would peel straight off the wall. It's starting to get incredibly hot in our bedroom.

"Jesus, Ava," he says, his hand resting over his heart. "You look exquisite. I can't believe you're my fiancée," he says, kissing me lightly on the lips. "This dress, angel," he says as I turn around and smile at him.

"Just like you envisioned it?" I ask and he nods.

"Better." He comes around me, touching the back of my neck where there's no fabric. His finger then trails slowly down my spine to right above my ass, where the back of my dress starts again. "Backless," he whispers against my shoulder and kisses it lightly. "Not that you need to know, but I approve. This dress looks lethal on you, angel." I turn around, watching him as he grabs his suit jacket and drapes it over his arm. He looks beyond delicious. He holds his arm out for me to take and I follow our team out to the waiting car. Clark helps me in and then sits down next to me. He smells absolutely edible. I'll say this, Clark in normal every day wear is already sexy. But Clark in a three-piece black suit? I'm dying. Literally DEAD. Seeing a man in a suit is, for a woman, what a woman in lingerie is to a man. He keeps looking away smiling, but I can't stop staring. From his incredibly styled hair to the bottom of his black Christian Louboutin's. He's perfection personified. Even in my high, high heels, I'm still almost six inches shorter than Clark. He's a god. The way he was looking at me earlier, I felt like the heat had been turned up to 100 degrees. He's looking at me like that now. I swear I have to cross my legs and close my mouth or I'll jump him here in the car.

"If the two of you don't stop looking at each other like that I swear I'm going to end up getting pregnant from all the way over here," Marco says in his strong Italian accent and we all chuckle.

"Yeah. You guys have all night in those clothes, so you'd better go ahead and chill out. I agree you both look yummy tonight, but calm down," Clayton adds as we take off down the driveway. Brooklyn was pissed that she was being left home with a nanny tonight, but I told her we would take her out for a treat tomorrow.

As we pull up to the gala, Clayton gives me the run through on how the press will work for the event. I know to keep my distance unless they ask for a picture with me in it. I'm not offended. Even though Clark keeps telling me to stay with him, I'd rather go wait at the table inside, but he wants me on the carpet with him. After at least 30 minutes of pictures, we head inside and Clark wraps an arm around me, pulling me tight into his side.

"You're stunning, Ava. You always are, but

you in that damn dress tonight might give a couple people a heart attack. There's not a man or woman in this place that hasn't turned their head when you walk by," he whispers as he grabs my hand, bringing his lips to my engagement ring.

"You sure they aren't looking at you, Grant?" I ask and he smiles, shaking his head. I reach down, squeezing his ass cheek and he laughs.

"Not a chance. They've seen me for years. You're something brand new and shiny. Didn't you hear them calling your name during press photos?"

I did. It was bizarre, but I've been trained by the best, a.k.a. Marco and Clayton. However, Clark is as delicious as any man I've ever seen on Earth. I'm definitely the luckiest woman in the room tonight. I get to share his bed tonight. After dinner and drinks we dance for an hour and then the host gets up to talk about the evening. Tonight's gala and fundraiser is for some film society. There are a lot of famous faces here tonight. I'm proud of Clark for coming tonight. He's such a good guy and the amount of people vying for his attention is a testament to his work ethic and the company he keeps. I have a few industry people approach me and tell me congratulations. I'm not sure if it's because of my engagement or the role I just landed. A few people are specific on what they're congratulating me for. The others I just nod and smile. I appreciate it. I just still don't know what to say to most of them. I recognize a lot of famous people in the room. Some are so kind and a few I could do without. I see Vivienne from Clark's last movie. She and I speak for a while, and I see people pulling Clark different directions.

"It's so nice to finally get to talk to you, Ava. I'm so happy for the two of you and congratulations on the movie role. Clark is so proud of you, which is the most adorable thing in the world!" she adds and I thank her. "I'd like to get together sometime. So seriously text me and we should grab lunch."

We exchange numbers and then I head to the table. I notice a lot of unhappy females staring at me when I get closer to Clark. I try to just head to my seat but Clark waves me over. He wraps his arm around my waist, pulling me close to his side. He leans down, whispers in my ear and I giggle.

"Dance with me," he says, and I nod. He takes my hand, and we head to the dance floor. I feel like all eyes are on us, but I couldn't care less. I have my Prince Charming and if this is my Cinderella moment then I'll happily live in the moment. Clark is an incredible dancer. I love and adore him. He leans down, kissing me passionately and then pulls back looking into my eyes. "I'm in awe of you, angel."

"I feel the same way about you, Clark," I whisper and he looks around the room.

"Let's get out of here! I think we've put in the time necessary."

When we get home, we head straight to the master closet. My feet are killing me even though I took my shoes off in the car. Clark offered to massage my feet, but I told him to keep his gorgeous, manicured hands off my sweaty, swollen feet. Clark unclasps the zipper of my dress and I let it fall to the floor.

"No underwear, Ava?" he asks, a little shocked, and I turn around smiling at him. "If I'd known that earlier I would for sure have had a coronary."

"Can't have panty lines, Clark," I add as I pull a tee shirt over my head and take my jewelry off with Clark's assistance. He hangs his clothes up in the closet and then pulls on some pajama pants. If I wasn't so tired, I'd for sure be all over him. He's delicious and I love undressing him normally. It's already past midnight and I'm exhausted. He lifts me up, carrying me to the bed and I groan. "I still have to take my make up off." I get up, accompanied by a lot of groaning on my part. It's crazy to me how men can just go to bed and women have like 20 things to take care of first. I take off my makeup and moisturize everywhere. Then head back into the bedroom. Clark is lying on his side, smiling at his phone and I stop in the doorway watching him.

"Something you wanna share with the class, Clark?"

"Yeah," he answers, showing me a photo of the two of us on the red carpet tonight and I gasp. We look great. I've never been on a red carpet, but I've got to say, this is so cool. The caption under the photo of us staring up at each other adoringly says: *Clark Grant has finally found his dream girl. Ava James, upcoming co-star to Dalton Calhoun in the biopic Sinatra. Ms. James has us green with envy in that Emerald dress with matching jewels. Envious as well for snagging Hollywood's most eligible bachelor. Word on the street is that they will be tying the knot before she heads to New York to shoot her first major film. Stay tuned for more info.* WOW! At least they were kind about it.

We are lying in bed kissing and embracing, looking at all the photos being posted from tonight when he leans over and pulls my face so I'm looking at him.

"Thank you for coming with me tonight, Ava!" He whispers in my hair, and I look at him like he's lost his mind.

"Thank you for tonight, Clark. Everything was perfect! And why in the world would you thank me? I appreciate getting to go. It was so glamourous."

"It was, but I'm glad you came with me. I haven't taken a date to an event in years. I have to say that was my favorite one by far!" He smiles at me, moving so he can take my foot in his hand.

He starts to massage my feet and I lay back groaning. He chuckles after a few minutes, moving to the other foot and then his hands trail up my leg, massaging my thighs. He finally reaches his destination, smiling at me as he gently starts to caress my sex. He leans over me kissing me gently as he enters one finger gently inside me and massages me from the inside. In no time at all he has my back bowing off of the bed as his lips capture my cries. After I've come back down from my climax, he kisses me gently on the lips and rolls over, turning off the lights. I'm out in seconds and completely sated.

It's Valentine's Day before we know it and I'm so excited. Clark got a nanny for tonight so we could go to dinner. Brooklyn again isn't thrilled but is excited because Clark bought her cupcakes. We head out for a really nice restaurant in Malibu. It's a somewhat far away but Clark says he's been dying to get me out to this restaurant. When we arrive, they put us next to the window so we can watch the sunset over the ocean during dinner. The seafood is absolutely delicious. We split an amazing calamari appetizer and she-crab soup. They bring out our entrees and I'm not sure I can finish all of my food. Clark orders the Swordfish and I order the Mahi.

It's been so long since I've had amazing seafood. As we are paying, Clark smiles at someone behind me and I'm scared to turn around. I hear Dalton's voice and then turn, smiling. Dalton is wonderful. We've spoken a couple times since I got the Ava Gardner role and he's been so supportive. I haven't met any of the other actors, but Dalton tells me it's an outstanding cast. He's excited about shooting in New York soon.

"Malibu, huh? Never thought I'd get you out here, Clark," Dalton jokes. Clark stands up, giving him a bro hug and then I stand as Dalton gives me a hug.

"I wanted to bring Ava somewhere special. We aren't moving out here. At least not yet," he says smiling down at me and winks. I roll my eyes. I'm surprised he doesn't already have a place out here. Dalton turns and introduces me to one of the most stunning women I've ever seen. She's older than me, but not by much. Maybe a little older than Clark but she's stunning. She reaches out a hand to me, smiling genuinely.

"I'm Rebecca. I've heard wonderful things about you, Ava," she says as I smile.

"Thank you. It's so nice to meet you," I reply as Clark and Dalton stare at us.

"Two of the most beautiful women in the world right here, Clark," Dalton says as Rebecca slaps her husband playfully on the shoulder. Clark laughs and then he and Dalton start talking.

"I'd love to grab lunch sometime, Ava. Please ask Clark for my phone number and call me. I'm serious. I'm so happy Clark has finally met someone as special as he is. He's happier than I've ever seen him. I think that's due to you." I blush and bite my lip.

"I love him more than I thought I could ever love anyone," I say looking at Clark who's deep in conversation with Dalton. I turn back to her and she's looking over at her husband. About that time someone comes up to Rebecca and asks for a photo. I move away and the lady shakes her head.

"I'd love a picture with all of you. I saw your photo in the green dress, Ava. You looked so beautiful," the woman says, and I can truly say I am stunned. How did she recognize me? I'm assuming because of who I'm around. This is the first time someone has wanted to get a photo with me.

"Did you know Ava is staring in my husband's next movie?" Rebecca tells the fan while smiling at me. "She's going to be fabulous."

"That she is," Dalton says as he and Clark come around us and get in a photo as well. The woman looks stunned to get a photo of the four of us and I smile kindly at her. She gives me a hug and I hug her back. I sit back down at the table as the lady asks Rebecca a million questions about some movie she once starred in. She leans over, kissing my cheek and then she and Dalton leave to go back to their table. Clark pays the bill and then turns back to me.

"Dalton is really excited having you in the film," he says, smiling proudly at me and I nod.

"I'm excited to be in the film too. So he can't be as excited as I am!"

"I'm not so sure, Ava," he adds, shaking the waiter's hand as we get up to leave. We wave goodbye to Dalton and his wife Rebecca. We walk out the front of the restaurant as a couple people snap inconspicuous photos of us as we walk to the car. I just keep my head down.

Clark asks me once we are in the car if I am cool with making another stop on the way home. I tell him of course and then we pull off the road. About 10 minutes from the restaurant, we turn onto another street and then Clark stops in front of a ginormous house.

"Do you want to go inside?" he asks, and I laugh at him. Are you kidding me?

"Do you own this?" I ask and he laughs but doesn't answer the question. "You didn't answer my question," I say as he gets out of the car, again ignoring my question. We walk up the stone steps to the ginormous glass doors and he unlocks the front door with a key. Oh. My. Gosh!

"I'm aware. After you," he says, motioning for me to go inside. He flips a switch and it's an empty house with floor to ceiling windows looking out over the beach. I can hear the ocean from the entryway, and I notice it's because the back glass doors are open. There's a table set up outside with candles and rose petals. I look over at Clark and he's watching me with a cautious grin. I walk out the back deck and feel the chill of the ocean on my skin. I take a deep breath. It's been so long since I've felt the ocean breeze on my face. I open my eyes and Clark grabs my hand.

"What do you think?" he asks and I shake my head, confused.

"It's beautiful. This is incredible. Did you rent it? Do you own it?" I ask warily and he smiles.

"Well… WE own it," he says, motioning for me to sit down. I sit down and he sits on the other side of the table. He lifts the silver tray covering and there are chocolate strawberries inside. "For you," he says, lifting one up and I take a bite. The flavors are overwhelming. That's not your average melted chocolate. It tastes really expensive. He grabs the champagne bottle from the wine chiller beside the door and pours us two glasses.

"We own this? You bought this?" I ask as I swallow my sip of champagne. Again, expensive.

"Maybe? I've been wanting to buy real estate out here in Malibu for a long time. About a month ago Brian told me about this property. I told him that I'd be interested in looking at the property for sure. I don't know if it would be our main residence or not, but I wouldn't make a final decision until you were able to see it. So, I want to know, what you think?"

"You want to know what I think," I replay his words aloud, laughing. "Clark it's amazing. It's beautiful."

"Would you want to live here with me?" he asks a little shyly and I have to laugh that this man is a little nervous about my answer.

"Yes. Of course. Wherever you want to live, Clark. I want to live there too. My home is wherever you and Brooklyn are," I answer, and he beams back at me. "How could you question that?"

"Well, I don't. I just didn't know if this would be something you would want. If you would even want to live in Malibu. We don't have to sell the other house in LA. I just want to know what you would like?" he adds and I roll my eyes.

"Clark. The past seven years I've lived in apartments, and you want to know if I would want to live here. In a beach front house. In Malibu. With you," I say sarcastically. "Can you see the humor there?"

"I can. But I don't ever want to assume, Ava. I know you want to live with me. Hell, my home is where you are as well. But you still can have an opinion if this is something you would want."

"You would want to keep both houses?" I ask

and he shrugs.

"We can. We can use this as a beach house and come here whenever we need a break from LA. Or come for the summer or holidays, weekends maybe? We don't have to make a decision now. I put an offer in and they accepted it. Would you like a tour?" he asks and I smile. He takes me around the three-story house and I'm giddy. All the walls facing the ocean are floor to ceiling windows. When we get to the master it takes my breath away.

"To wake up to this every morning," I say turning back to him and he's watching me. "Can you imagine?"

"I can relate, Ava. Waking up to you every morning with that view. A man couldn't ask for much more than that." I walk back over to him, rising up on my toes and kissing him tenderly. I lower my feet back to the ground and he places a hand on either side of my face. "To make love to you in this room, Ava, as your husband. Ever since I signed the papers and saw this very room on the listing, it's all I've been able to think about. To make love to you under the stars with the ocean breeze coming into the bedroom. I can't wait for you to be my wife, Ava." I literally swoon and kiss him hard before pulling back.

"Let's get married in Malibu," I say, and he opens his eyes wide. "There are a lot of vineyards and venues here. Let's get married the next opening they have. Small ceremony with just our friends and family. Then we can have our honeymoon here in our new Malibu beach house," I add as I pull out of his grasp, laughing and spinning in the middle of the master bedroom. He walks over to me, lifting me off the floor and spinning me around.

"I'll have Clayton call around town tomorrow and see what we can figure out," he says, smiling down at me. "I love you, angel. Happy Valentine's Day, my forever Valentine," he adds against my lips before he kisses me passionately.

Clark

April 3rd, I think to myself as Clayton FaceTimes Ava and I with the details. Less than two months away from marrying the woman of my dreams. I look at her and she's grinning. Marco is going to make her a one-of-a-kind creamy satin dress. Of course he has a lot of other ideas. I tried to stay focused during our wedding planning call with my team but watching everyone's excitement, specifically Ava's, is more entertaining to watch. Funnily enough, Brian is more excited than anyone. He's just happy this is all happening. I don't think he thought I'd ever find anyone. My mom is going to come and stay with Brooklyn for two weeks while Ava and I go on our honeymoon. Ava thinks we are staying at our new home in Malibu. We are currently furnishing the beach house and trying to finish it up before the wedding. I have a fun surprise for her that I think she will love. Everything that Clayton, Marco and Ava have picked out for the house so far has been great. Between Ava preparing for the upcoming movie shoot in May, auditions for the Bond movie with me, furnishing the Malibu house, Brooklyn's schooling and planning the wedding in April, we barely have time to sleep. It's between myself and two other actors for the Bond role. I'm not stressed about it. I'm just honored to be reading for it. Ava has run some lines with me for her movie. I can tell she's going to be perfect. She completely amazes me. I bought a grand piano for the front foyer so that the studio music director could come here and run through the musical numbers with Ava. To say I'm speechless when it comes to Ava is an understatement. I've been around talent my entire life, but Ava is a star. The most humble, honorable and genuine talent I've ever known.

The week of the wedding arrives and we are having a small get together at the LA house. Most of my co-stars, past and present. My business team, Shanna and Ava's team, have come over for a celebratory dinner. We decided not to do a rehearsal dinner since it's just going to be Ava and I standing at the altar with no wedding party. Clayton is going to walk her down the aisle and Dalton promised to sing a song at the intimate reception. I again have a couple surprises for Ava that I'm working on. Everything is coming along so seamlessly. Marco is all things hair, make up and gown. Brooklyn is so excited to get to throw flowers at people on the way down the aisle. We laugh every time she talks about what her role is for the wedding. My people make me so damn happy. Ava leans over to whisper in my ear as everyone is talking over the first course.

"I can't believe we actually made it to this week without having sex," she whispers in my ear, and I turn to her smiling.

"I can't either, baby. It wasn't the easiest thing I've done, but I'm also proud of us," I say, taking her hand and lifting it to my lips. "But I'd do anything for you. Hopefully you know that by now."

"I do! It's one of the reasons I love you so much." We finish our dinner surrounded by our family and friends. I see Brian is looking down at his phone concerned. He's never had a great poker face, and I do love that about him. He's great to play poker with. He can't lie but he can negotiate the hell out of a contract. I nod over at Brian and Ava looks over at him and then back to me. "Maybe you should make sure everything is okay."

"I'll be right back," I say as I head over to his

side of the table. He shakes his head trying to pretend it wasn't anything substantial. I stand there waiting for him to give it up and he finally stands up. We walk away from the table and turn our backs to everyone. "You can tell me," I say to him with a smile on my face. "You look like someone died Brian. What's up?"

"It's the week of your wedding, Clark," he says, putting his phone in his back pocket. "I didn't want to ruin the laid-back vibe tonight, but I think you need to hear this."

"I'm aware, and Ava and I are going to be fine. We have each other to get through whatever you or anyone else can throw our way."

"Okay. Well Kyle Wright's family is releasing his journal. They've turned it into a book. It's filled with all kinds of juicy details, specifically stuff about you," he says, and I wait. "And Ava," he adds. I feel my stomach drop a little.

"What do you mean Ava? He didn't know Ava," I add and he nods biting his lip. I can see he is deciding whether to give me the facts.

"Kyle was the one having Ava followed back when you were filming in Vancouver. He writes about having a private detective follow her. He was obsessed with the fact that you were with her. Mainly because he was in love with you, Clark. He talks about it in great detail in his journal. Apparently he was obsessed with the woman who finally turned your head. He got off on your protectiveness of her. He does not come across well, mentally, in his writings," he continues, and I stare at him. I blink a couple of times and then remember where I am. I turn my head looking over at the table and back. Most people aren't looking but Ava and Clayton are watching me. They are sitting beside each other talking and looking at me. "I'm only hearing about this because they released snippets from the book and a friend received an advance copy. I should have more on my desk by next week. But it's very dark and very sinister."

"When does the book come out?" I ask, looking over at Ava, winking and then turning my back to them again.

"Two weeks," he says. "You guys will be on your honeymoon, which will be good. You'll be away from this shitshow, but I'm not sure why his family is so intent on destroying what was left of his career. I mean, this is crazy, Clark. You know that right? The dude is dead."

"Yeah, I knew he wasn't well, but I didn't know it was like this."

"Supposedly there are also some photos. Not of Ava, but of you. On set. Hear me say we will respond, Clark. I know you know that. I don't want this ruining your week. Once I have more concrete information then we will make sure we respond appropriately."

"What kind of pictures?" I ask, looking at Brian and he shakes his head.

"I can only get descriptions. We are going to do whatever we can to protect the both of you. But I don't know what all is in this damn book. When I find out I'll let you know. Maybe not this week. You might want to give Ava a heads up. I can get with her PR people as well as the studio to make sure we do what we can. I'm sorry, Clark," he adds, and I put a hand on his shoulder.

"Not your fault, Brian. Some things can't be helped or controlled. I'll talk to Ava about it tonight. I don't want to keep anything from her. For now, put your phone away. We can deal with whatever this is tomorrow. Try and enjoy yourself," I say as he sits down and takes a large sip of wine. "There ya go," I add, laughing and patting him on the back. I head back over to Ava and she's watching me warily. So is Clayton. I sit down and tell her that we will talk after everyone leaves. Until then everyone is to enjoy the hell out of themselves. I'm marrying the woman of my dreams this week. She smiles at me, leaning over and kissing me on the cheek and then tells Clayton what I said.

After most of our guests leave, Clayton, Marco and Ava grab a bottle of wine out of the cellar and head out to the back porch. I put Brooklyn down for the evening and then head back downstairs. I stand in the kitchen watching the three of them lounging on the back porch, laughing hard, and it makes me smile. I couldn't be happier with my family. These people are my family. In a few days, Ava and I will be getting married in Malibu. Then I'll be taking her back to our house in Malibu to spend a couple days before I whisk her away on an adventure. When we get back, we will be heading to New York to watch Ava film her first major film. She's going to be absolutely incredible. I head out to the back porch and sit down, grateful to put my feet up. Clayton pats me on the leg and I smile over at him.

"Talk to us, Daddy!" Clayton says, looking over at Ava who is watching me warily. I sit up, placing my elbows on the table. I relay the information Brian told me and when I'm done it takes about a minute before anyone says anything.

"Are you serious?" Clayton asks, and I nod my head.

"That's literally all I know. Brian said the book is set to be released in a few weeks. We just have to take it as it comes. Can't freak out about it now. It won't change anything. Brian will let us know if we have any legal issues. I don't see us suing the publisher. It says more about Kyle than it does about us. But it makes me pretty sad that his family would want to come out with all of this. What do they gain?"

"Money," Ava whispers. I nod, rubbing my

thumb over her hand and she gives me a small smile.

We all take a deep breath and the guys head out after finishing their wine. Ava comes over, sitting down in my lap and we sit facing the twinkling lights of the city in the distance. She leans her head back on my shoulder and I enjoy having her so close to me, where I can hold her and keep her safe. I know I won't always be able to do that, especially now that she's venturing deeper into this world of mine. We sit in comfortable silence for a while and then she stands, pulling me to my feet. We clean up our glasses and head into the bedroom. Ava is quiet. I know she's got to be tired, but I also know that the news tonight is probably a little jarring. I head into the closet, changing into my pajama bottoms, giving her some time to process and then head back out to the bedroom. She's standing at the window looking over the backyard in nothing but her bra and underwear. I lean against the door frame of our closet in order to steady myself. The lights of the city create a beautiful lighting of her gorgeous body. I tell her not to move. I walk to my bedside table and grab my camera. Coming back to stand at the closet, I take a picture of her. The lights of the city in the distance are beautifully lighting her face. Moving to the side, I take a picture of her profile and then a few more photos. I pull her to the chair in the room and sit down.

"Ava, look at how beautiful you are," I say as I pull her into my lap so she can see the pictures. She smiles at me, a little embarrassed, and I shake my head. "Do you mind if I have some of these framed for our bedroom?"

"Not at all," she says, turning in my arms and kissing me lightly. "Thank you for making me feel beautiful."

"My honor, angel," I whisper, kissing her behind her ear. "Two more days, baby. Are you excited?" I ask.

"I'm so excited. I can't imagine being happier than I am now. I'm so excited to marry you, Clark. To walk down the aisle. For you be standing there waiting for me. To promise myself to you for the rest of my life. For you to make love to me for the first time and then every time after that," she adds, smiling at me. "To sleep in our new home. For Brooklyn to have another parent to love her," she adds, and I squeeze her to me tightly.

"God, baby, me too." I help her sit up so I can kiss a trail down her neck and then down her back. I unfasten her bra, letting it slowly fall down her body. I place my hands on her waist, standing her up so I can lean forward and kiss the rest of my way down her back to the top of her underwear. I slowly pull her underwear down her toned legs and kiss her lightly on each cheek of her beautiful, round ass. I turn her around so she's facing me, and

I smile up at her. "You have no idea how excited I am." I sweep her into my arms, carrying her to the bed and putting her under the covers with me. She curls into me as I wrap my arms around my soon-to-be wife, kissing her gently on the lips. I reach over and turn off the bedside table light and then kiss the top of her head. "Goodnight, baby."

Clayton

Today is the day!!!! It's finally here! Clark and Ava's wedding. It's been pretty hush-hush since it's a small ceremony, but I've already seen photographers around the venue. Our team has hired extra security, but we can only do so much. What we can control, we will. Everything else we are praying will go smoothly. Clark rented a couple houses in Malibu for the night so we can all be close to the wedding venue. This morning I picked up Ava to take her to Malibu with Marco and I. Clark, his mom and Brooklyn will come later. Ava already looks nervously excited as we are heading to the venue for a small brunch. The dress Marco designed for Ava is timeless. A classic cream satin dress. Cut low in the back like the emerald one. Except this one is a thicker satin material. I can't wait for Clark to see her in this dress. She's wearing her normal jewelry. The diamond studs surrounded by smaller diamonds in her ears and the matching necklace. I've seen the diamond wedding band Clark picked out for her and I have to laugh. She's going to be dripping in diamonds. The wedding band Ava picked out for Clark is a simple platinum band that will be perfect for him. Ava said she didn't care if he wore a band or not, but I told her not to be ridiculous. Clark will wear a wedding band. He's more than excited about it. She knows traditionally it's not as big of a deal in British culture as it is here. I just roll my eyes. It's Clark.

We eat a light lunch in our robes, overlooking the vineyard. The ocean in the distance from our balcony is gorgeous. Ava is looking as perfectly content as possible after a mimosa. I think she just needed a little help this morning taking the edge off.

"How are you feeling?" I ask and she smiles.

"I'm excited, but also really nervous. I'm glad there's only going to be like 80 people here today. I can't imagine having a big wedding. Not that I wouldn't want to get married in front of the whole world. I'm just nervous. I know once I see Clark everything will come together. I'll feel better once I can see him."

"It will be over before you know it. Trust me and we will make sure that we use some waterproof mascara today. I can only imagine all the tears between the four of us. We might flood this place. Not to mention all the tears of the women and men who will be crying that Clark Grant is officially off the market," I add, laughing, and she laughs too.

"That's so very true. I just want to say I do, kiss him and then celebrate!" she says, grabbing a grape off the table.

"Are you kidding? I can't wait to see his reaction when he sees you! I hope you know how stunning you look in that dress," I say as Marco comes around kissing Ava on the cheek.

"Yes. Thank you for letting me make your dress for your big day!"

"Are you kidding, Marco. I get a Marco Delaurentes original on my wedding day. I don't think I'll ever wear another designer," she says as Marco beams. He truly is talented and he's my husband! Yes, I'm still on cloud nine! With Clark taking a break this year from any major films, I'm going to get to spend more time with Ava while she's shooting. I love working with her and Clark, but being on set every day with Ava, my god the world doesn't know what it's in for.

Marco is zipping up Ava's dress when Brooklyn and Clark's mom, Chelsea come in. They both gasp when they see Ava in her wedding dress.

There's not a lot of frill to it. Her hair is in loose waves down past her shoulders and her make up is minimal and classic. She looks like Ava. Exactly the woman that Clark fell in love with. That's exactly who needs to be walking down the aisle this afternoon. I ask Marco if he can go and check on Clark. He nods, leaving us in the room. Brooklyn's flower girl dress is one for the ages. It's a cream satin dress with a pale pink tulle skirt. The satin bow in the back is the perfect touch. Marco tears up a little as the photographer snaps photos of us getting ready. She's the most precious flower girl in this world. Clark might even cry seeing his baby girl walking down the aisle before Ava. That is if she doesn't knock someone out with her flower petals on the way down. We tried to work on it, but this is Brooklyn we are talking about. Anything can happen.

We've got the ivory and pale pink rose petals ready. Brooklyn is raring to go. She keeps asking if we can go ahead and go and we keep telling her it's almost time. It's a great distraction for Ava. We are about 15 minutes away from heading down and I can see Ava is shaking her hands nervously. I grab her hands and she smiles at me. I kiss her cheek and she tears up. I wipe away a tear while she smiles up at me. Lydia comes in, surprising us both and Ava runs to give her a big hug. She really is the reason why we are standing here. Otherwise, Clark and

Ava may never have had the chance to meet. I turn to Ava, who is smiling at me.

"Lydia. I'm so glad you came," Ava exclaims to her, and she stands back taking Ava in.

"You have no idea how much I've enjoyed getting updates on the two of you from Clayton!" Lydia kisses her cheek and then mine. "I don't want to make you guys late, but I did want to say hello. I won't be able to stay for the reception since I'm visiting some friends but please know how happy I am for the both of you, Ava."

"Thank you, Lydia. I'm so grateful," Ava starts to say but then tears up. I grab her hand and she just nods at Lydia. Lydia tears up as well and I clear my throat. The wedding planner gives us the five-minute warning and Lydia runs out the door to get to her seat.

"You are the most beautiful bride, Ava. He's going to cry like a baby when he sees you. His sweet angel," I say as I look over at Marco who nods at me from the door. "Let's do this!"

We get into place as the final guests sit down. "Great is Thy Faithfulness" starts to play as Marco seats Clark's mom. He takes a seat next to her and then sits next to Lydia on the front row. I can see everything going on and Ava grabs my hand.

"You're making me nervous since I can't see what's going on," she whispers and I laugh.

"I'm sorry, darling. He looks amazing, Ava.

The Navy suit really suits his skin tone," I say as she giggles. I lean over, giving her another kiss on the cheek. "I do love you Ava and I'm so happy for you." She kisses my cheek and we both wipe away the tears from our faces. Brooklyn stands in front of the double doors like an actor waiting on her cue. She's ready and when we tell her to go, she goes with the confidence of a top model during Fashion Week. We both smile at her from the side so no one can see us. The doors close again and then Ava and I stand behind the door as the song comes to an end. Then another song starts. Ava smiles when she hears the music. Clark wanted to pick out the song since Ava didn't have a preference. Clark said he'd surprise her. I move Ava to the side so that she can see the screens set up on the sides of the platform. "Halo" starts to play, but it's not Beyonce's version. Clark had Dalton record a jazzy, big band version. Ava starts crying as photos of Ava and Clark start to appear. From Clark and Ava as kids, before they met, then to when they both separately moved to LA. There are pictures of Ava, Brooklyn, and then the three of them together. Clark and Ava dancing at the gala, mine and Marco's wedding and the video of Clark proposing to Ava. She wipes the tears away as the screen goes black. White script comes up with 'And this is Just the Beginning…'

I grab her hand and move her back to behind the double doors, checking her make up. We both take a deep breath and then she puts her arm in mine. The doors open as the last pre-chorus ends of the song. We start to walk down the aisle as the last chorus begins. The moment Clark and Ava's eyes meet I start to tear up. He already has tears rolling down his face and so does she. As we approach, I take her hand and give it to Clark. He's all smiles. I kiss her cheek and then go and sit next to Marco. Clark wipes a tear off her cheek and they stand at the end of the aisle smiling at each other.

Ava

Clark looks like a dream in his Navy three-piece suit. He leans over after taking my hands and whispers that I *LOOK BEAUTIFUL*. My hands are shaking, so Clark holds them in both of his, squeezing reassuringly. The pastor starts the ceremony, but I can focus only on Clark. We exchange our vows and I smile at him as he pulls the ring from his pocket. I haven't seen my wedding band yet. As he slides it on my finger, I look down at the diamond encrusted wedding band and then back up at him. He laughs and I shake my head. He's determined to keep me dripping – no, *drowning* -- in diamonds. Clayton hands me Clark's wedding band and I slide it on his finger. He smiles down at the ring and then into my eyes his eyes on fire with love and adoration for me. I smile at him as the preacher announces us husband and wife. Oh my gosh! We are officially Mr. and Mrs. Clark Grant. When Clark and I kiss, it's with a passion I've never felt from him. He takes my breath away and when I pull back he has fresh tears of joy in his eyes. He lifts my hand to his lips, kissing my hand and then we head back up the aisle. People cheer and slap Clark on the back. All I'm focused on is having a moment alone with Clark. We walk through the doors leading back inside and they close the doors behind us. Clark wraps me in his arms, tipping me backwards and kissing me passionately. We did it!!

"My wife," he says, leaning his head against mine. He's on cloud nine and so am I. "I love you, Ava Grant."

"I love you too, husband," I answer as he brings my left hand to his lips, kissing my wedding band.

The Venue's wedding director congratulates us and then takes us out to where we will get pictures taken. Brooklyn, Clayton, Marco and Clark's mom eventually join us. Of course, Clayton and Marco are in our photos. The venue's assistant goes to find Brian and his family for some pictures as well. He laughs, but enjoys his moment with us as well. We enter the reception to cheers as Clark pulls me onto the dance floor. I'm surprised to see Dalton onstage with the jazz band we hired. He winks at me. I look up at Clark, who leans down kissing me intimately. The intro to Mirrors by Justin Timberlake starts, but again it's a very Jazzed-up version. Clark. Freaking. Grant. He spares no expense. We dance till the sun starts to set, enjoying our time together with close friends. Shanna gives me a big kiss before chastising me for making her cry. Brooklyn runs over and jumps in Clark's arms. He gives her a big hug and then she heads back to the house with Clark's mom. Clark hired a driver to take his mom and Brooklyn back to the LA house since they'd be more comfortable there. That's just Clark. He thinks of everything.

We luckily don't have to stay the entire evening at the venue. I'm really wanting to get to the new Malibu house. We haven't stayed there yet, and Clark hasn't seen what all we've done with the house. I'm so excited to show him. That and…it's my wedding night! We pull into the driveway and Clark looks over at me smiling as he pulls into our garage. He tells me to wait in the car as he grabs our bags out of the back and takes them into the house. Coming right back out he opens my door, helping me out of the car and then picks me up, carrying me over the threshold.

"I'm old fashioned," he adds before he sets me down. I stand up, turning the switch on in the kitchen and see a surprise. "Also I had someone come by and do some romancing of the place for tonight," he whispers and I smile at him. I place a hand gently on his cheek and he smiles shyly at me. There's a bottle of Champagne chilling on the counter with two glasses that say His and Hers. I lean up against him and he smiles down at me. "I want to see what all you guys have done with the place, but I'm not going to lie, Ava. I really want to get you out of that beautiful dress." I turn around, grabbing the two glasses in one hand and the bottle of Moet before walking to the stairs leading up to the master bedroom. I turn around and Clark is watching me adoringly. I turn back around, heading up the stairs, slowly. I do not want to trip over my dress. He stops me before I can take another step up, taking the glasses and bottle of champagne out of my hands. "Please do not trip and get hurt," he says looking down at my dress and then up at me. I laugh, grabbing my dress, and continue walking in front of him up the stairs.

When we get to the master bedroom, I turn the light on to find rose petals on the bed and leading out onto our porch. There are candles lit around the room and it's perfect. He looks around the room, smiling at our newly decorated and furnished space and then back down at me. After placing the glasses on the table he turns to me, and leaning up against the chest of drawers he kicks his shoes off. He places his hands on either side of the chest of drawers he's leaning on. He's watching me. I smile and walk over to him and remove his suit jacket and then I begin to unbutton his vest. "This really is a sexy suit on you, Clark. You're so damn hot in it," I say as he continues to watch me adoringly. He loosens his tie, removing it as I start on his shirt. He removes the cuff links, placing them on the chest of drawers next to his tie. I smile to myself as I remove his shirt. He's standing there in his suit pants and I have to take a moment to take him all in. He removes his belt as I unfasten his pants, keeping my hand on his zipper after I've unzipped his pants. He looks down at my hand and then into my eyes.

"I love you, Ava. We will go slow," he whispers, and I grin up shyly at him.

"I'm not nervous yet," I say, my voice barely above a whisper. I pull his pants down over his fine ass and then they drop to the floor. As I put my hands on the band of his boxer briefs, he grins back at me.

"Then by all means," he says expectantly. I pull them down his legs and then stand back up. I take in my husband. In all his masculine glory and take another step back. All he's wearing is his wedding band and his signet ring with his family crest. I look down his body and see how badly he wants me and decide to not torture him any longer. I turn around and look over my shoulder. The zipper of my dress is only 3 inches as my dress is almost completely backless. Clark walks up behind me, placing a kiss on my shoulder, and runs a finger down my back along my spine, stopping at the zipper of my dress. "So I see no bra was necessary today. Let's see what else we might be missing," he adds as he unzips my dress, showing that I'm not wearing any underwear either. I look over my shoulder, winking back at him and he groans. He pulls the straps of my dress off my shoulders, letting my dress fall to the floor. Now I'm standing in nothing but my nude Christian Louboutins, a wedding gift from Marco and Clayton. I feel him step back, taking me all in. I look back over my shoulder and his eyes are burning for me. He comes to stand in front of me. He grabs my left hand and kisses my wedding band. "You're stunning, Ava." I back up to the bed and sit on the edge waiting for my husband to join me.

He gently presses my shoulders back so I'm laying down on the bed. He comes to stand in between my legs and kneels down. I feel my breath catch as he pulls my shoes off. I'm fully aware of where he is at all times. My senses are on high alert. I look up at him as he smiles sweetly down at me. "Scoot back, baby," he whispers his voice laced with seduction. I scoot back on the bedding, and he smiles down at me as he brings my foot up to his lips, kissing my ankle. Then he slowly starts to move his lips up my body. He's taking his time. He kisses up the inside of my thigh and I hold my breath, fully expecting him to start to kiss my sex. But he kisses my stomach instead and then up to my breast. He holds my face in his hands as he kisses me lightly. Suddenly I feel his hand trailing the same path his lips just took, but this time he rubs gently over my sex and I gasp as he sticks a finger inside of me. He groans into the side of my neck as he trails light kisses along my collarbone. I grab his face, kissing him passionately and he starts to gradually use more and more pressure. I feel a delicious sensation as my body is flooded with heat and then I fall gloriously over the edge. I open my eyes and he's looking down at me, caressing my cheek.

"That was beautiful, baby," he whispers as he starts to kiss back down my body. This time he doesn't avoid my sex. He kisses me there. Gently at first and I almost bow off of the bed. "Easy, baby," he whispers against my body. I didn't think I could go over the edge again, but within minutes I find myself falling again. I'm breathing heavy as I hear Clark whisper softly to me as he kisses back up my body. I grab his shoulders as he looks me in the eyes. He positions himself beside me. Kissing my face, my hair and then my shoulder. "You okay?" he asks and I laugh. He smiles at my reaction, and I reach down his body grabbing him gently. He doesn't stop me this time, but positions himself on top of me. "Your body is ready Ava, are you?" he asks, and I nod.

"Please Clark." I whisper and he waits a moment before gently guiding himself inside of me. I can tell he isn't fully inside of me. Then he holds my face with one hand, as he slowly and mercifully works himself deeper inside of me. "Please," I urge him as he leans down, kissing my lips gently. He pushes himself all the way inside of me and I feel a deep pinch at my core. I grab his shoulders and he stops. "Please don't stop," I say, opening my eyes.

"Give me a second," he grunts with a grin. I place one hand on his face bringing his lips to mine. "God, I love you, Ava," he says as he starts to move inside me. He's setting a pace for me to get used to. The pain eventually fades away and I'm left with a warm and delicious heat that starts to spread throughout my body. I place my hand on his ass and press him deeper inside me, this new rhythm making him groan into my mouth as I whimper aloud. I feel tingling in my chest, my body and mind are overwhelmed with love for my husband. My body begins to shake and my core tightens as I feel myself go over the edge. Clark joins me not long after I do. He stills himself on top of me, resting his forehead against mine. It takes me a second, but I smile up at him. He looks down at me with wonder and affection.

"I love you, Clark." I say, as a tear slips down

my cheek. I'm overwhelmed with how he makes me feel. And now all of this. He wipes my tear away, kissing me passionately.

"My wife," he says as he gently pulls out of me and wraps us in the sheet. He lays down beside me, pulling me onto his chest. I smile as I look out at the dark ocean through our window, laying in the arms of my husband, feeling closer to him than ever. I didn't think that would be possible. So this is what all the fuss is about. I can't imagine a better lover. I may be inexperienced, but I'm not an idiot. "Are you okay?" he asks as I turn over, resting my chin on his chest.

"More than okay," I answer as his thumb caresses my cheek.

"Good. I don't want you to be sore tonight. I want you to be able to recover because we have a few weeks of this, Ava," he says, smiling mischievously at me. "Also, we probably need to get you cleaned up," he says, standing with me wrapped in the sheets together. There's a small stain on the fitted sheet and I'm glad Clayton thought to make sure we had extras for tonight. I rolled my eyes at the time, not thinking I would bleed that much, but it looks like he wasn't wrong. "It's okay, Ava," Clark whispers as he turns the light on in the bathroom.

Before I step into the shower, I pull my hair up into a bun on top of my head, as Clark stands under the spray. I'm a mess with this man. I watch the hot water trickle down his skin and lean against the glass as the shower begins to steam up. Clark turns around, looking at me and I see he's ready to go again. He smiles and I walk into his arms. We clean up and as he's gently washing me, I know I'm safe here. He turns the water off, grabbing two towels. He wraps one around his waist and then one around my shoulders. I step out of the shower and Clark tells me he'll be right back. I forgot our bags are still downstairs. I sit on the bed looking around the room. So this is it. This is my new life, and I get to make love to Clark for the rest of my life. I feel the tears come before I can stop them. I cannot believe this is my life. I feel Clark in front of me before I realize he's even there. He's kneeling in front of me, and I slide off the bed into his arms.

"I can't believe how much I love you. How lucky I am that my first time was with you. Like this, with someone worshipping my body." He grabs my face, kissing me tenderly. He holds me in his arms as I get myself together and I feel the beating of his heart.

"I know, angel. I'm just as overwhelmed as you are. It's not like this for everyone. I love you."

We get dressed, and by dressed I mean I'm wearing Clark's pajama top and he's wearing the pants. I have lingerie for this week, but I don't feel like it's necessary for tonight. Maybe another night.

Tonight we are going to enjoy our first night in our beautiful home. Clark opens the champagne and pours us two glasses. We drink slowly, savoring the first night of our honeymoon. I sit looking out at the dark ocean, thinking back on this last year.

"You know this time last year I was moving into my apartment with my crazy roommates," I say as I take a sip of the crisp champagne. Literally a year ago," I add as he looks over at me smiling. "Yeah. A lot can happen in a year, Clark. I never would have foreseen this as my future." He grabs my hand and I squeeze his gently.

"And here you are now. My precious wife. And me, the luckiest man in the world," he adds as he takes a sip of his champagne.

"Who knew! One year later I'm moved into my Malibu beachfront home," I say laughing. "With my movie star husband." He laughs and then pulls my hand so I'm forced to stand in front of him. He pulls my legs so I'm straddling him. I lean down, kissing him passionately and then he picks me up so I'm still straddling him. I wrap my legs around his waist and he takes us back to our bedroom. I will always think of this place with a sweet smile and a flutter in my chest.

The next morning I head downstairs into the kitchen where I smell bacon. Clark is pulling a rack of bacon from the oven and when he sees me, he pours me a glass of orange juice while I sit down.

"I have a confession, Ava," he says, smiling at me, and I know it's nothing bad. It's Clark.

"What did you do?" I ask with fake shock. He laughs and then comes around to stand in front of me.

"I couldn't wait any longer. I wanted to look around. You guys did an amazing job on the house, baby," he says. "Anything you can't do?" he asks, and I laugh.

"Plenty of things. I can't play the piano," I answer and he smiles as he pours batter into the waffle maker. "I can't read music," I add and he looks up, shocked. "I know, right? It's not easy for me. I can follow along, but I've had to become a quick learner. When I hear the music once through, then I'm good to go. But it's why I was never able to play an instrument growing up. Man, I beat myself up for years and years over that. But it's my dirty little secret," I whisper, and he smiles kindly at me.

"You're still perfect to me, Ava."

"Oh, and I'm afraid of heights," I add as he comes over to run a hand up my leg.

"Anything else?" he asks, caressing my bare bottom. "Sounds like you're still perfect!"

"How about you, Clark?" I ask, kissing his chest.

"I'm not a good baker. I don't like driving fast. Mainly because I've seen some horrific stunts go wrong. I have to get over it, depending on the role I'm playing. I can't tap dance," he says, laughing at himself.

"Details, please," I say, putting my glass down so I don't spill it.

"I was in a musical in secondary school. High school to you," he says, lifting my glass up and taking a sip. "I was playing Gene Kelly. He's a great dancer. The singing, I could do," he says with a mock sense of pride. "But the tap dancing, that was hard as hell for me. I'm no Dalton Calhoun, but I did pretty well. At least the ladies thought so," he says, kissing my lips sweetly.

"Can't imagine that," I say sarcastically. "Will you sing for me one day?" I ask as he takes a waffle out and pours more batter in.

"Of course. Anything for you, angel! I'll even tap dance if it'll make you smile," he says as he places a waffle and some bacon on a plate and hands it to me. I pour some syrup on my waffle as Clark comes to sit next to me with his plate. "Sleep okay, my beautiful wife?" He asks and I smile. I just can't help it. I'm a wife. AND I'm Clark Grant's wife. Man, if my grandmother could see me now.

"I did. I slept very well. That bed is amazing. So is my bed mate," I say as he knocks his shoulder against mine. "You?"

"Like a champ," he answers as he finishes his waffle in seconds and I laugh. "Judgmental much, Ava Grant?"

We laugh the entire morning, when we aren't making love, that is. Clark is still very gentle, wanting me to get used to our bodies together. He's a very generous lover and he worships my body in a way I can't even begin to express. We walk on the beach later that afternoon. I hold his hand with both of mine.

"A girl can used to this," I say as we sit on the back deck watching the sunset a little later.

"Don't get too used to it," he says with a mischievous grin.

"Oh dear. What did you do now, Grant?" I ask as he laughs.

"We leave in two days for somewhere a little more, European," he adds, eyeing me warily. He's excited, but I'm not sure he knows I'm about to jump out of my skin with excitement!

"WHAT?" I exclaim, my face glowing. I start to giggle. "Where? Tell me! Tell me! Tell me!" I say as I get up and jump on him. He laughs as I grab his shoulders, making him look at me. "Tell me, Clark!"

"Well, first we are going to Paris for a couple of days," he answers as I squeal. He closes his eyes and when he opens them, they are alive with love for me and my excitement. Normally, I'd give him a hard time for spoiling me. But this is my honeymoon. OUR honeymoon. "Then we fly down to Monte Carlo," he adds slowly, "and then to a villa in Palermo, Italy, where we are going to stay for a couple of days. Until we move onto a yacht for the rest of our honeymoon to spend some much-needed time on the Mediterranean." I about faint. What is this life!

"How long are we going to be gone?" I ask as I wrap my arms around his neck.

"16 days," I rest my chin on his shoulder. "You okay, angel?" he laughs.

"Thank you!" I whisper as he wraps his arms tightly around me.

"Anything for you, baby! Did you honestly think that we would just stay here for 2 weeks?" He asks, laughing.

"Yes. And that would have been more than enough. Here in our beach house in Malibu," I answer, looking out at the ocean.

"That leaves us a little over a week to recover and get ready for New York when we get back. We will be jet lagged, Ava. Not sure if you've experienced that yet, but it's a real thing. Life will be an adventure Ava, but there's not another person I would want to do life with. I love you, angel," he says, whispering against my cheek.

When we arrive in Paris, I feel like I've stepped back in time. This place doesn't feel real. We walk into our honeymoon suite at our uber luxurious hotel, and the first thing Clark shows me is the view of the Eiffel Tower from our balcony. It's so close. I'm sure you have to pay top dollar for views like this. I turn around, running and jumping on top of Clark. Before he can even unfasten my dress, I'm all over him. I'm sure we put on quite the show for the birds outside on the balcony. But I don't care. I'm so fueled with passion for my husband that I could care less about who sees or hears what. I guess that's not completely true, but the birds outside of our window don't bother me. Clark and I lie on the plush bed in our suite and he rolls over so he's laying half on top of me.

"Baby," he says as I stretch, completely sated, in the afterglow of lovemaking.

"Yes," I answer as he leans down, kissing my hip.

"You're becoming a little sexual vixen," he states, and I cover my face. He reaches up, uncovering my face and kissing me gently on the nose. "I'm not saying that to embarrass you. It's bloody sexy. The sexiest thing I've ever experienced in my life. I get the full benefit of the confident woman you are, Ava. I'm just so damn happy," he says, leaning down and kissing my stomach. We spend the next few days sitting in cafes, exploring the city and making love with the view of the Eiffel Tower in the background. I can't tell you how perfect Paris is. Maybe it's because of Clark? Maybe it's the magic of the city? Or maybe I'm just the happiest I've ever been.

By the time we make it to the perfect blue waters of Monte Carlo I'm overwhelmed with this being my life. Clark knowing French seems to make things easier for us. Hearing him speak it fluently is almost as hot as exploring his body, and I've done a lot of that since my wedding night. We do a lot of sitting on the beach at the beachfront house he's rented. I've always been interested in Grace Kelly, so we do some museums and tours, as well as dine at a couple of incredible restaurants.

I'm sitting on the balcony of our rented home in Monte Carlo when Clark comes up behind me, wrapping his arms tightly around me. He just got off a FaceTime with Brooklyn. She misses us but is enjoying being spoiled by Clark's mom. I took a long bath, watching the sun set drinking a glass of wine. I enjoyed myself immensely. Clark is still kneeling behind me with his arms around me when I tell him to come join me. He shakes his head. He kisses the side of my neck and then looks down at my body under the water. He sighs contentedly and I giggle. I can tell he wants me and as nice as this bath has been, I want him as well. Afterwards we fall asleep with the cool breeze of the ocean ruffling the sheer curtains in our bedroom. I'm lying in his strong arms feeling so incredibly loved and safe. I always feel safe with Clark. It's the best feeling in the world. I'm trying to take everything in as it happens. I'm completely blessed and I thank God that he brought Clark and I together. I can't imagine not having him in my life. Clark rolls over, grabbing his camera and I kiss him passionately as he takes our picture.

The flight to Palermo is magical. I'm tired, so I go to the back of his jet where there's a cabin for sleeping. I wake up from my nap midair with Clark kissing down my neck. "I've always wanted to join the mile high club," he whispers as he unbuttons my dress. Leaving it open so I'm lying in my bra and underwear. He kisses down my body, removing my underwear and then kissing me passionately against my sex. It takes no time at all for me to wake up when he's devouring me like this. I cover my mouth with a pillow as I fall delectably over the edge. Clark pulls me so I'm on top of him. I sit up, straddling him and then slowly sink down on top of him. I gently move up and down, since I'm still getting used to being on top. Clark groans after a few minutes, falling over the edge and then pulling me down to lie on his chest. He presses his lips against my sweaty forehead, and I could fall asleep like this. He carries me to the bathroom and helps me clean up before we head back out to our seats. I blush. Not being able to look at the stewardess. I know she doesn't know anything, but I look out the window trying to clear my head. Clark looks over at me smiling, and I blush as he winks knowingly at me.

"Sleep well, angel?" he asks with a giant grin on his face. I reach over, digging my fingernails into his legs and he laughs, swatting my hand away. I look back out the window as we fly over Italy. I love how there's a map in front of my seat showing me where we are.

"One day I want us to come back and explore all of Italy," I say dreamily. Clark grabs my hand pulling it to his lips.

"I promise you, one day we will." He places a chaste kiss to my hand and then places it in his lap.

Two nights into our stay in Palermo and I can easily say that Italy by far is one of my favorite places I've ever been. The people here are so kind and hospitable. It's not that they weren't the other places we've been. It's just that it's on a whole different level here. The view from every window of our villa is absolutely stunning. We explore the areas near the Villa, but we don't venture far. I feel myself tiring easier as the trip goes along. I've never been this far out of the country. I'm a little on guard anytime we venture too far away from where we're staying. Clark has an ease about himself wherever we go. I cling to him, and he seems to love that. The food in Italy is so amazingly fresh. The pizza…I can't even begin to describe it. A few days later we move onto a yacht Clark has chartered. I know I shouldn't be surprised but this yacht is ginormous. It towers over all the other yachts in the area. I laugh when we pull up to it. Clark smiles knowingly over at me and I shake my head. As we board the "boat," if you can even call it a boat, they have a spread of food waiting for us. I run down to our room to change into my bathing suit first. I then head to the top deck and sit on one of the lounge beds, taking in the sights around me. Clark comes to sit down next to me, grabbing his phone and taking a picture.

"Gotta update our people. Let them know we're still alive," he says laughing. We've taken so many pictures while we've been here. I'm sure Clayton is so tired of getting them. We start to sail up the coastline and every port is beautiful. We "drop anchor" offshore during the day and then at night we move further and further up the coast. When we get to Capri we decide to stay and explore the Amalfi coast for a couple days on our way to Rome. We have just finished exploring the island of Capri when I turn to Clark at dinner and make him laugh. Like always!

"I think I've turned into an Italian, Clark. Not sure we can go back now."

"I get it, baby. I could stay here forever," he agrees as we watch the sun set. We start back to the boat and Clark stops us at a bench. We sit down and he pulls me into his arms.

"Thank you for everything, Clark," I say as I lean my head against him. "I love you so much!"

"I love you too, baby. We've got a few more days left on our honeymoon. Anything you wish we could do?" he asks, and I shake my head.

"You mean sexually?" I ask as Clark blasts out a laugh I've never heard from him. No one turns to look at us because no one here really cares. Everyone is loud and surrounded by jovial friends, family and lovers. It's pretty magical. Clark is so carefree here and I wonder if it's LA that makes him more cautious. Or if it's just the fact that here he feels a certain freedom that he doesn't have back at home.

"No. I don't mean sexually," he says, laughing and kissing the top of my head. "You kill me, Ava. In the best way possible. I didn't think I could be this happy." He pulls me onto his lap and kisses me with raw passion. I forget myself as I reach down grabbing him. He groans into my mouth and then pulls me so he's carrying me. "Let's get back to the boat before you get us arrested for indecent behavior. I love Italy, but I don't want to go to jail here."

We head back to the boat with our security in tow. I forget that they are even there. But Clark and his team insisted that while we are on shore to always have security. Clark doesn't have the luxury to walk around freely everywhere. People still take his picture, but no one comes up and bugs him. He's also very kind to everyone. I love how kind he is. I hope that if I'm ever in the same situation as Clark that I would also extend the same courtesy to everyone. I'm pretty impressed with Clark and the languages he knows. French, Italian, I'm sure there are others.

I'll never get tired of waking up next to Clark. Him sleeping in the nude is exactly as sensual and beautiful as you would imagine. There's no photoshopping where Clark Grant is concerned. Every inch of him is spectacular. I'm lying there admiring his physique when I remember one of the things I haven't done is to go down on him. He's definitely done more of that to me. I smile to myself, a little excited. He has no idea what I'm thinking. I touch him lightly with my hand as to not startle him. I wrap my hand around him, gripping him gently and slowly moving my hand up and down. Even in sleep he starts to grow harder at my touch. He moves beside me, and I hold him steady. I didn't know I could be this turned on just by touching him. But here I am, amazed as I watch his body come alive because of me. I lean over him, putting my mouth around him and slowly starting to take all of him in my mouth. I feel his fingers gently caress my hair. I smile and continue feasting on him until his hips start to move. He whispers my name and I smile as I feel him continue to grow harder. I think he's getting closer, but he grabs me under my arms and pulls me up, flipping me on my back. He pulls both of my arms over my head and then he's inside of me. We are both going over the edge together in no time at all. I smile to myself, rolling over as Clark laughs. He slaps me playfully on my ass before he goes to the bathroom to grab a washcloth to clean us both up.

"God, baby. What a wake-up call," he says, out of breath. "You never cease to amaze me, angel." I grab my swimsuit and put it on. I want to head up to the deck for some fruit and a tan. Shanna warned me not to get too much of a tan while I'm away. Because Ava Gardner had "flawless skin." I'm pretty cautious these days anyway with tanning, but I'm still going to enjoy myself. I mean the movie is a "Hollywood" version of Ava Gardner. As excited as I am to get to New York to shoot this movie, I've really enjoyed my time away with Clark. He comes up on the deck a little while later and we sit together looking at the coastline.

"I'm going to miss this, Ava, not gonna lie. But I'm also excited to head back. Are you getting excited about the movie?" he asks.

"I was just thinking about all of that. I'm excited of course, but I will miss this time away with you."

"I feel the same way. I'm ready to see Brooklyn. I've been away from her this long before. She's getting older and I don't want to miss her growing up. I know technically I'm not missing everything. I just don't want her to look back and be disappointed that I missed certain things," he says as I grab his hand.

"I don't think she will. This is part of your dream, Clark. It's what you love to do. A lot of parents travel for work. It's how they support their family. I think when she gets older she will appreciate that. You followed your heart. A lot of people don't do that, and then they're old and have missed the opportunity to follow their dreams, most of them end up resenting their kids because of it. You're an incredible father, Clark. I think Brooklyn will understand. If she doesn't follow your footsteps into the business as well," I add, and he leans over to kiss me.

"Thank you, Ava," he says as I lean back. "You always seem to know the right thing to say."

Clark

As we pull into Port outside of Rome, Ava and I debark and head to a waiting SUV. We spend the next 24 hours walking and driving around the city and it's absolutely brilliant. We have the best gelato I've ever had. Not to mention the carbonara we had for dinner one night. We are walking back to the hotel hand in hand when Ava turns to me, pulling me into a deep and passionate kiss. I lift her up, kissing her back more passionately as we lean against the side of a building. This time away with Ava has been beyond anything I could have ever dreamed of. Ava and I both are excited and sad to be leaving Rome in the morning. We are ready to get back. I know we both could also easily stay in our honeymoon haze for at least another month. When I'm old and grey I will look back on these last few weeks with a smile.

As we board our flight back to LA we've got at least half a day's travel ahead of us. Ava heads back to the bedroom to sleep once we are in the air. I sit reading different articles and news stories we missed while we were away and unplugged. I come across Kyle's book release details, and it stops me dead in my tracks. Back to reality. It's not great, but it isn't as bad as I was imagining. Poor guy never had a chance. He didn't have the support around him that he needed from his team or family. Part of me is disappointed and part of me is sad that I didn't try harder. Unfortunately, due to his obsession, I think it would have made things worse if I tried to intervene. No one in my circle saw this coming. He had over a thousand photos of me in a lock box that he had personally taken or someone he hired took. Pictures of me changing. Pictures of me and Ava. Photos of Ava driving with Brooklyn around town. Most of the pictures didn't make it into the book. The book leaves little to the imagination of what he was doing with those photos. His team was quoted as saying that he would become manic over the photos. Why someone wasn't trying to get him help is beyond me. What kills me is the interviews they did with his assistants and family representation on why they released all these intimate details. He was extremely in debt with his lifestyle, addictions and habits.

As they go into more grotesque details, I shut down my iPad and pull a book out of my bag to read. I can't go down that rabbit hole right now. Brian released a statement on behalf of Grant Productions.

> "Grant Productions is completely devastated by the loss of Kyle last year. As far as the details with the release of journals, materials, and his team's interviews regarding the depth of Kyle's health and mental state, our team and affiliates were not aware of any matter relating to this. We wish he could have received the help and support he needed. Grant Productions, nor anyone affiliated with our team, was not and are not connected in any way with the new release of information, specifically the behind the scenes details coming to light. We wish his team and family the best. We also pray that this information will lead to more awareness of mental health issues."

As the wheels touch down in LA, Ava is still lounging beside me reading a book. I fell asleep about halfway through the flight. Ava was just starting her book. Now she's almost done with the Ava Gardner biography she was reading. When I look over at her she smiles at me.

"Welcome home, husband." She grabs my hand and I lean over, kissing her cheek.

"Welcome home, wife. I can't wait to carry you over yet another threshold," I say as she squeezes my hand. We head to our Hollywood Hills home, and I text my mum to let her know we are on our way. On the way there I tell Ava the details surrounding Kyle's book, as well as the new information I read about it on the plane. She shakes her head in disappointment.

"He was a very sick and disturbed man, Clark," she whispers, leaning her head on my shoulder. "I hope you know that you couldn't have saved him or made it better. I'm sorry this is happening to you, Clark. Did Brian release the statement you guys talked about before we left?" She asks and I nod.

"He added a little more detail after more information came out, but yes. I don't want to pretend that we didn't know him. But I didn't know any of the information that's coming out now. The studio is also trying to figure out what to do. We can't pull him from the movies. It wouldn't be right to pull him from the film. But…I don't know. I'm glad it's not my decision to make," I add as we pull into the driveway. When we get into the house Brooklyn is in her pajamas and jumps into my arms. I hold her for maybe five minutes straight before she wants down to hug Ava. We also get the run down on what we've missed the last 16 days. Brooklyn is so full of excitement that it's 10 p.m. before she can settle down for bed. Ava has been doing laundry since we got home, even though I told her we could do it tomorrow. We have all weekend before Brooklyn has her last week of school next week. Ava said she's not tired, but I told her she has to try and sleep a little before we can get back on schedule. Jet lag is no joke.

Since being back it's been nonstop -- prepping for New York for Ava, catching up with what I've missed with Brian, getting the details from Clayton about our calendars for the next four to six weeks and then enjoying being a family of 3 with Ava and Brooklyn. I come behind Ava as she's looking over her script again. I kiss her shoulder, letting my lips linger for a moment before lifting back up.

"You're gonna be great, angel. I'll be in the study if you need anything," I tell her as she places the script down, smiling at me.

"Thank you. I feel ready. I know they can make changes before we even shoot. I think I understand my role for the movie at least," she adds as I smile tenderly at her. She's going to be wonderful.

"Just roll with it and do your best. We're all so

excited for you." Heading to my study, I sit in my chair and open up my email. I've offered to move the study around so Ava and I can share it, but she just laughs me off. She's special, that woman of mine. I do love our LA home. It's conveniently located. I just wonder if Ava would like to pick a home out with me. Instead of staying in places that I already have. Something to consider and also to discuss with her.

I call Brian and get the details on the apartment in New York. I've only stayed there a couple times in the last few years. I'm excited for Ava to see it and turn into something she would love. When I stayed there it was more of a bachelor pad. It's a three-bedroom apartment in Tribeca, not far from where Ava will be shooting. The studio will pick her up every morning and bring her and Clayton home to us every night. Brooklyn and I will explore the city and enjoy ourselves. Of course we will visit Ava on set, but for the most part I want this to be about her, not about me. I love that Clayton will be coming with us. He has taken the role of big brother and assistant to Ava. I won't really be needing an assistant as much as Ava will these next couple of months. We're all really excited about this trip to New York. Brooklyn's never been and it's been a while since I've spent some quality time up there. I love that Shanna has Ava all set and prepared. There are four other "unknown actors" in the film. So it won't just be Ava. Dalton reached out about grabbing dinner our first night in the city. He's been in New York for a couple weeks already shooting. I agreed and told him we'd love to.

New York in May is the perfect time to visit. The weather is beautiful, the birds are chirping, and everything is so green. Ava and Brooklyn both love the apartment in New York. They also love that we don't have to drive a lot of places. New York is so walkable. A couple people take notice of us, but for the most part let us be. I've missed New York. I forget how alive the city is. Ava heads to a table read the morning after we arrive. While she's gone Brooklyn helps me do some shopping for the apartment. I want to add a different touch to the apartment. It's filled with a lot of masculine furniture. Navy blues, dark grey and black. I've talked to Clayton and he's recommended a couple stores close by. We plan on heading there and then going for a nice lunch near Central Park.

Ava

I love everyone in the cast, they're all so nice. Dalton has a way of uniting everyone. Shooting began a couple of weeks ago, but we are approaching my scenes. I met the actress playing Lana Turner and I think she and I will be great friends. Gemma is about the same age as me. She's a little younger than I am, but she's really great. Our trailers are right next to each other, so we've spent a lot of time together. I love that the film will show that Ava Gardner and Lana Turner were great friends. They went out a lot drinking, smoking and getting into mischief. They both loved Sinatra and they both left him. Filled with that regret, they had each other to lean on. Those were some of my favorite scenes to shoot.

The hardest scene for me to film was the sex scene with Dalton. I knew it would be. The singing and acting parts were really a breeze. I really enjoyed those weeks of filming. Dalton has been so supportive. He's tried to make me as comfortable as possible with the sexual scenes. That week of filming was the hardest for me to shoot. I'm sure if I did those kind of scenes more often I'd get used to it, but this was my first onscreen sex scene. Ava and Frank had a very tempestuous relationship and so certain aspects of those scenes were fun to shoot. However, the rowdy sex scenes with Dalton weren't my favorite. Clayton told me I did a great job. He warned me that they are a little unnatural to shoot. I know Clark has shot love scenes before, so I asked him about it. His reaction was hilarious. Talking to your husband about how to shoot a love scene with another man is a pretty ridiculous conversation. We laughed it off, but I loved that Clark could see the professionalism behind it. At the end of the day, we got through it. Dalton and I even had some great laughs about it. He was as respectful as one could be in that situation. I came home with a couple of bruises from those scenes and Clark wasn't thrilled about that, but he understood. Frank and Ava had a VERY passionate and aggressive love life. That's all I'll say.

Tomorrow is my last full day shooting. At least my scenes here in New York. I still have my LA shoot days, but those come a little later this summer. Gemma and I are walking back from set when I learn more about how she got the role. She has a few more weeks of shooting after I wrap and then she's going back to her nine to five job. They aren't shooting the film in sequence, so she'll continue filming after I've wrapped my scenes.

"I took a six-week unpaid leave of absence from work in order to shoot the film. Honestly, I got the job because an agent here in New York spotted me. She was at the law firm I work for, in a meeting. She saw me at a desk and freaked out. Supposedly to her I looked like I could be Lana Turner's twin sister. Except at that time, I was a brunette. She asked if was an actress. So I said I could act," she says, recounting the conversation. "I mean, how hard is it to reenact the black and white movies of the 40's and 50's?" She adds laughing and we giggle about it. "We dyed my hair white blonde and she sent my photos and a video of me reading some lines with her to LA. All of a sudden, BAM, here I am. Playing Lana Turner in a movie about Freaking Frank Sinatra. It's crazy, right?" she says as I smile kindly at her. I love this girl so much.

"That is crazy, but I'm here as well. So maybe you and I were just meant to meet each other." We head into our trailers and then she comes over after she takes off her make up and costume. I change into some yoga pants and a tank top. It's much more humid here than in LA, but I love New York. I've missed it! We're sitting around talking and enjoying each other's company when Clayton comes in.

"Hello, you two," he exclaims as he comes in and puts his iPad and cell phone down. "Getting close to wrapping, Ava. You both look and sound amazing, by the way. The scenes of the two of you getting into mischief together I think are my favorite."

"Thanks, Clayton," I say, and Gemma smiles.

"Yeah. Thank you. This has been a blast so far. It's a little surreal to be here. I'll forever be grateful for this experience, and it doesn't suck to kiss Dalton Calhoun. Pretty unbelievable."

"What are you planning on doing next, Gemma? You're a great actress," Clayton says as he sits back on the sofa next to me.

"I'm going back to the law firm I work for. I'm the 2nd assistant to Blake King. Sounds fancy since he's part of one of the wealthiest families here in New York. He's actually pretty amazing. I'm pretty much an assistant to his secretary. I've only been there two months. Once I graduated from college I interned for a year at their uptown firm and then they asked me to join their team once I graduated. And yes, he's the younger brother to Brent King. People know his name better. Though I've only met him once and it was when I was taking the meeting notes for my supervisor when she was out of town.

Blake and I are actually pretty close. I wouldn't be here if he didn't make a huge exception for me to take a leave of absence."

"Wait. The Brent King? The Scottish hottie that was just on the cover of Forbes?" Clayton asks and Gemma smiles. "Wow. He's the most beautiful man I think I've ever seen. Marco let me put him on my hall pass list," Clayton declares to me and then turns back to Gemma. "I was really hoping he preferred men. Is he as hot as he is in his pictures?" he asks and she smiles.

"Even better. Half the company pretends not to look while the other half just can't help themselves. It's not that he isn't nice. He's just laser focused. I didn't go to school to be an attorney. I went to business school because I couldn't figure out what I wanted to do. And I had to get the hell out of town after high school. I live with three other girls in an apartment in Williamsburg. Living in the city isn't in the cards for me right now. This movie is going to help me pay off my student loans and then I'm probably going to save the rest."

"That's fascinating. I can't believe you didn't turn his head already. You're stunning, Gemma," Clayton says, confused.

"Well, that's sweet, but I've never actually spoken to him. I was in the back of the room when I was there. He's in the office down in the financial district, so we haven't had many interactions.

Blake, his brother, is great though. I can't imagine a better boss. But I actually like the blonde hair. I didn't think I would, but it's grown on me. I've learned how to do my makeup since I've been on set. Obviously I can't do it as well as the makeup artist here, but I've learned enough. I never really learned how to do make up. My dad raised me. He's still back in Georgia. But ya know, what's a girl to do?"

"Yeah. I bet he noticed you before. But I bet you $20 it'll be a completely different ball game the next time he sees you."

"Doubt it. He's used to dating super models and socialites. I'm just a regular girl," she adds, and I smile at her. Gosh how many times did I tell myself the same thing about Clark. The world has a funny way of bringing two people together that are meant to be together. I hope if that's the road she's supposed to take that it will happen for her.

"You're still the same girl, Gemma. Changing your hair just might catch his attention. You have to keep us updated," Clayton adds as we see our car pull up. I offer Gemma a ride, but she shakes her head in disbelief.

We head home and when we walk into the kitchen, we smell sugar. Cupcakes! Clayton and I head straight for them, but before I can get to them I feel my stomach turn. I run the other direction to the bathroom. I barely make it to the bathroom before I throw up everywhere, emptying the contents of my stomach. Oh, dear god why? Maybe it's the salad I had for lunch. It did have fish on top. Could be bad fish? I hear a knock on the door. I flush the toilet and then walk to open the bathroom door. It's Clayton.

"For god's sake, Ava," he says looking at me up and down. "Are you okay?"

"I think so. I mean. I feel better. A little nauseated still, but it came out of nowhere. I really wanted a cupcake," I say sadly before I turn around, throwing up again. Clark appears behind Clayton, walking into the bathroom pulling my hair back as I continue to empty the contents of my stomach. When I'm done, he sits me on the floor and hands me a wet washcloth. I press it to my face.

"Should I call a doctor?" he asks, and I shake my head.

"I think I must have had a bad salad for lunch?" I say and he nods. Clayton and I look at each other and then I lean back against the wall.

"Let's get you into bed, darling."

The next day I continue to throw up. On set, off set. Clayton is working overtime with the buckets. Poor guy. I'm exhausted and I wonder how long does the stomach flu or food poisoning last. Later that evening, after I wrap my last day on set in New York, I'm sitting in my trailer. Well, more like laid out on the couch, when Clayton comes in to tell me the car is here. At the moment, the thought of getting in a moving vehicle is the worst idea I've ever heard.

"Can we please walk back? I can't get in a car, Clayton," I murmur and he sits down next to me.

"Ava. Can we talk seriously for a second," he asks, and I sit up. I nod and take a small sip of water. I know what he's going to ask me before he even asks. It's the same thing I've been wondering since I threw up last night. "Could you possibly be pregnant?" he asks and I look over at him.

"We were so careful," I say, and he smiles. I've had my period since we've been in New York. So I know if I am, more than likely it happened while we were here in New York.

"Even the most careful people can get pregnant, Ava. Why don't we stop and get a pregnancy test on the way home. And of course, we can walk. I'll let the driver and Clark know." Clayton has already packed up the trailer with our stuff. So we put the bags and gear into the car to head back to the house on foot. We aren't far from the apartment. It's only a few blocks and I'm sure the fresh air will do me some good.

We head out, walking towards the apartment and the cool breeze makes me feel much better. Clayton stops inside a convenience store and brings out a bag. I haven't auditioned for anything else, so luckily I don't have anything else coming up. I know nothing about being pregnant. Talking to Clayton it's clear that he knows much more than I do. I love New York at night. The city's lit up and alive. It does something to my soul. When we walk into the apartment, Clark isn't downstairs. He must be in Brooklyn's room putting her down for the night. Clark has really been enjoying our time in New York and I must say I have too. I almost prefer New York to LA. We head to our bedroom, and I head into the bathroom. I pee on two of the sticks and then set them out. I'm a little nervous, but also a part of me is so very excited. I didn't realize how excited I would be at the thought of being pregnant. It didn't hit me until now. I close the bathroom door, like that will help the sticks have their privacy to make their epic decisions. I'm looking out the window at the New York skyline, and I feel so emotional in this moment. I don't even know what the results are, but I'm already crying. I think I'll actually be sad if it's negative. Clark comes up behind me, kissing my shoulder and wrapping his arms around my waist. Clayton tells us he will give us a minute, but I whip around.

"No. This will be a family moment. Please stay, Clayton," I say, reaching my hand out and he smiles. Grabbing my hand and pulling him towards us. "I want you here for this."

"We can probably go check," he says, and I nod. Clark wipes my tears.

"Clayton told me you guys were stopping for a pregnancy test. Are you okay, baby?" He asks, genuinely concerned. I nod, leaning my cheek on his chest. "Can I ask what has you upset? Is it the thought that we could be pregnant?"

"Yes. I think I'm just emotional, but I'm not upset that I could be pregnant. I think I actually want to be?" He smiles down at me, kissing me on the head and then lifting my chin so I'm looking at him. "I think I want to be pregnant, Clark," I voice as he leans down, kissing me gently.

"Well, it's a good thing," Clayton declares with a knowing smile on his face. He leans against the doorframe to the bathroom, and I walk in holding Clark's hand. We look down at the tests. PREGNANT! I gasp and then the tears are automatically falling down my cheeks again. These are certainly not sad tears. Clark holds me safely to him. I look up and he has unshed tears in his eyes.

"We're pregnant," I whisper against his lips, and he grabs Clayton's hand pulling him into our hug.

"Congratulations, you guys," Clayton says, and I giggle.

"We're going to have a baby," I whisper to the both of them and they both laugh with excitement.

"We're going to have a baby," Clark says back to me, and I jump in his arms. He kisses the side of head gently, swinging me back and forth. "How do you feel now," he asks as he places my feet back on the ground.

"Kinda sick, but excited. I mean, I know we didn't plan this, but I'm still so excited."

"I know. I'm excited too, Ava," he answers my lingering question in my mind.

"Are you sure?" I ask and he rolls his eyes.

"Ava, you and I are having a baby. I'm having a baby with the love of my life. Of course I'm excited. Please don't think anything else. It's still really early and we need to be careful. You probably need to get on some prenatal vitamins and find a good doctor while we're here. But yes, I'm excited. In fact, I'd say I'm ecstatic." He sits on the edge of the bed, and I sit in his lap.

"I already bought some vitamins," Clayton says going back to the bag and getting the bottle out. "They're actually a very reputable brand." I'm not surprised by this information. Clayton takes care of everything. I'm a little tired from all the throwing up and excitement. "Happy for you guys," he adds and then excuses himself. I'm sure he wants to go back to his room and get packed. He's supposed to fly back to attend an event with Marco, then they're coming back to spend some time in New York with us. With Marco's family in New York, they want to spend a good chunk of the summer here. It's going to be a blast.

A couple weeks later, Clark and I are so on cloud nine with the pregnancy. Besides the nausea and throwing up, I'm really happy. I meet with a doctor here in New York and she gives me something for the nausea. It helps a little but not a lot. I'm still throwing up a couple times a day. So far, it's manageable. We are eight weeks pregnant, and she tells me most morning sickness goes away by the end of the first trimester. I'm hopeful, but also fully prepared for this to continue the entire pregnancy. This wasn't planned, but this baby was created by two people so in love. Clark is delighted, which helps me to be as well when I'm really sick. We decide to stay in New York for the rest of the summer, just to be careful. I'm able to see Gemma a couple more times. I adore her. She's become like the sister I always wished I had growing up. I haven't told Shanna about the pregnancy yet. I want to get out of the first trimester before we share the news with anyone. We are walking in Battery Park, watching Brooklyn play, when Clark pulls me onto his lap.

"You know, Ava, you can still audition for roles. I'm sure you know that. Being pregnant doesn't mean the end of your career. Once the movie is released, you'll more than likely be approached about doing more projects."

"I know. I love that I have your support with all this. I just want to enjoy this pregnancy. The movie doesn't come out till next year. Probably a couple months after the baby's born. Then your movie will come out and you'll have a press tour as well. So next year will be pretty busy, but I know we can do it. We have the friends around us to make it work. I'm thinking I can take it a day at a time, like we did with this movie. When the right role comes along again, I'll cross that bridge when I get to it. In the meantime," I say, turning in his lap, "I just want to enjoy this time. In a couple weeks I'll let Shanna know so she'll get off my back about auditioning for every role that comes across her desk."

"Sounds like a plan, angel," he says, kissing me sweetly. "You are an amazing woman, Ava," he says, holding me in his arms. "I'm so blessed to have ever had the chance to be with a woman as strong, kind, and beautiful as you. I love you darling. On top of that, you're carrying my child," he says with tears in his eyes. "We will do this together. We will figure out our careers or whatever that looks like together. I wouldn't want to do this with anyone else. You're my angel. You have been since the day I met you," he says as tears stream down my face. He wipes them away with his thumbs, leaning in and kissing me. I turn back around and we watch Brooklyn playing on the playground, the beautiful and iconic New York skyline rising above us. I feel so safe here in his arms. I always have and I know I always will. The four of us. Our own little family, not to mention Clayton and Marco. I'm the luckiest woman in the world. I know that. I can't wait for what comes next because I know with our team surrounding us, I can do anything!

"You know what we should do on the way back to the apartment?" I ask as Clark kisses me behind the ear and I snuggle closer to him.

"What's that baby?" he whispers.

"Pick up some cupcakes!" I say giggling as Clark's chest vibrates behind me in laughter.

"Oh yea! I think that can be arranged!" He says as we wave at Brooklyn who's swinging on the swings. "Any particular reason you want to pick up some cupcakes? Craving?"

"Craving you and cupcakes!" I say as I turn my face towards him and giving him a knowing grin.

"Mmm…sounds delicious. Might have to ask for some extra frosting if you know what I mean!" he adds as I lean over and kiss him gently.

"I think we certainly can find something delicious to do with the extra frosting!" We both laugh and I think back to the first time Clark and I shared a cupcake. So much has changed since that moment and I wouldn't trade it for anything in the world!

ACKNOWLEDGEMENTS

To my Husband, Brad – Thank you so much for loving and encouraging me to pursue my dream of becoming an author. You've loved and seen me at my best and my worst. For that I will forever love you! I love you so much!

To Lisa Harris – My Fireball! Since day one you have walked with me every step of the way. For that and so much more I am eternally grateful. I love you more than words.

To KP Simmon – You have been an invaluable source of knowledge, direction and support. It is because of incredible women and authors like you that the rest of us are able to pursue and achieve our dreams.

To Shalyn Eyer – For believing and encouraging me to be the woman and writer I am today. You reading through my early drafts meant the world to me and showed me how much you truly care and believe in me.

To Ashley Ladd – Your friendship and insight during my journey here was everything I needed. You keep me humble and authentic. That's something I appreciate more than you will ever know. You have seen me through some of my darker days and yet you still walked with me.

To Jen Rooke – You make me a better woman and momma. Thank you for always knowing the right thing to say to help me make it through another week! Love you and our lunches!

To Julie Holt – My Editor and Partner in Crime (E.P.I.C) – I knew from the moment that we sat down to talk about my hopes and dreams as a writer that you were the woman for the job. I have a feeling we will be on this journey together long term. “We need more cupcake moments!” will always be my favorite editing note.

To Caroline Taylor – So grateful for you love! You have been such an incredible creative partner and your graphic design skills are unparalleled. Here’s to more fun in the future!

To my 1st Draft Readers – I appreciate your feedback and you taking the time to read different scenes and encounters as they were being dreamed up. I can’t express the love and adoration I have for you. So happy that you were able to read the finished book.

Finally, to my family and friends – I did it! Thank you so much for encouraging me on my journey here! I hope I make you all proud. I love you all immensely! Let’s GO!!!!

Honestly, the list of people I should thank or acknowledge would be longer than the book itself. To the readers, thank you, thank you, thank you! Your love, support and encouragement mean everything to me. A love for reading is such a vital part of who I am. When I say I appreciate you taking the time to read my book I mean it wholeheartedly. I am humbled and honored to be a part of the incredible list of authors who have also inspired me to follow my dreams. I hope I made you laugh and smile along the way. Now, onto our next adventure together!

CPSIA information can be obtained
at www.ICGtesting.com
Printed in the USA
LVHW080251100422
715631LV00011BA/371

9 798985 481501